FIRSTLIFE

Books by Gena Showalter
available from Harlequin TEEN

The Everlife Novels

FIRSTLIFE

The White Rabbit Chronicles

(in reading order)

ALICE IN ZOMBIELAND
THROUGH THE ZOMBIE GLASS
THE QUEEN OF ZOMBIE HEARTS
A MAD ZOMBIE PARTY

The Intertwined Novels

(in reading order)

INTERTWINED
UNRAVELED
TWISTED

FIRSTLIFE

by Gena Showalter

ISBN-13: 978-0-373-21157-9

Firstlife

This edition published by arrangement with Harlequin Books S.A.

For questions and comments about the quality of this book, please contact us at CustomerService@Harlequin.com.

Printed in U.S.A.

Dedication

To God and His dear Son, for inspiration (Luke 10:2, Mark 3:24) and boundless love (John 3:16).

To Pennye Edwards, for being one of the great loves of my life.

To Wendy Higgins, for the beta read and awesome feedback.

To Katie McGarry, for the perfect email at the perfect time.

To Roxanne St. Claire, my sister, my friend, my love, for the encouragement and support.

To Jill Monroe, the bestest best friend a girl could have, for just about everything. You make life better. (PS: I hid your name in the middle to ensure you'd have to search for it because *I'm* the nerdiest best friend, hahaha.)

To Kresley Cole, P.C. and Kristin Cast and Sarah Maas, for being the most fun people on the planet.

To Mike and Vicki Tolbert, Shane Tolbert, Shonna Hurt and Michelle Quine, for putting up with me. God really blessed you when He gifted you with me. Fine. He blessed me when He gifted me with you.

To Max, Riley and Victoria, for being you. I love you, always and forever.

To Deirde Knight, my agent, for believing in this series as strongly as I do.

To Lauren Smulski, for the read and amazing feedback.

To Natashya Wilson, my editor, for seeing a diamond in the lump of coal I originally sent you. Your guidance has been invaluable, and your love for the book/series a true treasure. You helped me in so many ways I'd need to write a new book just to list them all. You've always worked hard for me and always offered the most amazing suggestions, but this time, you surpassed yourself. Thank you!

It was the best of times, it was the worst of times, it was the age of wisdom, it was the age of foolishness, it was the epoch of belief, it was the epoch of incredulity, it was the season of Light, it was the season of Darkness, it was the spring of hope, it was the winter of despair.

—CHARLES DICKENS, *A TALE OF TWO CITIES*

TROIKA

From: A_P_5/23.43.2

To: L_N_3/19.1.1

Subject: Tenley Lockwood

Duuude. A heads-up would have been nice. Can you say *whack shack*?

If you failed to read my dossier, Nanne, I'm happy to bring you up to date on the highlights. I'm a well-trained and vastly decorated Laborer. Victory might as well be my middle name. What I'm not: a babysitter. Watching Tenley Lockwood is a waste of my many talents.

Oh, AND DID I FORGET TO MENTION SHE'S IN A WHACK SHACK??

With all due respect, I'd rather fish out my internal organs with a coat hanger than stay here. I'm officially requesting a transfer.

Light Brings Sight!
Archer Prince

TROIKA

From: L_N_3/19.1.1

To: A_P_5/23.43.2

Subject: Officially Denied

Mr. Prince,
I'm not your duuude. I'm your superior. You will only ever address me by my proper rank: General. Or the always appropriate *sir*.

You were selected for this mission for two very important reasons. You are young and (obviously) immature. Offense intended. Our older Laborers had trouble relating to Miss Lockwood, but you should fit right in.

On that note, continue "babysitting" Miss Lockwood, or I'll fish out your organs for you.

Also, I expect daily reports. I'm not overstating when I say convincing her to make covenant with our realm is essential.

Light Brings Sight!
General Levi Nanne

TROIKA

From: A_P_5/23.43.2
To: L_N_3/19.1.1
Subject: You Suck (& I'm WAY Mature)

Dear Sir,
Laborer is below your pay grade, but aren't you one of those "older" gents who failed with the girl? Just checking. (And prepping you for the time I succeed and rub it in your face.)

Anyway. I'm a good little robot, sir, so *of course* I'll do as you asked. Sir. Here's the thing, though, sir. If I have to watch/listen from the outside a minute more, I'm going to bleach my corneas and stab a pencil through my ears.

I want my Shell, and I want to go INSIDE the whack shack. Sir.

Also, here's the first report as demanded. I mean *so sweetly requested*. Sir. During the institution's version of creative writing class, your precious had to write a poem to express her feelings about life. I'm including a copy for your perusal. I defy you NOT to jump off a bridge after reading it. Sir.

The grave is the end
And I will never accept that
I have been set free from the chains that bind me.
I know
"Death has lost its victory"
Is a lie, because there is no greater truth than this:
"Life is hopeless"

Gotta say, I don't think Darkside McDowner is a great fit for Troika. I know, I know. We love the unlovable. We champion the weak. I don't need a lecture. Just tell me what makes her so "essential."

Your humble servant,
Archer

TROIKA

From: L_N_3/19.1.1

To: A_P_5/23.43.2

Subject: Poem, Among Other Things

I didn't fail with her, puppy, I cleared the way for you. There's a difference. Want to succeed? Learn it.

Expect a Shell at 0800. Just don't expect yours. I've selected one from GenPop. And before you reply with your typical flare—General Population? Are you kidding me (dramatic pause for effect), sir?—save your fingers the trouble of typing. I'm not sending what you want. I'm sending what you need. You may thank me later.

Also, in regards to the poem. Miss Lockwood understands there are two sides to every story. Why don't you? Do yourself a favor and read the poem again. This time, start at the bottom and work your way up.

And, Mr. Prince, the fact that I have to tell you what's so special about this girl means I need to schedule you for an emergency jackhammer to the brain. Do yourself a favor and pay attention to the pearls I'm about to throw. Light. Conduit. Loss...darkness.

Oh, and here's a good one: Moron. Again, offense intended.

TROIKA

From: A_P_5/23.43.2
To: L_N_3/19.1.1
Subject: Four Things

1) Sir Dude. I don't want to point out your obvious lack of intelligence, but Tenley Lockwood can't be a Conduit. Given your advanced age, you've clearly forgotten Conduits are raised by Troikan parents. They are the most loyal among us, from beginning to end.

2) And okay, okay. I read the poem from bottom to top, so I get your "two sides" theory. That doesn't mean the poem is any good. It doesn't rhyme.

3) The Shell arrived, and I honestly I think hate you. I'm pure male aggression, and you expect me to pass for a chick? As if *anyone* will be dumb enough to believe such a farce.

4) Myriad sent Killian. I've seen him skulking around in the shadows, watching the girl. Permission to slaughter?

TROIKA

From: L_N_3/19.1.1

To: A_P_5/23.43.2

Subject: Permission Gr… Denied! (Admit it. Your little-girl heart skipped a beat.)

You know our laws as well as I do. And what is at the heart of our second-most-important decree? Personal vendettas must be set aside for the good of the people. You are one of our people.

Do your job. Nothing else matters.

MYRIAD

From: K_F_5/23.53.6

To: P_B_4/65.1.18

Subject: My New Assignment

Hot and crazy, just the way I like 'em. Consider Tenley Lockwood bagged and tagged.

Might Equals Right!
Killian Flynn

MYRIAD

From: P_B_4/65.1.18

To: K_F_5/23.53.6

Subject: Show Some Respect!

You will speak of the girl with deference, or you won't speak of her at all.

I'm already close to pulling you from this assignment, Mr. Flynn. In fact, I have no idea why I allowed the Generals to convince me you can do what no one else has managed to do. You're too young, and your methods for success have always been inappropriate. But not this time! Persuade the girl to make covenant with us, but keep your pants zipped while you do it. And do not fail. *We need her.*

Might Equals Right!
Madame Pearl Bennett

MYRIAD

From: K_F_5/23.53.6

To: P_B_4/65.1.18

Subject: Fail? Not in This Lifetime <—See What I Did There?

You've never cared about my methods before, only the end result. What's changed? What's so important about this girl? If you've got inside info, do me a solid and share with the rest of the class.

And just so you know, we don't *need* anyone. We've never been stronger, and we outnumber the Troikans two to one. Also, this girl is basically an "it." When she dies, she'll just be one more cog in our wheel. But don't you worry your pretty little head. I'll sign her—my way. I always do.

In other news, Troika sent Archer. I'm going to cut off his limbs and beat him to Second-death with them.

MYRIAD

From: P_B_4/65.1.18

To: K_F_5/23.53.6

Subject: NO!

Control your temper until you've signed the girl. Afterward, I'll use my highest pair of heels to pin Archer down, and you can flay his skin to wear as a coat, if that's what you desire. Have I made myself clear? Do not engage. Not yet!

And the girl is so much more than an "it" and a "cog." Everyone is! But this girl...one day, she'll be your boss. She'll be *both* our bosses. If I were you, I'd be careful how I treated her.

MYRIAD

From: K_F_5/23.53.6

To: P_B_4/65.1.18

Subject: Sorry, but You're NOT Me

What you are? Too cute. Imagine me wincing in embarrassment for you as I say: I don't actually care about your permission. Consider my last message an FYI.

And you know better than most I treat my bosses the same way I treat everyone else. If you don't like it, Madame, you can absolutely reassign me. I have nothing to lose. I'm guessing you have plenty.

MYRIAD

From: P_B_4/65.1.18

To: K_F_5/23.53.6

Subject: Nothing to Lose?

How about something to gain? Sign the girl, and I'll give you what you've always wanted. Your mother's name and where to find her.

Though the End be Nigh

I've been told history is written by survivors,
but I know that isn't always true.
My name is Tenley Lockwood and very soon, I'll be dead.
This is my story—but my end is only the beginning.

chapter one

"You are better off Unsigned than a slave to Troikan law."
—Myriad

I've been locked inside the Prynne Asylum—where happiness comes to die—for three hundred and seventy-eight days. (Or nine thousand and seventy-two hours.) I know the exact time frame, not because I watched the sun rise and set in the sky, but because I mark my walls in blood every time the lights in the good-girls-gone-bad wing of the facility turn on.

There are no windows in the building. At least, none that I've found. And I've never been allowed outside. None of the inmates have. To be honest, I don't even know what country we're in, or if we're buried far underground. Before being flown, driven, shipped or dropped here, we were heavily sedated. Wherever we are, though, it's bone-deep cold beyond the walls. Every day, hour, second, our air is heated.

I've heard friends and enemies alike ask the staff for details, but the response has always been the same. *Answers have to be earned.*

No, thanks. For me, the price—cooperation—is simply too high.

With a wince, I rise from bed and make my way to the far corner of my cell. Every step is agony. My back hates me, but the muscles are too sore to go on strike. Last night I was caned *just because.*

I stop in front of my pride and joy. My calendar. A new day means a new mark.

I have no chalk, no pen or marker, so I drive the tip of an index finger over a jagged stone protruding from the floor, slicing through the flesh and drawing a well of blood.

I hate the sting, but if I'm honest, I'll love the scar it leaves behind. My scars give me something to count.

Counting is my passion, and numerology my favorite addiction. Maybe because every breath we take is another tick on our clock, putting us one step closer to death…and a new beginning. Maybe because my name is Tenley—Ten to my friends.

Ten, a representation of completion.

We have ten fingers and ten toes. Ten is the standard beginning for any countdown.

I was born on the tenth day of the tenth month at 10:10 a.m. And, okay. All right. Maybe I'm obsessed with numbers because they always tell a story and unlike people, they never lie.

Here's my story in a nutshell:

Seventeen—the number of years I've existed. In my case, *lived* is too strong a word.

One—the number of boys I've dated.

Two—the number of friends I've made and lost since my incarceration.

Two—the number of lives I'll live. The number of lives we'll *all* live.

Our Firstlife, then our Everlife.

Two—the number of choices I have for my eternal future.

(1) Do as my parents command or (2) suffer.

I've chosen to suffer.

I use the blood to create another mark on the stones. Satisfied, I head to the "bathroom." There are no doors to provide even a modicum of privacy, just a small, open shower stall next to a toilet. For our safety, we're told. For the amusement of others, I suspect. All cells are monitored 24/7, which means at any given time during any given day, staff members are allowed and even encouraged to watch live camera feed.

Dr. Vans, the head of the asylum, likes to taunt us. *I see and know everything.*

A good portion of teachers scold us. *Time waster!*

Orderlies belittle us. *Put on a little weight, haven't we?*

Most of the guards leer at us. They hail from all over the world, and though their language varies, their sentiment is always the same. *You are begging for it and one day I'll give it.*

Just some of the many perks offered chez Prynne.

Not everyone is horrible, I admit. A small handful even strive to keep the others from going too far. But it's no secret every staff member is paid to make us hate our stay, to make us want to leave *more than anything.* Because, the more we want to leave, the more likely we are to do whatever our parents sent us here to do.

My friend Marlowe dared to pawn her mother's jewelry to buy groceries, and she needed help with her "kleptomania." My friend Clay, a drug addict, needed to get clean.

The institution failed them both. A few months ago, Marlowe killed herself, and Clay… I don't know what happened to him. He planned an escape, and I haven't heard from him since.

I miss them both. Every. Single. Day.

I begged Clay not to risk a breakout. I tried to leave once, and I had help. My boyfriend, James, a guard high on the totem, arranged for cameras to be shut down, certain doors to be unlocked and other guards to sleep on the job. Still I proved unsuccessful.

For his efforts, James was shot in the head. While I watched.

Hot tears well in my eyes and trickle down my cheeks as I slowly strip out of my jumpsuit. Every motion comes with another blast of agony. When finally I'm naked, I step under a tepid spray of water. Modesty has long since been beaten out of me—literally!—but I wash as fast as I can. We're given a small ration of water a day. If we run out, we run out. Too bad, so sad. Something we're never given? Razors. I keep my legs and underarms smooth with threads I've pulled from old uniforms. I already feel like an animal; there's no reason to resemble one, too.

Not that a well-groomed appearance matters. While we're allowed to socialize with the opposite sex during mealtimes, I'd rather dig my heart out of my chest with a rusty spoon than date again. Yes, the rewards are tremendous, but the risks are more so. When everything comes crashing down—and it will—I'll be shattered into a million pieces. I'll have to rebuild. Again.

I should have resisted James's pursuit of me, but I'd been at a low point, desperate for any show of affection. He'd risked his job every time he'd disabled the cameras to sneak inside my room. He snuck in so many times, in fact, his memory still lives here. Every night when I climb into my twin-size bed, I'm reminded of the way he teased me out of my initial shyness. Of the way he cleaned my wounds whenever I was hurt. Of the way he held me in his arms, offering comfort and kisses. He'd wanted to do more. I hadn't. Not here. Not with a potential audience.

Forget the past. Concentrate on the present. Right.

I shut off the water and towel dry as best I can. I step into a clean, peed-in-the-snow-yellow jumpsuit, but only manage to bring the material to my waist, my arms refusing to work properly, my shoulder muscles giving up.

What am I going to do? I can't leave my cell like this.

The door suddenly slides open with a quiet *snick*. My blood flashes ice-cold as two guards march inside my cell, a flailing girl between them.

I gasp, my surprise giving me the strength I need to lift my hands and cover my breasts.

No, I'm not modest, but this is a special kind of humiliating.

The guards release the girl and push her in my direction. The first thing I notice about her? She has unevenly cropped pink hair.

"New roomie," one of them says to me. When he notices my partial state of undress, he grins. "Well, well. Vhat we have here?"

His Russian accent is as thick as ever, one of the many reasons I refer to him as Comrade Douche. Though my cheeks burn, I strive for a confident tone. "Vhat we have here is an underage girl who, upon her release, will ensure you rot in prison."

His grin only widens as he takes a step toward me. The pink-haired girl kicks him in the stomach, surprising me.

He focuses on her, raising his hand to deliver a strike. *"Suka!"*

Bitch in Russian. A word that's been thrown at me, as well.

She smiles and crooks her fingers at him, the universal sign for *bring it.*

The other guard grabs Comrade Douche by the arm and drags him into the hallway. Both men frown at me as the door slides shut.

Without missing a beat, the girl waves at me, looking almost…giddy. I blink in confusion. She's happy rather than scared? Really?

"Hello," she says, and I detect a slight British accent. "I'm Bow, your new best friend."

She's crazy. Got it. "I'm not in the market for a new friend." I hoped I'd remain solo. I don't like sleeping in front of another person but I have to steal catnaps to function. My last roommate told me I toss and turn, screaming about the torture I've endured or singing a number song my aunt taught me as a child.

Ten tears fall, and I call…nine hundred trees, but only one is for me. Eight—

Oh, no. I'm not getting lost in my head right now.

"Here." Bow stalks toward me, her stride long and

strong. Up close, I can tell her eyes are the color of freshly polished pennies. They're odd yet captivating, smoldering with an intensity that should be too much to contain. "Let me help you."

Out of habit, I step out of range when she reaches for me. But…zero! My favorite four-letter curse word. I don't think I can finish getting dressed without her.

She cups her breasts in a mimic of me and beams. "Boobs are awesome, yeah? Literal fun-bags. I don't know what you girls are always complaining about."

"Don't you mean *us girls*?"

Her hands fall away from her *fun-bags*. "Dude. There's nothing wrong with enjoying the equipment and getting a little some-some of my own goods and services. Seriously. I'm so hot even *I* want a piece of me."

Hot? Debatable. Bizarre, narcissistic and pervy? Unquestionably. She's the trifecta. In other words, I hit the probably-gonna-get-murdered jackpot this go-round. Yay, me.

"I'd rather not talk about your goods and services, thanks." Slowly I pivot, placing her at my back. This is a rarity for me. A low point, a moment of utter desperation. If she attempts a hit-and-run or a grab-and-stab—*anything* dirty—I'll make sure she regrets it.

She inhales sharply, and I assume she's studying the wealth of bruises I'm sporting.

"Sometime today," I snap, horrified by the perceived weakness.

She gently works my arms through the sleeves. "I hope you're prepared for the Everlife. Another beating like this could kill you."

Doubtful. Dr. Vans has the torture thing nailed. He knows when he's about to push a body too far. "Trust me. Death isn't the worst thing that can happen to me."

"Of course it isn't. If you haven't made the right plans for the Unending, you'll wish you ceased to exist."

The Unending, where Myriad and Troika—the two realms in power in the afterlife…aka the Everlife—are located. Where "real" life is said to begin.

Over the years, the world has been divided into two factions. Those who support Myriad, and those who support Troika. No one ever supports both. How can they? The realms are too fundamentally opposed—about everything!

Myriad boasts about autonomy…bliss…indulgence. To them, Firstlife is merely a stepping stone into the Everlife, everything happens for a fated reason and, when we experience Second-death—death in the Everlife—our spirit returns to Earth, the Land of the Harvest, to Fuse with another—brand-new—spirit.

They are willing to negotiate covenant terms to win over a human.

Troika, on the other hand, is known for structure…constant study…absolute conformity. To them, Firstlife matters just as much as Everlife, fate is a myth and, when we experience Second-death, we enter into the Rest, never to be seen by human or spirit again.

Troikans refuse to negotiate covenant terms, offering the same benefits to everyone everywhere without exception. The same laws, too. To them, what is right is right and what is wrong is wrong, for one and for all. Everyone on equal footing.

If one realm says the sky is cloudless, the other will say a storm is brewing.

They've been at war for centuries, the other's destruction the ultimate goal. That's why they fight so hard to win souls. That's also why picking the right side is so important. Someday, someone is going to lose.

Here on Earth, the Myriad and Troika supporters aren't segregated...exactly. They try to coexist, but it's in imperfect harmony and there's always an underlying hum of tension.

Sometimes riots break out, and the government is forced to execute martial law to prevent an all-out brawl.

A rare few people, like me, have no idea which side to back. We see merits to both sets of beliefs. We also see downsides.

We are called the Unsigned.

For us, there are rumors of a third spirit realm, the place we'll end up after Firstdeath. My parents used to tell me horror stories about it, stories whispered in the dark of night. The Realm of Many Ends, where nightmares come to life.

I've often wondered... Is Many Ends a made-up place intended to scare kids straight?

"Do you?" Bow asks as she zips up my jumpsuit. "Have plans for the Unending, I mean?"

"I'm not talking Everlife with you."

Her features scrunch with disappointment. "Why not?"

"I'll be here another three hundred and fifty-two days."

3 + 5 + 2 = 10

"And?"

And she will leave sooner rather than later. I recognize

her type. Extremely optimistic until something goes wrong. After her first beating, she'll cave and do whatever her parents want, guaranteed.

"Forget the next life. What about this one? Tell me why you're here." I motion to our illustrious cell with a tilt of my chin.

"My guardian sent me." She strides to the second twin bed and sits, and there's nothing graceful or feminine about her. "Told me to be a light."

Ugh. What I hear? Absolute conformity. "You signed with Troika, then." Not a question.

Her nod contains a thread of pride. "I did."

We're going to clash *so* hard. "What is light, exactly?" What's she going to be pushing on me?

"Whatever is needed to help someone find a way out of darkness."

Darkness. "Meaning Myriad."

She ignores my dry tone. "Meaning a problem, any problem."

Well, I've got plenty of those—though I tell myself this situation is fertilizer, and something good must grow from it.

"Why are *you* here?" she asks me.

"I refuse to make covenant with Myriad." Covenant—the equivalent of signing a contract in blood.

Sometimes, in an attempt to convince me to sign away my rights, I'm pampered. *Isn't this nice? This is what awaits you in Myriad.* Most times I'm tortured. *This is only the beginning of what you'll endure in Many Ends.* Not knowing what awaits me is the worst.

"Prynne is supposed to be unaffiliated with either realm," she says with a frown.

"It is." How else could Dr. Vans convince one kid to sign with Myriad and another to sign with Troika? Which he does. All the time.

She meets my gaze, a little surprised, a lot hopeful. "Do you want to make covenant with Troika?"

"Not even a little." As her shoulders droop, I add, "I hate to break it to you, but your guardian sucks. He—she?—sentenced you to hell. For nothing! No one here will accept your *light.*" *Trust no one. Question everything.*

"Maybe not, but I'll still make the offer. Yesterday, today and tomorrow, my actions matter."

In that, I agree with her. I'll even take it a step further. The most destructive or constructive actions begin with a single thought. And, ultimately, a single action can decide the direction our lives take. And our deaths.

I will choose my path. Me alone. My choice will affect no eternal future but my own.

She opens her mouth to say more, but I shake my head. Subject closed.

She hops up and walks around the room, studying every nook and cranny, finally stopping to gape at my calendar. "Seriously? You're using a finger pen? No wonder everyone calls you Nutter. You're the biggest nut in the whack shack."

She just got here. How does she know what I'm called? "Everyone calls me Nutter because of the size of my lady balls. That, and I tend to smear my opponents across the floor like peanut butter."

She thinks for a moment, frowns. "If your lady balls are

so big, why don't they call you Hairy Cherries? Or Furry Meatballs?" She taps her chin. "Well, duh. Because neither name describes your explosive temper. Oh! I know. I'll call you Sperm Bank! It covers the balls *and* the explosions."

I snort-laugh. She's brave, so gold star for that. In a place like this, lack of fear is rare and precious. Of course, if she threatens me in the slightest way, I won't hesitate to end her. Survival first, nothing else second.

"If anyone calls me Sperm Bank, my temper is going to explode all over *you*," I say. "Meanwhile, I'll be sure to call you Hatchet. The tool used to cut your hair, I'm guessing."

She fluffs the ragged ends of her *style*. "I used a kitchen knife, thank you very much. I'm confident the trim properly highlights my beauty."

Have to admire her positivity.

My internal clock suddenly goes off, the conversation forgotten. "Breakfast!"

She sighs. "Mealtime. Yay."

"Our cell will open in three…two…one."

The double doors slide apart.

"We have thirty seconds to exit the room," I explain. "If the door closes while we're still inside, we'll miss the meal." The food sucks, nothing but slop, but that slop has enough vitamins to keep us somewhat healthy. And really, anything is better than starving.

"So we're like dogs in a crate, taken out only at scheduled times so we won't crap on something important or chew on the furniture. Awesome."

Together, we dart into the hall. Our blockmates do the same. In total, there are twelve of us.

Twelve: the number of months in a year, members on a jury, and the hours on the face of a clock.

For a moment, we take each other's measure. Anyone going to uncage the rage today?

When no one makes a lewd or violent gesture—hey, this might be a good day—we head for the exit at the end of the hall.

Jane, one of the older inmates, mutters to herself and stops to bang her forehead against the wall. Skin splits at her hairline and blood trickles down her cheek. Everyone else keeps walking, head down and arms wrapped around the torso, as if to protect the vitals—or stop an avalanche of pain and misery from spilling out.

I march determinedly beside Bow, for the first time noticing she exudes a fragrant mix of wildflowers and lemon drops. I like it, but I know it won't last. Our water smells like chemicals, and the soap we're given smells like grease.

A high-pitched whistle cuts through the air, making me cringe. "Well, well," a voice says from behind me. "I just lost a bet I'd assumed was a *sure thing*."

"Like Becky," someone else calls, and snickers erupt.

I don't have to glance over my shoulder to ID the first speaker. Sloan "don't hate me because I'm beautiful, hate me because I plan to murder you" Aubuchon. She is Dr. Vans's favorite inmate, even though she's tried to kill him, oh, a dozen times.

From the things I've heard the good doc say to her, she's here because either (a) she can't control her temper or (b) she refuses to marry the old fart who will save her grandparents' estate. I've always leaned toward A. Arranged marriages still happen, but not often.

"Tenley didn't kill her new roommate at first sight, y'all," she continues, her Southern twang ridiculously adorable even while she's sneering. "Meaning, the newbie wasn't eaten—at least not literally."

Charming.

A few boos ring out, but so do a couple of cheers.

Bow turns and smiles at the girl. "What'd you lose? A few more IQ points?"

I almost sigh, because I can guess what's coming next.

A volcanic Sloan races forward to grab Bow by the collar of her jumpsuit, forcing her to stop.

Yeah. That.

I stop, too, unsure how I'll proceed. I've seen this song and dance before—eleven times, to be exact—and my reactions always differ. I've pretended to be blind and deaf, but I've also thrown a punch while screaming obscenities.

Sloan and I live by different philosophies. While I lash out only when provoked (usually), she attacks newcomers at the first opportunity to prevent challengers later.

Life sucks. We've adapted.

"Bless your heart." Sloan releases Bow to plant her hands on her hips. Tall, blonde and model-pretty, she's the girl every other longs to be. Until she opens her mouth, and her outer beauty can no longer compensate for her inner bitch. "You're not smart enough to realize I run this shit show. You'll keep your eyes down and your tongue quiet… or you'll lose both."

Bow flicks me an amused glance. "Hey, what do you call a blonde with only half a brain? Gifted!"

Am I really caught in the middle of this? "Have you

forgotten that *you* are a blonde?" And Troikan! Forgive and move on.

"So," Bow says, tapping her chin. "You're suggesting I blow in her ear for a data transfer?"

"That's it! Say goodbye to your tongue." Sloan pushes Bow with enough force to make the girl stumble.

Before she can do anything else, I react without thought, slapping her arm away. "Hands off." Guess I'm going to protest today. Which might do more harm than good. Like the rest of us, Bow has to learn to defend herself. There's no other way to survive.

Sloan's narrowed gaze focuses on me. "What are you gonna do, Nutter? Huh?"

"Do you really want to know?" I ask softly. Being the crazy girl in a place full of crazy girls certainly has its advantages. No one is ever able to anticipate my next move. "What I say, I'll do. No take-backs."

We've thrown down before, Sloan and I, and it wasn't pretty. Forget scratching and pulling hair, the quintessential "catfight." We punched and kicked and ripped at each other like animals.

We both bear the scars.

I'm not afraid of physical pain. Not anymore.

I'm hit with surprise when my roommate says, "Dude. Do you have any idea how funny this is? Sloaner the Moaner has a mouthful of number two while she's talking to Ten."

Another round of boos and cheers ring out.

Sloan forgets all about me, baring her teeth in a scowl. "Maybe I won't remove your tongue and eyes...yet. I want you to see what I do to you, and beg for mercy I won't give you."

"Enough!" A harsh voice booms from overhead speakers. "You know the rules, girls. There's no loitering in the hallways. Go to the cafeteria or go to the whipping post. Your choice."

I look at Sloan, who's glaring at Bow, who's smirking at Sloan.

Sloan bares her teeth and says to me, "You do know your boyfriend wasn't the only one capable of paying the guards to shut off the cameras, right? If I were you, I'd start sleeping with one eye open." With that, she turns on her heel and flounces off. Or tries to.

I grab her arm, stopping her, and get in her face. I keep my voice low as I say, "You sneak into my room, and I'll fillet you like a fish. No one will pay attention to your screams. *You* know *that*, right?"

You scream, I scream, we all scream. No one cares. The asylum's unofficial anthem.

Sloan jerks free and stalks away.

I cast Bow a humorless smile. "Welcome to Prynne."

chapter two

"Take comfort. Our laws are the same yesterday, today and forever."
—Troika

Bow laughs, which I don't understand. My temper is a bear that's just been poked with a stick. I don't like threats. And I especially don't like waiting to deal with threats. Yet, she's amused.

"Come on," I mutter, dragging her down the hall despite my physical discomfort.

There are multiple doorways, each painted puke green. The walls are medicine-tray gray, and the floors are some type of soil-your-pants brown. I know this for a fact. Last week, a guard threatened a new guy with castration and all hell broke loose…just like his bowels.

"Thank you for having my six." Bow bumps shoulders with me, only to mumble an apology when I wince. "Yeah, I could have taken her down, no problem, but you still put yourself on the line."

"Don't thank me. Just keep your head on a swivel and

your insults to a minimum. I don't want to mop up your remains."

Her grin slips a little. "I didn't enjoy lashing out at her. Sloan has some pretty big baggage. But her general nastiness triggered my inner bitch. I didn't even know I had an inner bitch! But yeah, okay, I should have handled the situation differently."

"How do you know about her baggage?"

"Uh, perhaps I misspoke. I mean, who *doesn't* have baggage, right?"

True. We all arrive with a couple carry-ons.

We pass through the commons, where our classes usually take place. There's no escaping high school, even here. There are plush leather couches and three different circles of chairs—which makes sense. (1) Thought, (2) word and (3) deed, the sum total of human capability.

Around the corner and through a wide set of double doors is the cafeteria. A colorless, utilitarian room with a sea of tables and benches that have been bolted down. The male inmates are already seated, eating from trays.

As Bow and I take our place at the end of the buffet line, I narrow my focus to the nitty-gritty. The number of inmates in the room: one hundred females versus ninety-seven males. It's uneven. I don't like uneven. The scales should always be balanced.

There are twenty guards—ten males, ten females—one "good guy" for every ten "bad guys." Despite the fact that outside these walls there's a Laborer from both Troika and Myriad for every one hundred humans, there are no Laborers here.

"Are you mathing?" Bow asks. "You look like you're

mathing. Well, here's an equation I think you'll like. There are roughly two billion people in the world, and twenty million Laborers. With those kind of odds, I never should have been assigned to stay in your room."

"Are you hinting life is a zero-sum game? You won, and I lost."

She snorts. "You basically won the lottery, and you know it."

"Or, your guardian paid extra to pair you with an Unsigned, preferably one with a Myriad background." Which is actually counterproductive to Dr. Vans's goal in my case. But when has the man ever resisted a bonus?

"Hey, look at you! Pretty *and* smart."

"And hungry," I grumble.

As we edge our way to the front of the line, multiple conversations take place around us.

"—too bad. I called dibs."

"—did you hide them? Tell me!"

"—don't allow Myriad scum near me."

How many of these kids are pro-Myriad? How many are pro-Troika? How many are Unsigned?

Bow clearly hasn't gotten the memo. Talking about the Everlife is forbidden. Well, only with each other. Dr. Vans's way of avoiding a riot inside these walls, I guess.

I deduced Sloan is Unsigned, which wasn't exactly hard to do considering she's said "I'd rather be a queen in Many Ends than a drone in the realms" countless times.

Okay, not countless. Twenty-three.

"We're going to be spending a lot of time together," Bow tells me. "Let's get to know each other better."

"No, thanks."

She persists. "How were you introduced to the realms?"

"The usual way." Since public schools aren't allowed to lean one way or the other, only private schools, children are told stories by biased parents. Also, different facilities offer virtual tours but, depending on who's running them, the tours are always skewed.

My aunt Lina is my dad's crazy twin sister who, I've been told, suffers from polyfused disorder, meaning the older spirit (supposedly) Fused to hers is strong enough to gain control of her body. When she isn't acting like a giggly ten-year-old who speaks in the past tense, she works for A Look Beyond, a tour company owned by Myriad.

I've seen night-kissed castles overflowing with orchid gardens. Bustling cityscapes with stone and metal skyscrapers intermixed with nightclubs and spas, everything connected by sleek silver bridges and tunnels illuminated by wrought-iron, dragon-shaped lamps. Vibrant white-sand beaches with a moonlit view of ruby, sapphire and emerald coral.

A bit of high-tech flare topped with old-world charm.

There's something for everyone, Aunt Lina likes to say on her sane days. On her *in*sane days? *The light bled into the darkness and the darkness died… I didn't want to die.*

On the other hand, Troika's version of Myriad is frightening. Darkness pervades. Darkness so thick it oozes over your skin like motor oil. There's field after field of dead trees, the limbs gnarled, the bark dripping crimson—bleeding. Any birds able to survive the lack of sunlight cry rather than squawk. The city is overcrowded, everyone packed as tight as pickles in a jar, and the beaches resemble life-size litter boxes.

Myriad's version of Troika is no better. Apocalyptic wastelands scorched by an unforgiving sun.

As a child, I was desperate to avoid Troika...until I heard my Troikan Laborer's description: dappled sunlight falling over intricate gardens, wildflowers and rainbows. A thriving metropolis both fantastical and futuristic, with palatial country estates and chrome-and-glass buildings in a variety of shapes and sizes.

"You might want to stop mentioning the realms," I finally say. "It'll get you punished."

She pushes out a breath. "Fine. I'll talk about something else. Something fascinating. Like the food. I'm pretty sure it's going to look the same coming out as it does going in."

She isn't wrong. "If you want a change of menu, the bugs in our room are always an option. Side note. Spiders taste like shrimp and cockroaches taste like greasy chicken."

"Okay, I now want to gag and hug you at the same time." She thinks for a moment, releases a dreamy sigh. "Maybe I'll have dessert snuck in."

"Good luck with that." Others have tried. Others have failed. "You'll be caught and—"

"Punished. Yeah, yeah. I know."

We're both given a tray. As we search for a table, a group of boys gives Bow a once-over. Snickers abound.

I stiffen, but Bow winks at them as we claim the empty table to their right.

"I think I heard the guards say her name's Bow," one of them says, not even trying to be quiet.

"It fits—unlike her uniform. Fatty Bow Batty," another mutters, spurring outright laughter from his friends.

Bow ignores them and stirs her slop as if she hasn't a

care. She's short and big-boned, a little plain, but she's a person with feelings.

I find myself snapping, "Integrity matters more than size, dreg." A derogatory name for someone neither realm wants.

He blows me a kiss. "Why don't you come sit on my lap, Nutter? I'll show you just how sizable I am."

Innuendos are always on the menu at Prynne, and I usually overlook them. Today, my fingers tighten around my spoon. We aren't given forks or knives, ever. Not that it matters. I can do bad, bad things with a spoon.

I glare at him and say, "Do you like having a tongue?"

He sticks his out and wags it at me.

I don't want to fight him—I'm too sore—but I will. If I lose, I lose, but at least I'll leave an impression.

Bow pats my hand. "Forget about him, Sperm Bank. He doesn't yet understand the outside is a shell for all of us. My beauty is on the inside, where it never fades."

She can't be this nice. She just can't be.

The boys return to their conversation, whispering among themselves, pretending what almost happened didn't almost happen.

"Plus," Bow adds, "he isn't even close to my type."

"Which is?"

She wiggles her brows. "Female."

Ah. Got it.

We lapse into silence. I remain aware of the people around us, always on alert, as I clean my tray. Gotta stay as strong as possible. Bow merely picks at the meal. One day soon, hunger will get the better of her and she'll be *thankful* for the slop.

One of the boys is trying to snag a bite off his friend's tray as we stand.

"Touch my food and die." The friend's snarl is pure menace.

"Here. You can have mine," Bow says.

The boy scowls at her. "Mind your own business, cow."

Trust no one. Question everything.

She shrugs, unaffected. "Your loss."

I'm not sure where to lump her in my mental files. Too good to be true? The real deal? Worth emulating? Or to be disregarded?

As we file out of the cafeteria, I'm sent to the commons for early morning therapy of the mind—*have to get my day started right*, I mentally sneer—and Bow is sent to the gym for early morning therapy of the body.

Sloan shoves another girl out of the way to claim the chair next to me. "You need to put your roommate on a shorter leash."

Going to pretend we didn't threaten each other? Fine.

"I'm not her keeper," I say. Her actions, her consequences.

"Don't be stupid," Sloan snaps. "In this place, your roomie should be your best friend. She's the one who's going to watch your back when yours is bruised." With a smirk, she presses on my shoulder, drawing a hiss from me. "Like now."

I bat her arm away, which only makes my pain worse. "I don't need your advice." *Trust no one...*

"Obviously you do. Word is, Vans will be gone tonight. Two guards have decided there's no better time to retaliate against you for choking their friend."

I stiffen. The choking incident happened four months ago, and the memory still haunts me. The guard in question snuck into my room. He thought I should earn his goodwill. I thought differently.

He left in a body bag.

I didn't enjoy killing him, even in self-defense, but I also didn't feel more than a few twinges of remorse. I've endured one too many beatings, or maybe I've witnessed one too many murders. Kids killing other kids. Guards killing kids. Vans killing James. We're desensitized fast. Here, it's survival of the fittest.

Guess Myriad and I agree on something. Might Equals Right.

"Thanks for the warning," I say, my stomach beginning to churn. I'm not ready for another battle. Not one of this magnitude. I'm not strong enough.

Doesn't matter. I have to find a way.

She scowls at me. "I didn't do it for you. The more prepared you are, the better your chances of killing two more of Vans's men."

Bloodthirsty girl. As always. "Also the better my chances of spending another thirty days in the pit, giving you a chance to strike at Bow without my interference, eh." The pit is a frigid hole in the basement where the only source of water is a rusty tap, and a bucket is the only piece of furniture.

"Hey. It's a small price to pay."

"Of course you'd think so. You've never spent any time down there."

"Not for lack of trying!"

I can't argue with that. I've often wondered why she's singular to Vans. Is she sleeping with him?

I've heard rumors about girls earning special privileges with their bodies. I've also heard about girls being threatened with harsher punishments if they refuse. Even the thought fills me with rage.

From time to time, a guard has propositioned me. I said no, flat out, every time. I've never had sex and my first time won't be a freaking business transaction. In my old life, some of my friends had often hit-it-and-quit-it, and it hadn't taken me long to notice most grumbled with disappointment while only a rare few sighed dreamily.

The loss of my virginity is a memory I'm going to carry into my Secondlife and dang it, I'm going to be one of the ones who sighs dreamily.

"You boning the boss?" I ask her.

Color blooms in her cheeks. Embarrassment? Shame? Both? She jumps up and snarls at me. "Oh, go to Many Ends, dreg!"

"And leave these luxurious accommodations? Nah."

She flounces off and chooses a new seat.

I remain on a razor's edge of calm through therapy...my different classes...lunch...and finally dinner. No one strikes at me, but all the guards are a little too *nice*. They smile every time I pass. They ask if I need help with anything.

That night, after Bow and I are locked in our cell, our lights out, I rush to cover the camera with a sheet—just in case—and gather my stash of shivs made from spoons and toothbrushes, hidden behind a stone in the wall.

No one tells me to remove the sheet, a sign in and of itself. The guards don't want anyone to record what's going to happen, and they can blame me for the lack of feed, maybe even claim I hurt myself in an attempt to incriminate them. Not that they'd get into trouble for hurting me.

"What's going on?" Bow demands.

I explain the situation. She waves a hand through the air, unconcerned.

"You won't need those," she says. "I've got this. You can sit back and simply enjoy the show."

As if.

I move to the side of the door, taking a sentry position. With a sigh, Bow does the same.

One hour ticks into another, but I remain in place. I've done this kind of vigil before, during the realm riots that occurred in my front yard.

My dad is a senator in the House of Myriad, responsible for ensuring Myriad-friendly laws are passed and Troika-friendly laws aren't.

Sometimes when a hot-button issue arose—like Myriad's desire to supersede the human government—Troikan protesters congregated on our lawn, threw rotten food at our doors and windows and screamed vitriol. I just had to wait for it to end.

The stress is the biggest obstacle. My limbs shake. My stomach twists. Sweat drips down my spine. At least I'm not cowering.

I'll never cower again.

"You sure they're coming tonight?" Bow asks, as blasé as ever.

"Yes. No. I don't know." Sloan could have lied to me. Her version of payback, I suppose. Although keeping us frazzled tonight so we're useless tomorrow isn't exactly her MO. She likes to use shivs of her own.

Finally the doors slide open. I tense, ready to strike. *Four* men wearing black masks march into the room.

They know where we're hiding. The two men in front swing their arms to deliver a brutal punch. One to each of us.

I'm slower than usual, so I fail to duck in time. I take a fist to the center of the chest, my heart skipping a beat… then another…before leaping into a too-fast rhythm. Bow manages to duck just fine, grab her guy by the arm and, using her elbow as a hammer, break his radius. As he howls with pain, she kicks out her leg, nailing my guy in the torso, causing him to double over.

I act quickly, slamming my knee into his nose. He goes down as another guy dives on me, knocking *me* down. Upon impact, agony consumes me. I can barely breathe, my lungs flattened, stars winking behind my eyelids.

Get up! I have to win this.

I try without success. Meanwhile, I hear a rustle of clothing, the crunch of other bones breaking…another howl of pain. Dragging sounds. A feminine grunt.

A shadow falls over me. I hold out my hands to ward off—

"It's okay," Bow says. "It's just me."

Relieved, I sag against the cold, hard floor.

"The men are out for the count and now in the hall."

Good, that's good. Guess she had this, after all.

Maybe I can trust her a little?

No, no. *Must resist the urge*. Despite what Sloan said—despite Bow's actions—no good can come from an alliance.

We're too different, and with Bow's support of Troika, she'll turn on me soon enough.

"I guess we're even," I manage to say. I had her back with Sloan, and she had mine with the guards. I got the better end of the deal, but that's not a me problem.

"Wow. You are one tough Nutter to crack. And that's *not* a compliment."

"I used to be nice," I tell her. My version of an apology, I suppose. "I was even shy."

I don't miss the girl I used to be; she's a stranger in so many ways. She was scared and weak.

With a strength that baffles me, Bow picks me up and carries me to my bed. She gently lays me across the mattress, saying, "What you need is—"

"Do *not* say light."

"Fine. A distraction from your troubles. Want to make out a little?" There's a teasing note in her tone. "This would be a pity session, nothing more. You may be female, but you're still not my type. You're way too mouthy. Oh! I know! I can teach you better uses for your—"

"Shut. Up," I say, trying not to laugh. Laughing will only make the hurt worse.

"Is that a soft no?"

"Hard no. I'm currently in a relationship."

She arches a brow. "You have a boyfriend?"

"No." *Miss you so much, James.* "I'm dating myself."

Bow snorts. "You want my advice? Break up with her. She's no good for you."

"Hey!"

"Well, it's true. Right now her priorities are seriously screwed up."

★★★

The next six days are surprisingly good. Well, as good as can be expected in a place as vile as Prynne.

The four guards were culled from the pack. Dr. Vans says they just up and disappeared, but that can't be true. He never punishes his men. I think the bastards are recovering in the medical ward. I just don't know why *Bow and I* haven't been punished.

I mean, we've been fed three squares every day, we haven't been singled out during any of our classes, and Sloan hasn't attacked us.

It's the little things.

My biggest complaint? Most of Bow's conversations begin with "If you sign with Troika, you'll..."

Discover the true meaning of joy.
Know peace for the first time.
Have access to the best advisors in the world.
Make friends who will always have your back.

Pick one. Pick all. Gimme. But too bad for her, Myriad makes the same promises.

I place my newest blood mark on the calendar and straighten with ease. My back is on the mend, my range of motion almost normal.

"Tell me something," Bow says as she ties her boots. I'm surprised she's lucid. She spent the entire night threatening the wall. *Go away. I'm going to kill* you. *Oh, yeah? Well, I can definitely hurt you.* "Have you met with a new ML lately? A boy? Maybe kinda sorta...handsome." She gags, as if the word tastes foul. "Maybe he pulled you aside in secret."

ML—Myriad Laborer. “No. Why?”

She hikes a shoulder in a faux-casual shrug. “I know Myriad’s MO. When a teenage girl refuses to do their bidding, they send a boy they think she’ll like. One who’s supposed to rev her engine.”

“My engine is set to idle, remember? Maybe permanently.” After James… No. Just no.

“Hey. Don’t say I didn’t warn you.”

My parents would never agree to…

Oh, who am I kidding? They so would.

“I guess it’s better than the alternative.” She stands, stretches her arms over her head and arches her back. “If Myriad ever considers you a lost cause, there’s a good chance they’ll send someone to kill you.”

Same with Troika. There have always been whispers about Laborers who poison the Unsigned to prevent a pledge to the other realm. “One, I’m not close to signing, period. And two, if I die here, Dr. Vans won’t get a bonus.”

The pro? The greedy bastard would take a bullet to save me. The con? It’s just a matter of time before he ramps my torture to the next level.

No matter what’s done to me in the future, I will hold out. I must. I’ll be released on my eighteenth birthday. Though my parents signed with Myriad before my conception, there was a special clause for the birth of a child.

When I came along, their contracts had to be renegotiated. Now their benefits are dependent on my decision. An incentive to raise me the “right” way.

If I haven’t signed with Myriad by the time I’m a legal adult, my parents will lose everything they love more than they ever loved me. Money, prestige. Homes. Cars. Boats. Not to mention the things they were promised in the Everlife.

Bow sighs. "Another day, another breakfast. Or a meal pretending to be breakfast."

A sense of doom overtakes me, a shadow I'm unable to shake. Bad is coming. Bad is always coming. But since six days have passed without incident—bad is coming *soon*.

Sounding resigned, she says, "Our cell will open in—"

"Three, two, one," I finish.

The doors slide apart, and we race into the hall.

Sloan spots me and flips me off. I know she's pleased four guards are missing, but she's also ticked about something—clearly—and lashing out.

I look her over and find finger-size bruises around her neck. Someone tried to choke her out. Been there, lived through that.

If I show her an ounce of sympathy, she'll try to throat punch me. I blow her a kiss.

"Come on," I say to Bow.

We make our way to the cafeteria, where I count the occupants out of habit. My gaze lands on a boy I've never before seen and oh, wow. Okay. He. Is. Gorgeous. Not that I care about a pretty face. Pretty can hide a monster. But I'm not overhyping when I say he's a living ad for every dream-boy fantasy every girl in the universe has ever had.

He has dark hair that hangs over a stern brow. I can't make out the color of his eyes, but just like with Bow, I can feel the intensity of them—because they're locked on me. His nose is straight, perfect, and his lips soft and pink. His jaw is strong and dusted with the shadow of a beard.

He leans back and drapes his tattooed, muscular arms

over the tops of the chairs flanking him, and smiles, a slow unveiling of perfect, white teeth.

In moments like this I miss Clay more than usual. He was—is!—such a good judge of character. He can take one look at a new inmate or guard and tell me if they have a heart of gold or one that's as wrinkled as a prune. We called him the heartalyst.

Where are you, Clay?

"Son of a Myriad-troll." Bow snarls, taking a step forward, about to move out of line. "How dare he show his ugly face!"

I shackle her wrist in a hard grip to hold her in place.

"Don't worry," she says, huffing and puffing. "I won't break the rules and murder him. I'll just introduce him to my fists—repeatedly!"

When she continues to struggle, I plant myself in front of her, forcing her to concentrate on me. "Calm down. Now. Or you'll be dragged out of here kicking and screaming."

She tries to glare at the boy over my shoulder.

"My TL once said hate is like drinking a vial of poison and expecting it to harm the other person," I tell her, and she finally settles. "You're not hurting the guy, only yourself."

"But…but… I'm justified," she says with a whine.

"So is everyone else, I'm sure." As I peer at her, curiosity fills me. "How do you know him? What'd he do to you?"

Stiffening, she turns away. "We've crossed paths a time or two. He's pure Myriad evil, trust me."

"He can't be that bad. I'm sure—"

In a flash of motion, she's facing me again, fisting my shirt, clinging to me, her copper eyes imploring me to understand. "He's worse than bad. Stay away from him. Okay? All right?"

I dare another glance at "pure Myriad evil." He's focused on Bow now, looking her up and down like he's a predator and it's finally mealtime. He smiles again, even more slowly, a lot more wickedly, and runs his tongue over his teeth, as if he can already taste her…and he only wants more.

I lose the ability to breathe.

"Move," the inmate behind Bow commands, giving her a push.

I snap to and toss the girl a scowl that rivals Sloan's, silently promising violence. Only when she's staring at her feet do I step forward and accept my tray from a creeper with greasy hair and an even greasier mustache. I'm pretty sure Dr. Vans purposely hires the scourge of the earth to scare us straight.

Bow accepts her tray and shepherds me across the cafeteria, as far away from New Guy as possible. I let her get away with it for only one reason: that stupid curiosity. Along the way we pass Sloan, who just can't resist the opportunity to stick out her leg to trip Bow. But Bow is a freak of nature. She jumps over the obstacle and kicks back, hooking Sloan's ankle between her feet and ripping the girl out of her chair.

As Sloan goes down, her elbow slams into her tray. Food pours over her head, and as she shrieks, the rest of the cafeteria grows quiet. Finally a chuckle cuts through the shock, and it's like a starting bell. The rest of the room explodes into squawks of laughter.

Bow doesn't grin over her triumph; she frowns. Once

again wishing she'd handled things differently? "I'm sorry," she calls over her shoulder.

What a conundrum she is. Smart, with sharply honed protect-yourself-at-any-cost instincts. But she also has a deep-seated need to soothe others.

When we find a table, she stares at me, intent. "Listen. Things are different now. Things you won't understand. You have to trust me, and you have to keep me nearby from now on. No matter what. Okay? All right? I'll see to your safety. If you'll let me."

"You can't see to my safety." No one can. "There are too many threats."

"Dude. I've already proved otherwise, and yet still you doubt me?"

"And," I continue as if she hasn't spoken, "I don't want you to try. I mean it. You'll only get yourself into trouble."

"Ten—"

"No. No arguments." I may be confused about my future, but I'm not confused about my present. I'll never place my well-being in the hands of someone else. Once, I trusted my parents. They sent me here. I trusted James. Since his death, I've been stuck with a terrible sense of loss. I trusted Marlowe, who'd been pro-Troika, but ultimately, she was so desperate to leave the asylum and enter the realm, she hung herself. She also abandoned Clay, who *loved* her.

Now I don't know if she's actually in Troika or Many Ends—if it's real. Suicide is expressly forbidden by both realms, and it can even render a contract null and void.

I trusted Clay, too. He managed to stay clean and sober until Marlowe's death. Afterward, he spiraled, doing I-don't-know-what to buy "happy" drugs from a nurse.

His mind roilin' and boilin', he asked me to escape with him. Said he'd paid the guards to do what they'd done for James. I'd already lost my boyfriend and couldn't bear the thought of losing another friend, so I turned him down and begged him to give me time to figure out a better way.

The next day, he was gone.

That was three months ago. Where is he? Free? Or was he caught? Is he somewhere within these horrible walls?

Sometimes I think I hear screams rising from my concrete floor.

"That boy...he's Myriadian, you know," Bow mutters.

She says *Myriadian* with the same inflection she might use with *cancer.* Does she hate him just because he signed with the other realm? "Have you ever heard of HART?"

"Humans Against Realm Turmoil? Yep. They like to protest the war between the realms in front of the House of Myriad, the House of Troika, and the White House."

"Right." From my History of the Worlds class, I know their ultimate goal is a treaty between the realms and the Land of the Harvest. I also know the first members got together soon after the realms revealed themselves...again.

Apparently, the realms did the whole "Hi, we're here and we're real" a few times over the ages, but humans—being human—romanticized the truth. Myriad has been called everything from Valhalla to Mount Olympus, while Troika was once known as Paradise. Then, around the 1500s, both realms began to insert themselves into everyday human existence, drawing us out of the dark ages.

"Why?" Bow asks, her tone cautious.

"Well, I'm wondering why members of the realms haven't agreed to a peace treaty. Or, you know, just hugged it out. I'm wondering why you hate a boy just because he's different. Or because he's hurt you for some mysterious reason. You Troikans claim you're all about forgiveness, right?"

"Forgiving someone isn't the same as letting him crap all over me. Dude. Have you ever heard the Myriad pledge of allegiance? *We won't rest until Troika is nothing but ash in the wind of eternity.* Also, the HART campaign is ridiculous. Light and darkness cannot coexist. A house divided cannot stand." She pushes her tray to the middle of the table, as if she's lost her appetite. "We'd be a two-headed beast, and we'd consume ourselves."

Speaking of consumption, she's eaten so little since her arrival I'm beginning to worry about her health.

"Distract me," she says.

"Eat," I reply.

"No. Distract me," she repeats.

"Want me to sing and dance for you?" I ask drily.

"Yes!"

"No way, no how. Not happening."

"Fine." She sighs with disappointment. "Just… I don't know, talk to me. Tell me something about your life before the asylum."

I don't want to share details about myself, but I also don't want her to starve, and it's now clear she requires motivation. "I'll give a nugget or two, but only if you eat everything on your tray."

"Are you kidding? It's gross and—"

"Trust me, you need the vitamins."

"Fine." With a grimace, she returns the tray to its proper place. "Now talk."

Where to begin? It seems like an eternity since I've revealed even a minor detail about my history. "I attended a Myriad-endorsed private school."

She waits for me to say more. I don't. She gives her tray another push.

I scowl at her. "What do you want to know?"

"How about your studies?"

"Besides the usual courses?" Easy. "The inner workings of the realm." Those classes were taught by Messengers, people responsible for spreading the word about the realm they loved.

Mostly, I'd been fascinated by the daily life of spirits. Unlike us, they have no need to sleep. They eat only one meal a day, a single piece of manna. A honeycomb-like wafer. Anyone under the age of eighteen attends school to learn more about their realm and its leaders. Kids are also taught the skills they'll need for whatever job they'll one day be assigned.

Everyone over the age of eighteen works an assignment nonstop until completion—even if the assignment takes years. Like undercover cops.

Bow swallows a bite of slop and grimaces. "What about your friends?"

"They were sheltered, like me." The answer leaves me without hesitation, as if I'm already used to sharing. "We could hang out together, but only with a parent or Laborer in view. We weren't to get behind the wheel of a car or even into a car with someone other than the person paid to drive us." At first, I accepted it. I thought, *My parents love me, want me protected.* Then came resentment. *My parents simply need me alive, whatever the cost.*

The day of my sixteenth birthday, after I refused to sign

with Myriad, I stole the keys to my mom's car. I'd never driven before, but autopilot made it effortless. I'd soared, and I'd never had so much fun.

But that kind of fun never lasts, does it?

The next day, I ended up at the asylum, scared out of my mind, shocked and confused.

"Does Troika choose humans the same way Myriad does?" I ask.

"Pretty much. Headhunters monitor people on the earth, searching for a certain trait."

Headhunter, a subdivision of Leader. "What trait?"

"Willingness."

"Willingness?" What does that even mean?

"Anyway," she continues. "Laborers are sent to protect the chosen and then, when the human reaches the Age of Accountability, they negotiate covenant terms and guide the human through the rest of Firstlife. With us, though, covenants are voided if the signer is coerced. With Myriad, a coerced signer must go to court to gain freedom."

Court? "There's a way out?" The news gives me hope.

"Yes, but too many lose the case, since the court insists both Troikans and Myriadians attend. The signer often cracks during questioning."

Well, a *little* hope.

"Now I know the before-Prynne Ten." Bow waves her spoon at me. "Tell me about the after-Prynne Ten. What are you going to do when you're free?"

Reveal who I want to be, rather than who I used to be? That one proves more difficult. "You first."

"As if you couldn't guess. I'm going to continue spreading light, and I'm going be the best Troikan Laborer—and the sexiest—in the history of ever."

I've struggled to pick a side for over a year. Here she is, unwavering in her belief. I'll just pretend I'm not writhing with envy. "How do you know you'll be a Laborer? There are four other jobs in the Everlife with multiple subpositions under each."

"I've known here—" she taps her fist over her heart "—all my life."

"And the feeling has never wavered?" Not once?

"Why would it? My position in life—and death—is part of who I am."

The envy I'm totally *not* feeling prompts me to say, "Or, fate has decided for you."

She scoffs, saying, "Don't get me started on fate! Fate is an excuse, a way to remove blame and therefore guilt for poor decision making. Free choice decides the outcome of your life, *not* fate."

Girl makes a good point.

"Why aren't you branded?" Those who make covenant with Troika are supposed to tattoo a three-point star on the top of each hand—not that everyone does. Those who make covenant with Myriad are supposed to tattoo interlocking jagged lines on their wrists. Again, not that everyone does. It's supposed to be an outward sign of an inward commitment.

"Oh, no." She shakes her head. "I answered your question. It's your turn to answer mine. What are you going to do after the asylum?"

I chew on my bottom lip as my mind whirls. I've never voiced my desire aloud, have held the secret close to my heart. “My grandparents left me a trust.” One my parents can’t touch. My grandparents were Troikan, which was how my mom was raised. When she met my dad, she decided Myriad was the place for her. “At eighteen, I’ll be set. I’ll be able to afford a house on the beach.” One with zero neighbors who force me to think about issues I can’t solve. “I’m going to…surf.”

I’ve never been allowed, could only watch other people from the safety of my bedroom. Anytime I asked to do something remotely “dangerous,” I was told I had to wait until I reached the Age of Accountability and signed with Myriad.

Now I crave excitement. The wind in my face, water beaded over my skin.

For some reason, as happiness buzzes in my veins, my gaze is drawn to New Guy.

He’s staring at me again.

Each of my pulse points leaps. Not knowing what else to do, I nod in acknowledgment.

“Wait. Are you *eye-screwing* him?” Bow demands.

What? “No!”

Somehow he hears our conversation over the chatter around us and calls, “Yes.” Then he winks at me.

I glare at him before I glare at Bow. I might have shared tidbits of my life with her, but that doesn’t mean she knows me or has the right to castigate me. “Do you want me as your enemy, Bow?”

Her jaw drops. “No. Of course not.”

I say nothing else, my point made. I stand and walk away from her…toward New Guy.

He smiles at me, but it's the wicked one, as if he knows a secret I don't, and it sets my nerves on edge.

As I pass him, I take a page from Bow's book, hook my foot around the leg of his chair and yank. The chair topples over, taking him with it.

His surprised laughter follows me out of the cafeteria.

chapter three

"There is no supposed to be, only what is."
—Myriad

There's a line in the hallway. As I take my place at the tail, Bow rushes up behind me, apologizing. I ignore her. As usual, some kids are sent to the gym to "lose a few pounds," and some are sent to the commons to "lose a little crazy." In either case, the time is considered a preclass "warm-up."

Also as usual, I'm sent to the commons.

A guard oinks at Bow and pushes her toward the gym. For the first time, she sidesteps him and tries to follow me.

I remember her warning. *You have to keep me nearby from now on.*

She's *that* worried about New Guy?

The guard—I call him Colonel Anus—grabs her. At the moment of contact, she spins, raising the arm he's holding and also cradling it against her chest while rotating her wrist, putting her palm just under her chin. She uses her other hand to latch on to the meaty part of *his* palm. Then she steps back, twisting his wrist.

He drops, hitting the floor with a thud, his arm now positioned behind his back.

Girl has even more skills than I realized. I'm impressed.

"I'm staying with my roommate today. Get used to the idea." She drops Anus's arm and steps on the back of his head to pass him. His nose slams into the floor, and he wails with pain. The problem? He has a friend I've named Ben Dover. Ben launches into action, grabbing Bow by the hair and yanking. She flails as she falls backward.

"Chubby girls don't get to spend their mornings chatting about their problems." He spits at her when she lands. "The treadmill is your best friend."

"Well, my fist is your worst enemy." She kicks out and nails him between the legs. "And my foot. Yeah, I probably should have mentioned my foot."

He loses his breath as he drops to his knees.

She sits up and draws back her elbow, clearly planning to knock out his teeth. New Guy runs past her before she can act and she goes still, as if her mind has clocked out for a smoke break. Did he do something to her? By the time she's all systems go, the guard has swallowed the nuts she drilled into his throat and reentered the game. He easily dodges her next blow and throws one of his own, popping her in the jaw.

A loud *crack* rings out.

As Bow crashes, other inmates move out of the way. Including me.

I want to help her, and I will—when I can actually do some good. *Know when to strike and when to wait. Or hurt.*

Two other guards and a nurse—a woman I affectionately refer to as Nurse Ratched—enter the fray.

Nurse Ratched pulls a syringe from the pocket of her lab coat. "A special cocktail for a special girl." Bow is held down and stuck in the neck. Her entire body begins to twitch, but she remain conscious. Most other kids pass out when they're drugged.

Guilt fills me. Could I have done something?

She would have done something for me.

"Show over." Nurse Ratched, another Russian, glares at me as if I'm at fault. "Move along. Now!"

No other choice. Well, no other *intelligent* choice. I head to the commons alongside the others. I'm trembling as I sit in my assigned circle in the back of the room, where chairs without cushions have been nailed down.

New Guy shoves someone aside to take the spot next to me. That someone—a boy named Hank—protests until New Guy gives him a hard thump to the throat. While Hank gasps for air, New Guy gifts me with that slow predator's grin.

I breathe him in: peat smoke and heather. Exotic, with a hint of musk, and I swear it's like I've just been transported to the British Isles after a rainstorm.

His eyes…they're as bright as the sun I haven't seen in over a year, and they are the most mesmerizing shade of gold with flecks of crystalline blue.

In one, there are five flecks. In the other, three.

Five. The number of our senses. Sight, sound, touch, taste and smell.

Three. A trinity. We have a spirit, soul and body.

In an octave, the fifth and third notes create the basic foundation of all chords. How appropriate. Those eyes have somehow made my blood sing. Or I'm simply malnourished and on edge, and my brain is overcompensating.

Yeah. That.

This close, I can almost count New Guy's individual lashes. They are long, spiky and jet-black…and I'm staring at him, I realize.

"That wasn't a very nice thing to do," I say.

"And knocking over my chair was?" His voice is low and husky with a slight Irish lilt, and it's almost as smoky as his scent. "Let's do the introduction thing so my heartbeat will finally calm down. I'm Killian. And you are stunningly beautiful."

Before he's finished delivering the (clearly) practiced line, I'm already building walls. "I think you mean I'm attitudinal."

"Definitely not. But now I'm certain you're irresistible."

"I think you mean unsuitable."

"Or adorable."

Oh, crap. Are we flirting? "All right. Enough."

The corners of his lips twitch. "Are you playing hard to get, lass? It's never happened to me before, so I need clarification."

"I'm not playing anything. And I'm *impossible* to get."

He rubs his hands together with something akin to glee. "Well, then. Challenge accepted."

I open my mouth to protest, but my gaze lands on his wrists. Myriad brands. They are the loveliest I've ever seen, the links slanted rather than rounded, creating languid eyes. And up close like this, the tattoos on his forearms appear to be Technicolor. They are spectacular, but there are too many to count without a more intense study.

I want to do a more intense study.

And…there's something odd about the images. Something more than simple aesthetics. The arrangement, maybe? There are lines through the skull with tears of blood. More lines through the cracked and crumbling moon, with pieces falling into the stars. Are they telling a story? Like hieroglyphics?

"Into tattoos, lass? Well, I'm happy to offer you a private unveiling later."

My cheeks flare with heat. I duck my head to hide the reaction.

I'm not usually into tattoos, no. Even though I have one myself. A small rendition of planet Earth on the back of my neck. I was fifteen when I got it—snuck out with my friends in my first real act of rebellion—but I'm not sure why I thought a globe was "a perfect expression of my turbulent emotions, and something I'll *never* regret."

"You're still staring," he says.

I grind my teeth. "Where are you from?" Like the staff, inmates hail from all over the world. I'm a native of Los Angeles, where the House of Myriad resides—where my dad wields a massive amount of power. The laws he helps push through affect both humans and spirits.

My mother is an artist in high demand. Her paintings of Myriad always sell at auction.

I sometimes wonder what the two have told their friends about my absence. Boarding school? Rehab? Or the truth?

"Where do you want me to be from?" Killian rasps.

Irritation sparks. "Why are you here?" I always ask the newcomers, even though I rarely receive an answer. Bow, Marlowe and Clay are the exceptions.

He shrugs. "Would you believe I saw something I wanted and decided to come in and get it?"

My blush returns, and I lament the fairness of my skin. Not to mention my inability to hide even the slightest reaction. Most of all, I lament his effect on me. "Let me guess. You wanted the five-star cuisine? The frequent whippings? The voyeuristic staff?"

Nonchalant, he drapes his arm over the back of my chair. "Perhaps it was your friend. What's she calling herself these days?"

His odd phrasing throws me. "Her name is Bow, if that's what you mean."

"Bow." He laughs, low and intimate. "An archer uses a bow and arrow. How cute."

Again, I'm thrown. "What's the deal between you two?"

"She's a bitch, and she can't be trusted. Don't worry, though." He leans close enough to graze the tip of his nose against my ear. "I'll protect you."

I jerk away, severing contact.

"Are you afraid of me? I'm disappointed." Killian pouts at me. "Where's the firecracker who once choked a guard with his own belt?"

I don't have to wonder how he obtained his info. In here, the gossip train never stops running. I'm sure he heard about my punishment, too.

"I'm not afraid of you. I just don't like to be touched without first granting permission." I meet his gaze dead-on, a clear challenge. "And if you want an introduction to the firecracker, I can arrange it. She's a little ticked you called her roommate a bitch."

He accepts the new challenge with eagerness. "Yes, please. With a cherry on top of me."

He's laughing at me, isn't he? He's even relaxed enough to twirl a lock of my hair around his finger, the black strands a lovely contrast to the bronze of his skin.

I slap his hand away. "You're positive? She's heartless."

"You're only whetting my appetite, lass."

Not just laughing, but mocking. It makes my next action easier. "Don't forget. You begged for this." I punch him in the throat, a quick jab that causes him to gasp for breath he isn't able to catch. Payback for Hank. The action should stop…whatever this is.

I smile at him. "Just so you know, even an animal in a cage can strike back."

He recovers swiftly and—shocker—returns my smile with one of his own. His amusement appears genuine and, dare I believe it, tinged with a bit of respect.

He opens his mouth to reply, but Sloan glides into the empty seat beside him and pats his chest. She doesn't appear to enjoy the connection, but she doesn't end it, either. "Hey there, sugar bear." She gives him a patented I'm-not-wearing-any-panties wink but it, too, seems faked. "I thought I'd save you the trouble of asking around for my info. I'm Sloan Aubuchon."

His attention never leaves me. "No, thank you, lass. I'm only interested in Ten."

His accent is thicker now, pure seduction, but the sweet words are actually a threat. I sense it. Too bad for him, I'm far from cowed. He has no idea the horrors I've endured. I'm not a wilting flower. Not anymore.

"Ten kisses from me?" she asks.

"To you," I tell him, "I'm Tenley." What's in a name? Only everything. Nicknames allow an intimacy I don't want to share with him.

"Or you can call her Nutter," Sloan says, helpful as ever. "Everyone else does."

His gaze rakes over me. "For the size of your balls, or the nutty goodness of your taste?"

Through gritted teeth, I say, "Do you require another introduction to the firecracker?"

He's smiling as Dr. Vans enters the room.

Quiet descends over the circle as the most hated male in the asylum sits in the only cushioned chair. His narrowed gaze finds Sloan, and he pats the empty seat next to him. The one always saved for her.

She raises her chin and remains in place.

I don't like the way he's looking at her. I lean into his line of sight, claiming his attention with my glare. He runs his tongue over his teeth before looking away from me.

He's a tall, lean man in his late thirties. His short brown hair is always meticulously styled, his clothes impeccably tailored underneath his lab coat.

"Are you *protecting* your enemy?" Killian asks me. "Lass, you're getting more interesting by the second."

"You mean I'm getting more bristling," I mutter.

"More riveting."

Dang, he's quick.

"All right, everyone. We have a new member of our family. Please stand and tell the group three facts about yourself, Mr.—" Dr. Vans glances down at his notebook "—Flynn."

Killian stands without hesitation. "I hear it's best to picture your audience in their underwear." He winks down at me. "Nice choice." As the other kids chuckle, he adds, "I enjoy long walks on the beach, swimming in the ocean and surfing. I used to have a weakness for blondes, but I have a feeling that part of my life is over."

He surfs? Seriously?

What are the odds?

A brunette on the other side of the circle fans her face. Sloan signs *call me*.

Vans notices and scowls at her.

"Also," Killian adds, "I'm a Myriad boy through and through. If you give me an hour, I'll convince you to sign in the first five minutes, and we can spend the rest of our time celebrating your decision."

I give him a thumbs-down.

Hank raises his hand and, with challenge in his eyes, says, "I accept. Your cell or mine?"

"Like you could handle me, boy-o." Killian sits.

"I like your enthusiasm, Mr. Flynn. Perhaps Ms. Lockwood needs to spend quality time with you." Vans makes a notation in his book. "Yes. I'm already sold on the idea. I'll make the arrangements."

I bite my tongue to stop a shout of negation. Of course Vans wants to pair me with a Myriad loyalist.

How would Killian, my parents or even Bow like it if I actively tried to convince them to join the world of the Unsigned?

I drum my fingers against my chin. "I think quality time with Mr. Flynn is *exactly* what I need…to finally push me in Troika's direction."

Killian snorts, as if he knows I'm bluffing.

Vans purses his lips but doesn't reply directly. "All right, everyone. I'm here to listen to any problems you've been having. Talk to me. Help me help you make your stay here more enjoyable."

More enjoyable for *him*. For us? More agonizing.

As different kids list their grievances—things I've heard a thousand times before—I distract myself with the childhood song that's never far from my mind.

Ten tears fall, and I call...nine hundred trees, but only one is for me. Eight times eight times eight they fly, whatever you do, don't stay dry.

"—don't like that you're still alive, Vanniekins." Sloan runs a fingertip down each cheek, mimicking tears. "Let me remedy the problem?"

An-n-nd as usual, he moves on without chastising her.

Seven ladies dancing, ignore their sweet romancing. Six—

"—spiders in my room," a girl bursts out, as if she can't hold in the words a second longer. She shudders with revulsion.

Dr. Vans makes a notation.

Oh, honey. You have no idea what you've done. Next time she's due for punishment, she'll find *thousands* of hologram spiders in her room. Her mind will think they're real, and she'll willingly peel the skin from her body to remove the critters.

"You have to send someone to remove them," she adds. "I can't go another night—"

"Shut up," I snap. Cruel to be kind. "Pretending to be afraid of spiders is—"

"I'm not pretending."

Fool! She doesn't get it.

Sooner rather than later, she will. She'll remember this moment and cry.

Dr. Vans focuses on me, his dark eyes narrowing. "Miss Lockwood, you seem eager to speak. Do you have any complaints about your treatment?"

I pretend my middle finger is a tube of lipstick and apply a first and second coat. I'll never willingly offer ammunition to be used against me. He knows this.

Still he says, "I'll give you five seconds to voice your biggest complaint. Continue to remain silent, and I'll be forced to penalize you."

Finally. The sword I feel poised at my neck every second of every day will slash, and I'll experience the next round of torture.

I become the sole focus of every person in the room, but I keep my eyes on Vans.

"One," he says.

"I think I'm going to barf every time I look at your face." *How's that?*

"Only a *legitimate* complaint will be heeded, Miss Lockwood."

"Excellent. I was completely serious."

"Two. Three."

"She would like the guards to keep their hands to themselves," Killian says. To pull attention from me? "I know I would. I'm more than a piece of meat."

I kind of admire his balls. Figuratively! Only figuratively!

"Miss Lockwood?" Vans prompts.

I raise my chin in a mimic of Sloan. Denying him is one of my favorite indulgences. My hope is that, at the end of his life, when he's lying in his sickbed, choking on his own vomit—a girl can dream—he'll look back and bemoan the fact that I'm his biggest failure.

"Four, five," I say with a smirk.

Sloan shakes her head at me, all *bless your stupid heart.* Maybe I should've played along. All I had to do was complain about something I hate, or lie about something I hate, but the truth is too important to me. I hate lies almost as much as I hate Vans. The worst of the worst lie. I won't emulate them, even to save myself from a boatload of grief.

A few inmates snicker. This enrages Vans, who leaps to his feet. He motions to Ben Dover and Colonel Anus with a tilt of his chin. "Take her."

Killian jumps up and steps in front of me, shocking me. He frowns at me over his shoulder, as if he's in shock, too, then he scowls at the guards. "She stays. I'm not done talking with her."

He, a stranger, is…guarding me? And he's doing it even after I refused to guard Bow. Way to rock my world.

I stand and give him a nudge into his chair. "Don't worry about me," I whisper. I don't want him hurt on my behalf. "Worry about yourself."

He glares but remains silent as Colonel Anus takes my left arm and Ben Dover takes my right. I'm hauled to my room. Bow is there already and she's still in a drugged sleep, but now she's on her bed, her wrists and ankles shackled to the posts with cuffs that glow more brightly than a lamp. Aka fetters.

Vans enters the room behind me. My stomach churns, as if it's trying to make butter from bile, but I swallow back pleas for mercy. This man has none.

I'm held immobile as he paces in front of me. "Ten,

Ten, Ten," he says and sighs heavily. "Ever the troublesome child. Why do you force me to hurt you?"

"Your choice. Your actions. Don't try casting blame on me."

"This isn't the way I like to treat my patients, but I'm willing to do whatever proves necessary to save you from the Realm of Many Ends...or an eternity as a Troikan slave."

"*You* are Unsigned." He must be. "I've heard you tell other kids you'll do anything to save them from eternity as a Myriad drone, one of countless souls overpopulating a dying realm."

He shrugs. "What's right for one isn't right for another."

No. No! He has an answer for everything and though this one sounds good, I cringe as if he scraped his fingernails over a chalkboard. There has to be absolute right or there isn't absolute wrong.

This place is wrong.

This *man* is wrong. He misleads and misdirects without regret, caring more about a monetary payoff than the long-term health of the kids under his "care."

Troika would tell me to forgive him.

Myriad would probably tell me to attack without mercy.

That. I like that. Strike before he can strike at me.

With a roar, I lunge at him. The guards hold me in place, squeezing my shoulders so roughly the joints nearly pop out of place. Pain lances through me, and for a moment, I see stars. I don't care. I struggle with all my might, desperate to reach my target.

"Did you get your degree at Discount Psychology?" I

throw at him. "You only make half a difference and even then it's a bad one."

Direct hit! A muscle flexes in his jaw.

Two other guards enter the room. D-bag and Titball. How sad. No Comrade Douche today.

"Perfect timing," Vans says, gloating now.

Both males carry a bucket of water and a rag. They stop in front of my blood-covered wall and dip the rags in the water—

Understanding dawns, and I gasp with horror. *Not my calendar. Anything but my calendar.* Those numbers have been the only constant in my life. My only friend. I can't lose another friend.

"Apologize for insulting me. On your knees," Vans says. "I'll *think* about forgetting your behavior today."

I actually consider it. My numbers…they aren't just my friends but my only diversion from the horrors of the asylum. My only real hope. Through them, I can see the light at the end of the tunnel. My next birthday…and my ultimate escape.

But. There's always a *but* with me, isn't there? I won't be able to live with myself if I give this man—this travesty of a human being—what he wants. Because, if I do, the light at the end of the tunnel will no longer be so bright.

I lock my knees, remaining on my feet.

"Very well." He nods, almost anticipatory.

The guards begin to wash the lines away, and my horror is renewed and redoubled.

Not ready to say goodbye. "Stop. Please. You have to stop!" I kick out my legs, but I'm jerked out of striking distance. "You have no right to destroy my property!"

They continue washing, and my emotional pain cuts worse than any physical pain I've ever endured. Flesh heals. The soul can fester.

"If you don't want to lose anything else you value, Miss Lockwood, you need to leave Prynne. And soon. All you have to do is sign with Myriad," Vans says, and the guards pause. "Nothing has ever been easier."

A crimson drop of water trickles down the wall. A bloody tear. My beautiful calendar is dying, and with a single word I have the power to save what's left of it. How can I not just say—the—word.

Say yes. *Yes, yes, yes.*

See? It *isn't* difficult.

The word bubbles up… "No," I end up saying. "No, I won't sign."

What is *wrong* with me?

Vans vibrates with rage, but quickly manages to calm himself. "I know that isn't what you planned to say, Miss Lockwood. Last chance. Sign with Myriad."

Moonlight…castles…and one day, a return to the Land of the Harvest, Fused with another soul…living out my fate…

Might Equals Right.

Sunlight…wildflowers…an eternity of Rest after I fulfill my covenant duties…my mistakes my own…

Light Brings Sight.

Right now, I would rather know the truth—who is right and who is wrong? I would rather not ruin my future. As I've learned, the wrong decision can lead down a road with more bumps and slumps than I'm equipped to handle—can cost far more than I'm willing to pay.

"I won't," I grit out between clenched teeth. I can't allow a momentary pain to eclipse an eternal decision. Feelings are fleeting, no matter how earth-shattering they seem; they never last, always change. A covenant is forever.

Vans curses at me. D-bag and Titball return to work. I go still and quiet, watching as every precious line disappears.

When there's nothing left, the group leaves, though Vans pauses in the doorway to say, "I want to be your advocate, Miss Lockwood, and yet you insist on making me your enemy."

"*You* insist." My eyes burn with tears. I blink away, refusing to give this man the satisfaction of knowing he broke me. "I simply oblige you."

He taps his fingers on the door frame, the only indication his irritation hasn't faded. "Perhaps one day Myriad will decide they don't want you, after all. Kind of like your parents decided *they* didn't want you, yes?"

A sharp pain nearly slices open my chest. Vans knows just how to wound for maximum damage. "Has torture ever worked for you?" I ask, but I already know the answer. I've noticed the fast turnaround. Most kids stay only a month or two.

"More often than not."

"Might Equals Right, eh?"

My derision causes him to tap faster. "One decision can change your circumstances, Miss Lockwood. Just one."

I smile a little too sweetly at him. "One bullet can change yours."

The smile he gives me is just as sweet. "Up to this point, I've been easy on you. Keep pushing, and you'll see my worst." He reaches into his pocket and throws what looks to be a black button at me. A button that hits the floor because I don't even try to catch it. "Almost forgot. This is from your mother."

Why would she give me a button?

He leaves at last, locking me inside the room.

My tears long to break free, and my knees long to buckle, but I maintain my tough-as-nails attitude. The cameras…

With a trembling hand, I pick up the button. A flash-scribe, I realize. A way to send a recorded message. Now I'm even more confused. What does the mother who abandoned me, not visiting for seven months, wish to say to me?

Ignoring a swell of eagerness—*have to know, now, now, now!*—I stuff the device in my own pocket and stumble to Bow to check the fetters for locks. I find none. Good. I can free her, but oh, it's going to hurt.

What's a little more pain, right?

The outside of both cuffs is heated, and—I hiss—by the time I press the release button on each one, seven blisters decorate my fingers and palms.

The glow of the metal dwindles, the needles on the inside of each device detaching from bone and ejecting from her skin.

Clink, clink. The cuffs fall away, but she doesn't wake. I'm glad. I'm not in the mood to deal with her.

With a curse, I tumble onto my squeaky mattress and stare up at the ceiling. Life sucks.

A muted scream suddenly echoes from the floor, and I jolt.

Isn't Clay, isn't Clay, isn't Clay. He's safe. He made it out.

Will I?

The flash-scribe is practically burning a hole in my

pocket, my eagerness overtaking me. I withdraw the device and press my thumb into the top. As soon as my print registers, my mother's voice fills the cell.

"Hi, Ten. Bet you never expected to hear from me, huh?"

My heart thumps against my ribs, and my gut clenches.

"I know I haven't come to see you in forever, but there's a very good reason for that. A beautiful secret. One that's taught me how to be a mother again. I'm sorry, sweet girl. I'm sorry for everything, and I love you, I really do. Your dad loves you, too, but he's scared of losing his job and—well. That's not your problem. We'll be coming to visit you soon, and it's my hope we'll take you with us when we leave."

Hope flares, only to die a quick death. This is a trick. Has to be.

A baby cries in the background. My mom says, "Shh, shh," as if there's a human being with her rather than a television, and I frown. No one under the age of eighteen—besides me—has ever been allowed inside the house. My mom's rule.

And I get it. She prefers not to look at what she isn't allowed to have: another kid. She wants one as fervently as I want a sibling—someone to love me unconditionally, just because I'm me, not because of what I can do. But, long ago, the realms made a deal with the human governments. To prevent overcrowding in Secondlife, where spirits can live for centuries, even millennia, there is a one-child-per-family limit during Firstlife. In return, the realms share their advanced technology, like this flash-scribe.

My mom clears her throat. "I've got to go, sweetheart. I

know I screwed up with you, but I'm going to give my—child a better life. You have my word."

Why the hesitation before *child*?

I toss the device across the room. She doesn't love me. She can't. And there's no way my dad even likes me.

Are you sure about that?

A memory takes center stage in my mind. My dad carries me on his shoulders as I stretch my arms overhead, doing my best to capture a star in the sky.

"Almost got it," he says with a laugh.

My mom claps and calls, "You can do it, sweet girl."

All right, maybe they loved me once. The emotion has withered. Like my heart.

A moan escapes Bow. A second later, she comes up swinging, panting for breath. Her gaze is far from disoriented as it finds mine.

"Are you okay?"

Her first thought is of my welfare? Even though I did nothing as the guards knocked her around? My guilt returns. "I'm fine. What about you?"

"Fine, no thanks to Killian."

I remember the way he raced past her. "What'd he do?"

"Doesn't matter." She plays with the edge of her blanket. "Vans is right, you know. At least about this. One decision can change your circumstances."

"I know, but—" Wait. "How do you know what he said?"

"The body—I mean, *my* body—might have been drugged, but I was still aware."

How'd she manage that? I've been drugged before, and I was out for the count.

"Sign with Troika, Ten." Those copper eyes beseech me. "You'll never regret it."

"Prove it. Give me a guarantee."

"My word isn't good enough?"

No. "Why do you want me, anyway? Why do *they*?"

She inhales deeply, exhales sharply. "Have you ever heard of a Conduit?"

"Yes. Someone or something used as a means of sending something from one place or person to another."

"Right. And in Troika, a Conduit is the highest type of General, second only to King. Conduits are rare and precious, powerful both here and there. They absorb sunlight from Earth—which is more than just heat and illumination—and direct the beams to the realm. There are whispers about you," she says, only to go quiet.

"Whispers suggesting I'm a Conduit?" Someone rare and precious? Powerful? I laugh at the absurdity. "Wrong."

"How do you know?"

"Better question. How do *they*?"

"Like you, I don't have all the answers." She sighs. "Let's forget the Conduit thing. There's a lot about you to admire. When you fight, you go balls to the wall. When you believe in something—like your right to choose—you can't be shaken. You're too stubborn. And whether you admit it or not, you'll never be okay with the Myriad way of life, the strong taking from the weak."

"You can't know—"

"I can. Because that is what's happening here, and you hate it."

"Not every Myriad supporter is like that." James never

took without asking. "Just like not every Troikan is forgiving."

She pinches the bridge of her nose in a show of fatigue. "Yeah. There's that. I try to remind myself that everyone has their damage and no one is perfect. Except me."

At least she didn't try to deny the problems. "Both realms need a personality makeover." And the thought of making a difference in one…kind of intrigues me.

"A makeover of any kind requires the proper tools, honey. And talent."

"Are you saying I'm currently toolless and talentless?"

"Oh, good. You understood."

We share a smile.

But her amusement doesn't last long. "Sign with us, Ten, and you'll be one of mine. I'll get you out of here."

"One of yours?"

"My friend. A member of my team. My family. Those I protect, whatever the cost."

I laugh even though, deep down, a need to belong to *someone* plagues me. To be cared for and finally, truly loved…to be first rather than last. "Trust me. I'm not someone you want in your family." I'm bad news. Everything I touch turns to rust. "And let's be real. You can't even protect *yourself*. Not here, not all the time."

"This?" she says, motioning to herself, then the room around us. "What you see? It's not even close to reality. Stop trusting your eyes and start listening to your heart. It sees more than you ever will."

"Heart…as in emotions?" Troika is usually more concerned about law.

"Heart, as in spirit. The real you."

That's just it. Who am I? Ten? Or soul-fused with someone else?

My mom once speculated about my "other half." *With the way Myriad is acting,* she said, *it must be someone powerful.*

How do you know I'm Fused? I remember asking.

Everyone is Fused with someone, sweet girl. It's a way to give those who originally signed with Troika a second chance...a way to give those who signed with Myriad a chance to win more souls.

Before all this, I was pro-Myriad all the way. The fairy tales she wove about an enchanted land where daylight never intrudes and the royal ball never winds down, where candlelit castles are standard housing, and marrying a prince is a very real possibility, enthralled me.

The dirty little secret I kept from her? A part of me has always been Troi-curious.

Is the realm poverty-stricken? Does sunlight always glare? Are the homes basically cardboard boxes? Or is the sun bright and glorious, offering comforting warmth? Does the sweet scent of wildflowers saturate the air?

My (former) TL told me deception is Myriad's greatest weapon. The hungry wolf hidden by a lamb's skin. I haven't heard from him since my incarceration.

To my parents' consternation, it's illegal to prevent a Laborer from speaking with a potential candidate if said candidate is willing. No matter the Laborer's realm.

I'd mostly ignored my TL, not wanting to cause trouble at home...until a friend admitted she'd signed with Troika. In a moment of startling clarity, I'd realized we were—for all intents and purposes—enemies. I would be expected to excise her from my life. Even hate her.

I'd wanted to know why. So I risked chastisement at long

last, going to a Troikan center, where humans in need of aid could request a meeting with a TL.

Before we parted, the TL assigned to me asked me a question that cracked through a hard outer shell I hadn't known I'd erected.

Are you living your parents' dream…or your own?

I'd scoffed at him then, but that night and every one after, I'd wondered… Why do I believe what I believe? What is truth and what is lie? What is real? What makes me right and so many others wrong? What if *I'm* wrong?

The wily bastard had planted seeds of doubt in the rich soil of my brain, and the more I searched for answers, the more those seeds were watered…the stronger they grew. Now the leaves are so thick I can't see past them.

If I'm Fused, I'm not me. I'm part of someone else. Or several someone elses. But if I *am* me, I alone am responsible for my problems. Who wants to suck *that* badly?

But the thing I wonder most? Do I have a set fate, or can I change it? In other words…can I mess it up worse?

chapter four

"What is isn't always what's supposed to be."
—Troika

I watch him. At lunch and dinner that day, I watch Killian. When he talks to girls, he seems utterly absorbed in the conversation, as if every word spoken is a secret he has to know. And the girls eat it up. He makes them feel special, I can tell. They preen for him. But those girls…they aren't special to him. I can tell that, too.

He's too aware of the world around him, his hand never far from his pocket, as if he has a weapon hidden inside. As if he expects to be ambushed at any moment. As if he wants to be ambushed.

Anytime the girl looks away from him—which isn't often—his gaze finds me. He winks. He knows I'm watching him, and he wants me to know he knows.

His confidence lends him an aura of power and, someone please help me, I admire it.

Later that same evening, Vans does as promised and arranges my "date" with Killian. The doc is upping his game.

First, Nurse Ratched delivers a dress to my cell. A pink sundress. Pink. With ruffles and lace. I grimace. I'll be the prettiest princess in the asylum.

Her parting words are both a threat (to me) and a triumph (to her.) "You can wear it…or you can go naked. Your choice."

A red haze descends over my vision. A choice that isn't really a choice is a violation of my rights.

What rights?

"Wow," Bow says, looking me over after I've changed. "A make-out session would *not* be out of pity today."

"Um. Thanks?" I smooth my hands over the ultrasoft fabric. "I feel ridiculous."

"What's the occasion?"

As I explain today's therapy session, her eyes narrow.

"Son of a Myriad-troll," she mutters. She's sprawled atop her bed. "Wonder how much Mr. Flynn had to pay for *that* privilege."

I spread my arms wide. "Because wanting me is completely unfeasible?"

She closes her eyes as she shakes her head. "Sorry. Sorry. You're hot. You're awesome, and I know he craves a taste of you. Who wouldn't? But he's a piece of scum, and he always has ulterior motives."

A grumbled apology, but an apology nonetheless.

"You're forgiven. I guess." I mean, even *I'm* wondering why Killian has turned his predatory sights to me. "Tell me your history with the guy."

She growls low in her throat. "He sucks. That's all you need to know."

This girl has repeatedly pried open my secrets with a

crowbar. She doesn't get to keep her own. "Don't you want to help me build extra defenses against him?"

"Are your current defenses in danger of crumbling?"

No. Absolutely not. But… "Do you really want to take the chance? There's something about him…"

She points a finger at me. "Is that *breathlessness* I hear in your tone, Lockwood?"

What? "No!" Me? Breathless? Never! "I'm as hard as steel."

She punches her mattress, the springs squeaking. "You want details, fine. He stabbed his best friend in the back—twice! He's selfish and cruel. He uses girls to get what he wants, and then he discards them."

"Are you one of the girls he used and discarded?" I ask gently.

"No! Gross! I've never jonesed for his scones." She shudders. "It's just…he'll sleep with you and leave you brokenhearted in the rubble that has become your life."

Bow, who is obviously biased, has probably seen a distorted version of the truth. She's never seen into Killian's heart.

Or maybe I'm making excuses for the guy.

"If getting down and dirty is his main objective, I'm the last girl he should target." I possessed the common sense and wherewithal to stop James every time his hands wandered past my shoulders, and I *loved* him.

And unlike Killian, James looked at me as if he adored me. He smiled with me, not at me. He whispered beautiful things in my ear…

So lovely.

So soft.

So perfect.

I'd been as mesmerized as I was flustered.

"I'll never say yes," I add.

"Famous last words. If you find yourself tempted, remember Killian is selfish in bed," Bow says, as smoothly as if we're discussing our favorite kind of donuts. "Oh. And I hear he's small. Like, micropenis small."

I roll my eyes. "Can you tell me something about him that doesn't have anything to do with sex?"

"All right. For starters, he's going into this thinking you're going to fall for him and do anything to spend eternity with him."

"Why does he even care? He's human. If I sign with Myriad to be with him—" no boy is ever going to factor into my decision, because they don't come with a guarantee, either "—he won't be rewarded."

She stands and walks over to pat me on my cheek. "Wow. You're, like, Super Naive Girl."

In the back of my mind, I note the temperature of her skin. Like James, she's too cool, as if she's incapable of absorbing heat.

Try to warm me up, James used to say.

"So… Killian *will* be rewarded?" I ask.

"Well, yeah. Everything we do has a consequence. Good or bad. In Firstlife and Everlife." She tilts her head and studies me more intently. "Who's your ML?"

"I've always had two at a time. Many have come and gone, but one has always remained the same. Madame Pearl Bennett." A flawless blonde with a warm smile.

Distaste darkens Bow's features. "Madame is the title for a Leader, which is step above a Laborer."

"Yes." A fact I'd pointed out to Madame Bennett as soon as I learned about the different positions. She'd smiled sweetly and said, *You, my beauty, are special. I want to oversee your case myself.*

I'd asked what made me so special, and her smile had only grown. *You remind me of someone I loved and like her, you're going to do great things for our realm.*

I'd adored her. Once. She was the one who told my parents to send me to Prynne. I'd heard them talking. At first, my dad resisted the idea. When Madame promised him the experience would toughen me up, help me become the person I was meant to be, and snap me out of my pouty teenage refusal to sign with Myriad, he finally relented. Then he convinced my mother.

"Well," Bow says, and I can't tell what emotion she's projecting. I only know it's negative. "You must be as important to Myriad as you are to Troika. No one I know has ever had two MLs."

Me, either. But… "Myriad doesn't have Conduits."

"No, they have Abrogates. Those who extinguish the light. The most powerful people in their realm." She glares at me. "If you sign with Myriad, you won't only deny Troika a Conduit, you'll drain the Conduits we do have."

I rub the back of my neck. "What would happen then?"

"Troika would plunge into darkness right alongside Myriad. It's what the other realm has always wanted. It's what we've always fought." Bow bites her lower lip. "Are you sure you can resist Killian's…charms?"

"Definitely." *His eyes make my blood sing…* "Possibly. Hopefully." *His smirking mouth and blatant innuendos make my blood boil…* "Definitely."

She pushes out a heavy breath. "Do you have *any* experience with the opposite sex?"

"I've had a boyfriend," I tell her, suddenly defensive.

"Here? He was human?"

"Of course."

"How do you know?" she asks.

"How else? I was allowed to touch him." Every Laborer comes to earth in a Shell, a humanoid outer casing that somehow makes a spirit tangible to the physical world. Despite that tangibility, we're forbidden from touching the Shells for any reason. Without being told why!

She crosses her arms. "What was he like? This boyfriend?"

"His name was James. I met him my first week. He snuck me food when I was starved and salve every time I was beaten." The true miracle? In the quiet of the night, he made me laugh. "Why the curiosity about him?"

"Duh. I'm nosy. You know this. Was he Unsigned?"

"No. He was secretly a Myriad loyalist—" Vans would have fired him if he'd known "—but he rarely talked realm business with me." He saw *me*, not a potential realm-mate.

"Ah." She makes a face as she nods. "He was doing the long con."

"Excuse me?" What did *that* mean?

"The long con requires more planning and preparation. A longer window of interaction with a target as well as a longer period of time to execute the main objective—signing you."

White-hot anger sparks. "Not everyone is obsessed with eternity."

"Yeah, but wouldn't the guy who claimed to love you

want you to be with him forever? And you once mentioned bonuses… I bet staff and inmates alike receive them."

She…she… Oh! She's ticking me off!

"What else did you like about him?"

"Screw you. I'm done with this subject."

She gives a regal wave of her hand, all *the queen wishes you to proceed*. "Was he staff or inmate?"

"Staff. And he lived for me—then he died for me." Apparently I'm *not* done with the subject. My chin trembles, my defensive tone echoing in my ears. "He was killed when he aided my escape attempt."

Nine months have passed since Dr. Vans shot him in the chest.

A baby spends nine months in a mother's womb. The phrase "on cloud nine" means to be happy or euphoric.

I'm anything but happy. Maybe I *should* sign with Myriad. I'll get to see James again.

Part of me expected him to visit at least once. Even though the realms claim loved ones can damage a cause far worse than a stranger, so laws are in place to prevent after-death interactions.

"You saw his actions," Bow says, "but not his heart."

Is she serious? "Actions *reveal* heart."

"Not always. Deception is all about perception."

Okay. That's it. "I'm done with this subject." I mean it this time.

"Of course you are." With an unfeminine grunt, she falls onto her pillow. "You're a runner."

The words are like a punch to the gut. "I'm a fighter."

"Ha! Fighters take a stand."

I throw myself on my bed and peer up at the ceiling,

wishing I lived in a time before the realms existed. Not that there *was* such a time. There is and has always been a Firstking. He created both Myriad and Troika, a realm to give each of his sons. Then he created the Land of the Harvest and humans. Subjects to inhabit the kingdoms—*after* they picked a kingdom.

Of course, one brother soon plotted to destroy the other, hoping to rule *both* realms, and a war ignited.

Guess who says which brother is at fault?

Many Ends was (supposedly) created for criminals, but ultimately became the home for the Unsigned.

"Tenley Lockwood. You are expected in the commons." The heavily accented female voice suddenly spills from the speakers strategically placed in our ceiling. Next, the door opens.

Well, zero. The time has come.

I give myself a pep talk: *A pretty face won't sway you, and pretty words won't affect you. You will remain distanced. No boy is worth the hardships that accompany him—not here.*

"Be careful." Bow's anger drains, and worry takes its place. "Do you have steel panties? If yes, put them on *right now.*"

I snort and rush into the hall, where I find Killian waiting for me. His eyes aren't on me, but Bow, and they're crackling with fury. His hands are balled into fists, ready to deliver.

Bow remains in place, staring back through slitted lids, but *her* hands aren't balled, and she doesn't try to sneak out and murder him, so I consider it a major improvement.

Like me, Killian has been relieved of his jumpsuit. He's wearing a black T-shirt and a pair of jeans, and both fit him to perfection. I mean, wow. If he was beautiful before, he's exquisite now. He's a boy—man—without equal.

"How old are you?" I find myself asking.

"Nineteen." When his blue-gold gaze finally finds me, he gives me a once—twice—over and smiles. "For once, I'm glad for my lack of years."

So he can score without being a major creeper? "You're a legal adult."

"And you're not. I know. Opposites attract."

"I *mean*, no one can force you to do anything you don't want to do. Why are you here?" I asked before, but he only fed me a bunch of bull. "If you want to survive the evening with all your parts intact, answer honestly."

His smile returns as he stuffs his hands in his pockets and hikes his shoulders in a shrug.

Irritating! "Be a big boy and use your words."

"Maybe Vans is paying me to beguile you. That's what you're thinking, isn't it?"

Yes! And what if James was paid to do the same?

Argh! Bow! She's in my head.

Killian offers me his tattooed hand. "By the way, you should *always* wear pink, lass."

My stupid heart stutters and my stupid hand trembles as I link our fingers. His skin is as cold as Bow's and James's. That's weird, right? Or am I the weird one?

"I shouldn't have to mention this, but hey, why leave anything to chance? This isn't a real date."

"Don't like the label? Fine. We'll give it a new one. How about pants party for two?"

I almost laugh. Almost. "I'm not wearing pants."

"Underpants?"

"I think I prefer the term *death match*."

"Death match, it is. And look at me, willing to compromise. I really am the perfect guy."

I do laugh this time. He's shameless.

He leads me down the hall, into the commons, just not the commons I'm used to seeing.

One corner of the room has been transformed. There's a small candlelit table with two cushioned chairs placed side by side. Platters of food occupy every inch of the tabletop. There's even a bottle of wine and a chocolate cake.

Cake! Is this heaven?

Killian doesn't lead me to the table. No, he leads me to the left, where a virtual tour is playing over the wall. One I've never seen before. A moonlit beach so realistic I can almost smell the salt and sand.

"You're going all out, right from the start," I mutter. Waves dance over the shore, leaving lacy foam behind. Pinpricks of light crawl toward the water—glow-in-the-dark turtles! I coo with delight. "They're so beautiful."

"Wouldn't you love to hold one?"

An-n-nd my delight fades. "Do you really think I'll be so easily manipulated?"

"You say *manipulated*. I say *rewarded*. You love the water. Don't try to deny it."

I go rigid. Either he eavesdropped, which isn't likely—I would have noticed him nearby—or Vans's cameras and mics picked up what I said to Bow, and the information was given to Killian.

The leash on my temper begins to unravel. Needing distance, I walk to the next wall. People have set up camp around a crackling fire pit—people who are talking and laughing, enjoying Everlife.

At the next wall, a different group is playing a game that looks like a cross between volleyball and football. Tackle folleyball?

"This," Killian says, tapping the fire pit, "is what awaits you in Myriad."

"Unless Troika is right, and *this*," I say, tapping the net, "is just an illusion."

When he offers no reply, I turn to him. His gaze is locked on the pit. No, not the pit, I realize, but the people around it. Is that *longing* I detect from him? Maybe even a hint of envy?

"Earlier, you mentioned surfing," I say. "Who taught you?"

A muscle tics beneath his eye. "I taught myself."

I've most definitely stumbled onto a sensitive subject. "What about friends? Your parents?"

"What about *your* friends and family?"

Oh, no. We're not playing that game. "I'll answer your question if you answer mine."

Several seconds pass in silence. Finally he says, "My father never wanted me, and my mother—" He presses his lips together, shakes his head. "Thought I could, realized I can't. I won't ask personal questions and you won't ask personal questions. Deal?" He takes my hand and ushers me to a chair.

"Deal." I sit without protest and, as my heart aches for him—*poor boy, his dad never wanted him!*—I remind myself of a very important fact: Killian isn't my friend; he's bait.

I *must* remain detached.

My mouth waters, the scents stronger. "Let's eat."

He claims his own chair and snaps his napkin over his lap. "Ladies first."

"You'll probably come to regret that." I fill my plate *and* a bowl with all kinds of goodies I haven't had in over a year. A slice of chocolate cake—priorities!—a scoop of chicken potpie, slice of chocolate cake, scoop of yam casserole, slice of chocolate cake, two scoops of mashed potatoes, a slice of chocolate cake, a scoop of buttery green beans, a slice of chocolate cake—

"Going to save any cake for me?"

"No, actually, I'm not. Mine." I point my spoon in his direction. "You don't touch."

He lifts his hands, palms out. "How long have you been a chocolate addict?"

"Since birth. The struggle is real." I return my attention to my task. Now. Where was I? Oh, yes. Ten grapes, a slice of chocolate cake, ten strawberries, a slice of chocolate cake, and finally, to give this meal a health kick, a spoonful of pasta salad.

The problem? I have an odd number of cake slices.

I go ahead and take the final slice to even things out.

"There's no way you'll be able to eat all that." He pours me a glass of wine. "You're too little."

"I'll eat every crumb. And I'd like water to drink, please."

"Well, I'd like your dress to spontaneously combust, but we don't always get what we want, now, do we?"

Zero! Or maybe this time around I should use *Vans* as my favorite four-letter curse word. Killian's one-track mind is going to cause *me* to spontaneously combust.

Is the plan to get me drunk? Make me vulnerable to suggestion?

"I'm underage." Eighteen, the legal age for everything nowadays, can't get here fast enough. "If I drink any alcohol, I'll be breaking the law."

"Sorry, lass, but that sounds like a you problem."

So it's wine or nothing. Whatever. I'll sip. I won't let myself get drunk.

He *tsk-tsk*s. "Don't look so gloom and doom. Two or more glasses of wine a day can severely reduce your risk of giving a shit."

Nice. I accept the glass and take my first taste of something alcoholic. Mmm. Wine is tasty. Notes of raspberry and walnut, sweet yet earthy. "Just so you know, I'm not discussing the Everlife with you."

"What *are* you willing to discuss? You know what, never mind. You'll probably suggest the many ways to murder me." He pushes his food around his plate before pinning me with a laser stare. "What if I said your allegiance to Myriad is a matter of life and death? Would you discuss the realms then?"

"Yes, but only to say you're being ridiculous, trying to give me a god complex so I'll feel important and believe that one measly girl will make a vast difference."

The handle of his spoon bends. "One measly girl? Try one *stubborn* girl. Your continued refusal is causing all kinds of—" Once again he presses his lips together. "Myriad obviously needs you. They're going to a lot of trouble for you."

I catch another hint of the longing and envy. Does he

think no one needs him, no one would go to any trouble for him?

I sigh. I'm reading too much into his expressions, aren't I? Seeing what I want to see. Or even a reflection of my own emotions.

"How about we sit in silence?" I ask.

A voice spills over the intercom. "You will continue your conversation about the realms." Dr. Vans, reminding me of where I am, who I'm with and the nefarious purpose of the evening.

My fingers tighten on my spoon with so much force I fear my knuckles will pop free of my skin. Of course Vans is listening to our every word, watching our every move.

"Did you know?" I ask, glaring at Killian.

"No," he says, his teeth gritted. "He definitely isn't part of my plan."

Well, well. An outright admission that there *is* a plan.

Intent on ignoring both males, I sling one arm around my plate, guarding the contents, and shovel in heaping bite after heaping bite. First the cake slices disappear…followed quickly by, well, everything else. When I finish, I moan with satisfaction. And regret. Mostly regret. I probably should have saved *something* for Bow.

As I wipe my mouth with my napkin, Killian chuckles.

"What?" I demand.

"*Now* you're a lady?"

I pat my stomach. "What? My gastrointestinal clock was ticking. I wanted a food baby."

"Good thing I poked holes in the cake."

A smile tugs at the corners of my lips, and I can't stop it. I don't want to like this boy, but dang it, he's witty.

Then I remember Vans, and the urge to smile diminishes.

I gasp when Killian throws a plate at the cage-covered camera in the corner. A plate that clatters to the floor without shattering. The cage is unaffected, as well. Even still, the action makes us both feel better, and we share a look of understanding.

"What do we do now?" I ask.

"I could remove my shirt and do push-ups, impressing you with my manly strength."

I think he's kidding, but I'm still tempted. Watch him ripple and sweat? Yes, please. I force myself to say, "No, thanks." An idea strikes, and I go with it. "I want to talk about your parents." He's here to lure. I can't allow him to enjoy the experience, now, can I? "And I'm sticking to our rules. I'm not asking questions. I'm demanding."

He flicks his tongue over an incisor. "Pick a different topic. Otherwise you'll be bored."

"You mean adored."

He snorts, even relaxes. Then he sighs, his stare seeming to drill into my soul. "My mother died before I had the chance to meet her, but my birth was recorded. I've watched the video so many times I've memorized every detail. At the end, she nuzzled my cheek and told me she'd never forget me. Now I wonder..."

A lump grows in my throat. Now he wonders, what? If she's Fused? If she remembers him?

I reach over and pat his hand. "I'm sorry for your pain."

He searches my eyes—for what? "I think you mean that."

"I do."

We go quiet again, but this time, awareness crackles between us. Crackles over my skin, making me tingle.

"If you're not going to discuss the realms, you're going to do a trust-building exercise." Vans's insistent voice makes us both flinch. "Ten, stand in front of Killian and fall backward. Killian, catch her before she falls."

You've got to be kidding me.

Killian pops his jaw but stands. "If I wasn't eager to get my hands on you, I'd hunt the bastard down and choke him with his own intestines."

My brain locks on one thought: Killian will soon have his hands on me.

I drain my glass before I, too, stand. What? I'm thirsty. A fog spills through my brain and a sweet voice whispers, *His towering height is a very good thing, there's nothing to be afraid of, and maybe you should hold on to his shirt. For balance.*

No! I call foul!

The fog is clearly a whore galore, and I decide to teach her a lesson by stepping back…into my chair. Oops! My butt hits with a little too much force, and I wince.

Killian pulls me to my feet. "You're not getting out of this, lass." He leads me away from the table. As he moves behind me— or rather he tries to move behind me— I turn with him. I don't want him at my back.

He has to know the problem, but rather than castigating me, he distracts me. "What kind of punishment were you given this morning? I've wondered all day."

His blue-gold eyes sizzle with a shocking amount of anger. Anger on my behalf.

He has a protective streak, doesn't he?

Finally I turn. I don't give myself time to think about

my actions. Here goes nothing. I…lean…back. My stomach leaps into my throat, and I honestly expect to hit the ground.

He catches me and smiles. "Well?"

I'm so relieved, I find myself saying, "I kept a calendar on my wall." RIP, sweet calendar. "Vans had it washed away."

Killian's brow furrows as he helps me straighten. "You screamed because of a calendar?"

"Well, it was a good calendar," I say, defensive.

"Noted." He twirls a finger, silently telling me to turn around. "What else has been done to you during your stay?"

"Just about everything you can imagine. Whippings, beatings. I've even been fried with a cattle prod." I turn more easily this time. "Oh, and let's not forget the time I was waterboarded. So fun!"

Shut up! common sense shouts. I'm oversharing when it's time to be a vault.

Oh, who cares? This is a wonderful day, and I love absolutely *everyone*!

"Dr. Vans has *waterboarded* you?" Killian asks, his voice so low, so silky, I'm almost hypnotized by it.

"Yep. But here's a better question. Are you ready for me?"

"Can anyone ever be ready for you, lass? But don't worry. I won't let you get hurt. You have my word."

I hold my breath as I fall…fall…

Killian catches me again. This time, he spins me around, so that we're face-to-face. "Do you want me to kill Vans for you?"

Maybe. I step closer, intending to reveal the most important piece of information in the history of the universe: his eyelashes are pretty and I'd like to measure them. Who am I kidding? I already know how long they are. Perfect inches. But I say, "There's a pond in my brain, and a lovely fog is dancing over the water."

Killian looks at me as if I'm the best birthday present ever.

Wait. I planned to tell him something... "Eyelashes."

"You're drunk," he says.

"How dare you. I'm only *probably* drunk." I reach out and trace a fingertip around each of his eyes. *Soft* eyelashes.

Frowning, he clasps my wrist and places my hand at my side. "Why didn't you fight back today?"

Fight back...fight back? Oh! Vans. "There's only so much I can do. I bet you've never been on the receiving end of an attack. You're so big."

"Oh, I've been on the receiving end of an attack." His anger returns in a flash. "I've also gone back and repaid the person responsible a thousand times over."

I'm shivering. Why am I shivering? "Not one for mercy, huh?"

"Victors are adored, failures are abhorred."

As many times as I've failed to escape the asylum and save myself from more pain, well, he must think the worst about me. "I'm going to disrespectfully disagree with you. If victory is achieved the wrong way, it's not really a victory at all."

He arches a brow and sneers, "Your opinion is very en-*light*-ened."

Ugh. Do I sound like a Troikan? Bow must be rubbing off on me.

"Your turn," I say. "Turn around."

"You really think you can catch me?"

"I'm stronger than I look."

"And yet I'm still not reassured."

I twirl my finger.

He rotates slowly, reluctantly. "By the way, victory is victory. I end up on top, not the bottom."

"On top of what? The pile of heartbreak and suffering you leave in your wake?"

He opens his mouth, closes it with a snap—and falls.

I catch him, but he's heavy, heavier than I expected. He keeps falling, taking me with him. We hit the ground and he laughs, then I laugh. We remain on the floor in a tangle of limbs.

"I'm beginning to think," I say, "Might Equals Right should mean the strong are tasked with the protection of the weak, because the strong aren't always strong and the weak aren't always weak. Everyone stumbles. And one day, when *you* stumble—and you will—you'll need someone to help you stand. Will there be anyone eager to do so, or will there be a line of people hoping to kick you while you're down?"

His amusement does a disappearing act. Abracadabra... gone! He glares at me. "I'm done with this topic."

The words are thrown at me. The same words I've thrown at Bow every time she's hit a nerve; I know I've reached him, whether he's willing to admit it or not.

"Okay, I'm going to break my own rule and discuss the realms." I stretch out over the floor, more comfortable with him than I should be. And I can't blame the alcohol. Stupid game! Killian caught me when he could have let me fall. "What made you side with Myriad?"

He leans back on his elbows, watching me warily. "There are too many reasons to list in a single evening."

"Give me the highlights, then." When he shakes his head, I say, "The top ten? Top two?"

"Why bother? My reasons won't affect your decision."

"So? Tell me anyway. I'm curious." What remains unsaid: *about you.*

He gaze heats, as if he heard what I didn't speak. "One. I'm more at ease in the dark. Two, Troika claims soul-fusion is a lie, but I know it's real."

Excitement turns the wine I've ingested into champagne—or what I imagine is champagne—the potent brew suddenly bubbling and effervescent in my veins. "You have concrete proof? Even though no other spirits have seen it happen and, from what I gather, the only way the people in Myriad know who's Fused with whom is through guesstimates, matching the deaths in the realms with the births here."

"I don't have to see to believe. I'm sometimes pulled in two different directions."

I wait for him to say more. He doesn't, and my excitement fizzles.

Treading carefully, remembering his mother, I say, "I'm often pulled in two different directions, but that doesn't necessarily mean I'm Fused. It means I'm divided, the potential for good and evil running through my heart."

He scowls at me. "Someone who refuses to see the truth will accept the lie."

Well. That's kind of deep for a boy who presented himself as a shallow he-slut. Also, it's kind of true. "Someone who accepts the lie will never see the truth."

"I have to be Fused. My *mother* has to be Fused." His accent is thicker. "*That* is the truth."

Poor boy, I think again. He's holding on to his hope with everything he's got. "I hope you're right," I say and I mean it.

He nudges my hip with his foot. "Half the things that come out of your mouth make me want to punch a wall, and the other half make me want to kiss you…and only sometimes to shut you up."

I reel. He wants to *kiss* me? "I gather you don't like someone mucking around in your head."

"Is that what you're doing?"

"Not intentionally. Maybe." His pretty eyelashes throw shadows over his cheeks, but the flicker of candlelight spilling from the table continually chases the darkness away with beams of gold.

He could be a poster boy for both realms. One moment he's surrounded by darkness, the next he's set free of the gloom. Radiant.

I lick my lips and ask, "Have you ever been in love?"

He gives me a strange look. "Why do you want to know?"

"Simple curiosity."

"There's nae such thing as simple curiosity. Either you're analyzing me, or you're interested in me."

"Analyzing," I rush out. *Yes, yes. Surely that.*

"Very well. The answer is yes I have, but no, I won't give you any other details. Unless you're willing to trade? My life story for your agreement to sign with Myriad."

Zero! I'm beyond curious, but his price is too high. "You have to tell me without strings. We're on a date, aren't we?"

"No. We're on a death match."

Right. "So tell me about the girl, or I'll scoop out your eyes with my spoon."

"I'm pretty sure you ate your spoon."

A statement I can't refute, considering I don't see the utensil anywhere.

Okay. That's it. Wine and trust exercises make me stupid. Let's put an end to this.

I push to my feet, sway just a little. I mean to say, *I'm sure we've wasted enough of each other's time. We're parting ways.* But he peers up at me, those long lashes teasing me, and what I end up saying is, "You should probably shave your eyelashes. They're distracting. Good night."

"Sit down, Ms. Lockwood," Dr. Vans commands. "The date isn't over."

Killian snaps his teeth at the camera before he stands. He peers at me, his eyelids hooded, his lips pink and moist—he's just run his tongue over them. "I could make you feel good, Ten. After you sober up." And his voice...his voice is already in bed, naked and waiting for me.

I don't want a naked boy in bed, waiting for me. Do I?

Oh! Oh! And his scent. Peat smoke and heather wraps around me, a delicious smoke that joins the fog in my head.

"You want to feel good...don't you?" He's practically purring.

I try not to shiver. I shiver *a lot.* The charmer is back, and he's turned on high.

Turned on? Bad choice of phrase. What is *wrong* with me?

"I can make myself feel good," I say and stop breathing.

Please tell me I didn't just utter those words. "How long will you make me feel good?"

"Does it matter? Good is good."

A nonanswer that is more telling than he probably realizes. He'll hit and run, and I'll be left to deal with yet another rejection. "It matters, because *I* matter. To me! You'll be done with me the moment I sign with Myriad. Well, I'm going to tell you a secret, and you have to keep it." I cup my hands around my mouth and whisper-yell, "I may *never* sign with one of the realms." Take that, Vans.

Killian's features twist in a glower. "Why would you do that to yourself? Many Ends offers only pain and suffering."

"Many Ends may not be real." I push him away, but he's strong and backs up only because he chooses. "I just want the freedom to make my own choice without interference. That's all."

"You have freedom. You have freedom right now. You had freedom yesterday, and the day before and the day before that. No matter where you are or what you're doing, you have freedom of choice. You're so afraid of making the wrong decision, you're actually stagnant."

I'm now astounded. He—the evil charmer—nailed it. I have the power to make my own decision any day...any second, but I haven't done it, because I've let my doubts become quicksand at my feet.

Needing to get away before I throw myself at him and hug him, I inch around him. "I'm going to think about what you said...tomorrow. Or maybe the day after. I'm pre-hungover."

He follows me, reaches out and sifts the ends of my hair through his fingers. "I don't want you to go."

"Too bad," I say, now backing away from him. "This death match is officially over." Sadly, I didn't win. But then, neither did he. We've reached a draw.

"Ms. Lockwood," Dr. Vans says.

I flip him off via the camera, continuing down the hall, heading for my cell.

chapter five

"Your mistakes do not define you, only the emotions you feel."
—Myriad

It's no big surprise when, over the next three days, Bow and I are locked inside our cell. It's my fault, and I know it. (1) I didn't sign with Myriad during my date with Killian and (2) I insulted Vans.

Starvation is clearly my punishment. Bow is collateral damage, and there's nothing I can do to help her. Every morning, the knowledge guts me anew.

On the fourth day, a knock sounds at our door soon after the other girls are let out for breakfast. As I shamble over, curious, the knock comes again, louder and harder. Through the glass in the center of the door I see Sloan's pretty face.

She presses a piece of paper to the glass. *Enjoy—K.* She points down before ducking out of view.

Frowning, I look at the floor and watch, mesmerized, as a thin protein bar slides under the crack. Food! My dry-as-the-desert mouth suddenly waters and my hands tremble as I pick up the prize. So the gift has touched dirty concrete. So what. True hunger isn't a twist in your stomach accompanied by an embarrassing grumble. True hunger makes you feel as if razors are slashing through your gut. There's a hollow sensation you can't ignore, your body growing colder and weaker by the minute. Weaker in a time and place where only the strong survive.

Might Equals Right. But as I told Killian, it shouldn't.

Hunger has even caused Bow to hallucinate more vividly. Before, she would talk to the wall. Lately, she snarls at air, saying things like, *You can't come where you're not invited. Go!* and *You're not getting this one, prick.*

By the time I straighten, practically crying with relief—screw the cameras—Sloan is gone.

I admit I'm tempted to hoard every nibble, but I have enough faults. I don't need to add greedy and selfish to the mix. I'm trembling as I split the bar and throw half to Bow.

Her mouth forms a small O. She's lying on her bed, the covers bunched at her feet. "You're *sharing* with me?"

"You say that like I've complained you've been using half our air." I stuff the bar in my mouth, my eyes closing in bliss as I chew and swallow. Oh, wow. Oh, yes. I owe Killian big-time. My hunger fed on my hope, each day becoming more depressing than the last. Right now, I could sing and dance through the cell like a freaking Disney princess.

I guess I owe Sloan, too. She risked punishment to help me.

Wait. Why did she risk punishment? And why did

Killian send her, of all people? Are the two friends now? *More* than friends?

My hands curl, my nails digging into my palms.

"You've been living on shower water." Bow still sounds shocked.

"So have you." If Vans shuts off our pipes—and I have a sinking feeling that will be his next move—we'll be reduced to drinking from the toilet.

"You're wasting away while I have untapped resources." She smooths a hand over her rounded belly before tossing her ration at me. "Here. I'm not hungry."

How can—

Whatever. I'm not going to argue with her. I devour the offering.

She anchors her hands behind her head and peers at me. "I know your parents want you to sign with Myriad, but why send you to a place like this to get the job done?"

"My dad is desperate. He loves his job and the money he makes, the power he has."

If I *do* sign with Myriad, maybe I can get them to rejig their slogan/motto/whatever. I'd go with… I don't know… Sharing Is Caring!

The thought makes me smile.

"He actually thought paying someone to beat you into submission was the perfect solution?" She snorts. "Has he met you?"

I hike up my shoulders. "Fear makes people stupid."

"For sure. Fear destroys. Hope is always the answer."

I like that. "When I was a kid, my mom used to say something similar. She grew up with Troikan parents."

Bow perks up. "What made her sign with Myriad?"

"My dad, mostly. Oh. And the rigidity of Troikan law. She complained a lot."

"Well, don't believe the hype. No civilization can thrive without rules of conduct, and all of ours fall into one of three categories. King, realm and self. But everything boils down to this. Treat others the way you want to be treated, and hold no grudges."

A tri-tier of rules…which makes sense. *Troika* means a group of three people working together, especially in an administrative or managerial capacity. My numbers-obsessed mind makes the connection, and gives me a little thrill.

"In a word," I say, "unconditional love."

"The foundation of all good things." Sheepish, she adds, "As you've noticed, I sometimes have a wee bit of trouble with the grudge thing."

"Yeah, but that aside, I thought Troika was anti-emotion."

"No one is anti-emotion." She crosses her arms over her chest. "Feelings matter, but they can change in a blink, making them an unreliable guide."

Over the intercom, the usual voice announces, "Tenley Lockwood. Your parents are waiting for you in Dr. Vans's office."

I tense with nervousness, maybe even a little eagerness. My mom actually kept her promise?

My dad has visited once every other month. When I asked him about my mom, he said, "We're currently separated, living apart. She's decided seclusion is better than family."

She left him…and me.

Bow climbs to her feet. "If at any time you decide Troika

is the place for you, verbalize your allegiance. That's all you have to do. Your word is your bond."

Right. Troika offers the same terms to everyone. Part of the "no exceptions" thing.

"The realm will provide health care, schooling, therapy when needed, financial assistance and even protection services upon request," she adds.

I think I prefer Myriad's MO. They offer different packages and bonuses. If you want bigger and better, you have to work for it. But greater risk, greater reward.

She pats me on the shoulder. "Don't worry. I'll be with you in spirit."

There's a thread of amusement in her voice. A thread I don't understand.

Whatever. Dread replaces my eagerness, my blood morphing into fuel as I approach the door. All I need is a match, and I'll catch fire and burn. The lock disengages, the metal block opening, allowing me to step into the hallway.

No one is waiting for me. Knowing I'm being watched on a panel of monitors, I make my way to the left, snake around a corner, bypass the empty commons and enter the overcrowded cafeteria, where the scent of slop makes my mouth water. Really, the protein bar was only an appetizer.

When I spot Sloan, I nod my thanks, but she quickly looks away.

I search for Killian, finding him easily when he stands. Our gazes merge. He's bigger than I remember. Like, *really* big. Loaded with muscle big. The kind of muscle found in a gym only after years of training.

My heart skitters into a faster rhythm, and tingles rush through me. I shiver. For a moment, I want to run to him.

I'm falling down a pit of despair…confusion…darkness, and because of the trust exercise, I know he'll catch me.

I resist the urge.

His cunning gaze assesses the situation as if he's already considered three ways to destroy everyone present.

His closet protector is coming out to play.

I mouth, *Thank you.*

He frowns and gives a clipped nod.

"Chop, chop," Nurse Ratched commands from the gate blocking "patients" from the offices.

As soon as I reach her, she pivots on her heel and presses her index finger into the ID box. After a quick scan, she swipes her card across the side and punches in a code. The gate buzzes open, and she stalks through.

My surroundings change in an instant, as if I've stepped through an invisible portal into a fairy tale. From cold and impersonal to warm and inviting. The walls are vibrant baby blue rather than medicine-cabinet gray. Six portraits hang throughout, three on each side of me. Each bears a different-colored rose, meant to add a touch of beauty to a bona fide hellhole. A large wrought-iron candelabra is twisted into the shape of a dragon. The creature's mouth is open, his teeth monstrous, but he spews blackbirds rather than fire, the metal flock stretching to the door at the end of the hall, where Nurse Ratched stops and smiles coldly at me.

She's tall and big boned, with frizzy red hair framing a face that is littered with acne scars. Over the past year, I've had plenty of time to observe her in her natural habitat and I've come to realize she uses her job as a way to obtain what she's never gotten outside these walls. Power.

Myriad must be her wet dream.

"Go ahead," she says. "Fight your future the way you always do. Insult Dr. Vans and your parents with that viper tongue."

"I will, thanks." Whatever happens, I'll survive. My parents need me alive.

How sad is that? The best I can say about the people who created me is that they need me to continue breathing.

The girl I used to be would have curled into a ball and sobbed. The girl I am raises her chin and presses on.

"Afterward," she adds, "we have extra-special plan for you."

Last time, I was tied down and beaten with brass knuckles. *Extra-special* scares me.

I ignore the fear, as always, knowing it will only help her sense of empowerment.

"So sweet of you." Like Sloan, I trace fingertips down my cheeks. "Tears of joy."

She pats my cheek with a little too much force. "Enjoy the meeting, Miss Lockwood. I have feeling you won't enjoy *anything* for long time to come." With that, she knocks on the door and strides away.

I want to vomit.

The door to Vans's office slides open, and cold fingers of dread crawl down my spine.

I can do this. Whatever "this" is. I remind myself of the three most important facts of life.

(1) Firstlife, good or bad, is fleeting, even if we live a hundred years. Numbers never lie. A hundred years is nothing compared to thousands of years in the Everlife. So a few hours...days...weeks of pain? Means nothing. Because—

(2) pain is temporary, just as Bow said. It won't follow me to the other side.

And (3) what happens after death will be forever, making the afterlife far more important than anything that happens here and now.

Still, I break out in a sweat as I step inside the spacious office, where everything is ornate and overdone. An arched ceiling with a crystal teardrop chandelier dangles above a desk the same size as the conference table. The walls are made of light stone and dark wood, the two framing multiple bookshelves and a marble fireplace with legs carved to resemble lions. Lions with golden collars clamped around their necks, their heads bowed.

Gossip claims there's a door to the outside world hidden somewhere in this room.

Vans is already seated at the conference table, alongside my parents. Yes, my mother is here. A pang of homesickness overtakes me. Homesickness, along with regret and sorrow. The painful deluge nearly chokes me.

Fat tears stream down my mother's cheeks as she meets my gaze. She's gained at least twenty pounds since last I saw her, yet she used to flip out over a single ounce. Priorities change.

I cut off a bitter laugh.

As I stare at her, silent, a sob leaves her. When I was a little girl and someone said an unkind word to me, she would whisper, *You don't have haters, sweetheart, you have prefans.*

"Ten—" she begins.

"Tenley," I correct, my tone cool. "Only my friends call me Ten."

"Yes, yes, of course." Her chin trembles as she struggles to control her reactions. "I understand."

I hurt her. Good. *She's* hurt *me.*

Sorrow has marred features that are strikingly similar to mine. We both have pale skin with a smattering of freckles and eyes almost too big for our faces, though hers are a rich chocolate brown. Our cheekbones are high and sharp, our noses small but pert, our lips heart-shaped. She has a shoulder-length crop of auburn hair artfully cut while my last trim came from a butcher knife courtesy of Nurse Ratched.

"Are you here to take me home?" I ask.

She looks down at her hands and shakes her head.

"Not unless you're ready to sign the contract," Senator Lockwood says. He sits rigidly in his chair, his features strained as he looks me over.

He's aged. There are new frown lines around his eyes and mouth, and his once-olive skin is sallow. His hair, so black it gleams blue in the light—an attribute I inherited from him—is now salted with gray. His mismatched eyes, one green, one blue—another attribute I inherited—watch me with determination.

Despite his shortcomings, he's still a handsome man. Women everywhere have always thrown themselves at him. Girls, too. My friends would giggle about him behind their hands. *So sexy.*

At the table, only one chair is empty, and it's on the opposite side of the others. Their way of saying *we're a unit, you're alone.*

I sit with all the dignity I can muster.

"Tenley." The senator pulls at the collar of his shirt. "It's nice to see you."

"I wish I could say the same."

His flinch is slight, but I notice. Does he ever wonder if he made the right decision sending me here?

Vans pushes a digital pad my way, putting my forced breeziness to shame. "Are you ready to sign with Myriad?"

"Nope. Now, if we're done here…" I stand.

"Refuse," he continues as if I haven't spoken, "and I'll be forced to punish Killian for sneaking food to your cell."

I gasp. The cameras. Or he and Killian planned this, thinking I'd feel so guilty about the boy who caught me when I fell, the boy who fed me when I was hungry, I'd finally cave. "No mention of Sloan?" I grit out.

"Who is—" my mom begins.

The senator shakes his head. "We don't need the details."

Correction: he doesn't *want* the details.

I ease into the chair and cross my arms. "You want me to sign, Senator? Convince me."

His next flinch is more noticeable. He's always hated when I use his title. He reaches up to give his collar another tug but catches himself. "I've tried. Look where we ended up."

"We?" That's rich!

My dad pushes out a heavy breath. "You have no idea what it's like to grow up in poverty, the child of Unsigned. I had nothing. Not even friends. Myriad changed everything. I owe them. *You* owe them."

I flash back to the night I heard my parents arguing about my grandparents—my mom's parents. The Troikan loyalists.

"They just want to spend time with their granddaughter," my mom said.

"We can't risk it," my dad replied. "They'll fill Ten's head with nonsense, the way they once filled yours."

"They won't. They only want to make memories with her."

"Don't be naive, Grace. Everyone has an agenda."

"You're wrong. And cynical! They're wonderful people."

"If they're so wonderful, why did you reject everything they taught you?"

"To be with *you*," she'd whispered.

I glance at my mom. She's still crying. Does she ever wish she'd sided with her parents instead of my dad?

"Myriad will take care of you," he says, his desperation showing. "They'll take care of us all."

He's deceived, a voice whispers in my ear. I detect a slight English accent and immediately think of Bow. Only the voice belongs to a boy. *You'll be used up and thrown away like garbage.*

I jerk my head left, right, then behind. No one stands near me.

"Are you all right?" My mother reaches across the table to clasp my hand.

I lurch back, avoiding contact. A single touch will be more than my fragile state of mind can handle.

She presses her lips into a thin line.

"Think," Vans says. "Once you agree, there'll be no more pain. No more hardships."

"And Killian?" I demand.

"He'll be pardoned."

Zero! Dr. Vans knows me well. If there's a chance Killian is a victim of his manipulations, I can't allow him to be hurt.

Trepidation crawls the length of my spine. Am I actually considering doing this? "Give me a minute."

My dad nods eagerly. "Yes, yes. Of course."

I swivel my chair and face the door.

I know this present life is hailed as a simple dress rehearsal. A test, some say. A type of school, others believe. Either way, if I sign with Myriad, I might be able to live for the very first time.

I'm ready to live.

My parents believe Myriad is the right choice. As much as I resent them, I admire their confidence. And dang it, I still love them. They're as worried about their future as I am about my own.

"If you were to sign with Troika," Vans says, "you would be on the opposite side of the war. One day, you might even be tasked with killing your parents."

I resent the pair, but I could never kill them. Even temporarily.

I spin back around, finally ready to do it. To say yes. I mean, why not? When I open my mouth, however, no sound emerges. After everything I've endured—physical hunger, weakness and depravation, mental exhaustion and trauma, emotional upheaval—my decision comes down to their needs over my own?

"I'm sorry," I whisper. "I can't. Not yet."

My dad closes his eyes, his shoulders hunching in. A position of defeat. He's known among his peers for his indomitable strength and unwillingness to back down. "I only want the best for you. Why can't you see that?"

"Maybe because there's usually blood in my eyes," I snap, unmoved by his unusual display of emotion. And wow, when did I become so cold and callous?

Oh, I know. The day I arrived at Prynne.

His nostrils flare. He glares at Vans, unloading a shotgun full of fury. "This is your fault. You promised us results."

The doctor dons an impassive mask. "I've asked repeatedly to take my efforts to the next level. You refused."

What? My dad actually prevented certain tortures?

"I even advised you against the massages and other privileges."

What!

"Say the word, and I'll hurt her in ways you can't even imagine—without breaking her, of course."

I clutch my churning stomach.

"No," my mom says, shaking her head. "Absolutely not."

"I won't kill her," Vans assures them. "She won't be violated. But an increase in pain is the only option we have left. All I need is your permission to proceed."

My father pinches the bridge of his nose.

I tremble in my seat. *Say no, Daddy. Say no.*

"Yes," he croaks, and I have to bite my tongue to stop myself from screaming. "I don't want to proceed this way, but you've left me with no other choice. One day you might even thank me."

I don't… I can't…

I blink rapidly, fighting tears. "Fathers are supposed to protect their little girls."

"That's what I'm trying to do," he shouts. "I'm trying to protect your future."

Right words. Only, they are a lie. He's protecting *his* future. Mine is shattered, just like my heart.

"You'll be pleased with the results, Senator Lockwood." Vans lifts his famed digital pad. "I'll send you pictures documenting the procedure."

Sign with Troika. The voice hits my awareness again, so distinct that I can't pass it off as my imagination. *Swear allegiance right now, and I'll get you out of here. No one will hurt you.*

"Who are you?" I demand.

Vans frowns at me. "Is someone speaking to you, Ms. Lockwood?"

My parents share a look of shock. Well, the senator is shocked. My mother is almost…hopeful.

"Is there a Laborer in the room?" My father looks around.

A Laborer? But—wait! A memory sparks. Laborers are sometimes allowed to visit a human while in spirit form.

Please, the voice says. *End this travesty before it starts.*

"Does no one else hear him?"

A chorus of "No" rings out, each individual negation tinged with a different emotion. Irritation, relief and confusion.

So. A TL is here to help me. And all I have to do is hand over my eternity.

To Dr. Vans I say, "What are we waiting for?" I clap my hands, as though overcome with excitement. "Stop the unnecessary chitchat and get this party started."

chapter six

"What you know and feel matters, but what you do matters more."
—Troika

There are days a smart mouth gets you into trouble, and you wish you could travel back in time to glue your stupid lips shut. For me, this is one of those days.

The sad thing? Even if I'd remained silent during the meeting, I would have ended up in this position.

My parents are escorted out of Vans's office. In the doorway, my mom stops to glance back at me. Her cheeks are stained with tears, several droplets caught in her lashes.

Stay strong, she mouths.

Help me, I mouth back. I'm not too proud or foolish to ask while I have the chance.

Eyes welling, she ducks her head and leaves. As her sob drifts through the quiet of the room, my heart crumbles. My one chance for no-strings aid is gone.

Comrade Douche and Titball enter the room. Without speaking a word, they grab my arms and drag me into the hall. I offer no protest. I catch a glimpse of my parents slipping through the door in the opposite direction. Are they headed to a nice hotel? Going to stop for a delicious brunch?

I'm taken to a small sterile room devoid of furniture. Two chains hang from the ceiling, and both have fetters at the ends…just big enough for my wrists. I can deal with anything except chains.

At last I begin my struggle for freedom, but it hardly matters. I'm malnourished and weak, and I'm subdued easily, my wrists soon encased. The outside of the fetters begin to glow as little needles extend from the inside, drilling past skin and into bone in seconds. I hiss. The pain is substantial but nothing I haven't endured before. The problem is the mental anguish.

Trapped! No way out!

The guards pull the chains taut, lifting me off my feet. My shoulders scream in protest, the pressure more and more agonizing. Finally, all I can do is breathe…in…out…in…

Comrade Douche whispers, his accent thicker than usual, "You need strong man to take you in hand. I come for you tonight and prove, yes?"

Now I want to vomit again.

Vans discards his lab coat and rolls up his shirtsleeves, displaying a patchwork of scars from one of Sloan's attempts to kill him. The impassive, even affable, mask he'd donned for my parents' benefit is stripped away, revealing the monster I've come to despise.

"You know," he says as the guards march out of the room—Douche pauses to blow me a kiss. "I've always admired your spirit, Ms. Lockwood. It's a shame I have to damage it."

I can't give him the pleasure. *Get it together. Stay strong.* "Go ahead. Do your worst."

Common sense shouts, *What? Take that back!*

"Your best has only ever tickled," I add. Common sense and I are currently bitter enemies.

Anger flickers in the depths of his eyes, and I know his overinflated pride has been injured.

My satisfaction is minimal, considering the circumstances.

Nurse Ratched wheels a large silver tray inside the room and the door closes behind her, sealing the three of us inside.

Stay calm. Think. Stall, stall, stall. "You don't have to do this. You said there are no other options, but that's not true. You can give me the time I asked for."

"Time is running out." He smiles. "No, we're going to do this. Money buys happiness, and anyone who says otherwise is lying. I want my money."

"Aren't you afraid of what awaits you in the Everlife?"

He lifts his shoulders in a shrug. "I've never cared about tomorrow. Only today."

"Is that why you're Unsigned?"

"In part. Troika's benefits aren't worth my time, and Myriad hasn't offered me enough."

"So you want to wait for a better deal, but I'm supposed to accept the scraps thrown my way?"

"Yes. Exactly." He slants his head in my direction. "As your father said, one day you'll thank him for this. One day you'll even thank me."

Never! "You're lying or deluded."

"I believe the word you're searching for is *right*. I've been where you are, Ms. Lockwood. My father ran this institution, and his father before him. Everything I've done to you has been done to me. And look at me now. I'm strong, unbreakable. Drop me in any situation—war, famine, plague—and I can survive."

"Living shouldn't be synonymous with surviving."

He pops on a pair of gloves. "You have my permission to scream as loudly as you'd like. These walls are soundproofed."

I swallow the lump growing in my throat. There will be no more stalling, then.

"*You* have *my* permission to scream," I tell him. Looking past the pain in my shoulders, I arch my back for momentum and naturally rock forward, kicking both my legs as high as they'll go and nailing the good doctor in the jaw. His head whips to the side, blood leaking from the corner of his mouth.

He grunts. His eyes narrow as he licks the crimson from his lips. "You'll regret that." The words are filled with promise…and anticipation.

I raise my chin with as much dignity as I can muster. "I only regret your birth."

He slaps me across the cheek, and the taste of copper trickles over my tongue.

We are nose to nose a moment later, his hot breath fanning my split lip, burning me. "Say another word. I dare you. Your parents have given me permission to do anything I wish to you. You heard them. I can even cut out your tongue, if I so desire."

He's just cruel enough to do it.

I glare at him, but I don't speak another word.

Triumphant, he backs away from me and nods to Nurse Ratched.

She lifts a syringe and thumps its belly, only to freeze as the room—the entire building?—begins to shake. The walls rumble, and dust plumes the air. Both Vans and Ratched stumble and fall, and if not for my chains, I would have gone down, too.

The shaking stops as suddenly as it started, and the pair climb to their feet.

"The realms must battle nearby," Nurse Ratched says, dusting off her pants.

She's probably right. Whenever Troika and Myriad engage in battle, the violence spills into the Land of the Harvest through earthquakes, tornadoes, tsunamis and, during the worst of the confrontations, asteroids.

Nurse Ratched swipes up the needle she dropped and approaches me, her dark eyes glittering. "Adrenaline and others goodies to enhance your experience."

I struggle against my bonds, trying yet again to ignore the pain shooting through me, but I'm already sluggish, and with my limited range of motion, it isn't long before she's able to shove the needle deep into my arm. A sharp sting registers—minimal to everything else—followed by a wash of cold…then heat, such horrible heat. Sweat beads over my brow and upper lip, igniting a fire inside me. When the flames reach my heart, the organ bursts into a raging gallop, knocking so hard against my ribs I'm certain they'll break.

Only momentary, I remind myself. It doesn't help.

Vans waves a thick metal syringe in front of my face. "You've heard of the poison the realms use to kill humans,

I'm sure. This little concoction is a variation of it. *Baiser de la mort*, it's called. The kiss of death. You'll *want* to die, but you won't."

Fear courses through me—*beg, plead*—but still I manage to smile. "Is the big, bad doctor afraid to get his hands dirty? Don't think you're strong enough?" If he wants to take my tongue, fine. Do it. It's only ever gotten me into trouble. "You're a little bitch, aren't you? That's why you use poison."

"Hold her," he snaps.

While Nurse Ratched cradles me against her body, effectively caging my head and arms, he sticks me in the neck.

I tense, expecting an immediate reaction. The injection hurts, but I've experienced worse. I relax; I even offer the pair another smile. "Aw. Looks like you're destined for another failure."

He offers no reaction, but then, he knows what I do not: I've spoken too soon. My blood begins to boil, every cell in my body becoming a flame, my veins close to total disintegration.

My skin bubbles, melting like cheese on a pizza. Surely.

"This is only the beginning," he gloats.

I open my mouth to reply—but I scream. All at once, I feel a thousand razor-sharp pinpricks in my veins, my head, as if bugs are crawling through me, their dagger-tipped legs tap, tap, tapping where they don't belong. My muscles knot. I think my bones crack. Pressure builds in my temples, and when it becomes too much, warm liquid leaks from my eyes, ears and nose.

I'm bleeding, and I'm dying. I have to be dying. No one can survive this.

Momentary...just a blip. But a single heartbeat might as well be a hundred years.

Don't care. Stop. Have to make it stop.

I'll do whatever he wants. I'll sign with Myriad.

Stop, stop, stop.

If I change my mind about my future later on, I can go to court. Bow mentioned the possibility for the coerced. Yes, yes. Too many lose, she'd said, but I'm willing to take the chance.

Stop!

"I—" My mind breaks, disconnected with me, disassociating with reality—a memory becoming my new truth. I'm seven years old. My dad is home, but he's pacing in his office, worried about money. *How are we going to pay this, Grace? We're tapped out.*

My mom is painting in her studio, preparing to sell one of her pieces earlier rather than later, leaving me in Aunt Lina's care. She's come for a visit. We're alone in my bedroom, and she's twirling. She's Loony Lina today, the personality that is blind. Blind and yet, somehow she manages to avoid bumping into my furniture.

"I'm sorry the poison hurt you so bad," she says in a little-girl voice, despite the fact that she's twenty-seven, like my dad. "But I'm glad the doctor died."

"Poison?" I ask, confused. "Doctor?"

"You escaped!"

Loony Lina always says crazy things.

Now I'm baffled. Ten years ago she mentioned poison and escape? But...but...back then, she couldn't have known this would happen. Right?

Vans pinches my chin between his fingers, jerking me

from my thoughts, forcing me to face him. I'm unable to focus, my vision too cloudy.

"You know what to say to make the pain stop."

Stop…stop…yes, that's exactly what I want. Will do anything! Panting breaths wheeze through my mouth as I try to tell him—

What?

My parents' dream…or mine?

"No," I manage to croak.

Rage contorts his features. He snaps his fingers in Nurse Ratched's direction. "Give her another injection."

Another? *No, no, no.* I struggle to contain my whimpers of protest.

"You kill her?" Nurse Ratched asks. "That is what happens next."

"Give her another injection!"

No! *Bow,* I try to scream. She said she would rescue me. She promised. I just… What do I have to do? Say the word—what word? Troika?

Nurse Ratched hurries to the tray and, after rooting through the utensils scattered across the top, returns to my side. Another sting. Another wash of cold followed by intense heat. The terrible sensations in my head magnify a million degrees, and I release a bloodcurdling scream that springs from the depths of my soul.

Over and over Vans tells me to sign with Myriad, and over and over I somehow find the strength to deny him. *My dream…dream…* He pokes and prods at me. He hits me with a closed fist, backhands me with an open palm. He slices at my arms and legs with a scalpel but through it all… *dream, dream, dream…* I resist.

Finally he has two choices. Stop, or watch me die.

"Let her down." His disgust is clear.

Nurse Ratched adds slack to the chains until my feet touch the floor. My legs are the consistency of jelly, and I can't hold myself up. I sag, my head falling forward, my chin pressing in my sternum as my arms continue to bear the bulk of my weight. Then the fetters are removed, and I crash, knocking out what little air I managed to collect in my lungs.

Vans is right about one thing. I really, really want to die.

"You damaged her." An all-too-familiar voice slashes through the silence. A male voice with a slight Irish lilt.

Killian is here?

My relief is boundless. A savior! I don't even care that I'm a damsel in distress.

I can't lift my head, but I find the strength to pry open my eyes. A cascade of blood obstructs my vision. All I see are two shadows standing face-to-face.

"This is a restricted area," Vans barks. "Leave. Now."

"Unfortunately for you, you aren't the one who pulls my strings," Killian says. "Do you know who you *are*? The bastard who used my actions against the girl. Oh yes, I heard about that."

A third shadow appears. "Your services aren't necessary, Killian." Bow's voice! She's come for me, too. "You can leave. I've got this."

A menacing growl from Killian. "I'm not going anywhere without Ten."

"You'll get her over my dead body."

"Agreed. But first I'm going to dispose of the trash."

"Now wait just a—" Vans begins.

"Don't kill—" Bow says.

Both go silent.

Different sounds hit my awareness. Rustling clothes. The whoosh of air. Gurgling. A loud *snap*. A louder *thump*. A whisper.

"Things will be better now, lass." A soft brush of fingertips through my hair as Killian's scent fills my nose.

My whimper is barely audible.

"Get your filthy hands off her," Bow demands.

"Why don't you make me, Little Bow Peep Show?"

More rustling clothing. When it ceases, I hear panting.

"Vans should have been locked away," Bow shouts.

"Do you truly believe he deserved a second chance?" Killian asks. "Or is your realm speaking for you?"

"I happen to agree with my realm. You don't deserve a second chance, and yet you live."

"I've never asked for a second chance. I am what I am. I *like* what I am. In this case, I'm the victor."

Bow blows out a frustrated breath. "We need permission from Ten or someone in her familial line to intervene on her behalf—any more than we already have. Until then, our hands are tied."

"*Your* hands are tied. Her mother gave her own ML permission to protect the girl from mortal harm. Permission that's been passed to me. I just protected Ten from mortal harm. Which I'll continue to do outside these walls."

"You can't escape with her."

"I can. Your laws aren't mine. You should have convinced her to leave days ago."

"You want an Unsigned out there? She would have died sooner rather than later."

Huff, puff. "With me, the level of danger doesn't matter," Killian retorts.

A curse from Bow, then a curse from Killian. The two go silent. I hear…typing?

Bow grunts and walks closer to me. I hear splashing. She crouches to do…something. Her hand is moving. She's writing? On what?

"What are you doing?" Killian demands.

"Her grandmother has requested I clear a path of escape. The girl will choose whether she stays or goes."

She's delusional. My grandmother is dead. Both of my grandmothers are dead, in fact. One is in Troika, and one is in Myriad.

"So much for keeping an Unsigned inside these walls, eh?" Killian's dry tone seems to suck any humidity out of the air. "Guess what? My new orders just came in. I'm supposed to stop you—put your claws away. I won't obey."

"Thank—"

"Don't thank me, Archer. I won't let her leave with you, either."

Archer?

"She'll leave with *me*," Killian continues. "If you get in my way, well, I'll happily kill you."

"You can try."

Footsteps. Muttered arguing. Then…nothing.

I'm not sure how much time passes. I drift in and out of consciousness, but finally…*finally* I'm able to move. My fingers twitch. I roll my shoulder. I lift my arm, wipe my eyes to clear my vision and—

Scramble backward.

A few feet away from me, Vans is on his back, motionless, his dull eyes staring at nothing. His mouth is open, crimson dried at the corners of his lips. He's…dead? He must be. He's lying in a pool of blood. One of his hands has been removed, and it's cuddled up next to my ankle, like a puppy.

Did Killian do this?

If you get in my way, well, I'll happily kill you.

I bolt to my feet, different parts of me threatening to revolt.

Killian and Bow are gone. They saved me…then left me behind?

Clear a path of escape…

Frowning, I stumble to the open door and peek into the hall. Two guards lie motionless on the floor.

Bow's doing? Or Killian's?

Does it matter? There's no better time to escape. *Go, go!*

I rush through the room. The problem? My rush is actually slo-mo. I'm weaker than I realized, operating on empty. I manage to swipe up the lab coat Vans dropped and, despite the pain shooting through me, shove my arms inside the proper holes. The doctor's key card is attached to the lapel. Perfect. I stuff the scalpel in my pocket, grimace as I pick up the severed hand—the number 830543 is scripted across the top. A message from Bow?

A composite number. A prime number. The prime factors are: 7, 59, 2011

My brain wants to dissect each of the individual numbers, but there's no time. I drop the hand beside the scalpel and beat feet to the best of my ability, heading for Vans's office.

The number of obstacles in my way: two, at the very

least. Nurse Ratched will be nearby just in case Vans has need of—

I trip, landing with a hard thud, losing my breath. I look over my shoulder and discover Nurse Ratched slumped against the wall, her neck at an odd angle.

Ooo-kay. One obstacle. The lock on the office door.

In the distance thunders a stampede of feet, the wild cheers of inmates, the thud of furniture being turned over. An alarm screeches to life.

My best isn't good enough; I have to do better. I scramble up and lurch into motion, hobbling instead of running.

"Ten! Ten!"

The voice comes from behind me. I turn. Sloan is beating at the gate that separates the prisoners' wing from the offices. Her features are ablaze with a combination of excitement and strain, her fingers curled around the wire so tightly, her knuckles are bleached. Behind her, several kids are beating Colonel Anus and Ben Dover into pulp and powder. Fists are flying. Feet are kicking. Nails are raking and teeth are biting. The guards struggle…at first.

"Get your ass over here!" Sloan demands.

The kids responsible for beating—killing—Anus and Ben appear beside her, blood smeared on their faces, coating their hands.

Do I attempt to rescue, despite my weakness? Or do I flee while I can?

As if I don't already know the answer. I needed help, and Killian and Bow stepped up. These kids need me. I have to do my part.

"Have you seen Killian or Bow?" I ask, limping over.

"No." Sloan glances behind her. "Hurry!"

I press the severed hand against the ID pad, swipe the card along the side, but…the door remains closed, exactly as I feared, as the screen asks for a code. What should I do?

Frustrated, I beat Vans's hand against the pad. My gaze is drawn to the number. The number! Could it be the code? With a quivering finger, I jab at the keypad. Success! The lock disengages, and the kids are able to shoulder their way past me.

I return the severed hand to its place and move down the hall.

"Idiot!" Sloan shouts. "You're going the wrong way."

"Have to find Killian and Bow," I call. Can't leave them here to clear the way for me, endangering themselves further, when my way no longer needs clearing.

Kids, kids, are everywhere, fighting the guards and orderlies with equal fury; they are winning, but there's no sign of my helpers. I step over a motionless, bloody body—Comrade Douche has a baton stuffed down his throat.

Someone slams into me from behind, pushed by someone else. I trip forward and knock into yet another person. An inmate. His gaze is wild as he swings around, his fist already cocked and loaded to issue punishment. A rush of adrenaline loosens my sore limbs and I duck, avoiding contact, then dart past him.

I search every open cell, every corridor. Still no sign. Zero! Maybe they've already left?

I brave the boys' ward with no luck and return to the gate. The crowd has thinned considerably, but D-bag and Titball have taken posts on either side. Both men wield a baton, beating on anyone who comes into striking range. Namely three girls and two boys desperate for freedom. So desperate, they continually throw themselves at the guards despite the fact that their bodies are already bloody and battered, their energy almost completely depleted.

Dread floods me, and I grind to a stop. New obstacles in my way: two.

A pair. The atomic number of helium. Once again my number of choices.

Fight or flight?

My trembling magnifies. I want out, and I won't leave the kids behind; I have to fight.

Deep breath in…out… I square my shoulders, take stock. D-bag is holding one of the boys on the floor with one hand and beating him with the other. Titball has pinned the others in the corner, but his eyes are locked on me.

Kill him.

Killian's voice whispers through my mind. A hallucination, I know. And why not? I'm Nutter.

Disarm him and move on.

Now I hear the disembodied voice from Vans's office.

My mind flashes back to every leer, push, punch and battle. Every time I was dragged down the halls. My calendar. Today's chains and poison.

Obstacle. I'll kill! My wrists and shoulders scream in protest as I rush forward. Along the way, I grab the scalpel I stole from Vans. One second I'm twisting to avoid being grabbed by Titball, the next I'm stabbing him in the neck. *Jab, jab, jab.*

He drops to the floor, his body twitching.

I expect satisfaction. Instead I want to cry.

I'm panting as the inmates move away from D-bag *and*

me, peering at me as if I've done something both horrifying and amazing—as if I'm as bad as our enemy.

"Stay here or follow me." I pull out the severed hand and key card. "Your choice."

chapter seven

"Fear keeps you alive. Fear reminds you that you *are* alive."
—Myriad

Alarm blasting.

Blood soaking my hands.

Kids babbling at my sides.

Problems mounting one after another.

Because I worked the locks, I'm the last to make it through the secret door that's hidden behind the fireplace in Vans's office. I race down a long narrow hallway, the walls and floor made of concrete. I pass another open door and enter…hell on ice. Zero! The thin lab coat and even thinner uniform offer little protection from the harsh winterscape now surrounding me. I'm on a mountain. There's snow at my feet, in the trees and dancing in the wind.

A loud *boom* suddenly assaults my ears. As a bolt of lightning cuts through the sky, the land below me vibrates. The realms are still fighting?

My eyes tear from the cold—the tears instantly freeze. With only a single breath, my nose, throat and lungs burn as if they've been scalded by acid. Goose bumps rise from my head to my toes, and I shudder. Kids I've ignored and fought, liked and disliked, are running in every direction, but they aren't running fast. Hypothermia is already setting up camp, their blood turning into sludge.

How long can we survive out here? A few hours…perhaps an entire day if we're hearty?

We're not hearty. Me most of all.

Whatever. Have to try. Can't go back.

I motor forward.

Boom! The noise doesn't come from the sky but the ground. A few yards away, an inmate—just—explodes, bits and pieces of…of…human flying in every direction. I flail for purchase, but the ground is too slick. I skid while swallowing bile as those bits and pieces plop all over the ground.

Screams of fear erupt. Chaos reigns.

Another battle between the realms, or maybe land mines? To my knowledge, a realm battle has never ripped a person into a thousand pieces. "Be still," I shout, but no one hears me. We have to take a minute, figure this out, search for other bombs.

I scan the area and manage to find the ignition site. Smoke curls toward a sky that's set ablaze by a dipping sun. Oh…my… Daylight! For a moment, I forget where I am, forget the horror of what just happened and the trials I've endured. The colors—gold, pink, blue—are mesmerizing.

Is Troika like this?

Warmth strokes over me, seeping through my skin and dancing over my bones, seeming to strengthen me. Pinpricks of gold and blue dot the sky. Stars so bright you can see them during the day? I stretch out my arm, ghosting my fingertip through a brilliant ray of light. Dust motes twirl through the air, somersaulting just out of reach.

When I see the blood on my hand, I snap back into focus. The asylum. Escape. Bombs.

"Guards!" someone shouts.

And now we're being hunted. Wonderful. I dart forward, constantly examining the ground for any sign of another bomb. I pass a charred sandal with a severed foot still strapped inside and gag.

There are one, five, ten, eighteen kids ahead of me, running, running. Eight others have stopped to catch their breath and figure out the safest course of action. Bad news, gang. Both choices suck. We can keep going, even though we're without proper clothing and provisions, or we can allow the guards to return us to the hornet's nest.

Am I being chased? I glance over my shoulder, my eyes going round with shock, my jaw dropping. The institution is massive, both tall and sprawling, with thirteen stories made entirely of gray stone, the front of the structure protruding from the mountainside, the rest hidden deep in the rock face.

There's more to the place than I ever realized.

None of the guards have focused on me, at least.

Movement at the corner of my eye. Is that—

Yes! Bow! She races toward me, a backpack bouncing over her shoulder. She isn't slow like the others, but swift and sure. I shout her name. Our gazes lock.

Boom!

There's a seismic shift as a white-hot blast of air throws me backward. For a moment, I'm warm, and it's nice. Until

I land and my lungs empty. When I'm able to breathe, the air is heavy with smoke. I cough as debris rains. I don't have to do an in-depth study to know another kid just bit the dust. *Don't be Bow. Please, please don't be Bow.*

She clears the smoke and comes up beside me, grabs my arm without slowing and yanks me to my feet.

Thank the Firstking! "Careful," I tell her as we shoot forward.

"Careful will get you caught." She runs faster. "Come on!"

I return to scanning the ground for anything out of whack. A stone, a frozen branch. The glint of metal—there. "Bomb," I shout, jerking her around it.

"Thanks," she mutters.

Step, step, step…stone…branch…metal! A pattern. A numerical rhythm my mind instinctively captures. One step, two, three, stone. One step, two, three, four, five, branch. One step, two, three, four, metal. They aren't laid in a straight line, of course, but staggered. Which also presents a pattern. Left, left, right. Right, right, left.

I pump my arms faster, taking the lead, leaping over the next bomb and dragging Bow with me. When we reach the bottom of the incline, heading toward a densely populated forest, I stop looking for explosives and start praying I accidentally trip one. A burnt body is a warm body, and right now the cold feels like a thousand needles pricking at my skin. Shudders begin to rack me, one after the other, barely a pause between. My teeth chatter. Snot trickles from my nose and, like my tears, freezes.

"What's in the pack?" Too much to hope for a battery-operated heat lamp? At this point, I wouldn't say no to fetters.

"Essentials" is all she says. The temperature hasn't affected her in the least. She isn't shivering. Her teeth aren't chattering. Her eyes and nose are free of tears and snot, and there's no hint of blue on her lips. How is that possible?

We reach a bank of tall, thin boulders. In the center, two lean against each other, forming an upside-down V—creating a doorway. There's an enter-at-your-own-peril vibe. Where *are* we?

I release Bow and slow down. "Got to take…a minute to rest. Not sure…how much…farther…"

"No, no. We can't stop," she says. "When I left the asylum, every guard inside was gearing up to come after us. And there were a lot of 'em! An entire army was training in the underground levels."

An entire army to elude? Zero!

Can't risk capture. I draw from a reservoir of strength I didn't know I possessed and soldier on, tripping past the rocks. Icicles are extended like swords and cut at my face, but it doesn't matter. Even the needle-prick sensation is fading, my skin numbing.

"Do you…know where…" My foot catches on a fallen branch and I tumble, landing in the snow and dirt face-first. Bow helps me stand, and I realize the "branch" is actually a leg. A human leg.

Hank, the kid Killian punched his first day at the asylum, is sprawled on his back. He's motionless, his eyes glassed over with a sheen of ice. His skin is the color of the morning sky I've missed so much, and there are crystals protruding from the end of his nose.

Bow crouches to place her hand over his heart, not to feel for a beat, I don't think, but to…mourn a lost life? "Light Brings Sight," she whispers to him. "May the Everlife reward you for your kindnesses during your Firstlife."

Her words humble me. Life is precious to her and yet, fifteen minutes ago, I ended one.

My guilt returns.

Her gaze brims with sadness as it meets mine. "He's in the Everlife now. Let's keep you out of it." She straightens and draws me deeper into the forest.

Where did Hank go? Troika? Myriad? Many Ends?

Bow turns a corner. She seems to have a destination in mind, and I'm glad. My thoughts grow hazier by the second, and my eyelids are heavy. Fatigue settles in my bones.

"Keep up," she commands. "We're a two-man team. Do your part."

Right. My part. But every step adds another pound to my feet until they are too heavy to move, and all I want to do is… "Nap," I say. At least, I think I say it. I can no longer feel my lips.

"No! No sleeping." She winds her arm around my shoulders to hold me up. I expect the heat of her body, even as little of it as there is, to warm me, but…no. There's only cold, cold and more cold. "Just a little bit farther."

My head lolls forward, my chin hitting my sternum. I manage another step, then another, counting as I go. One, two, three…all the way to one hundred and fourteen, before I begin to fall…fall…

"No!" she shouts. "Snap out of it, Ten. Stay awake."

Sorry, I try to say. There's an explosion of black inside my head, and it's lights-out for me.

★ ★ ★

The ground shakes, waking me with a jolt. I jerk upright and gasp out, "Four!"

The sound of my voice startles me. So does the number. Four?

The number of directions I can go. North, east, south and west.

Four elements. Earth, water, fire and wind.

And in my song: *Five times four times three, and that is where he'll be.*

A bead of sweat trickles down my temple. I'm sweating? Last thing I remember, I was morphing into a Popsicle. I wipe at my brow, the action setting off a domino effect, which ends with a terrible ache in my temples.

Grimacing, I scan my surroundings. I'm not sure what I expect to see. I only know *this* isn't it: a cave smaller than my cell at the institution. In front of me, a fire blazes, throwing golden rays of light over rocky walls that are splattered with...dried blood? Paint? Bow's backpack rests at my feet.

"Bow?" My voice echoes, but there's no return greeting.

She left, clearly, but she didn't take the backpack with her. Why? Where could she have gone? How much time has passed since I fainted?

The entire cave shakes again as I dig inside the pack. Another battle between the realms taking place nearby? "Essentials" consists of a digital notepad, a necklace with Troika's symbol, a tank top and pair of jean shorts, a pair of combat boots too big for my feet, six cans of buffalo wings probably taken from the staff lounge and a bottle of vodka.

Mostly useless!

But can I really get mad? Those cans… I'm so hungry, absolutely starved. I open and devour the contents of one. Only one, and only for strength. I resist the temptation to eat the other five. So freaking good! Bow needs nourishment, too. Dang it, where is she?

I switch on the pad, hoping to find a note or something to point me in the right direction. I'm not disappointed. In strong, bold calligraphy, I see:

Ten,

You naughty snoop. I knew you wouldn't be able to resist taking a peek. Good for you. Knowledge pays. Eat, write the world's most depressing poem, count rocks or whatever it is you like to do, but stay in the cave. If other inmates are out there, I'll find them and bring them "home." Don't worry. I've got Troika on my side!

Light Brings Sight!

Instead of signing her name, she's drawn a picture of a man holding a bow and arrow. An archer.

Her name is Bow, I once said to Killian.

Bow, he replied. *An archer uses a bow and arrow. How adorable.*

And then, when I lay on the floor of Vans's torture chamber, Killian and Bow had argued, and Killian had called her Archer.

I shake my head to dislodge the confusing memories. Can Bow find and save any of the other inmates without aid? Well, human aid. Maybe, but not likely. Not only must she face the elements and the guards, she must convince the kids to trust her.

So. Yeah. I have a poem for her.

I am alone.
Never will I believe
You care for me
The truth is
Having faith in you is foolish
I don't think
My well-being is your first priority
I know
We'll protect each other
Is just silly. I believe
Remaining on my own
Is the smartest course of action
Staying with you
Is the fastest way to Firstdeath
Walking—no, running—away from you
Won't be easy, but I'm willing to do it
And I know that
We're better off together
Is a lie. For I'm certain of this:
I am alone.

Two sides. The read down, and the read up. The negative and the positive. For once, I'm leaning toward positive. Bow needs me. There's always strength in numbers.

I use the scalpel to cut the tank top into multiple strips of cloth, then wrap the strips around my feet and exchange my regulation sandals for the boots. I return the scalpel to my pocket, then double-check to ensure it's there. As my only weapon, it's priceless.

Okay. All right. I push to wobbly legs, blood rushing out of my head, making me light-headed, even dizzy. I wobble as I make my way to the opening of the cave. Before she left, Bow set up a drape of leaves and twigs to seal me inside, and she did a very good job; I have to fight my way free.

Morning sunlight greets me, and oh, wow, it's gorgeous—but it means I slept the night away. A first since my incarceration.

Unfortunately, the air is so cold none of the ice has melted from the terrain, and my muscles instantly protest, knotting up. At least there aren't any guards around or booted footprints in the snow.

"Bow!" I shout. If I draw unwanted attention, I draw unwanted attention. The faster I find her, the better. "Bow!"

Eerie quiet taunts me, broken only by the occasional whistle of wind.

"Bow!" As I make my way forward, a storm erupts in my chest. The thunder of my heartbeat, followed by a downpour of acid, scalding everything in its path. What if something's happened to her? I'm certain the guards aren't our only worries. Any surviving inmates could have ambushed her, thinking to loot her belongings. Or worse. An animal could have mauled her.

A twig snaps. I stiffen. "Bow?" This time, her name is little more than a whisper.

A brute of a man steps from the foliage—along with two of his friends. They are Big, Bigger and Biggest, and they are covered in grime. I can overlook the grime. Each man has something I desperately want: a coat.

I hope they speak English. I hope they're friendly. But I don't count on either.

Still, I try to barter. "You hungry? I'm willing to trade a can of chicken for a coat." More than fair.

The one in the middle licks his lips—and I'd bet it's not at the thought of dining on chicken.

Self-preservation instincts scream, *Run!*

I'm about to do just that when a violent gust of wind nearly sweeps me off my feet. Worse—or better—Bigger's coat blows open, and I catch a glimpse of chopped pink hair. Bow! She's clutched against his beefy chest, unmoving, and my heart shudders with fear.

Judging by the leer the men throw my way, I can guess what they want from two lone girls, and it's not witty conversation. I know the odds of defeating them suck. Three brutes against one wily scrapper. At least six hundred pounds of muscle against one hundred and five pounds of me.

"Did you hurt her?" My words are gritted.

Biggest grins, revealing crooked, yellowed teeth. "We capture escapees for doctor." His accent is thick and Russian. "We take back to asylum…but not before we have fun."

Now Vans's hidden door makes a whole lot of sense.

"Come nicely, girl." Big. "We have fun with you, too."

"No harm." Bigger. "Unless you misbehave."

No harm, my ass. I free the scalpel from my pocket, hiding the glint of metal behind my arm. My teeth chatter, and the goose bumps return to my skin. "Counter offer. You drop the girl and walk away, and *I* won't harm *you*."

Bigger and Biggest guffaw as Big's eyes flare with glee. He likes a challenge. Noted.

Big moves toward me, and I realize I'm not the only one hiding a weapon. There's a wicked-looking dagger clutched in his hand, but I hold my ground…hold…

There's no other way to save Bow.

The closer he gets to me, the more his excitement *grows*. Literally.

He swings at me, aiming for my shoulder. If his punch lands, it won't be a deathblow, but it'll make me scream.

Now! I duck, avoiding impact, and slam my scalpel deep into his femoral artery. I may not remember everything from my human anatomy class, but I *do* remember the smallest nick to the femoral can be fatal.

He bellows in pain, blood spurting from his leg. As he crumples to his knees, I try to roll out of the way, but he manages to tangle his fingers through my hair and yank me to my back.

His friends step toward us. He holds up his free hand—the one with the dagger—stopping them. Then he gives me a cold smile…and strikes.

This time he's serious, and he's mad. His target? My heart.

I suddenly see the merits of Troika's way of thinking: being led by emotions can do more harm than good.

I raise my arm to block the blow, and the blade slices through my wrist, coming out the other side. Pain consumes me in a brutal flash, stars glittering behind my eyes, dizziness overwhelming my mind. I fight to remain conscious. If I pass out, I die.

The color in Big's cheeks is draining fast. He teeters back and forth, close to passing out, too. But first, he wraps his fingers around my neck and squeezes. *No!* I swing the scalpel at his throat, but he bats my arm away, nearly dislodging my already bruised shoulder.

Come on! As I buck and flail against his hold, he only tightens his grip. The stars behind my eyes are replaced by spiderwebs of black. This can't be it. This can't be the end. Here one second, poof, gone the next. I didn't survive Vans's torture just to be strangled on a mountain.

"You want my help, lass?"

I recognize that gravel-and-smoke voice, that seductive Irish accent. Killian is here! In an instant, joy consumes my fear.

"Lass?"

I can't speak, can only nod.

It's enough. He says, "You'll want ta let her go, lad. Consider this your one and only opportunity to walk away. After this, you won't even be crawling."

I can make out his silhouette. He's tall, but he's not as tall as the brutes. With three against one, he could get seriously hurt. Or worse! I don't want him hurt.

"You leave before too late, boy," says one of the brutes.

"Wrong answer."

Suddenly I'm free, Big ripped away from me. Gasping for breath, I scramble to my feet, ready to fend off Big before he's able to pin me again, but I find him on the ground, his eyes closed, a pool of blood forming around him.

Killian is focused on the remaining brutes. Whatever he did to Big scares the other two greatly.

Bigger drops Bow to the ground. "She yours. Take, take."

A small gasp leaves the girl. She blinks open her eyes as she struggles to sit up. One second…two…she proves unsuccessful, as if her body has turned to stone.

"Malfunction," she manages to grit out.

Bigger and Biggest hold up their hands, palms out, and take a step back.

I race forward, but Killian beats me to Bow's side. He raises his arm, his own dagger glinting in the sunlight, and angrily meets my gaze. "These men are Unsigned, which makes them your brethren. Is this really what you want for your life? Do you wish to spend eternity with them?" I expect him to throw the weapon at the brutes—but he says, "Show her who you really are, Archer," before slamming the blade deep, deep into Bow's chest.

TROIKA

From: A_P_5/23.43.2

To: L_N_3/19.1.1

Subject: Ten, Ten, Ten

Bow is toast. The inferior Shell malfunctioned, allowing the Unsigned to overpower me, and Killian to stab me.

Speaking of the worst spirit in the Everlife, Killian has the girl all to himself right now—and that's the good news. She's intrigued with him, just like—never mind. I can see it in her eyes, and I know any attempt to keep the two apart will only make the intrigue stronger. How would you like me to proceed? What have I been cleared to do?

Archer Prince

TROIKA

From: L_N_3/19.1.1

To: A_P_5/23.43.2

Subject: Your Capacity to Forgive Is Humbling

You need to let go of your anger with Mr. Flynn. Miss Lockwood was right. It wounds *you*. And if you aren't careful, one day it will wound innocents.

I'll send you another Shell. As generous as I am, I'll even send one from your personal collection.

And yes, you're right. Finally! Attempting to keep Miss Lockwood away from Mr. Flynn will do more harm than good, but try to remember that Mr. Flynn is his own worst enemy. He'll destroy her intrigue all on his own. After all, pushy people get pushed, and Mr. Flynn's actions will speak for him. Let yours speak for you.

Her grandmother has spoken with the Generals and, because Ten has admitted she needs help, you have permission to help her through any means necessary—

unless, of course, the girl dismisses you. Unfortunately, we still can't stay where we aren't welcome.

Also, watch your six...or rather, your ten.

General Levi Nanne

TROIKA

From: A_P_5/23.43.2

To: L_N_3/19.1.1

Subject: Does Every Moment Have to Be a Teaching Moment?

It's annoying.

Anyway. I'm getting through to Ten, I know I am. And yet she's still drowning in a sea of doubts, unwilling to trust her own instincts. If she won't grab hold of the life raft I've thrown at her, we ARE going to lose her.

I've grown to like her. I don't want to lose her.

TROIKA

From: L_N_3/19.1.1

To: A_P_5/23.43.2

Subject: Prepare for Another Teaching Moment

I remember the day Miss Lockwood was born and the uproar it caused in the realms. She absorbed and released so much Light our monitors were blinded. You remember the day, too; you simply weren't told why such a bright light cut through our realm. Myriadians claim she glowed so brightly because she was Fused with one of their Generals. Though they also claim to love the darkness, they want our light. They always have.

And I know, I know. Miss Lockwood isn't exactly glowing right now. Darkness shrouds her. But we don't give up, Mr. Prince. Ever. And while we have permission from the Generals to do what needs doing, Miss Lockwood's will comes first. What she accepts from you, give. What she rejects, try again another way. If she won't grab hold of your life raft, throw her a rope. If she won't grab hold of your rope, throw her a branch.

TROIKA

From: A_P_5/23.43.2

To: L_N_3/19.1.1

Subject: I Really Hope…

I'm not this irritating to Ten.

chapter eight

"Fear is the enemy at your back with a knife to your throat."
—Troika

I'm numb with shock as much as cold. Killian—the boy who saved me from Vans and potential rapists—just stabbed Bow in the heart.

Killian just stabbed Bow in the heart!

Rage peeks through my numbness. Sorrow bulldozes through it.

One blow. One life—now gone?

After everyone Killian killed at the asylum, I should have seen this coming.

He spits on Bow before turning to the giants.

As I dive on top of the girl, hoping to protect her from further harm—*can't be too late, just can't be*—hoping there's some way I can save her—*too late, already too late*—the mountain men realize Killian has just relinquished his only weapon.

"Stupid boy." They all smile their hungry smiles, no longer afraid of repercussions.

"Come, try to take me down," Killian says with a smile of his own. "Welcome your Firstdeath with open arms."

They attack with a brutal clash of fists. A mistake. A *pop, pop, pop* sounds as Killian breaks their bones. He laughs as he punches, parries, then punches again and again, going for the nose, the throat and, as the men howl in pain, the kidneys and bowels. He reminds me of a bear playing with its food.

When Bigger abandons the fray to concentrate on me—planning to scoop me up and run?—Killian stops laughing, stops playing and delivers a lethal blow. A kick so powerful one side of the man's head caves in and his eyeball pops out.

Horror claws at me, and fear eats the remains.

I shake so forcefully I probably look like I'm having a seizure. Killian has revealed his true nature. He's a black-hearted snake, and he's going to win this battle…he's going to turn his attention to me. What will happen then?

I shouldn't wait around to find out, but I can't bring myself to leave Bow, even though she's gone.

With a war cry, Biggest dives on Killian. The two hit the ground and roll toward me. I scramble back to avoid a foot to the face, watching as the mountain man loses all control, fueled by rage and adrenaline as he pounds his fists into Killian like a jackhammer set on high. Bile burns my throat.

Killian shows no signs of tapping out. Or even pain! He doesn't try to protect his face from the next blow…or the next and the next…as he grips the man by the neck. I feel like I take the blows for him, my entire body jerking. He flings Biggest deeper into the trees, ensuring I'm no longer within the man's reach, and my heart flutters with equal measures of relief and panic.

A kind gesture from a murderer.

I quiver as I smooth pale locks of hair from Bow's brow. What the…? Confusion slaps me, overshadowing everything else. I've seen death, and this isn't it. Her eyes are open, but she has no irises, no pupils, doesn't even have whites. The sockets are just *empty.*

My heart stops fluttering and starts galloping as I brush my fingertips over one socket, then the other. They aren't actually empty, I realize, but covered by a film as clear and smooth as glass. I bend down to peer past the film. Inside her head I see no blood, tissue or brain.

I don't understand.

I look her over more carefully. At the moment of death, *everyone's* bladder and bowels release. It's just a fact of life. A final humiliation, I guess. Death's ultimate F-you. But her jumpsuit isn't wet or stained between her legs.

Is she *alive*?

Hope flares, even though I know the thought is impossible. Those sockets…

I turn my attention to the blade protruding from her chest. There's no motion to indicate she's breathing. An-n-nd, not a speck of blood discolors her jumpsuit around the blade. There's a wet spot, but it's covered by…diamond dust?

What is going on?

My mind is spinning but getting nowhere fast as I yank the collar, ripping the top to her navel. The blade is buried hilt-deep in her heart, but there's still not a drop of blood. There *is* more liquid diamond dust.

I don't know what to think…or what to do. I'm too

fogged by pain, fatigue and uncertainty to make sense of anything.

A grunt captures my attention. A snap. Another pained howl.

I focus on the battle still raging and swallow a whimper. The boys are back in the clearing, and Biggest is doing his gold-star best to land a blow *anywhere* on Killian's body. But Killian is too fast—it's like comparing a horse-pulled wagon to a race car—ducking and punching with mesmerizing rhythm. His skill is masterful, and the part of my brain enamored with numbers sits up and takes notice, even sighs dreamily.

Punch, punch, duck. Punch, punch, kick. Punch, punch—wow! He uses every part of his body to inflict maximum damage. He is a lethal weapon.

I flinch as he executes a perfect head-butt. As his opponent reels, he dives into the guy, his teeth ripping into a tender throat…and he's beautiful, so terribly beautiful while he does it. While Biggest howls, he breaks the guy's beefy arm and, with a well-placed elbow jab, breaks the man's already-broken nose.

Biggest drops, but he's not yet out for the count. He snarls and crawls toward Killian. "Will…kill…"

My mouth goes dry—*up, get up, do something!*—but Killian laughs his gut-chilling laugh devoid of humor. "You won't. If you want me to end you quick, you'll give me your coat before I have to bloody it further. Otherwise your pain will only get worse."

As he speaks, the ground shakes. His gaze slides to me. To ensure I'm okay or that I'm watching? Is he showing off or does he fear I'll run?

Run…yeah, I should probably run. He's proved to be homicidal, untrustworthy and just plain crazy.

Pure evil. Bow tried to warn me.

If I stay, we're going to fight. Definitely verbally, maybe physically. And the bottom line? I'll lose against him. *Gotta slay a lion before you can slay a dragon.* He's far more experienced at combat. My knowledge is limited to cafeteria brawls and guards who won't take no for an answer.

At the moment, however, none of that matters. I stay put, despite the danger. I have questions—a whooole lot of questions—and he might have answers.

As a precaution, I use what little strength I have left to wrench the blade from Bow's chest. A blade bearing zero drops of crimson. I'm flabbergasted all over again. Her wound gaps open, but there's no muscle or bone underneath her savaged skin but…pulsating electrodes?

Confusion bombards me, my mind spinning all over again. I don't… How… Why?

"Just want girl." Biggest takes a swing at Killian and curses in Russian when he misses.

"Aye, I know that." Killian lands a punch to the guy's jaw, causing him to whirl while spitting blood and teeth. "Problem is, I've never liked to share my toys."

So I'm a toy now?

Forget confusion. Hello, rage. I'll cut first and ask my questions later.

Biggest lumbers to his feet, preparing to launch another strike, but I've had enough. Playtime is over. I'm still weak, and I'm still trembling, but my goal is simple. Get in and out without either guy noticing—until it's too late.

I race into the fray. Or rather, I try to race into the fray.

The frigid cold has turned my blood into sludge, slowing my movements, and it doesn't help that the injuries Vans inflicted on me are swollen, my skin stretched taut over every wound.

Biggest notices my approach and pivots toward me. So much for stealth. As I raise the blade, intending to go for his already injured throat—far too late to turn back now—he swipes out his arm to backhand me. I duck, but I'm not fast enough and end up taking the blow at the side of my head.

Pain explodes inside my skull as I fall. Thankfully a surge of adrenaline floods my veins when I collide with the ground. Determined, I roll toward him, reaching up to stab him. The blade sinks into his side, blood spurting. He yowls and reaches for me.

Killian kicks his arm out of the way and jabs a dagger deep into his eye socket. Biggest's next howl makes a mockery of his first. Then he goes quiet.

I collapse on the ground, gasping for breath. It's over. The battle is over.

One of them, at least.

A shadow falls over me. I stiffen, my gaze roving up, up to Killian's blood-spattered face. Blood-splattered, even though I see no real injuries on him. Even stranger, he's far more beautiful than before, because his smooth veneer has been stripped away. His charm and seduction are replaced by savage determination.

For some reason, the fear leaves me. Whatever happens, happens. I'll deal. I've dealt with worse.

His hands fist at his sides. "I had everything under control, lass."

"Yeah, well, you were taking too long."

“Complaints? I saved your life.”

“*Why* did you save it? To kill me yourself—the way you killed Bow?”

“Bow overstayed her welcome.” He kicks the girl in the stomach and grins with satisfaction. “You, I’m not going to hurt. Why would I? I now own your soul. Isn’t that the save-a-life rule?”

And now the charmer is back. “You’re with Myriad. You’re anti-rules.”

“For you, I’ll make an exception.”

“How sweet. But, no. *Hard* pass.”

“You might want to reconsider. There are cuts and bruises all over your face, and there’s a lump on your jaw. You, Tenley Lockwood, are currently hideous. You’ll scare all other potential rescuers away.”

“A risk I’m willing to take.”

“Too bad.” He extends a hand to help me up—the very hand that slammed a blade into Bow’s chest. I crab walk backward, but he sighs and follows me. “I’m going to help you, lass, and that’s that.”

Zero! With every inch I gain, my bleeding wrist screams anew. Finally I stop. I have no other option, my body refusing to cooperate. Moving did me no good, anyway. “I’m a mess. How are you so…fine?”

He chuckles. “I’m fine, am I?”

Not going to respond to that. “You have no cuts, bruises or lumps.” His short dark hair is slightly rumpled. The flecks of blue in those eyes of molten gold are glowing with different degrees of menace despite his amusement. “Just thirteen streaks of blood.”

In the ancient past, thirteen steps led to the gallows. A

hangman's noose has thirteen knots. At thirteen, children are considered teenagers.

No wonder the number thirteen is hated worldwide. If there were thirteen months in a year, the thirteenth would probably be called Helluary.

"Counted, did you?" Killian crouches in front of me, his determination only growing. "I've noticed your affinity for numbers. A little obsessive, a lot cute."

"I've noticed your affinity for cold-blooded murder." He's not going to distract me or win me over. Answers followed by escape. That's my plan and I'm sticking to it.

He isn't the least bit abashed. "Hardly. The mountaineers were self-defense, so they don't count. Archer—Bow—is still alive."

The lack of blood…the sparkling liquid…those clear eye sockets…the electrodes under her skin…

"Impossible," I say, but there's a tremor in my voice.

"Trust me. You'll see him again."

"Him? Are you trying to tell me Bow is—was—a guy named Archer?"

"I'm not trying to tell you anything, lass. I'm simply stating facts."

However improvable, I think… I think there's truth to what he's saying. Bow isn't Bow…and maybe Bow isn't dead. "How will I see her—him—again? In the Unending? And why did you stab him?"

Show her who you really are…

"A thousand different reasons." He shrugs. "At the top of the list—I knew it'd feel good."

Irritation is like a bull with horns, ram, ram, ramming

my calm facade. "Victors are adored and failures are abhorred, right?"

He ignores my dry tone and nods. "Exactly."

"Meanwhile, you have no idea how wrong you are. Victors can be hated."

The bull with horns begins to ram *him*, I think. He snaps, "Your precious Bow is my enemy."

"No. She's—"

"A Troikan Laborer."

The statement echoes between us. "Im-impossible." Right? "I touched her, and she never protested. Never accused me of committing a crime."

"Think, lass. Why would the law exist if not to hide those who wish to pass as a human? When undercover, a Shell is allowed to touch whomever he or she desires. Have to blend in, don't you know."

The coolness of Bow's skin…just like the coolness of James's skin…and the coolness of Killian's.

I lick my lips. "Are you a Myriad Laborer?" No, no. He can't be. He's not a Shell.

Shells can't have sex with humans. Can they? And yet, he's bragged about his conquests.

He eyes me intently as he says, "What do you think?"

"Are you?" I insist, bordering on desperation now.

"What. Do. You. Think?"

"Just tell me!"

He stretches out his hand. "Just touch me. Then *you* tell *me*."

I give a violent shake my head. Touch him? No way, no how. Not ever again.

He smiles without humor. "I like you, lass. I shouldn't,

but there's something about you. You're smart, and you make me think. Now use your brain and figure this out, because we both know you're not going to believe anything I tell you."

My hand flies to my heart and rubs. What did I know beyond any doubt? "You love Myriad. You were able to give me a virtual tour unlike any other. Dr. Vans paid you to target me, but you killed him."

"Oh, yes, I most certainly did kill him," he says. "With relish. But he wasn't paying me. He had nothing I prized.

Easy to say, hard to prove. "How do you know his mindset if you weren't working for him?"

"I wired the entire building and listened to his every conversation. As soon as I tapped into your final torture session, I began looking for you. He thought it was okay to hurt you, to use my actions against you. I taught him the error of his ways."

A violent gust of wind blows between us, so strong it sends me skidding into the base of a tree. Air bursts from my lungs, my bruises screaming in protest.

My gaze looks past Killian. I have no idea what to say to him.

Is he or isn't he?

I lumber to my feet. My teeth chatter as I trip around him and crouch beside Big. He's the smallest of the three and, even better, his clothing has sustained the least amount of damage, despite Killian's best efforts. There are only a few drops of blood on his coat. I remove it with quivering fingers. My wounds protest as I shove my arms through the holes and pull the hood over my head.

"Stealing clothes from a corpse?" Killian sounds impressed. "That's pretty hard-core, yeah?"

"You planned to do it."

"Yes, but I'm actually hard-core." His accent has changed. No, not changed, not really, but the more intently I listen, the more I detect accents from different parts of the world.

Branches snap, though neither of us moved. Is someone out there? One of the kids from the institution? One of the guards? Another mountain man? I shudder, sway. And zero! Dizziness is knocking on the door of my mind.

I do my best to focus as a large shadow slips over the leaves, moving slowly, a mere inch at a time. Gnarled fingers of dread creep down my spine. I'm not sure how much fight I have left.

"Killian," I whisper. "Someone's coming."

His scowl is dark, a promise of violence. "I know. Tell him to stay away from us."

Him? "Who's out there?" An inmate?

"Tell him he's not wanted here."

A guard? "Words won't do any good. We have to—"

"In this case, words are all you need."

All *I* need. Not him? Though I don't understand, I lift the knife he used on Bow. "We're armed. Don't come any closer."

"You can do better than that, lass. Tell him you want nothing to do with him."

Why? Something about this situation is *wrong*, I feel it in my frozen bones, so I say nothing else.

"Very well. I'll work with what I've got." Killian clasps my wrist and drags me away. "Let's get you to a safe place."

The shadow follows us, but maintains the same distance, as if he won't—or can't—come any closer.

Along the way, Killian sends my blade flying with a single bat of his arm. "You won't be needin' this."

My shoulder vibrates with pain, and I whimper as I wrench away from him.

The noise makes him flinch. "I'm sorry," he grumbles. "I didn't mean to hurt you."

I offer no reply. I still have the scalpel, but I don't use it as he turns, picks me up and cradles me against his chest, his arms strong, intractable bands around me. I even sag against him, surprisingly docile. I'm tapped out. Got nothing left. I'll fight tomorrow.

He heads toward…my cave, I realize. He knows where I spent the night?

The fire is low but still crackling. He sets me down and stokes the flames with logs hidden in the shadows. When the flames are high enough, heat wafting through the air, he wrestles me out of the coat.

"What are you doing? Hey! Give that back! It's mine. I stole it fair and square."

"I'm going to tend to your wounds. You couldn't pay me enough to wear the coat. I have standards."

Then why was he trying not to bloody it during the fight? For me?

The idea throws me for a loop.

He adds, "I suggest you dig deep and find your own." The derision in his tone…

As if we're playing a game. Enough of his games! They keep me off balance and—

They keep me off balance. Well, no wonder he plays them.

I go still. If he *is* an ML, he won't hurt me. He'll do as he claimed and tend my wounds. Because I'm the one with power in our relationship. I'm the one with something he wants: the key to my future.

He settles in front of me and claims my wrist in a grip as intractable as his hold. Like Bow, like every time before, no heat radiates from him.

"Are you afraid of me?" he asks, and there's now an edge to his tone.

Does he actually care about the answer? "I was. Now I'm not exactly sure."

"Do you think I'll take advantage of you?"

"Maybe. I don't know you. Not really. Wait. Scratch that. I know you're a murderer."

"Still harping on a few measly kills?" His expression is gentle as he meets my gaze. "I will *never* hurt you. Not again. All right?"

I nibble on my bottom lip. "Are you a Myriad Laborer?" I ask again.

"If I were, do you think the powers that be would allow me to admit it before you figured it out?"

Maybe. Maybe not. "If you are, you should know I can't be charmed or frightened into making my choice. My allegiance has to be earned."

"Are you *certain* you can't be charmed?" He brings my hand to his mouth and kisses my knuckles, making me shiver. "Or is it my charm that frightens you?"

"No?" Ugh. Just ugh. A question? Really?

He's smiling as he releases me and pulls a thin black cloth from his back pocket. When he unwinds the material, I see syringes, a spool of thread glowing as brightly as fetters, packaged cleaning wipes, thin tubes of ointment and bandages.

I remember the vodka in the backpack and though I would love to drink my way to oblivion, I decide not to indulge. Too vividly I remember my wine-buzzed attempt to caress this guy's eyelashes.

Besides, the warmth of the fire is helping to clear my thoughts, and the answers I don't want to face are beginning to crystallize, battering against what remains of the disbelief. I may not want to accept the truth, but I must.

Bow without eyes…without blood…the electrodes…the name Archer…my doubts shed one by one until I'm left with the only bare-naked truth.

She—he—*is* a TL. He came to Prynne to recruit me. He befriended me, spied on me and tried to manipulate me.

I was just too dumb to see it.

And then there was James, whose body was as cool as Bow's and Killian's. Was he—is he—an ML? Did he purposely mislead me?

The long con…

An arrow of uncertainty leaves me bleeding. I genuinely loved him, but that doesn't mean he genuinely loved me.

The uncertainty expands, creating a fresh wound in my heart. He told me stories about his childhood, how he played hide-and-seek with his teddy bears, pretending they were brothers and sisters, and I'd related. I petted his chest while he admitted being a guard at Prynne was merely a stepping-stone to becoming a detective.

I sobbed for him after he was shot. I lay awake night after night, tossing and turning, blaming myself for what happened to him. I'd wanted so badly to escape, to start a life with him. A real life.

I still mourn him.

Killian cups my cheeks and forces me to face him. He's frowning. "What's caused this upset?"

I tell him the truth. Why not? "James."

A muscle ticks under his eye, as if he's angry. "The boyfriend."

"Yes." And oh, zero. My eyes are burning, my chest constricting and my temples throbbing. My entire world has been turned upside down and inside out, and my mind is about to break. I hurry to change the subject before I break down. "Were there any other kids out there?"

"A handful." He offers no more as he lifts the tools he needs from the cloth.

"How many were alive?"

"Less than a handful. Others were captured by mountaineers." He smooths a clear gel over my wound.

A sudden tide of nausea nearly doubles me over. I breathe past the pain, saying, "What will happen to them?"

"I don't know. They aren't my problem."

"Well, I'm not your problem, either." A plan takes shape. Save the inmates captured by the mountaineers, deal with my injuries later. Time is of the essence.

But isn't it always?

When I try to stand, Killian holds me down.

"You're not going anywhere. You *are* my problem." His gaze meets mine and stays locked, the air between us thickening. "You know why. Say it."

"I...do know why." Finally I vocalize the admission. "You... You're my ML."

A cascade of relief accompanies the words. *And the truth shall set you free.*

"I am." He reflects the relief back at me. "There are many different kinds of Laborers. My subdivision isn't to confess our origins unless and until the human figures it out, enabling us to move in and out of lives at will, making our mission less complicated."

My cheeks heat as I ask, "Do you really have sex with your humans?"

He gives me a half smile. "Shells feel. I've experienced every human sensation but bleeding. I've only ever hemorrhaged."

"Hemorrhaging isn't bleeding?"

"Not for spirits." He brushes his thumb over the pulse in my wrist. A pulse that only beats faster. "Let me show you more of my realm. I'll answer any other questions you have, and you'll see how perfectly you fit. You'll understand how important you are to our cause."

"I can guess how important you think I am." Do I sound as bitter to him as I sound to myself? "Troika considers me a Conduit, which means Myriad considers me an Abrogate."

"I didn't see it at first. Thought you were just another army drone. But you're so much more, lass, and we need you. You'll command a legion of Leaders and Laborers, plan strategic attacks and lead your personal army into battle."

"So, an *easy* job."

His next smile is megawatt.

"Maybe my first act as Abrogate will be ensuring you're publicly flogged."

He shrugs. "Wouldn't be the first time."

The throwaway admission actually...*saddens* me.

"If Troika wins you, their light will intensify and encroach into our realm. It's happened before. Only once, but we lost millions. Our spirits cannot survive in light, just as theirs cannot survive in darkness."

The fate of the war depends on my decision? No, absolutely not. The pressure…it's too much. "I've seen you in the light, and Archer in the darkness."

"No. You've seen my *Shell* in the light and his Shell in the darkness."

Pressure…growing… "I'm not interested in another tour or answers." Not right now. I'm in the middle of a tug-of-war, the rope wrapped around my neck, and every answer he gives me removes a little more slack. "There's too much to do. As soon as you've patched me, I'm going after the other inmates."

"We'll see about that." Killian cleans the gel he'd applied with a moist towelette, and it stings, but only at first. There must be some type of numbing agent soaked into the cloth.

He selects a syringe, and when his finger makes contact with the belly, the liquid inside begins to bubble. Bubbling liquid he injects deep into the wound. All hint of numbness wears off, foam rising from the center and spilling over the sides. I hiss.

"Would it break your heart to discover Saint James is a Laborer?" he asks as he works. "That he was sent to convince you to sign with Myriad?"

Mind…threatening to break down again… "He loved—loves—me."

"Are you sure? You would stake your life on that fact?"

"Yes," I start to say, only to hesitate. Zero! I can't overlook evidence just because I don't like it.

"Did he?" I ask softly. "Does he?"

"You tell me."

Not this crap again. I need the truth, even if it does shatter me. At least I'll be able to put myself back together. "I admit he's a Laborer, okay. Now *you* tell *me*. Was I simply a mission to him?"

He gazes at me with heat growing in his eyes, and it's like a fever suddenly overtakes *me*. "Remember, the truth hurts for a little while. Lies hurt forever." His voice is as soft as mine. "Yes, you were merely a mission to him. I'm sorry."

I…believe him. I believe him because he has no reason to lie and every reason to hide such a damaging truth.

James used me. Tricked me. Those stolen moments of comfort, so precious to me, were as much a tool of manipulation as Vans's torture. But the worst part? Vans, a vile mercenary, was honest about his intentions, while James, who professed to love me, only ever deceived me.

How he must have laughed at me, the blind, desperate fool.

"I'm sorry," Killian repeats. "James uses a script. A method of deception for getting what he wants."

A long con.

My dream of happily-ever-after with him, one I hadn't known lingered in my heart despite his supposed demise, dies a thousand violent deaths.

For once, a death really is the end.

Keep it together. "You also have a script," I say without any inflection of emotion.

"I never lied to my assignments. And I *had* a script. Show you a part of Myriad I knew you'd love, impress you with stories of my strength. My script worked as well as his." Killian weaves the spool of glowing thread through my skin—threads that are as hot as fetters, cauterizing the wound after drawing my flesh together. "Now I'm doing something new. I'm winging it."

Sweat beads over my brow, and another hiss escapes me. "That's not going to work for you, either."

"We'll see about that, as well." He flicks me a small smile that hints at a wealth of secrets. The past he'd only begun to share. "Your threshold for pain surprises me. I thought you'd scream."

"Why would I scream? Physical pain will never compare to mental anguish."

The amusement drains. "I'm sorry," he says again. "You should only ever be pampered."

Is he *flirting* with me? Here, now? Or is he simply *winging it*?

"Just stop, okay? Unlike your other targets, I realize the fickleness of human attraction." I may be led by many of my emotions, but not lust. Never lust. "The body doesn't always crave what's good for it. That's why attraction will never be enough for me. That's why there has to be more. Love. Devotion. Determination. Things *you* can't offer me."

"How do you know what I can offer? And you only *think* you can overcome lust. If you'd ever experienced true physical pleasure, you'd realize how ridiculous you sound."

My temper—a wild thing—blasts free of its cage. "Dreg! You have no idea what I've experienced. You'll *never* know." I huff and puff in an effort to calm. "Lust will never be more important than commitment. Commitment stacks the odds of a successful relationship in my favor."

Still he scoffs. "You think relationships can survive centuries? There are many tasty treats out there…many beauties to be sampled."

"Beauty fades." Beauty, Bow once said, was simply an outer shell. Heart and respect—those last forever. "Character lasts forever."

One of his brows wings up. "Are you politely telling me you like my outside but not my inside?"

"I was polite? Well, score one for me. Unintentional counts for something, right?"

He chuckles softly as he finishes the stitches. Gently he wraps my wrist in a bandage. "There. All done."

I hate to say it, but gratitude is owed. "Thank you."

"Oh, lass. Don't thank me yet." He smiles again, this one all about seduction. "Once you're healed, I'm coming after you with everything I've got."

A warning. A challenge. My heart performs a series of flips inside my chest. "You forget," I say. "I've seen you in action. You're no match for me."

His smile only widens. "Is that so?"

"That's so. Prepare to experience your first defeat, Killian."

chapter nine

"The end will always justify the means."
—Myriad

I pull my injured wrist to my chest, ending all contact with the guy who's proved to be a cornucopia of contradictions. Kind yet cruel. Amiable yet acerbic. Concerned yet uncaring. For someone living in a realm where emotions are practically gold, he doesn't seem to know how to manage his. And maybe that's the point: releasing his emotions purges them.

But purging always leaves you empty.

Empty, you can be filled.

I expel a breath. Will I ever stop this tug of war?

Killian studies me, his expression unreadable as he says, "What makes you think losing you would be my first defeat?"

He might have been able to mask his expression, but he can't disguise the threads of bitterness in his voice, and I'm intrigued. "What—or who—did you lose before me?"

One second slips into another, tension sparking between

us. Tension…and an undeniable awareness. It's as if I'm seeing into his soul and, despite what I said earlier, there's beauty inside him. He's a boy with hurts as strong as my own and dreams just as vivid.

"Right now," he finally says, "I'm beginning to lose my patience. You know Myriad is perfect for you, and yet you resist making covenant. You know you fit with us. Know you'll be happiest with us."

Moonlight…sunlight.

Vengeance…forgiveness.

Fused…solo.

He's wrong. How can I *ever* know?

I stand, swaying when my knees shake. "I'm finding the other inmates and—"

"No, lass, you're going to sleep." A certain command. "The medicine will—"

"Do me a favor and don't be here when I return," I interject. As I step forward, a wave of black sweeps over me. I fall. What the—

"—activate any second," he finishes as his strong arms catch me. He eases me to the ground, and I know nothing more.

Gasping, I open my eyes and jerk upright. A collage of memories rush in at once. My escape. The fight with the giants. My rescuer, who is seated across from me, the fire crackling between us, tendrils of smoke curling to the roof of the cave. The walls are shaking, but soon stop. Another realm battle?

Killian doesn't seem to notice. He's comfortable in the darkness, a phantom within familiar depths.

A blue light emanates from his wrist, but with a single tap of his fingers, the light dies.

"You…that…" I stammer.

He dismisses my bafflement with a wave of his hand. "Sleeping beauty awakes at last."

Irritation blooms. "Earlier you called me hideous. Basically a she-beast."

"Earlier you *were* hideous. An *absolute* she-beast. Now the medicine has kicked in."

The medicine… "How long was I out?" I ask with bite.

"Roughly six hours."

There are six points on the Star of David. Six, the atomic number for carbon. A six-pack of beer—what I could use right now.

"Here's a better question," he says. "Do you feel as good as you look?"

I…do feel good, I realize. The wound on my wrist is nothing more than a long, thin scab, the stitches absent. Dissolved? The knots in my muscles have loosened, and when I gingerly pat my jaw, I note the swelling is down.

"I'm not going to say thank-you," I mutter. He helped me for *his* gain, not mine. "Not again."

"You prefer to thank me with action instead? Well, I accept."

I give him a double-birded salute. How's *that* for action?

He laughs outright, the sound of it rusty. "I've never understood the insult of showing off your middle finger. I'm number one in your book—what's to hate about that?" As he speaks, he reaches over, slides the scalpel from my pocket and turns, flinging the metal across the cave.

I gasp with surprise and confusion. Then I see the scalpel embedded in the throat of an intruder. A pained grunt echoes as the masked man falls to his face.

Killian jumps to his feet. "Stay here, lass. I want you protected at all times. Knowing you, however, you'll decide to run. If so, all you have to do is stay alive. I'll find you."

My heart knocks against my ribs as he flies through the exit.

I rush to the injured man's side to rip off his mask, and a chill skims over me. He's a guard from Prynne. He worked there four months, six days and eight hours, during which I endured sixteen eyebrow wiggles, twenty-seven lewd grins and three invitations to the party in his pants. If I "sucked him off," he said, he'd give me a candy bar.

A candy bar. As if that's all I'm worth.

The memory still boils my blood.

He peers at me, frantic, a rush of crimson gurgling from the corners of his mouth.

You don't know his heart. He's capable of change—we all are. Give him a second chance, Archer would probably say.

Remove his junk and stuff it in his mouth, Killian would definitely say. *He can eat his own candy bar.*

"I'll help you. For chocolate." My anger is speaking for me, more powerful than my capacity to forgive. "Don't have any on you? Aw, too bad." By the time I've relieved him of his winter gear—mask, goggles, insulated coat, heated gloves and socks…everything but the blood-soaked scarf—he's dead.

I don't feel guilty. I don't!

Except dang it, I do. He never showed me a bit of compassion…and I acted just like him.

I dress as quickly as possible before stuffing the giant's

coat in the backpack, hoping to share my bounty with other inmates. Screw Killian's order to stay here. Kids just like me are being hunted. I'm doing what I originally planned and finding as many inmates as I can. We'll make our way… somewhere else. Somewhere far away from the asylum. Far away from our parents. Far away from Laborers who use without thought.

I yank the scalpel from the guard's throat and clean the metal with the dry end of his scarf—a scarf I throw into the fire after returning the scalpel to my pocket. A weapon has never been more important.

I anchor the backpack over my shoulders, mentally polish the nuts I'm so infamous for, and step out of the cave. Night has arrived with a vengeance, the moon shielded by the tall canopy of snowcapped trees. My surroundings are nothing but doom and gloom…until the goggles switch on automatically and illuminate the world around me. A computerized scanning system even pinpoints Killian's footprints. Great for me, but bad for the kids the guards are chasing. I head in the opposite direction, and lo and behold, the rest of the gear works wonders, keeping me warm and toasty.

The problem? The farther I get, the more a sea of dark thoughts bombards me, soon so loud I'm surprised I'm not surrounded by a crowd of people. Or…maybe I *am* surrounded. By people I can't see. Messengers. Without Shells, they are spirits and therefore invisible to me.

I've heard Messengers are sometimes posted around homes and buildings to stop members of a rival realm from gaining entry.

Guess they can also be used to keep flight risks inside caves.

Go back, go back, one says. *It's not safe out here. You'll die. You're going to die, die, die. Turn around, before it's too late. Go back! Your time is running out!*

The words elicit fear, and as I'm learning, fear is Myriad's greatest weapon. My heart sprints toward a nonexistent finish line. Fire burns the center of my chest while ice freezes the blood in my veins. I begin to pant, sweat beading on the back of my neck.

Almost too late…go back!

The ground shakes, and the whispers suddenly stop. I breathe a sigh of relief and continue forward. I'm not going to die, and I'm not going to pander to fear, giving it power over me—power to direct my actions.

What I do will be my choice, not the choice of my emotions.

One point in Troika's favor.

And while the odds aren't currently in *my* favor, I'm not helpless. I have my wits.

Trekking down the mountain, I count my steps. One, five, ten…twenty…fifty…one hundred. One hundred percent, the full amount. One hundred degrees Celsius, the boiling temperature of pure water at sea level. The sum of the first ten odd numbers. (1 + 3 + 5 + 7 + 9 + 11 + 13 + 15 + 17 + 19 = 100)

Any lingering fear finally drains, my physical reactions returning to normal. *Good, that's good.* I pick up the pace, going another two hundred steps. Two hundred—bicentennial. The Latin word for this number, *ducenti,* also means "to the leading man." Numerologists claim this particular number signifies insufficiency.

The ground shakes again, harder than before, throwing

me off balance. I topple to my butt, pain vibrating through me. Dang it! How many battles are the realms going to fight today?

I shamble to my feet and resume my counting. Two hundred and fifty…two hundred and seventy-five…three hundred—a triangular number and the sum of a pair of twin primes: 149 + 151. A perfect score in bowling. The number of Spartans famous for fighting an army of two hundred thousand Persians.

At step three hundred and eighty-one, I wind through a tangle of trees. The ground is slippery, but my boots have a thick rubber frame with metal studs on the soles, helping me remain steady.

At step four hundred and six, a high-pitched ring blasts through my head, making me cringe. I stop and rub at the cloth covering my ears. The ring fades, and I hear—

"—another one, sir." An unfamiliar voice. "He's already dead."

Gasping, I spin to see who's come up behind me, but I'm alone. There's not even movement to indicate someone is hiding in the trees.

"Take him back to the facility," another voice commands. "His parents will need to be notified."

Realization dawns. The voices are spilling from speakers attached to the sides of the mask. I'm now hooked up to Prynne Radio.

"No sign of the girl," yet another voice says.

The girl. Me? Surely not. There are others out here.

"Don't worry about her. You see her, you walk away. *Without* harming her."

"But, sir—"

"No arguments. The order came from up top. Just… find the others and go silent. Our frequencies have been compromised."

I pick up the pace and push through a jumble of gnarled limbs. Up ahead, I spot a glow-in-the-dark lump. One I recognize. The Prynne uniform. An inmate! Has to be. Relief gives me the strength I need to run…run. When I'm close enough, I drop to my knees and skid across the ice. I reach—a boy. He's lying on his side. With a gentle push, I roll him over.

His glassy eyes stare into the distance. Ice shimmers in his hair, and on his nose, mouth and chin. The rest of him is tinted blue.

I'm able to overlook my panic as I cling to hope. This doesn't mean he's dead.

With my teeth, I rip off my glove. I feel for a pulse, but…

My hope withers. He *is* dead. His spirit has already moved on.

Is he in Myriad? Or Troika? Or was he Unsigned, like me?

Is he in the Realm of Many Ends?

A crunch of ice sounds behind me, but I don't have time to investigate. Or prepare for an attack. Something—someone—collides into my back, knocking me to my face. On impact, a jagged piece of ice cuts my cheek, and my lungs are flattened. I fight for breath I can't catch, stars winking behind my eyes.

Anger engulfs me. No more abuse! With a roar, I jam my elbow into his torso. A bellow of pain echoes through the night, the heavy weight lifting from me in a blink. I turn and kick, nailing the culprit in the chin.

He falls, landing on his butt, and I look him over. A guard! We're wearing the same mask, coat and boots. But… why would one guard attack another?

"Big mistake," I say through gritted teeth.

"Ten?" He tears off his mask, revealing dark hair and a blood-smeared face I recognize. A fellow inmate. Clayton Anders—Clay! Undiluted joy brings tears to my eyes.

He climbs to his feet, very much alive.

"Clay." I jump up and tear off my own mask, the cold nipping at my skin and freezing the tears. My teeth chatter. "You're here. You're with me." We close the distance and hug each other with complete abandon. "I'm so happy to see you."

"Ditto, number girl. I've missed you every day. Thoughts of you kept me going." His grip on me tightens. "Why is six afraid of seven?"

I laugh. This boy! He's always loved to tease me. "Why else? Because seven eight nine."

He buries his head against my shoulder. Even through my coat I feel something warm and wet. Tears of his own? "I'd hoped you escaped. Sometimes I heard screams…"

"Yeah." A tremor rocks him and seeps into me. "Yeah. I did escape. I made it outside the asylum, but last time I was unprepared for the cold. A group of Russians caught me. They did… The things they…"

"I know. I know." I can imagine. I stroke his hair. "It's over, done. You're safe now."

His next tremor is stronger. "The next morning, they brought me back to Vans. I was locked in an underground facility where the guards are trained."

I pull back and fit my gloves over my hands. "How'd you get free yesterday?"

"Some pink-haired girl came through and opened my door."

Bow. I owe her. Him. Whatever! "Have you found any other inmates out here?"

His voice is low and filled with countless regrets as he replies, "No one living. You?"

"The same." There has to be more we can do. I won't accept failure.

A moan drifts on the wind, and I turn toward the sound. "Did you hear that?"

Another moan, softer but no less agonized.

"Yeah." He fits his mask over his face. "Come on," he says and races forward.

I replace my mask, as well, and though I hate to leave the dead kid out in the open, I follow Clay. Take care of the living, and let the dead take care of the dead. The sound leads us to a small clearing surrounded by thriving evergreens, but there's no sign of the Prynne uniform.

I take a risk, calling, "This is Tenley Lockwood. I know someone's here, but I'm having trouble finding you. I don't want to hurt you. I just—"

A pile of rocks rattles, and a trembling, gloveless hand reaches out.

"Here!" I shout to Clay, desperate as I sprint over. I dig through the stones to discover—

Sloan. Her partially frozen face is tinted blue, but she has a pulse. Faint, but there. She's not shivering, and I know that's a bad, bad sign.

Clay falls at my side and helps me pull her the rest of the way from the rubble.

My desperation escalates as I grab the coat from my backpack and wrap it around her shoulders, then remove my gloves yet again to shove them onto her hands. "Do you know how to start a fire?"

"No, but even if I did, the guards—"

"If they find us, we'll fight them, but we have to get her warm *now*." The cave is too far away. She won't survive the uphill trek, and I'm not sure we're strong enough to make it.

"All right. Okay. I'll do my best."

Zero! "We need help," I mutter.

If telling Archer to stay away actually forced him to stay away, maybe summoning him would force him to appear?

A girl had to try.

"Archer," I call. "Bow. Whatever your name is. I'm asking for help." I remember what I shouted to the shadow at Killian's bidding, the restrictions I put in place, and add, "If you can hear me, you can come closer now."

"Oh, I can hear you." Ice crunches in the distance.

I jump to my feet, the scalpel clasped and ready for action. Just in case. Clay moves beside me, holding a rock, just as ready. I remember his withdrawals, how unsteady he was. Now he looks clean and sober.

A guy I don't recognize steps into the clearing, both of his hands lifted, palms out. A sign of surrender. His hair is the color of spun gold, and he's impossibly handsome. He has the kind of face you'd see on a magazine. *World's Sexiest Male.*

He is the saint to Killian's sinner.

Like Killian, he's without a coat. He's wearing a T-shirt that hugs the massive cut of his biceps. Also like Killian, he's tall and gloriously muscled.

"Stay where you are," Clay commands. "I don't want to hurt you, but I will."

"Why would you hurt me? Ten asked for my help." The newcomer takes one more step, landing in a beam of moonlight. "Here I am."

"You heard her call for Archer, could have decided to pretend you're him to take advantage of her."

His gaze locks with mine, his eyes odd yet captivating, the color of copper, and smoldering with an intensity that should be too much for any one person to contain. They are *Bow's* eyes.

"I *am* Archer."

I detect a slight English accent, the very voice that once whispered through my head, and I reel anew. Killian told me I would see Bow again—Bow, as a male named Archer.

Well, I'm seeing him.

"What are you?" I want to hear him say it.

He smiles. "You know what I am… Sperm Bank."

I lurch back.

"Well, *I* don't know who you are. Why are you talking about a sperm bank?" Clay turns to me. "And what do you mean, *what* is he?"

"You're a TL," I say to Archer. "My TL, to be exact."

His nod is relieved and resigned at once. "And you're going to have to trust me, at least for a little while, if you want Sloan to live. I can get her warm and hide her from approaching guards."

I'm just as relieved, just as resolved, but I'm also angry

all over again. How dare he pretend to be a girl, invading my privacy? How dare he pretend to be my friend?

I *don't* trust him, not anymore. He's as bad as Killian, only wanting one thing. But I give him a clipped wave over anyway. At the moment, he is Sloan's best and only chance for survival.

He needs no more encouragement and springs into motion. Clay and I stand in place, watching as Archer crouches, holds out his hands and taps his fingers over the top of his palm. A bright blue light springs from his flesh—like the one I saw on Killian—and my jaw drops.

"What do you really look like?" I ask.

"Exactly like this." He dances his fingers through the light, as if he's typing. I think… I think he *is* typing. He stands, moves a few yards away and repeats the process, crouching and typing. He does this four times in total, until he's formed a square with us in the center.

"What's happening?" Clay asks, his incredulity as fierce as my own. "How are you *glowing*?"

"One of the perks of the job. I'm always hooked to the Grid."

Grid?

He advances until he's inside the square with us then types into the blue light one more time. The light vanishes—only to reappear in the four corners he created. Beams shoot up, out, over and under us, forming walls and surrounding us with heat, such delicious heat. And the walls are so freaking beautiful, sparkling with diamond dust. I can almost convince myself the sky fell on top of us and stars are glimmering.

I reach out with a trembling hand and ghost my fingertips over the wall. And that's exactly what it is. A wall of air with a jellylike consistency—jellyair. *Trademark pending*, I think drily. I can joke or sob. How is any of this possible?

Ripples spread from one wall to the other, entrancing me. "How are we hidden?"

"We see the light." Archer crouches beside Sloan and measures her pulse. "Others see the reflection of the forest."

"And if they bump into us?"

"They won't. The moment the light activated, Troikan Messengers arrived. You can't see them, but they're there."

"Fear based?" I ask, still resentful of my encounter with the Myriad Messengers.

He gives me a look, all, *Who do you think you're dealing with, puny human?* "Distraction based."

"Messengers." Clay rubs the back of his neck. "That's the job my ML and TL said I'd have in the Everlife."

"Have you signed with one of the realms?" I panic at the thought. What if we end up on different sides?

"Not yet. But I've had a lot of time to think, and I'm leaning toward Troika. My family is Troikan and I'd like to spend eternity with them."

"But… I thought you hated your family for sending you to Prynne."

He peers at his feet. "I hated *myself*. And as horrible as my experience at Prynne has been, I can't regret coming here. I'm sober. I met you…and Marlowe."

Marlowe, who might or might not be in Troika right now.

"After I help Sloan, I can give you a tour of the realm." Archer takes a dagger from a sheath at his ankle and slashes his wrist. He holds the wound over Sloan's lips.

"Wait. What are you—" He's not doing the vampire thing, at least. Glittery liquid leaks out rather than blood.

"I'm giving her Lifeblood," he says. "She'll heal."

As droplet after droplet trickles into her mouth, she gives no reaction. But Archer appears satisfied by the time his wound mends. Mends, right before my eyes, the flesh weaving back together. I've never seen anything like it.

He lowers his arm and smiles at Clay. "Now for the tour."

The words are for Clay, but the tour is for my benefit, I'm sure. My anger with Archer hasn't lessened, despite his cool tricks, and I currently want nothing to do with his realm.

He types in his arm again, and a few seconds later, images begin to play over the walls. Like Killian, he shows me a beach. Only this one is sun-drenched, revealing the crystal clarity of rainbow-colored water. When I see surfers riding waves—and whales!—I close my eyes, every muscle in my body clenching. He's using the information he gathered against me. Information he shouldn't have.

Can no one like me just because I'm me? Will I always be a commodity to win rather than a person to love?

chapter ten

"Grass isn't greener on the other side. Grass is greener when you water it."
—Troika

A bead of sweat trickles between my shoulder blades, and I remove everything but my uniform to use as a cushion, creating a cozy spot to rest beside Sloan. She's still unconscious, but I'm happy to note rosy color is seeping into her cheeks. Archer's Lifeblood worked.

I guess he's not a total ass.

Clay does a similar strip after the tour, sits beside me and focuses on the TL. "I refused to speak with my TL for years. A way to punish my parents, I think. Maybe myself. I've regretted the decision for a while now."

"If you'll accept me, I'll be happy to be your TL by proxy."

"You can do that?"

"I've already requested and gained permission."

"I'll accept you, thank you." Clay looks down at his wringing hands. "A covenant was offered to me years ago.

My parents told me the offer was revoked. I'd done too much..."

"No," Archer says. "No. An offer is made to every child and once made, it remains active until Firstdeath."

Expression agonized, Clay whispers, "But...you don't know the things I've done."

"I don't need to know. Nothing you've done can compare to the things I did, and yet, when I was ready, I was welcomed with open arms."

Hello, intrigue. What did Archer do? He's so by-the-book, I can't imagine him purposely breaking a rule.

"I just... I want to make up for my mistakes before I pledge." Clay scrubs a hand through his hair. "Want to be worthy."

"Why?" Archer walks over, pats him on the shoulder, clearly surprising him with the forbidden touch. "It's not necessary, and you never know how much longer you have left in the Land of the Harvest."

Realization suddenly hits me. *Harvest* is a farming term, and here, Troika and Myriad reap souls. At the moment, I'm not sure if I'm insulted or flattered.

"I'm young. I'm finally clean. I've got time," Clay says.

Archer's shoulders hunch in ever so slightly. He's like a kid who's just been denied his favorite dessert. "Be careful. No one knows the day or the hour."

Two Prynne guards approach our well-lit square. Just before they reach us, however, they veer to the left, as if deep, deep inside they know to avoid what their eyes cannot see.

Messengers in action. I can't see them either, but I can see the result of them.

Surprise! There's more to the world—worlds—than I ever thought possible.

"Neat." Clay yawns and stretches.

The yawn is contagious. Despite my earlier rest, I'm operating on nothing but the fumes of an adrenaline surge that has already crashed and burned. The medicine Killian used on me is wearing off, my soreness coming back. I'm also hungry, cranky and weak.

"You're tired. Both of you." Archer gives me a pointed look. "I'll keep you safe. Sleep for once. Don't fight it."

Another reminder that he knows more about me than he should. "You should have told me you were a guy before I showered in front of you," I snap at him.

Unabashed, he says, "You're in a mood. Is it that time of the month for you, too? Have our cycles finally synced?"

Oh, them be fightin' words.

I yawn again, my jaw cracking. Okay, fine. Them be fightin' words *tomorrow*. "What about Killian? He'll stop at nothing to find me." At the mere mention of the boy's name, my blood heats and crackles like the fire, making me tingle. Foolish! "Or to keep me from signing with you."

"Killian?" Clay asks.

There's a flash of resentment in Archer's copper eyes. "The epitome of Myriad evil. And he can't see us, either."

Good. That's good. Of course.

Archer's gaze narrows on me. "Have you accepted your importance? Have you realized you're the final drop of water that causes the cup to overflow?"

Pressure... I turn away from him without saying a word.

Clay blows me a kiss before refocusing on Archer. "How old are you, Mr.—"

"Call me Archer. And I'm nineteen."

"How long have you been with Troika?"

"I was raised in a realm."

In "a" realm. The odd phrasing catches my attention, but I let it go. I'm too tired to match wits with him, and besides that, I don't want his attention returning to me.

"I've always known people age in the Unending." Clay frowns. "But no Laborer I've ever seen has looked older than thirty."

"Unlike physical bodies, spirits are eternal and never decay," Archer says. "They reach a certain threshold—the Age of Perfection—and freeze."

Like our Age of Accountability, only better.

My eyelids grow heavy, and I finally give up the battle, stretching out on Sloan's other side. I'll catnap. My circumstances have changed, yes, but my mind-set has not. No matter how much I trust Clay and, okay, all right, in this regard I trust Archer, too, I can rely only on myself.

My mental lights go out…

And switch back on—

A needle jabs into my neck, and pain shoots through me. Vans laughs in my face. I try to kick him, but the chains on my wrists limit my range of motion—

"Ten. Ten."

Hands on my shoulders, shaking me.

"Wake up. Now!"

Danger! Under attack!

My eyelids split open and I jolt upright, swinging my arm.

Sloan ducks, avoiding a punch to the cheek. "Wow. Not a morning person, are we?"

I'm panting, my heart a jackhammer in my chest. I scan my surroundings—the glowing square. Archer stands at the farthest edge, his arms hanging at his sides. Sloan sits at my right, facing me. Clay sits at my left, his knees drawn to his chest, his eyes closed. No enemy lurks nearby. No one's trying to hurt me.

Calm. Steady. The torture...only a memory.

Sloan, despite her teasing, is pale and trembling, but at least she's alive.

"What's wrong?" I reach for my scalpel.

"You were screaming in your sleep. What is this?" She motions to the glowing walls, then points to Archer. "Who is he?"

Right. She missed yesterday's intros. "That's Archer."

"Great. Wonderful. But that bit of info tells me nothing. *What* is he?"

Looking him over a second time, I notice details I previously missed. He's as still as death, unblinking, and his eye sockets clear as glass. So. His spirit is no longer inside the Shell. He can leave it at will?

Where did he go?

There are multiple articles of clothing scattered around his booted feet, and it's clear he took down an entire contingent of guards while we slept.

I start with the most important fact. "He's on our side."

"Good. He's hot," Sloan says in a stage whisper. Hoping he'll hear and respond? Then she gives up all pretense of timidity and makes grabby hands. "Yummy yum yum, give baby some sugar."

I roll my eyes. "You know him better as Bow. The girl you tried to trip at breakfast."

She blinks in astonishment. "You lie."

"Oh, and he's a TL."

Now she grimaces. "He just lost a few thousand do-me points. I'd say both realms can stuff their values where the sun doesn't shine, but Myriad would be happy to comply and Troika wouldn't take offense."

Her jaded makes my jaded look like a fluffy baby bunny.

She shakes her head, as if dislodging cobwebs. "I think I'm in shock. Mr. Bow Archer is a hot slice of beefcake."

As Clay stirs, I scan the forest outside the square. So much for sleeping a minute or two. Obviously, I slipped into a coma for *hours*. The sun is high in the sky and gloriously bright. Trees are still covered in glistening ice, but there are no signs of guards.

"Well?" Sloan brushes the dust from her palms. "What's the game plan?"

I snap to attention. Right. We need a game plan. "Mine is simple. Eat breakfast. Ditch Archer, avoid Killian." I'm sick of being pressured. "Oh, and escape the mountain without getting shot. Survive till I'm eighteen." Maybe I'll even go to college and study to become an accountant.

Mind porn! I shiver with a sudden burst of excitement.

Maybe by then I'll have figured out my Everlife.

How do others choose? What seems like a great idea one moment can become a nightmare later on. I know this. I've seen pictures of my teenage mother's new perm—hello frizz. The nap I just had to take in the hammock a few years ago—hello severe sunburn and possible melanoma. The tattoo I got at fifteen—hello planet Earth I can never wash off. And none of those things mean anything in the big scheme of things. This does.

"Sounds good. I'm on board." She rubs her temples. "And before my brain explodes, I guess I should tell you… thank you? You saved my precious." She waves a hand to indicate the curves of her body.

"I didn't save you. He did." I motion to Archer with a tilt of my chin.

"Oh, thank goodness. I would rather smell like fart for all time than be in your debt for a single minute."

I snort. "What makes you think you *don't* smell like fart?"

Frowning, she lifts her arm, sniffs her pit. I laugh out loud, and she flips me off.

"I *don't*," she says.

A *boom, boom, boom* sounds, as if fireworks are exploding in the sky. The ground shakes, and Sloan gasps. Normally, we can go months without any kind of sign of violence from the realms. What's happened the past few days, well, it doesn't bode well for us, does it?

Things are escalating up there. And where do the realms actually battle, anyway? Spirits bonded to Myriad can't get inside Troika, and vice versa.

Clay stands and stretches. "I'm going to excuse myself from this particular conversation." He walks toward Archer, tentative, and glances over his shoulder, his brow furrowed with confusion. "What's wrong with him?"

"Besides looking good enough to eat?" Sloan joins him at the Shell and reaches out, only to drop her arm just before contact, the no-touch rule ingrained. "No one seems to be home."

"Those in the Everlife must be able to enter and withdraw from a Shell at will," I say. Which explains why Archer cursed at Killian in our cell. I couldn't see the Irish seducer, but he could.

Also explains why I heard their voices at odd times. They were trying to help me…and manipulate me.

My hands curl into tight little balls.

"You're correct. We can, and we do. Often." Archer's voice rings out. "As easily as slipping a hand out of a glove."

Sloan screeches and stumbles backward.

Clay grins. "I'm suffering from serious Shell envy right now."

Archer offers Sloan a helping hand, but she shakes her head no, adamant. With a shrug, he steps around her, his otherworldly copper gaze landing on me. "I found a town to the south of us. If we leave now, we can make it before nightfall."

"I'm not going anywhere just yet." Maybe I won't ditch him right away. Maybe I'll use him the way he used me, let him take me where I want to go. "I have to eat." My stomach rumbles. I dig through the backpack and hand both Clay and Sloan a can of food. Archer refuses his, reminding me of the time he turned down the protein bar. "You don't need to eat, do you?"

"Only manna."

"But you ate the asylum's slop." Even mentioned it looked the same going in as it did coming out. "Sometimes."

"The Shell has a compartment that allows me to ingest and expel at will and—"

"I'm interested in what you're saying, I really am." I can't tear my gaze from my can of chicken. "But I'm actually *not* hearing anything you're saying." Food!

I pop the top, Clay and Sloan following suit, and the

scent of hot sauce and blue cheese wafts on the breeze. My mouth waters.

Like savages, we shovel nugget after nugget into our mouths.

I force myself to slow the closer I get to the bottom of the can, but it doesn't help. Soon the can is empty. Well, zero. One gram of protein per bite, twenty-three bites. Enough fuel to get me through the day? We'll find out.

Clay rubs his stomach, hot sauce smeared all over his face. "Best meal I've had in forever."

"That's sad," Archer says.

"Can we go now?" Sloan says, and she sounds bored. "We've got a Laborer to ditch and a mountain to descend." She bats her eyelashes at Archer, more determined than coy. "Oops. Now we've lost the element of surprise. Whatever shall we do?"

Clay shakes his head. "We need Archer. We won't survive without him."

Archer stares at me, accusation in his eyes. "You planned to leave me?"

"I did." And I won't feel guilty about it. "Then I changed my mind. Now. I need a moment of privacy." My bladder is demanding serious attention.

I stand on surprisingly steady legs and say, with my head high, "If you'll excuse me."

"Once you step out of our square of tranquility, the cold will crash into you." Archer swoops down and tosses my coat in my direction. "I'd dress first, if I were you."

Right. I don the coat, gloves, mask and goggles. I'm still wearing my boots, but I exchange them for a better fitting pair found scattered at Archer's feet.

"Here." He pulls a necklace out from under his shirt then over his head. A small vial dangles at the end. He closes the distance between us, extends the vial. "Liquefied manna."

Considering what I just ate for breakfast, my morning breath has to be at DEFCON Five. I angle my face away from him before I say, "You're giving me spirit food?"

"Yes. Drink it. If you dare."

The challenge is unmistakable. "Let me guess. I'll drink it, and I'll either fall head over heels in love with you or I'll end up with explosive diarrhea. Punishment for wanting to give you the stinky boot."

"You should know me better by now."

Do I detect…displeasure? And dang it, I *do* feel guilty about this and the whole ditching thing.

I grab the vial before I can talk myself out of it, pop the cork and drain the contents. The liquid is warm and sweet, like melted honey but not as thick, and as it washes through me, I feel hugged from the inside out. My veins begin to tingle, as if my blood is fizzing.

"What's happening to me?" I demand.

"I'm sure you noticed that I smelled good while living in the asylum. Manna not only nourishes, it cleanses."

And addicts. *More! Gimme!*

"This particular variety of manna is found *only* in Troika," he adds, and I glare at him. Manipulated again. "Go. Do your thing." He gives me a little push, and I end up outside the square.

The jellyair appears wet, and yet I emerge on the other side completely dry. And within seconds, I'm close to frostbite. I trudge behind a tree and take care of business. As

I'm fastening my pants—my butt stinging from cold slaps of wind—a snap of twigs. My heart stops. I go still.

Danger!

A familiar scent wafts to my nose. Peat smoke and heather… Pure seduction.

Killian? Nearby?

My heart kicks back into gear, beating hard and fast. Did he watch me pee?

My cheeks burn.

To him, I'm nothing but a soul to be won, I remind myself. One soul in a long line of souls. A number.

Oh, the irony.

He hates defeat almost as much as he hates Archer. No matter how sweet he can sometimes be, my best interests will never be his main concern.

I sprint back to the square—only to realize I can't see the square. Zero! What am I supposed to—

Archer appears a few feet in front of me, my backpack slung over his shoulder. Sloan and Clay step forward, suddenly flanking his sides. The former inmates are dressed in winter gear, but Archer hasn't changed out of his T-shirt and jeans. His beautiful features are twisted in a scowl, the stars branded on the palms of his hands glowing bright blue.

"Killian," we say in unison.

"Want me with you now? This way." Archer launches into motion, and we do our best to remain close to his heels.

"Killian…the new kid?" Sloan asks, already wheezing. "Why are we running from *him*? He's hotter than Bocher! That's Bow plus Archer, in case your puny brain isn't hip to my hop."

"He works for Myriad," I explain. While I'm not yet wheezing, every step is more difficult than the last, my thighs burning and straining.

"Know what I just heard?" she asks. "He's young, hung and dumb. My type!"

"Your standards need work," I say, and okay, yeah, I'm wheezing now.

"Can't improve on perfection but ow, ow, ow, blisters! I'm not sure how much farther I can make it."

Archer grins at me over his shoulder. "Why don't you recite a poem and distract Sloan from her *total* lack of stamina? Something uplifting for once. And make sure it rhymes. The best poems *always* rhyme."

Is he serious? "One poem, coming up." I clear my burning throat, as if I'm about to say something profound. "You suck in so many ways, but at least our association pays. You kept us warm and away from the swarm, and you've got a really nice form. But you are a major pain in the ass, and that's not just sass—it's a bitch slap of truth from a sweet little lass."

He chokes on his one tongue. "That was *not* uplifting."

"Then you must not have been listening. I feel better already." Sloan clutches at her heart as if she's having an attack. "Only problem is I think I'm dying."

Archer glances at her then Clay, and he frowns. "Clay?"

"When we reach the town, or wherever it is we're going," Clay announces with no hint of levity, "I'm going sign with Troika. No more waiting. You were right."

I trip over my own foot, barely managing to remain upright. "Why the rush? Yesterday you said you had time and—" *No! Zip it!* His future is his own. I have no right to pressure him the way others have pressured me.

It's just…deep down I want him to wait until *I* make a decision, want him to pick the realm I pick.

I'm just as bad as my parents.

"I thought about it all night," he continues, "and then *this* happened. We're on the run again. None of us know when the end will come. And no matter how many mistakes I've made, I want to be ready for mine."

His assurance makes a mockery of my uncertainty.

"We do this now." Archer leads us into a small cave. "There's no need to wait until we reach the town."

For several heartbeats of time, no one says a word. We're too busy panting. And gagging. The canned chicken has challenged my stomach to a blood feud.

Archer types into his arm, a soft blue light radiating from his flesh. Jellyair falls from the top rocky ledge of the entrance, finally hitting the icy ground and sealing us inside. "You ready?"

Clay nods. "What do I need to do?"

"Offer a simple pledge of allegiance. Nothing more, nothing less."

"But remember," I say as I clutch my side, "that simple pledge is permanent. There will be no going back."

Pressuring him again. Stop!

"Don't be an idiot." Mist wafts in front of Sloan's face as she continues to labor for every breath. "The realms only want worker bees and soldiers for their war."

"Does that really matter? He has to pick a realm. His only other option is Many Ends." I shudder, knowing I can deny its existence no longer. Something I'd done because

I hadn't wanted to accept the possibility I'd end up there. "The realm is the Prynne Asylum of the Everlife, nothing but punishment and pain. I just… I don't want to end up as your enemy, Clay."

He tugs at a lock of my hair. "You won't. Not ever."

"You're both buying into the hype. Many Ends can't be as bad as Laborers claim," Sloan says. "Eternal punishment simply for choosing not to sign with Myriad or Troika? Bullcorn!"

Archer looks at her with pity. "A pledge to Troika creates a bond to the realm. Same with Myriad. A bond that grants entrance into the realm. The Unsigned are bondless, so their spirits have only one place to go. Many Ends."

I've heard this before, but for the first time I wonder… "Are the kids of the Unsigned sent to Many Ends?"

"No. Children are somehow bonded to both Troika and Myriad. I've often been assigned the task of sitting with a dying child so that I'm there at the moment of death, able to escort the spirit into Troika. At the Age of Accountability, the bonds are broken and the spirit is allowed to choose us or Myriad, just like a human."

Sloan hunches over and waves her hand as if she has more to say, but she's too winded to care anymore.

I lean against the ice-cold rocky wall, happy for Clay, sad for me. "I'll support your decision," I tell him. "Whatever it is."

Archer pats him on the shoulder again. "All of Troika will become your family. When you need our help, you have only to ask for it. And when you enter the Everlife, you will be trained in the position most suited to you. Messenger, I think you said."

Clay is all but salivating. And then he does it. He utters the vow all children are taught by at least one of the Laborers—the vow that will forever decide the course of his life. "With my heart, mind and body, I believe Troika is the realm for me. I pledge my Firstlife. I pledge my Everlife. All that I am is Troika's, and Troika is mine."

"And so it's done," Archer says with a big grin.

Just. Like. That. A future now forever charted.

I expect bright lights, or cheering to echo from some secret place. Something. Anything! But nothing happens.

Archer cups Clay by the nape and pulls him close for a bro-hug, the two patting each other on the back.

"Welcome to the family, my friend," Archer says.

"Thank you." There are tears in Clay's eyes as he smiles up at the Laborer, and I'm almost knocked over.

This. This is what I was waiting for. The moment is so… momentous. I hadn't known the heavy weight Clay used to carry on his shoulders until just this second—because it's gone, the weight is gone. His head is higher, his shoulders no longer hunched but squared and proud. Contentedness radiates from him, as if he's shed years of fatigue.

I want that. I want that so badly.

"In Troika," Archer says, "you'll be rewarded for your deeds in this life. I'm not saying your deeds affect the benefits you receive while you're here, only that the sacrifices you make for us will never be forgotten."

"What kind of rewards?" Sloan rubs her hands together, suddenly intrigued. "We talking jewels? Cash? Gold?"

The scent of heather drifts on the wind, and in unison Archer and I stiffen. Oh…zero! "I'm pushing the pause button on this conversation. We've got to go."

"She's right." Archer disables the wall of jellyair.

We follow him back into the frigid cold. We run and run and run, sunlight glistening off the ice at our feet. My wheezing returns, only it's a thousand times worse, the burn in my lungs soon competing with the one in my thighs.

"Changed my mind…need another break."

A light erupts from Archer's wrist. He doesn't slow as his fingers dance through it, typing, typing. Up ahead, a blue beam shoots from the sky and slams into the ground, leaving something behind when it fades.

Archer grabs that something as he runs past it. "Here." He tosses each of us a length of rope. "Knot them around your waist. You're going to need them."

I don't ask questions. As I run, I do as commanded.

A new noise erupts behind us—a howl of rage. A war cry?

Something dark whizzes past me and slams into Archer. The Laborer is thrown into the side of the mountain with so much force there's a vibration at my feet. When he lands in a tangle of punching fists and kicking feet, I catch a glimpse of dark hair and an arm sleeved with intricate tattoos.

Killian found us.

I slide to a stop, grabbing hold of Clay and Sloan as they do the same. Together we stand or together we fall.

"I'm going to kill you." Killian delivers a viscous jab, jab to Archer's nose. "You had no right—"

"I had every right!" Archer ducks, avoiding the next round of fury. He lands three punches to Killian's side. "She doesn't want you."

"She doesn't know what she wants."

She, meaning *me*. My stomach twists.

"I won't let you hurt her the way you hurt Dior," Archer says through gritted teeth.

Dior?

"By the time I finished with your darling," Killian says, his tone nothing but silk and heat, and yet I pick up the underlying note of his rage, "she was begging me for more."

That rage...over a girl... Killian is doing his best to hide his feelings, but he's failing.

He loved Dior, didn't he?

Mind scramble!

The vicious fight rages on, the boys hitting rocks and razor-sharp ice as well as each other. I cringe as flesh is torn from both Shells, every tattered piece shimmering with diamond dust. Lifeblood, Archer called it.

"Let's not wait around to crown the winner." Sloan pulls on my arm.

"I can't leave. I have to help Archer." Clay is already moving forward. "He's family!"

I don't understand the bond he feels so quickly. "Clay—"

Boom!

The explosion echoes from the sky, and again, it sounds as if fireworks have been unleashed. A battle is happening up there at the same time one is happening down here. Maybe... Archer's friends are throwing down with Killian's? Is that how it works?

"Wait." I tighten my grip on Clay's wrist to hold him in place. If we get in the middle of two savage animals intent on killing each other, we won't be walking away—we'll be crawling. And that's if we're lucky. And...and...

Are the vibrations at my feet getting stronger?

"How many times did we sit on the sidelines and do nothing when other inmates needed us?" Clay's eyes beseech me. "I can't sit on the sidelines anymore." He pulls from my clasp as Sloan gives me another tug.

The counterforce sends me careening. I don't mean to, but I take her to the ground with me. The impact is jarring, and even maybe knocks a little sense into me. Clay is right. No more sitting on the sidelines. If I can help Archer and Killian, I have to help them—before they send each other into Second-death.

As I stand, another loud boom echoes from above. I look up and realize this one didn't come from the sky but the mountain, heralding the beginning of an avalanche. The sky is nothing but snow, ice and rock—and falling straight for us.

chapter eleven

"Without an end, you cannot have a new beginning."
—Myriad

Life is all about the numbers.

Today those numbers are the seconds we have to reach safety. The tons about to crash down upon us. The feet/yards/miles we're about to fall, unable to stop ourselves.

"Come on." I grab the end of Sloan's rope and run as fast as I can. She isn't prepared, and I have to drag her behind me. When I reach Clay, I grab his rope and drag him, too. We aren't yet connected, but I try to remedy that as I run; I'm shaking too badly. "Archer! Killian! Come on!"

Numbers never lie, and the center of a mass like this is always heaviest, so that's where the avalanche will move the fastest and hit the hardest. If we can get far enough to the side, we can maybe, hopefully, avoid being buried.

I glance up. Zero! We're not going to get far enough to the side.

There are no trees nearby to act as an anchor for our ropes. Not that we'd have time to tie ourselves to the trunks. What should we do next? Brace?

The rumble of snow grows louder until I'd swear a freight train is hidden beneath the flakes. Yes. Brace. I recall a book I read and shout, "If you're swept away, start swimming uphill as soon as you can." The longer we're buried, the harder movement will be. "Don't stop until—"

Impact!

I'm thrown down, down, down by what seems to be ten thousand pounds of snow. I grip the ropes with all my strength as I tumble around like clothes in a dryer. Common sense tells me to keep a hand in front of my face—I might need to dig a tunnel to breathe—while keeping the other lifted above my head to help with disorientation. But I have a choice, always a choice. Help myself or help my friends by maintaining my grip on their ropes.

I maintain my grip.

When finally I stop, snow and debris are piled on top of me. I try to catch my breath but there's not enough oxygen. Desperate, trying not to panic, I thrash with my legs, propelling up…up…

Am I going the right way?

Does it matter? If I'm buried under a foot or more, I won't make it to the top on my own. That's just fact.

What seems an eternity later—yes!—I break the surface and suck back as much air as my lungs can handle. I'm frantic as I scan the sea of white, seeing no sign of the others. "Clay! Sloan!" No response. "Archer! Killian!" Again, no response.

I tug one rope, then the other, and realize the two are on top of the snow, both facing the same direction. I use the lengths to fight my way through the rest of the deluge…

“Ten!” Clay calls, beyond frantic. “Help me. You have to help me.”

I lumber to my feet and follow the sound of his voice… skidding to a halt when I reach the edge of a cliff. Hanks of snow and rock fall over…and just keep falling.

“Ten!” He’s clinging to a tree that’s been knocked over the edge, the roots the only thing keeping it in place.

“I’ve got you.” I dig in my heels and try to pull him up with the rope. “Don’t worry.”

“Ten… Ten…”

A whimper at my right. I turn my head and see Sloan, and I almost lose my breakfast. She’s hanging over the same cliff, and like Clay, she’s white-knuckling a tree branch with every bit of strength she possesses.

“Pleeease. Help me.”

My panic returns with a vengeance. I won’t be able to pull them up at the same time. They’re simply too heavy. I have to pick one and pray the other holds on just a little longer.

Another hated choice. A sob lodges in my throat, constricting my airway.

I love Clay. We’ve laughed together, and we’ve cried together. He’s kind, honest and, as he just proved today, willing to help when needed. I can picture him at my seaside home, surfing alongside me.

Sloan, on the other hand, has been a thorn in my side for a little over a year. She’s a pain in every sense of the word. She’s irritating and combative, and I can’t imagine ever trusting her at my back.

But Clay now knows where he’s going when he dies. Sloan will wind up in Many Ends.

"I'm so sorry, Clay. I'll pull you up next, okay? Just hang on. Hang on!" I release his rope, hating myself, and grip Sloan's with both hands. As my feet slip, I look around—everywhere but at Clay. There are no boulders or rooted trees within reach, which means I can't anchor myself. Okay. All right. Can't be helped.

"Ten," she cries.

"Let go of the branch," I shout at her. "Please."

"No, no—"

"Do it! I can't pull you up if you're clasping the tree." A tree that is teetering. "Sloan! I've got you, promise. Just let go!"

"I can't," she says as she weeps.

"You must. Help me help you."

She only weeps harder.

Rage joins my deluge of emotions. "At the count of three, I'm helping Clay. One. Two."

She lets go, giving me the full brunt of her weight. My feet slip closer to the edge, leaving me unable to balance. I crash to my butt and slide faster. A terrified yelp escapes her.

Come on, come on. I dig my boots as deep into the snow and ice as I can, managing to stop my momentum and pull with all my might. I gain an inch…then another…she can't weigh more than one hundred and twenty pounds, but my shoulders burn and shake as if they're lugging a couple of tons. Muscles I didn't know I had spasm.

Survival instinct demands I release her and save myself, but I just keeping pulling…pulling…

Just a little farther…

So close to assisting Clay…

When the tops of her hands reached the edge of the cliff, I grit out, "Grab the side and climb up."

As soon as her grip is steadyish, she kicks up a leg. A few seconds later—an eternity—the top of her body clears the side.

"Hurry! Please." Mist dances in front of my face as I pant, and tears well in my eyes. I glance at Clay as snow topples over the cliff edge. He is desperately trying to inch his way along the tree trunk—a tree trunk that teeters a little more with his every action.

"Ten." Clay's panic is worse than mine. "Please."

"Sloan," I plead. "Come on!"

Her arms shake and strain as she claws the rest of the way, finally safe. Thank the Firstking! I release her rope and reach for Clay's, the movement sending another mound of snow over the edge. He's close enough now that it hits him right in the face…and it's strong enough to knock him loose.

"No!" I dive down, my arm extended. I'll catch him, I have to catch him, but something latches on my ankles, keeping me from going over the edge as I encounter air, only air. "Clay!"

He shrieks as he falls…falls…and the sound rips me up inside, but it's better than the terrible silence that comes next. *No. No, no, no.* He's not—he can't be—but I see him. He landed on another plateau, and he's unmoving, a crimson pool growing around his oddly contorted body.

Horror overwhelms me. I just found him, and now he's gone?

Sloan pulls me up. "We can't stay here. It's not safe."

She bands her arm around me, forcing me to stand. "Move with me!"

Now she's in a hurry? I fight to remain in place. I can't leave Clay. I just…can't.

From the time he lost his grip on the branch to the time he hit the bottom of the mountain—roughly eight seconds. If I'd had two more, if I'd let go of Sloan just a little sooner, I could have caught his hand.

Two. Seconds. That's all I needed.

She slaps me across the face. "Ten!"

I taste the copper tang of blood, but I don't care. He's down there. My friend is down there. He deserves so much better.

"You listen to me." She grips my shoulders and shakes me. "I'll drag you kicking and screaming if I must, but we're leaving. You saved my life. Now I'm saving yours."

I saved her, but I didn't save Clay. There's nothing I can do to bring him back. But her words have the desired effect. Finally I allow her to lead me away. Dead, I'm no good to Clay.

"We're going to be okay," she says through chattering teeth. "After what you did for me, I'm basically your bitch for life. I'll get you out of here even if I have to sleep with a bunch of sexy guys to do it. I know, I know. I'm a giver."

As I go numb, I lose track of time. I know we descend the mountain. I know Archer joins us when we stop to rest, but not Killian. Archer explains we're hidden from the ML, but I don't respond. I don't care. I know we stop a second time so Sloan and I can eat, but I don't know where we are or what I put in my stomach.

"—going to be okay?" Sloan asks.

"She's strong," Archer replies.

Strong? Me? I'm not. I'm the weak link. I let my friend die—but I'm not the only one to blame.

Flames of wrath spark, melting some of the numbness.

"You didn't save Clay." I shake my head, blink and meet Archer's copper gaze head-on. Melting... "You promised to be there for him, to be his family, his brother, to help him when he needed you. Well, he needed you!"

Archer flinches. His Shell is damaged, but nothing like before, the flesh—or whatever it is—once again in the process of weaving back together. "I can do a lot of things, Ten, but I can't be everywhere at once, and I can't override free will."

Melting...gone! "Are you saying Clay chose to die? I assure you, he didn't. He *begged* me to save him." He begged me, and I failed him. My tears return, my chin trembling.

"He begged you, but didn't ask me."

I'm about to punch him when he adds, "I'm saying this is my fault, not the fault of my realm. I was told Killian neared, and I wasn't to engage. I disobeyed, and my new brother died because of it. I'm saying I chose to engage my enemy rather than call for reinforcements, a fact that will haunt me for the rest of my days. A mistake I'll never make again. I'm saying you had two options, and you did the right thing."

"I let my friend die," I say slowly, softly. "That will *never* be the right thing."

"He's not in any pain. He's happy, preparing for his homecoming."

I try to picture Clay smiling. I just see him lying in a pool of his own blood.

"I would have found myself in Many Ends," Sloan says, wrapping her arms around her middle. "Have you ever… visited?"

We're seated inside another four-by-four square, but I take no comfort in the warmth. I deserve the cold.

"No. I've tried," Archer tells her. "We hear the screams of the people inside, and we've even attempted to follow spirits through the veil, but we're always blocked."

Sloan shudders, and maybe she even rethinks her no-realm stance.

"If there's a way for one to enter," I say, my tone now hollowed out, "there's a way for others to enter."

"You would think so, yes." He stands, lifts his hand, the star in his palm glowing. He types inside the light, saying, "Come. We have four more miles to traverse."

The walls around us fade, and the cold sweeps in.

We remain silent as we hike, and I'm glad. My mind is churning. Like Sloan, I'm one of the Unsigned. If I die right now, I'll end up in Many Ends, most likely exchanging one torturous existence for another. But…

Maybe that's better than the alternative.

Archer failed to rescue Clay. Strike one, Troika.

Killian's actions led to the avalanche that put Clay in danger in the first place. Strike one, Myriad.

My parents. Enough said. Strike two, Myriad.

Rules that prevent TLs from saving a human life without being asked. Strike two, Troika.

We make it to the little town Archer mentioned about two hours after sunset. Heaters mounted to the tops of silver poles line the streets and illuminate our path with a soft red glow. Golden light shines from a multitude of box-shaped buildings carved into the side of the mountain. Every building is connected through some type of tunnel. There are no windows, no real *personality.*

Archer stops as the light in his hand flares. He moves into a shadowed corner to type.

"What are you doing?" I demand.

"Responding to a message from my leader."

Jellyair creation...communication between Earth and a realm. What else can the device do?

"I have to make him understand..."

Archer's frustration is clear, and I'm suddenly glad the cell phone implanted behind my ear was deactivated the day I arrived at Prynne. Vans hoped to make me feel isolated. Trapped. His mistake. If I can't be reached, I can't be tracked or ordered around.

"While you're wasting our time," Sloan says, batting her lashes at him, "would you be kind enough to tell us where we are?"

"The Urals." His typing speed increases, his fingers jabbing at invisible keys.

The Urals. A mountain range that runs through western Russia. My mind whizzes back to one of my first history lessons. Almost a century ago, snow covered the mountains, but unlike every year before, the deluge didn't melt with the change of season. The climate worsened, becoming so harsh trees and wildlife soon died. The realms finally stepped in and planted sustainable foliage.

"This town is like any other. There's a mix of Troikan and Myriad loyalists as well as Unsigned. A few weeks ago, there was a riot among the three and tensions are still high." The light fades, and Archer drops his arm to his side. His shoulders slump as he turns and shoves a bag of coins into my hand. "I'm sure the asylum has people living here, as well, to keep tabs on the citizens and in case inmates escape and live long enough to get here."

Wonderful. "We need weapons. Good ones."

"And you'll get them. At the end of the street is a bed-and-breakfast. I know the owner. He'll have everything you need… He'll get you wherever you want to go."

"He's trustworthy?" Sloan asks.

"He is."

Good. "You can go now," I tell him. I'm done with him, with all of it.

He opens his mouth only to snap it closed. He can't override free will. Part of the "love people unconditionally" law, I'm sure.

"Goodbyes are sad," Sloan says, dragging her fingertips down her cheeks in her signature move. "Let's wrap this one up before we start craving ice cream and start nomming on the streets."

I meet Archer's gaze, the copper irises haunted—and haunting. "We'll be okay on our own."

"Will you really?"

I'll make sure of it. "Go."

"I have a minute or two of leeway before I'm forced to obey." He offers me a sad smile. "Without me, Killian will be able to reach you. And he will. He's coming for you."

"I can handle him." It's the truth. It has to be the truth. "Who's the girl? Dior?" I'm not sure why the question leaves me now. Actually, I do. Killian is coming for me, and I want all the info I can get. Information is power.

A slight hesitation before Archer says, "Invite me back, and I might tell you."

"Oh, no. You don't get to play the intrigue card. You owe me."

"Just as you owe me."

How dare he! "I don't owe you any—"

"You're lying to yourself, or you're lying to me. Which is it?" He doesn't give me a chance to reply. He places his right hand over his heart and his left over his right, and a second later, he's gone.

MYRIAD

From: P_B_4/65.1.18

To: K_F_5/23.53.6

Subject: Daily Means DAILY

Not only did you kill Vans before we finished with the resource, you have now missed several reports, Mr. Flynn. Miss Lockwood is important to me—to all of us. Tell me how you're progressing with her NOW. After your fight with Archer, the Generals are debating your reassignment, among other things.

I'm debating whether or not to forget the identity of the person Fused with your mother.

Madame Pearl Bennett

MYRIAD

From: K_F_5/23.53.6

To: P_B_4/65.1.18

Subject: Threaten Me, and I'll Ruin You

You want to reassign me? Please. I've been in the field since the age of fifteen. That's four years, in case you're having trouble with the math. In those few years, I've bagged more Firstlifers than Laborers who've worked for centuries. The Generals need me, and they know it. No one else will get through to this girl. No one else had better try. They do, and I'll kill first, ask questions later. She's mine.

She's different from anyone I've ever dealt with, and I need more time to figure her out.

Also, if you try to use my mother against me again, I will do as I promised in the subject line.

Killian Flynn

MYRIAD

From: P_B_4/65.1.18

To: K_F_5/23.53.6

Subject: WHO Are You?

Usually you make snide comments, but you rarely become angry. And you've NEVER cared if we allowed another Laborer to take a shot at your assignment. You've always seen it as a personal challenge, a way to prove your superiority.

Are you falling for the girl?

That makes sense, I suppose. The General she's Fused with is my daughter, Killian. You loved Ashley once. Remember? Because I do. I've never forgotten.

Work harder to sign Ten. Please. The longer she remains Unsigned, the more time Troika has to win her. We can't allow her to side with the enemy. We just can't.

I'll kill her myself before I allow that to happen. Then I'll kill your mother.

I, too, make promises rather than threats.

MYRIAD

From: K_F_5/23.53.6
To: P_B_4/65.1.18
Subject: Your Inner Bitch Is Showing

What I remember? Nine Generals died in a single battle. Yes, your daughter was among them, but she was like a sister to me. Nothing more. She isn't the one Fused with Ten Lockwood. I'd know it; I'd feel it.

I don't.

And I *will* sign Ten. Now leave me alone and let me work.

chapter twelve

"Your Firstlife sets the stage for your Second."
—Troika

I motor through the mountain town, sticking to the shadows, Sloan on my heels. I'm a girl on a mission. (1) Avoid detection. (2) Acquire shelter. (3) Regroup.

By the time we reach the bed-and-breakfast, situated in what looks like a miniature nuclear power plant, my feet throb and my back aches. While the other buildings are box-shaped with three tiers and crumbling stone, this one is tall and round, like a cooling tower, steam wafting from the top.

Inside, lavender-scented warmth envelops me and I check number one off my list. Murals cover the walls, a summer garden here, a spring meadow there. The carpet is a stunning shade of green, made to resemble the softest grass. There are people milling around a small kitchenette that offers free tea and cookies.

Sloan pushes her way forward and snags one of the cookies. She pops the entire thing in her mouth—and gags. "Oh, gross. This is the worst thing I've ever had in my mouth."

"You must be a Myriadian, then," says the woman next to her, and judging by the derision in her tone, I'd wager she's the chef. "They wouldn't know a good thing if it bit them."

"I'm currently Unsigned."

The woman steps away from Sloan as if the girl has a contagious disease. "A clear indication you have poor taste. My cookie is packed with nutrition."

"Hate to break it to you, but *nutrition* is just another word for *feces*."

I leave the two to their argument and close in on the old lady manning the back counter. When I ask to speak with the owner, she gives me a *tsk-tsk*.

"You wanting a piece of him? Don't try to deny it. Girls just can't seem to keep their hands off his goods and services." Mirth glows in her pretty dark eyes, making her appear slightly younger than her two million years—or however long she's lived. With her stooped shoulders and heavily wrinkled skin, I'm not sure I've ever met an older human. "Mr. Brando deserves to be treated with respect, he does."

"I'll be respectful, promise. I'm..." I lower my voice, whispering, "Archer sent me." There's no need to use my own name. "I'd like a room." Among other things.

She doesn't ask for any other information but holds out her weathered hand in silent demand for money. I offer one of the coins the Laborer gave me. An Amethyst geode, cut to the size of a quarter. The deep purple glints in the light, and there's a crown engraved in the center. This came from Troika, and it's worth more than most people make in a year.

"Is that… It is! We're rich," Sloan says, coming up to my side. She stares at the old woman. "That coin better cover dinner, too. A feast fit for two queens. And clothes. We definitely need clothes."

Another *tsk-tsk*. "You'll get what you get and you'll like it, you will."

At least we'll get, and I'll be able to check off number two on my list.

"In the morning," the woman adds, "you might or might not get a visit from the owner." She smiles with another hearty dose of mirth. "I'm sure he'll see you either way."

Ten tears fall, and I call. Nine hundred trees, but only one is for me. Eight times eight times eight they fly, whatever you do, don't stay dry. Seven ladies dancing, ignore their sweet romancing. Six seconds to hide, up, up, and you'll survive. Five times four times three, and that is where he'll be. Two I'll save, I'll be brave, brave, brave. The one I adore, I'll come back for.

As I toss and turn, unable to sleep, Loony Lina's song plays through my head. A silly rhyme we recited while holding hands and spinning in a circle. As soon as we uttered, "The one I adore, I'll come back for," we collapsed on the floor and giggled. But Loony Lina's giggles had always turned into sobs.

I'm sorry you had to die, especially so horribly, she'd say. *I missed you.*

Always she'd spoken in past tense about events that had never happened. Loony Lina. So much older than me, but not any wiser.

I'm not dead, I'd tell her. *I'm right here with you.*

When I turned thirteen, my dad stopped letting her come around. He stopped talking about her completely, in fact, as if she no longer existed. And anytime I asked about her, the subject was abruptly changed.

Another conversation rises to the forefront of my mind.

You didn't become an accountant, silly. The lost dream that never should have been a dream, she'd said. *So sad.*

At the time, becoming an accountant hadn't even been on my radar.

"What *do* I become?" I'd asked.

"A somebody!"

A somebody…like a Conduit or an Abrogate?

Finally, morning sunlight pushes through the window. I give up trying to snooze and ease upright, scrubbing a hand over my eyes. A new day. A new trial to face.

I frown when I notice the digital note glowing above the nightstand.

Ten,
In case you ever want to strangle Archer.
Yours,
Killian

He snuck into the room, and I failed to detect him.

I jerk my hand through the light, and the words vanish. Two leather wrist cuffs rest on the nightstand, each with a small metal hook in the center. When I tug the hooks, a wire extends, forming a…garrote.

Zero! The bracelets are perfect for me. Absolutely perfect. I owe him…the way I owe Archer, who saved me from the cold. I admit the truth at last, even though I don't like it.

I anchor the leather beauties in place and pad through the room, a garden paradise just like the lobby. Portraits of roses hang on the walls. Wildflowers are sewn into the comforter, and lilies are woven throughout the emerald green carpet.

In the bathroom, I shower, blow-dry my hair and brush my teeth. Instead of putting my clean body in dirty clothes, I slip into one of the robes I find in the closet. By the time I'm finished, Sloan is awake.

"Hate mornings," she mumbles. "And afternoons. And evenings."

As she showers, I order breakfast and—giving it another shot—new clothes. Everything arrives an hour and a half later, but Sloan still hasn't emerged from the bathroom.

I knock on the door. "You okay in there?"

"Fine, fine," she says. The door swings open. Like me, she's wearing a robe. She's tense, her cheeks pale, but she brightens when she spies breakfast. "Food!"

The meal consists of eggs, bacon, pancakes, biscuits and gravy, everything straight from a can and absolutely delicious. In my old life, I would have rather starved.

In my old life, I was stupid.

When there's nothing left, I rub my full belly. "How are you feeling?"

"Like my clock is about to zero out, ya know?" She tugs on a buttercup-yellow shirt that has blue stripes along the sleeves, and bright blue tights decorated with lilies. "Vans won't stop looking for me."

She doesn't know. "Vans is dead."

Her eyes go wide with hope—and disappointment? "Are you sure? How do you know?"

"I saw his body. And I used his severed hand to open the gate and free you."

"Who had the honors?" Her voice is strained.

"Killian." My motions brusque, I dress in an outfit very similar to hers. A pink shirt that has green flowers sewn along the sleeves and green tights with pink stripes. The material is lightweight but stretchy, molding to my body like a second skin.

"I wanted Vans dead, but *I* wanted to be the one who killed him," she says and stomps her foot. "It's not fair."

"If life was fair, Clay would be alive."

She blanches and turns away. "So. What's the plan?"

"Meet with the owner of the hotel whether he wants to or not, weapon up, and find a way off the mountain."

"Yeah, but to where?"

"As far away from the institution and our families as we can get. I need to hide out until my eighteen birthday, and I'm sure you do, too. After that, I'm buying a house on the beach."

She thinks for a moment, nods. "Sign me up."

"You ever surfed?"

"No, and I never want to. I'll soak up the sun and cheer you on while drinking margaritas. Then, after I turn eighteen, I'll go home to Savannah and—"

Knock, knock.

I share a concerned look with Sloan before palming the scalpel I've managed to hold on to and making my way to the side of the frame. "Yes?" I call. There's a peephole, and I steel a quick glance.

A little boy?

"Have you seen my mommy?" He's trembling and looks like he's going to burst into tears at any second.

"You've got to be kidding me," Sloan mutters.

I open the door to find the boy—probably three or four—clutching a stuffed teddy bear to his chest. He's the cutest thing I've ever seen, even when he wipes his snotty nose on his shirtsleeve. His curly dark hair resembles a mop, and his eyes are big, slightly darker than his skin. They are familiar eyes. Where have I seen them?

"We haven't left our room, kid." Sloan walks over and crouches to meet him eye to eye. "We have no idea where your mom is."

He hiccups. "But…but…"

"We can help you find her," I add in a rush.

His expression changes in an instant, from somber to gleeful. He tromps into our room, saying, "Dude. I'm getting so good at this."

My brow furrows in confusion.

He snickers. "You can't tell I'm a Shell? You should be embarrassed. Well? Don't just stand there. Shut the door," he says, dropping the teddy bear to the floor to use as a stepping stool. He perches at the edge of the bed.

"You're a Shell?" Sloan shuts and locks the door. "Okay. That does it. I feel like a chicken with my head cut off. Pissed as hell and kinda lost."

Realization floods me. Those eyes…they belong to the old lady who manned the counter last night.

I move in front of the boy—woman, whatever—with my I-used-to-live-in-a-crazy-house face on. "Who are you?"

"The one who's gonna save your skinny ass. Archer said

you two are looking for a way off the mountain." Such a sneering tone is *weird* coming from such an adorable face.

"You know Archer." A statement not a question.

"Of course." He kicks his legs, one after the other. "I'm Steven, and I own this place."

"You own it?" Sloan presses a hand to her forehead. "How old are you? Really?"

"I'm seventeen." His chest puffs up with pride. "A *mature* seventeen."

This cute little snot-nosed kid is my age. I think I need to avoid the world today. There's no way I can adult. My mind is scrambled again.

"I did *not* just get played by a seventeen-year-old punk," Sloan mutters.

"An *experienced* seventeen," he adds, wiggling his brows.

I try not to vomit in my mouth. "You're with Troika?"

"Ding, ding, ding," Steven says. "Though I'm currently on sabbatical."

I stare him down. "Which means…?"

"I might or might not have gotten in trouble for selling black-market Lifeblood." He buffs his nails on his shirt. "I might or might not have called it TOP. Taste of Pleasure."

"And you're, what, planning to help us out of the goodness of your sweet little heart?" Sloan might have used a sugar tone, but she gives the boy the stink eye. "Only later we'll realize you expect us to hand over rights to our Everlife, right?"

"Weren't you listening, blondie? Or is the air in your head clogging your ears? I'm not on duty, so I'm not signing no one. All I expect from you is a hand job." He wiggles his brows.

Ugh! I do throw up in my mouth. I also throw a dirty sock at him.

He grins. "Fine. My help has nothing to do with you." He hops down and toddles to the closet—to a hidden panel with a minibar. He offers up a bottle of vodka and when we turn him down—in our sitch, sober girls survive—he drains the contents. "I owe Archer a favor. He called it in."

To trust this odd little stranger or not to trust? A choice. Not one I like, but one I'll make of my own free will.

"I've got a car out front ready to whisk you to our version of an airport, where a plane is being prepared to fly you stateside. Anywhere you'd like to go. Oh, and there's a gun for each of you below the floorboard."

Trust, I decide. For once I'll take the easy road. "Thank you."

"Yeah, yeah. My job is now officially done."

Sloan isn't so easily convinced. "Maybe I'll scoop you up and take you with us. You'll be our shield, just in case you've set any traps."

"Go ahead. Would you like a preview of what's gonna happen when you carry me outside the inn?" He tosses the empty bottle at the trash can, misses, then skips over to scoop up the teddy bear. He meets Sloan's gaze, his bottom lip turning down in a pout. Tears well in his eyes. "I tried to s-stop her, officer, but she t-touched my private p-place."

"Why you little—" Sloan launches forward, but I grab her wrist, stopping her.

Steven, eyes now dry, cackles as he strides to the door. He has to stretch on his tiptoes to reach the doorknob. He steps into the hall and pauses to look over his shoulder. "Archer visited while you were sleeping. He cashed in a favor and asked me to help you. Otherwise, I would have let you fend for yourselves." With that, he skips away.

Archer couldn't help me directly, so he was helping me remotely.

Zero! I don't want to like him. Not after everything that's happened. But I do. He's a good guy, and maybe… maybe he truly cares about me, not just my decision. Or maybe I'm deluded. How am I ever to know?

Sloan and I gather our meager belongings, don our new coats and make our way outside. The air is as bitterly cold as I remember, despite the bright rays of light and warmth spilling from the sun, but with every blast of wind, our clothes actually *heat.* I scan the surrounding sidewalks for Archer… Killian. There's no sign of either boy.

Archer can't approach me until I invite him back. Killian can show up at any time.

As promised, a black sedan waits at the curb. As we step forward, the back door opens without outward assistance. I hesitate only a moment before sliding onto the cushioned leather seats.

The partition blocking us from the driver is shaded, hiding our identities. And his. A fact that makes me nervous, but I say nothing, merely remaining on alert. Get to the airport, get to the States.

We motor forward, soon twisting and turning along a thin, treacherous road that offers no railing to prevent a plummet over the side of the mountain. There are signs posted along the way.

Light Brings Sight!

Might Equals Right!

We HART You! Humans Against Realm Turmoil!

Don't Believe the Lies! Realms Are Simply a Way to Control You!

Sloan looks away from the window and sighs. "What are you going to do after you buy your beach house and learn to surf?"

"Stuff myself on Twinkies and Ding Dongs and finally figure out my eternal future." And it'll be easy...maybe. There will be no one to pressure me.

She gives me a double thumbs-down. "I'm going to marry the first unsuitable suitor I can find." She spreads her arms and throws back her head, laughing. "Granny will be soooo ticked."

"Did she really try to force you to marry some old fart just to save her estate?"

"Oh, yes, she surely did." Anger and bitterness twist her expression. "One day, I'm going to burn down the ancestral estate. But I don't want to discuss my revenge."

Afraid I'll try to change her mind? "No prob. You were boring me, anyway."

She snorts. Then she shifts nervously in her seat and rubs her hands over her thighs. "So... I wanted to wait until I had my head wrapped around the details before I talked to you about this, but, well, I'm too eager. I have new Laborers. My TL is Deacon, and my ML is Elena. She visited before my shower, and afterward I actually called for my TL. Just said, *I'd like to speak with someone from Troika*, and he appeared."

I go on higher alert. "And?"

"Myriad offered me a house of my own design, any car I desire and a hundred-thousand-dollar bonus deposited straight into my bank account. For my Everlife, I'm to train as a Laborer."

My heart flutters. "Did you accept?"

"No, but for the first time in my life, I'm actually thinking about it. I'm not sure Many Ends is as bad as we've heard, but if there's a remote possibility, well, I need a new Everlife plan."

"What did the Deacon guy offer?"

"Same thing Archer offered Clay. Family, aid whenever requested, you know the rest."

"You interested in that?"

"Are you kidding? I hate my family. Why would I willingly sign on for another one? But, girl, Deacon is hot, so *of course* I said I'd think about it. I'm considering allowing him to plead his case…in bed."

I roll my eyes. "You're as bad as Killian."

When the car stops, I peer out the window to see a line of caves—the airport? Seriously? In one of the caves, I can make out the nose of a plane, the wings retracted to fit inside the smallish hole.

"I think we have a talent for going from bad to worse," Sloan mutters.

"Agreed." Up ahead, there's a long stretch of flat ice. Most likely the runway. Seems *perfectly* safe.

The door swings open, but this time it's courtesy of a man—the driver.

"Hallo, Ten." Killian smiles at me, slow and wicked. "So good to see you again."

Butterflies dance in my stomach a split second before anger mows over them, shredding their wings. I glare up at him. "Your actions led to the death of my friend."

His smile vanishes. "Clay is in the Everlife now. We should be happy for him."

Happy? *Happy?* "Your favorite little motto—Victors Are Adored and Failures Are Abhorred—is garbage. You might have won your skirmish with Archer, but you lost my respect."

An unreadable mask falls over his features. "I said *should be*, Ten, not that I am. I haven't been able to forget your words. *If victory is achieved the wrong way, it's not really a victory at all.* I didn't want your friend to die. Especially not that way."

"And yet you helped kill him."

His gaze lifts, staring at the other side of the mountain. "One day, you'll see him again."

"That doesn't negate the loss I feel *now.* His Firstlife mattered. To me! To him! He had hopes and dreams." I swallow a sob.

If I ultimately choose Myriad, Clay will become my enemy despite his claim to the contrary, and I hate the very idea. But war is war.

"Firstlife matters," I repeat.

"Hear, hear," Sloan calls. "I'm looking forward to wrinkled skin, gray hairs and most especially the use of diapers."

"Maybe it does matters," he says, acting as if she didn't speak, his attention steady on me, "but it's still not the end. When you live as long as we do, loss is inevitable. You have to learn to let go."

Never! "Some things are worth clinging to, no matter the cost. If you have nothing to lose, well, I pity you."

He scowls at me. "*Never* pity me."

I blow him a kiss. "Pride is a weakness."

His scowl deepens as he offers me his hand.

I take it, asking through gritted teeth, "How did you know about the car?"

He remains directly in front of me, keeping the sunlight out of my eyes. "Steven owed me a favor, ta. I cashed it in."

His accent is stronger than usual, his voice huskier. "A Troikan owed a Myriadian a favor? How did *that* happen?"

"With great skill." The mask falls away, and he looks at me with something akin to desperation. "I spy, and I wait. When circumstances appear hopeless, I offer hope…for a price. I'm owed *thousands* of debts."

A deal with the devil. But…part of me suspects he's trying, once again, to impress me with his strength, reverting to old habits. It may be kinda sorta endearing, and it softens me when I want so badly to remain fortified against him.

His gaze sinks to my wrist, and he practically vibrates with happiness. "You like your present."

I sigh. "I do." I'm not one of those girls who can't accept a gift. Gimme. "Thank you."

Sloan slides out behind me, saying, "Maybe you didn't see or hear me, handsome. Surprise! Here I am! I'd love to catch up." She moves around me to link her arm with his and draw him away from me.

He allows it, frowning at me over his shoulder, as if he's unsure how to proceed.

Again, it's endearing.

"We've been so *vulnerable* on our own," she continues. "We're so weak, and here you are, a big strong slice of beefcake, ready to save the day." When they reach the wall of the cave, where the nose of the aircraft peeks out, she pushes him with all her might, and presses a toothbrush shank against his carotid. "Or not. Lookit. I know your type. Sweet when things are going your way, but meaner than a wet panther when they're not." The sugar has abandoned her tone completely, leaving only anger. "I'd rather die than allow you to hurt Ten. Rephrase. I'd rather kill you than allow you to hurt Ten."

"Is that so?" In a lightning-fast move, he grabs her wrist and rotates her so that her back presses against his chest and her cheek against the icy, rocky wall. "Let me tell you what *I'd* rather do."

"Don't harm her," I shout, rushing over.

He lets her go in an instant, holding up his hands, palms out, and my relief is palpable.

A scowling Sloan pivots, pointing the shank at him once more.

"No," I say, moving between them. "Put the weapon away, Sloan. He's not here to hurt me."

He yanks me behind him, safeguarding me from the shank. As if she'd hurt me now. Still. The protective gesture is—freaking—endearing.

I'm so sick of the word!

"Enough, you two. Please." I wait until both nod before leaving them to their own devices and entering the cave.

There's someone checking something under the plane.

"Hello," I call, a sense of unease sliding over me. I'm not sure why. Kind of reminds me of the fear I experienced when I ran from Killian, and yet I'm not fearful. Just wary.

Are Messengers from Troika here, attempting to guide me?

"I thought I heard voices out there." An unfamiliar man

closes the hatch and strides over to greet me. He's tall with gray hair and craggy skin. "You must be my newest cargo."

"Yes." I extend my hand for one reason and one reason only, and it's not to be friendly. We shake, and I conclude he's human rather than a Shell, his skin calloused and warm. He's also an Unsigned, his hands and wrists free of brands.

But…my unease only grows stronger. I ignore it, determined to leave this place.

"Where are we headed?" Killian asks, his voice devoid of emotion.

"I've got enough fuel to take you anywhere you want to go."

"Hawaii," I say, making a split-second decision. I'll be far from LA—and my parents—but close to water.

"It's settled then," the pilot says. "Go ahead and board and we'll take off."

chapter thirteen

"Reality exists within the scope of your senses.
If you feel it, it's real."
—Myriad

We're in the air fifteen short minutes later. The aircraft is small and the flight is bumpy, and I'm laid bare by a certainty I'd rather not face: I'm afraid of heights. Well, afraid of falling.

The way Clay fell…

I shudder.

"Cold?" Killian asks. He's perched in the seat next to mine, toying with the ends of my hair. "Or frightened?"

"Screw you," I mutter. Why can't I be like Sloan? She's as happy as a boss in the copilot seat.

Fear hinders, never helps. Look past it.

"I can distract you," he says. "Or we can sit in silence."

"I pick silence."

"Very well."

True to his word, he says nothing *for hours.* Despite my annoyance, I manage to nap for several more. But, after I wake up, another hour slips by as I shift uncomfortably and visualize the many ways to die in a plane, I finally admit the cold-shoulder treatment is only hurting myself.

I give up, saying, "Earn your keep. Do something to distract me."

His chuckle is warm, not the cold thing I expect. "Dance, monkey, dance?"

"Good. You understand."

"How about we negotiate terms for your covenant?"

Why not? I'm a little curious and a lot desperate. "All right. Tell me what, exactly, Myriad is willing to offer me."

He goes still. "You're serious?"

I swallow a snort. "Yes. I'm serious."

As if he's afraid I'll change my mind, he rushes to say, "Your contract will last your Second-death. We will ensure your Firstlife is filled with fame and riches that far surpass anything your parents ever achieved, and in your Everlife, you'll be given a place of honor inside the palace, as well as any other home you desire. If you want it, you get it, even if it's occupied. You will never lack for anything. You will have servants, and you will answer only to our King."

"I have no desire for fame and riches." I've already experienced the heavy cost of each. "And I don't want to steal someone's home."

I think I've surprised him again. He regards me quizzically. "Name your desire then. Your wish is my command."

No way I'll tell him about the beach house. I want to buy it with my inheritance and owe no one. "What about a job?"

"As an Abrogate, you'll need to train for other positions.

Messenger. Laborer. Scout. Leader. The more you know about each, the better Abrogate you'll be."

"But…how do you even know I'm an Abrogate?"

"For starters, you're Fused with a General."

He drops the news as if I'm supposed to coo with excitement. Thing is, I'm not even slightly startled. I should have guessed this was always about the spirit I'm supposedly Fused with, not me.

"Again I ask how you know—beyond any doubt."

A slight pause. "We…don't. We can only guess, but all our Generals were wiped out at once, and their Second-death coincided with your birth."

"Yeah, well, I'm sure my birth coincides with a lot of Second-deaths."

"Yes, but your spirit glowed through your skin. That only happens when a soul is Fused with one of the more powerful positions."

"Or, as Troikans believe, the soul is a Conduit." At least, I'm guessing.

He gives a formal nod.

"Abrogates are Generals, and Generals are decisive, right? They make battle plans. They lead the masses. They aren't torn about a major decision. Like me."

"You don't know *what* Generals are. You've never spoken to one." He pauses. "Would you like to? I can arrange a meeting."

Again curiosity gets the better of me. "Yes. All right. But only if you answer one more question for me."

"Anything."

I lick my lip, a small tremor moving through me. "Do you like me, or am I just a job to you?"

He grapples for a response, finally settling on, "The two aren't mutually exclusive."

No, they aren't. "Do. You. Like. Me?"

"I...do," he says and scowls, as if the admission is painful. Maybe it is. Friends have the power to hurt you in ways enemies never can.

He curses suddenly and throws a glance over his shoulder to the seat in back. "Enough! Leave us."

My eyes go wide. "Someone's here?"

He faces me again, his expression stony. "No."

Word games. "Who *was* here?"

"One of my Flankers." He flicks his tongue over an incisor. "Before you ask, Flankers are a subdivision of Laborer. They follow me to chronicle my exploits."

One, I'd had no idea he had a tail. And two, someone actually *chronicles* his *exploits*? Like he's what, a knight of the days of old with a troubadour?

I laugh at him—I can't help it—and soon, he's laughing with me.

When we hit a particularly nasty bump, I gasp. He winds an arm around my shoulders and I let him, offering no protest. I even lean against him of my own volition, resting my head in the hollow of his neck, where the scent of peat smoke and heather soothes me.

"Why don't you take another nap?" he says. "I like listening to your one-sided conversations."

He's heard my sleep talking? Great! "What have I said?"

"Ten's tears fall..."

"No. Ten tears fall. The number ten."

"No. You clearly said *Ten's tears*. Your name."

I did? "Yeah, well, you leak liquid glitter when you're injured."

"Glitter? How dare you. My manliness is offended."

"Your manliness will survive."

He caresses my shoulder, almost as if he's petting me. "A spirit doesn't function like a body. While we have muscle and bone, we're sustained only by Lifeblood, and when we lose it, we hemorrhage power."

I try not to react to his touch…yeah, I *try*. "So, when you lose all your Lifeblood…"

"We experience Second-death."

"So you can die, even inside the Shell."

"Yes. I've lost many friends that way."

The news…isn't welcome. What happens afterward? Fusion, or the Rest?

Another air pocket causes us to lurch, and I go cold inside.

He attempts another distraction. "You should drop Sloan. She'll always put her wants above your needs."

"Someone else's actions will never decide my own." A facet of my free choice. One I embrace wholeheartedly.

The blue light flashes on his wrists, and he curses.

"A message?" I ask.

"Yes."

"You aren't going to respond?"

"No. It's from Madame."

"Madame…what?"

"Madame Arse Pain." His teeth are clenched, his tone filled with disgust. "She's my Leader."

"Don't like working for a woman, huh?"

"Don't like her, period."

"What'd she do—"

"Oh, no. I'm not airing my dirty past with her. You still have to deal with her."

Ah. Madame Bennett.

The light flashes a second time, and he slaps his wrist. "She wants another progress report."

Another. Just how many of our interactions has he shared with her? "Full disclosure. I'm walking away from *you* when we land."

"Me? What'd I do?"

"What you know, Myriad knows and what Myriad knows, my parents know."

"Your parents haven't been told of your escape…yet."

That's something, at least. "Why the reprieve?"

"Prynne has only informed parents of the deceased, and I requested Myriad keep quiet about you. Your parents… annoy me. Your mother is hiding something, and your father is an adulterous prick."

Shock and horror nearly choke me. "He's cheating on my mom?"

Killian goes still. "You didn't know?"

I shake my head as the plane hits another nasty air pocket, the nose dipping. My internal organs shrivel and for a moment, my mind spins round and round on a carnival ride.

He tightens his grip on my shoulders. "Turbulence is natural, lass. We aren't going to crash."

"Don't use the C-word!"

His chuckle is as beautiful as the rest of him. "I think everyone in the realms heard you. But don't worry. I'm the big strong manly man and I'll keep my weak little girl safe."

"Jerk," I mutter, but I begin to relax against him. I won't

think about my dad's infidelity and the mental hatchet job it must be doing on my mom.

Killian leans down, his mouth hovering over my ear. I think he's going to kiss the lobe but he whispers, "Do us both a favor and sign with Myriad."

My heart hammers as I lift my head. "Killian—"

Our gazes connect, the air between us heating, crackling. He presses his forehead against mine and cups my nape, his thumb stroking up, into my hair and down, under the collar of my shirt.

"I don't just want you," he says. "I *want* you."

"I don't understand the difference," I tell him honestly. Even still, his admission makes me tingle.

"The first I can easily walk away from. The second… you make me feel—*you make me feel*."

The words aren't pretty, but they're ragged. His tone isn't sweet, but raw.

I'm nearly undone. Is he being for real? Or is this just another con to win me over?

The plane jiggles again, but at first, I don't really care. Not anymore. When it continues, growing increasingly more violent, I freaking care. I freaking care *a lot*. The bin above us pops open and my backpack spills out as the nose of plane dips at a more acute angle. If not for our seat belts, we would have pitched forward.

This isn't normal.

I'm nearing full-blown panic when the pilot steps from the cockpit, a bag slung over his shoulders. He moves swiftly, avoiding our gazes.

Killian releases me, saying to the man, "What are you doing?"

The pilot wrenches open the side door and I'm blasted by a cold punch of wind and a hard kick of shock. My hair slaps at my cheeks as he—

Jumps!

"Help! Help! Killian, Ten. He hit me!" Sloan's screaming voice cuts through the brutal bellow of the airstream. "He's gone!"

Yes. He's gone. He, our only means of landing. The shock collides with panic, and my brain nearly shuts down. I focus on Killian. "What should we do?"

"Stay here." He jerks at his seat belt, his expression grim. "And sign with Myriad. Verbalize your agreement to the terms I presented. Don't risk your Everlife, Ten. Please. If I can't land the plane..." He shakes his head, as if he's unwilling to consider the possibility. "Please," he repeats.

I remind myself I'm no longer a damsel in distress. I can think this through. What I can't do? Base my decision on fear. Because, while I might be free to make my choice right now, I'll never be free from the consequences of that choice. And I think I'd rather wind up in Many Ends than in Troika, warring with Killian, or in Myriad, warring with Archer and Clay.

"D-do you know how to fly a plane?" I shout over the squall.

He remains grim-faced. "As a Laborer, I've trained for all kinds of situations."

I'll take that as a no.

His buckle finally gives, but the plane has taken another dip and dive. He bangs into the wall that divides front from back. A wall he grips, pulling himself around the edge; a Herculean task considering the gale-force wind.

He disappears from sight and a few seconds later, Sloan peeks out from behind the wall. Foolish girl! She's going to be sucked out!

I lean over and stretch out my arms. "Grab the hooks on the bracelets!"

As soon as she has a firm hold, I tug while she kicks at the wall. Midair, her body begins to edge toward the opened door. I yank with all my might, using a reservoir of strength I didn't know I possessed.

She plows into Killian's vacant seat. Shaking, she buckles up. She's pale, her cheeks stained with dried tears.

Eyes haunted, she asks, "Do you think we're going to die? Say no, and I'll believe you. You never lie."

I meet her gaze and remain silent.

She covers her mouth with an unsteady hand. "We should pick a realm, either realm. Many Ends..."

"Yes," I tell her. "Choose." Not knowing what else to do but remembering Archer's final words to Clay, I whisper, "Archer. I'm asking you for help. Please."

There's no bright light, and he doesn't magically appear.

Sloan must have read my lips. A tremor rocks her against me. "Where is he? Ten, *where is he*?"

Her panic is kindling for my own, but I manage to tamp it down. "We don't have to see him to know he's here." I've learned the hard way.

"What if he's only allowed to help Troikans?"

"We're potentials. We qualify." We must.

"I want to see him. I *need* to see him."

I...don't, I realize, shocked. I trust him. Despite everything—or maybe because of everything—I know he's doing everything within his power to save us. The real question is—will it be enough?

The plane continues to plummet. My pulse points race harder and faster, as if I've been injected with a thousand vials of *baiser de la mort*.

I glance out the window and see no sign of clouds—only land. Green. Lush. Pretty. We are going to crash. There'll be no stopping it. Any moment now…

"Brace for impact," I tell Sloan.

"Ten." Tears cascade down her cheeks.

"Have you chosen?"

Long locks of her pale hair slap her cheeks as she shakes her head.

Some people say your entire life flashes inside your head just before the end. Mine doesn't. I don't have an amazing epiphany with all the answers. I know only that I'm not ready to die, and that I won't—I can't—allow courage to fail me. Today I fight to live and live to fight.

I *won't* die.

I tuck Sloan against me and wrap myself around her and notice—

No. Dang him, no!

Killian struggles to return to us. The blue flecks in his eyes are completely overshadowed by the darkness of his pupils.

"Leave," I shout. "Leave now." I won't let him die inside his Shell. "Go. Go!"

He doesn't, using his leeway the same way Archer did.

"Sign with Myriad. Please." He throws himself over us—

Boom!

I'm pitched back and forward almost simultaneously, the

force so powerful I'm surprised I'm not snapped in two. Metal grinds and crunches, the sounds an assault to my ears. Fire dances through the belly of the plane as both engines explode. My adrenaline is so high, I shouldn't feel a lick of heat or the bite of the belt or the slam of my body into the seat in front of me as the plane compacts, but the pain…it consumes me in an instant, swallows me—

I open my mouth to scream for help, but end up swallowing a mouthful of water. Water? We crashed into an ocean?

Crazy thought: *Now I can surf.*

I laugh hysterically as dizziness sweeps over me. Darkness is fast on its heels—

I come to with a realization that I'm floating…no, I'm dropping, down, down…*thud.*

Lying on my back, I crack open my eyes and discover I'm in the middle of a moon-drenched jungle, gnarled trees and thick foliage all around me. The only light comes from thousands of lightning bugs, many of which are buzzing around me.

Ouch! Several land on my arm, burning me. Not lightning bugs, after all. I think they are…living embers? I wave my hands to shoo them away and find blisters in their place.

The air is dry, white-hot, and sweat is pouring from me. Screams, so many screams, waft on the breeze. They are pain-filled, agonized, a story as certain as numbers—this is suffering in its purest form. Snakes, their forked tongues hissing at me, slither along branches that are stretching, stretching in my direction. Some kind of monkey-like creatures are highlighted by the ember-bugs and they are staring at me from between leaves that look like they have razor-sharp teeth.

Where am I? This doesn't look like *any*place I've ever been.

"Sloan?" I call her name as I scramble to my feet. "Killian? Archer?"

There's no response.

The monkeys jump to the ground a few yards away from me, and I realize they aren't monkeys, after all. They have the bottom half of a giant spider—which is a nightmare all its own. Eight legs, each hairy and lined with sharp ivory horns.

I take a step back. They follow me.

This isn't part of the Land of the Harvest, is it?

Could this be Many Ends?

For once, an answer is easy. No. This isn't Many Ends. I'm not dead; I'm very much alive.

Boom!

The ground shakes so hard I'm knocked off my feet. The monkey-spiders dart behind the foliage, many of the stems now withdrawing into turtle-like shells. I turn to see a thick, horribly dark cloud mushroom toward the sky, and when it reaches yellowed clouds, it tips over like a waterfall and rains down, down, down upon the tops of the trees, where it breaks into a million pieces, those pieces darting in every direction, the smoke somehow morphing into big, black birds with skeletal bodies, spiked beaks and metal claws.

Snakes are grabbed with those claws. Monkeys are snagged with those beaks. I swallow a scream and run, counting my steps and turns. Eight steps, right turn. Eleven steps, left turn. I'm not sure how I got here, or how I'll leave, but I need to know how to return to the spot I first arrived. Just in case it's the key to going home…home… Where is home?

Twenty-three steps, another right. Some patches of air are shimmery, like curtains, but I feel no different when I pass through them, so I'm not sure what they do.

Six sharp pinpricks spear me in the back as I'm swept into the air. I scream and flail, panic threatening to overtake me. Ember-bugs slam into me, leaving blisters behind.

What should I do? What should I do!

Fight!

Right. I palm my scalpel—zero! I came with the clothes on my back, but not my weapon. *Okay, it's okay.* I grab hold of a branch as we pass, our momentum allowing me to rip off the tip as well as the skin on my palm. Which doesn't bleed, I notice, but leaks a thick, shimmery liquid.

Lifeblood.

I *am* dead. And this…this *is* Many Ends.

The knowledge rips through me, tearing my insides to shreds. I reel, the shock of my new reality almost too much to process. This means… No, no, no. My Firstlife is over, and I've officially entered the Everlife.

I can't… I don't… I need to…

Get it together!

A freak-out isn't helping. My strength is draining—hemorrhaging—and I have to act quickly. I can worry and lament whenever I'm free.

I twist as best I can, take in a face that is nothing but a thorny beak and pitted bone, and swing up my arm, stabbing the branch into the creature's side. A squawk rings out, as warm, black liquid gushes over my hand, burning like acid. Those claws open, at least, and slide out of my back. I drop.

When I slam into a patch of gnarled treetops, I lose my breath and quickly roll into branch after branch…finally landing on the ground with a thud. A rock has gouged my side, stealing what little oxygen I managed to suck in.

Though the dizziness has returned with a vengeance, I'm able to sit up and take stock of my new location. I frown. *Nothing* is different. Same gnarled trees, same toothy plants now slithering toward me—it's as if running and turning this way and that and being flown roughly three hundred feet took me right back to where I started.

A groan escapes me as I stand. A flock of the bone-birds squawks overhead.

Sticking with my calculations of three hundred feet, I backtrack. Bugs buzz around me—lizard-like bees, flies with saber teeth—and I pass through countless shimmery patches of air. The placement of trees and the fall of branches remain the same.

Go somewhere, yet go nowhere.

My ears twitch as a high-pitched scream pierces the air, one that is louder than all the others. One that is closer to me. Is someone else here?

"Sloan?" I call. Guilt slaps me. Did I lead her here?

A rustle of tree limbs. A hard weight slams into me from behind, pushing me facedown. I gasp, but when I look around, there's nothing and no one there. More rustling sounds. Another *slam, slam*, as if I'm being punched. I wheeze and spit dirt and—water gushes out of my mouth.

I'm forced to my side as I cough, my throat coated in acid, my lungs on fire.

"That's it. That's the way." Hard hands continue patting at my back, and I expel another gush of water. The black fades from my vision, revealing a rocky beach, a large body of water with metal and debris, smoke rising from the top, curling toward a wealth of skyscrapers. "You're alive. You're alive now."

I am? I died and came back to life?

Again, my shock is almost too much to process. This time, I can't stop my freak-out. I was dead. I was dead, and I was in Many Ends. Many Ends is real. A real place. A gruesome, awful place.

I don't want to return. Ever.

"Sloan," I manage to croak.

The hands smooth over my back more gently, offering comfort now. "She's alive." Archer's voice registers.

He came! Sloan survived!

"You died," he says, as unsteady as I am, "but you're back. You're back, and you're all right."

Tears of relief burn my eyes. *I'm all right, I'm all right.* The words echo through my mind, but I'm not sure I believe them. And oh, no, no, no, did my bowels release? I jerk my gaze down, expecting the worst. I'm soaked with ocean…lake?…water but I'm clean. My spirit must have stayed connected to my body, despite the distance between the two.

"My friend Deacon is seeing to Sloan's care," Archer says.

"Killian?" I ask.

A pause. A pause that grabs hold of my heart and squeezes. Then—

"His Shell is toast, and his spirit isn't in the area."

I almost grab him, almost shake him. "Tell me his spirit survived."

"I…can't. If he disconnected from the Shell before impact, there's hope. Did he disconnect?"

I swallow a sob. The boy who once considered Firstlife a nuisance did his best to save mine. He stayed with me every second, keeping his strong arms wrapped around me.

He didn't want me to wind up in Many Ends. And he might have lost his Secondlife for it.

chapter fourteen

"If you can see or feel it, you can change it."
—Troika

I'm not ready to move or stand but Archer says, "We need to go before the authorities arrive," so I do both. With the movement, the cuts I've sustained tear deeper into muscle, and my bones vibrate. My limbs are waterlogged. They weigh two tons, at least.

"The plane was on fire when it crashed into the water," Archer says. "If we hadn't buffered you, you would have died."

"Thank you." The words aren't good enough, but they're all I've got. I grind my molars as pain shoots through me. "Where are we?" Had the pilot gone off course?

"East Coast. New York." He leads me to Sloan, who's seated inside a circle of rocks, her knees drawn up to her chest as water froths around her feet. There's a cut on her forehead and obscene streaks of blood over each of her cheeks. Her gaze is focused above, where rainbow beams of light dance through the sky. Either the northern lights have moved or there's another realm battle going on.

"The pilot told me he was sorry, but he'd been offered the only thing he ever wanted." Her chin trembles. "I didn't understand at the time. He hit me, and when I opened my eyes, he was gone and we were…we were…"

"I know." He willingly, purposely signed our death warrants. But…why? "Who would want us dead before we'd signed away our futures?"

"Myriad," Archer says. "They're tired of waiting for you to make a choice and don't want to risk a covenant with Troika."

No. "I don't believe that. Killian fought to save us." He's alive. He has to be alive.

"Yes, and I'm sure he'll be punished for it. He's been different with you, going against orders, even killing Vans."

Rocked to the bone, I look up to the sky and shout, "If Killian is hurt, I will *never* sign with Myriad."

There's a whistle of wind, and it scrapes against my nerves. But there's no voice. No eruption of lights that spell out, *He's safe.*

A really tall, really muscled guy—Deacon?—approaches us. His features are rough; they are those of a warrior who's lived on the battlefield and danced in the blood of his enemies. His hair is cropped and dark, but his eyes are the color of summer, green and lush with life, the perfect foil to his ebony skin. His nose is a little too long and his mouth a little too thin but both work for him, and work well. He'll never be on the cover of a magazine, but I'm willing to bet he's the star of many fantasies.

He assists Sloan to her feet and drapes a jacket over her

shoulders, speaking to Archer in a language I've never heard before. A beautiful language that rolls from his tongue.

Archer replies in the same language.

"Come," he finally says to me.

"What—" I begin.

He already knows what I'm going to ask. "The Troikan language. That way, if any spirits from Myriad lurk nearby, they won't understand what we're saying."

We're hustled to a van he's procured. The back is empty, perfect for lying down.

The driver introduces himself—yep, he's Deacon. As he takes corners a little too swiftly, Archer does his best to patch our wounds. He doesn't have the most delicate touch, and the bumpy ride only makes his inelegant ministrations worse. I wince when he ties the bandage around my arm a little too tight.

Boom!

The van rattles, and both Sloan and I gasp.

"A battle between the realms," Archer confirms. "My boss's men are stopping Madame Bennett's men from getting close to you."

No wonder the battles seem to follow me. They are. "What about Killian?"

"No one has reported seeing him."

Fear and disappointment combine, threatening to flatten me. "Why don't you just give us your Lifeblood?" That's how he healed Sloan of her frostbite.

"We lost too much fighting our way to you before the crash and even more as we fished you out of the water."

Now that I've hemorrhaged, I understand.

"If we lose any more," he says, "we'll be useless for days.

Since your injuries aren't life threatening, I'm not going to weaken myself. You need me strong."

"I get it," I say, and I do.

We lapse into silence. Sloan is shivering, so I draw her closer. I should be as traumatized as she is, but despite everything, I'm somehow calm. Well, calmish. And tired, the vibrations from the road doing their best to lure me to sleep. I fight to remain awake. Part of me suspects I'll open my eyes and find out I'm back in Many Ends.

"All right, folks." Deacon's voice echoes through the van as the vehicle comes to an abrupt stop. "We've arrived."

I sit up gingerly and exit with Archer's help. Deacon climbs into the back, scoops up Sloan and carries her out. We're—in the middle of nowhere, nothing but green grass and mountains for miles. It's pretty, but it's not my idea of a well-guarded hideout where we can recover in peace.

Silver lining: I'm not freezing.

"This way." Archer steps forward and vanishes.

Right. Jellyair. With a sigh, I follow him and suddenly I'm standing in front of a dream come true: a two-story log cabin with twinkling lights strung around the roof. Fields of lavender scent the air. Lush green trees have actual beehives hanging from the branches. Around the cabin itself are troughs with wild strawberries overflowing from the sides, and my mouth waters for a taste.

This is a *home.* Where doting parents sit on the porch, rocking in handmade chairs while watching their children run and play.

Archer takes the lead but stops with his hand on the doorknob and looks over his shoulder at me. "This is a

Troikan safe house. No one from Myriad will be able to pass through the borders."

Meaning, Killian. "What keeps the Myriadians out?"

"The beams are infused with light. A Myriadian touches them, and they burn. Badly."

"But Shells aren't burned by light." Only spirits, according to Killian.

Deacon laughs as if I've said something funny. Have I? There's so much I don't know about the realms.

"This is a special light," Archer says with a glare directed at his friend. "Myriad Shells disintegrate in seconds." He stomps into the house, done with the conversation.

I stay where I am, looking past the wall for any sign of Killian.

"We have safe houses all over the world. They aren't opulent, but they should have everything you need." Deacon comes up beside me and sets Sloan on her feet. "Go inside, girl."

"As long as this place has hot water and a tub," she says, trudging forward, "this can be a slaughterhouse for all I care."

When she's on the porch, I say to Deacon, "Do you bring humans here often?"

"Only the ones who have been marked for death. You're welcome, by the way."

"So high and mighty. Troika is just as likely a suspect."

"That's not the way we roll." Deacon looks at me, adding, "A lot of people have gone to serious trouble for you, but they'll let you go if that's what you want."

"Even though I'm a Conduit?" Supposedly. More than

ever, I *don't* feel like one of the most powerful people on the planet.

"Even though. We'll die to preserve your right to choose. If your choice destroys you—destroys us—so be it. And it will. Destroy us both, I mean. We've lost two Conduits in the past five hundred years. We have only two others. If even one is killed, we won't have enough light to sustain our people for more than a few decades."

Pressure…

He sighs. "I hope you're worth everything we're doing."

"I'll save you the trouble of wondering. I'm not." I'm undecided and pretty much changing sides as often as I change underwear.

Considering the scare I just had, I'm probably due for another.

"With that attitude?" he says. "No. You're not."

"You'd rather I do the narcissistic song and dance? I'm so amazing and wonderful." I fluff my hair and bat my lashes at him. "*Of course* I'm worth the trouble."

He rolls his eyes. "You have your moments, but I'd rather you saw yourself as Archer does."

"And how is that?" Maybe I would, too.

"When he was first assigned to you, he saw you as a spoiled rich girl with a little too much crazy. Mommy and Daddy are mean to me, boo-hoo. All this torture, wah-wah."

"Screw you both. Pain is pain, and if you've never been whipped or beaten or injected with poison, your opinion in this matter doesn't mean jack."

"I make light, because you didn't have to go through any of it. You could have signed with us—"

“I could have, yes, but I didn’t because I don’t know where I fit. I don’t know where I belong.”

“You do. Everyone knows. Everyone always knows. Deep down, where it matters. But they want something else, a seemingly better offer, perhaps, so they talk themselves into doubt and confusion—darkness of the mind. Then, finally, the doubt and confusion morph into certainty you were wrong to begin with.”

“No.” I shake my head.

“I’ve lived longer than you. I’ve seen more. I know, and you know. You just don’t want to face the truth.”

“And what if the truth is Myriad?”

“Then for you, it’s Myriad.”

I scoff at him. “You’re not going to try to change my mind?”

“I never debate the truth. You know your answer, so grow a pair of balls and accept it. Stop wasting our time. Now, are you going to let me finish telling you my story?” he asks.

I wave my hand in regal command.

“After the institution, Archer told me there’s something about you…an inner strength very few people possess. A goodness untouched by the evil around you. A generosity of spirit that allows you to put the safety of others above the safety of yourself. And I hope he’s right, because word came down today. For Archer’s part in your friend’s untimely death, he will experience the Exchange.”

I use my time at the safe house to recover from my wounds and plan my next move.

Myriad wants me dead and without Troika’s assistance,

I can't hide from them. I'm only human. But then, I don't want to hide from the realm, and I don't want to rely on one over the other. I want to see Killian, thank him, maybe hug him and slap him for risking his life.

There's been no sign of him, no rumors about his life—or his death.

I absolutely refuse to consider he died and he's now Fused with a newborn, that he has a new Firstlife tied to someone else. He's out there. What's he doing?

I miss the jerk.

By the dawn of the seventh day, I realize I have only one viable option. It's simple, but it just might work. I will request the one thing I've wanted since this whole travesty began: time to think without interference. I'll promise to voice my decision the day before my eighteen birthday. Of course, the closer we get to the date, the more danger I'll face, the realms fearing my defection. But the fact remains: any time I gain is more than I currently have.

It'll mean saying goodbye to Killian and Archer—shredding my heart when I lose the best friends I've had in forever—but it'll only be for a little while. At least for one of them.

With a sigh, I press the tip of a steak knife into my finger, a drop of blood welling. A drop I wipe on the wall beside my bed, leaving a smear of crimson behind.

My new calendar. Sunlight streams through my bedroom window, highlighting the numbers.

"Do you not know how to relax?"

Archer's voice fills my room, and I slowly pivot to face him. He's standing in the doorway, arms crossed.

"No. Just like you don't know how to share important

details with your friends." I'm miffed with him. He refuses to tell me anything about the Exchange.

"Fine. It will be bad. Blood for blood. A crime was committed, and a punishment must be meted out. That is law, even for Myriad, though they would deny it. Every human is precious, priceless, and I'll pay a price that reflects that. Happy now?"

Not even close. Maybe the crash knocked some sense into me, because I no longer want him penalized. He's suffered enough. "What about mercy?"

"Trust me. In this, I'm being shown great mercy. I should be dead, like the one I helped kill, and yet I live."

"But—"

"This is justice, Ten. You can't pick and choose the parts you like and ignore the rest. That opens the door for partiality."

He makes a good point. Not that I'll admit it. "Why are you here?"

"Two reasons. The first, to ask if you want to reactivate your cell phone. I'll have to put you to sleep but it won't take more than a few minutes."

"No, thanks." I still don't want my parents or Prynne able to call or track me.

"Now the second. I'm going to teach you how to fight."

What is it with these Shell boys and their lack of respect for my *skills*? "I know how to fight." I hold up the butcher knife. "Want a demonstration?"

He nods. "I do. But allow me to amend my statement. I'm going to teach you how to fight…and win."

"I know how—"

"Win *every time*," he adds.

Fair enough. I could use the practice before I leave him. I sheathe the blade at my waist. "What's this lesson going to cost me?" Let's get the nitty-gritty out of the way.

"Only a poem. Something cheery for once."

I arch a brow. "Does it have to rhyme?"

"Of course. Good poems *always* rhyme."

He and Loony Lina would adore each other. "All right. Here goes." I clear my throat. "You, the he-man, will teach me how to fight. Me, a little girl with little might. But what you don't know about this lass is that she's super determined to kick your ass."

He barks out a laugh and waves his fingers at me. "Come on, then. The toll has been paid in full."

I slide my feet out of my favorite house slippers, a luxury I haven't experienced in over a year. Funny how I used to take such things for granted. I've known great wealth, and I've known great loss. I've had tastes of happiness and sorrow in both states.

Emotions never discriminate.

I tug on a pair of combat boots and follow him downstairs. I've memorized the layout of the house to ensure I'll be able to find my way to any room blindfolded. Never know when something like that will become necessary. There are four bedrooms upstairs, each with its own bathroom. Sloan has spent the bulk of her time in bed, and Deacon has spent the bulk of his seeing to her wounds and coaxing her to eat.

"You'd choose Troika again today, even if you were given the chance to change your mind," I say. "Wouldn't you?"

"I would. I love my realm. I love my family. I love my job."

Would Killian say the same?

Killian. Where are you?

We stride through the spacious living room furnished with an oversize leather sofa, two recliners and a blazing fireplace. Archer swipes a large black bag from a coffee table made from logs. He turns left, and the scent of bacon and eggs almost draws me in the opposite direction. If I were to go right, I'd enter the kitchen, a paradise of gray stone, rose-veined marble and oak cabinets, rustic yet opulent. Deacon must be cooking breakfast.

"Later," Archer announces, sensing the direction of my thoughts.

I whimper like a spoiled baby.

He stalks outside and, a few yards from the house, drops the bag. His legs are encased in leathers that reveal every flex of his muscles as he crouches to dig out a gun, two daggers and a thing I can't identify.

I really like this guy. He's more emotionally secure than Killian, but then, I think he's had a better support system. He doesn't need me, but I'm pretty sure he could use me, and not just because of his realm. After the way he handled those boys in Prynne, the ones who called him names, I can guess how badly he wants to dish out Troikan light to those in need. And even to Myriadians. He just hasn't found a way to do it. He needs a bridge.

He glances up, notices I'm staring and smiles slowly, his copper eyes alight with amusement. "Please don't tell me you want a piece of me."

"Gross! I most certainly do not."

"Good. What about Killian? You wanting a piece of him?"

I…think I do, but I also think Archer isn't ready to hear the answer.

He wags a finger at me. "I'm not going to warn you about him. Not again."

Guess my expression gave me away. "Thank you. I appreciate—"

"But I *am* going to tell you about my feud with him. He—"

I'm about to tell him to spill now, now, now when a tornado rolls over the top of the dome. I gape. Fence posts and other debris swirl inside a vortex of wind I can't feel.

"Only an F-2," Archer says. "There's a battle going on between the realms, but it hasn't reached critical."

"What's the battle about this time?"

"Myriad wants you out of our safe house."

The fact that I'm the cause is a weight around my ankles, pulling me deeper and deeper into a sea of guilt. Soon I'm going to drown. I hate the thought of innocent people being hurt because of me.

I make a decision to leave the safe house *tonight*.

I'll send a flash-scribe message to Madame about my intentions, and I'll leave a note for Archer. Can't take a chance they'll try to stop me.

"Well. Tell me about your feud with Killian," I say.

He works his jaw. "There was a girl."

Nailed it. "Dior?" I ask, remembering the name the two spat at each other.

"Yes. We were both assigned to her. I loved her. When she laughed, she had a dimple right here." He touches his cheek. "She dreamed of being a doctor, of tending anyone of any realm who couldn't afford medical care."

Hesitantly I ask, "He stole her away from you?"

His nod is clipped. "Then he tricked her into signing with Myriad."

I almost can't breathe, my chest is so tight, but I manage to say, "He was just doing his job, what he thought was right."

Archer's nostrils flare. "Usually Myriad Laborers earn more for getting humans to accept the least possible amount, but he ensured she received the worst possible deal just to spite me, adding fine print she didn't understand."

"So she didn't get a fancy house or car. So what? There's more to life."

"*You* don't understand. She's in medical school right now, but even then, if she saves the life of a Troikan loyalist, she earns a penalty in Firstlife *and* Everlife. There's nothing I can do to help her."

What Killian did...yeah, it was bad. There's no getting around that fact. But he's not the same Killian. Firstlife didn't mean anything to him back then. Now he's learning to value human life. Why else would he put himself in harm's way to save me?

"Can you get her out of her contract?" I ask. "What about court?"

"I begged her to demand a day in court, but she's too afraid of the repercussions of losing."

"I'd like to meet her." Somehow I'd like to help her.

"I'll arrange it." He straightens, waves a hand over the weapons. "Now. Where would you like to start?"

"I don't know what half those things are."

"This is an Oxi." He holds up one of the guns. "With a single blast, it causes Shells to decay."

And what if I misfire and hit *myself*? "No, thanks."

"This one, the Stag, shoots darts that, when embedded in a Shell, trap the spirit inside it and shut down mobility. This is a shield with rotating razors at the edges."

"What about a sword of fire?" I've heard they are the ultimate spiritual weapon.

"I can wield a sword of fire. You cannot."

Bummer.

"So. Back to your choices. There's also a dagger, a—"

"That. A dagger." I'll go with what I know. For now.

"Very well." He swipes up one of the daggers. "Lesson one."

I blink, and something cold and sharp is pressing into my neck, Archer directly in front of me. "You... How..."

"Distraction kills as surely as this blade," he says. "Concentrate."

Now I smile sweetly at him. "Cockiness kills as surely as this knife." I use the tip of my weapon to give his berries a little pat.

He barks out a laugh. "Touché. Or should I say testies?" Backing up a few steps, he says, "Let's do this again. This time, when I lift the blade, block with your right arm and stab me with your left."

"Really stab you or just—"

But he's in front of me a second later, the blade at my neck.

He huffs with disappointment. "Again."

We spend the next several hours training. He isn't gentle, but he isn't overly rough, either. He shows me the most vulnerable spots on a human as well as a Shell, then comes at me with the dagger, with his fists, with well-aimed kicks. My still-healing body aches and shakes, but I don't let it slow me down. I like this. I need this. And Archer is good about explaining how he was able to knock me down and how I can prevent it from happening again.

When we decide to quit for the day, I'm sweaty and shaky. I collapse on the ground, letting the warm sun caress my exposed skin. And I have a lot of exposed skin. For the first time in over a year, I'm wearing a tank top and shorts.

He walks to my side, his shadow covering me. "I've asked our Watchers to find out who ordered the plane crash, but they haven't found the answer."

Watchers. No need to ask what *that* job entails. "I don't recall a Watcher on the list of Everlife jobs."

"They fall under the subdivision of Scout."

So much to learn. So much to keep straight.

I open my mouth to respond, but a motion at my left catches my attention and I turn—and gasp.

Killian is alive, and he's outside the jellyair!

chapter fifteen

"Without us, you have nothing."
—Myriad

I run. Archer calls my name, his tone exasperated but not angry. If Killian is here, it means one of two things. The Troikans lost the battle in the sky or my TL allowed my ML to get close. My guess? Archer logged in a request.

I think—hope—he sees me as more than a conquest. Well, a possible conquest. I hope he sees me as a friend.

"You are such a pain," he shouts. "You know that, don't you?"

Oh, yes. He sees me as a friend.

I'm grinning as I pass through the jellyair. A shower of warmth. A silken caress. Then I'm standing in the gloom of darkness, fat gray clouds hanging in an onyx sky, trees knocked over from the earlier tornado. Locusts are singing and crickets are chirping. A frog croaks. A breath of wind rattles tree branches together, causing leaves to dance.

Anticipation uncoils inside me, but Killian is already gone. I spin one way then the other, finding no sign of him.

Dang it! Where is he? I know he couldn't see me through the jellyair, but surely he wouldn't leave.

"Well, well. Look who finally decided to show up."

I do another spin and find myself facing a short black girl. What she lacks in stature she makes up for in curves, and her face…wow! She looks like a living doll with big brown eyes that are heavily lashed, heart-shaped lips that are even now pulling tight in a snarl, and round cheeks.

"I gotta say," she adds after scanning me up and down, "I expected you to have a third boob or something."

A boy steps up beside her. He's the taller of the two, but not by much, and leanly muscled. He's Asian and beautiful, his dark hair dyed red at the ends and styled in a mohawk.

He gives me the same up-and-down scan. "You must be wearing your jealousy goggles, E, because I can totally see her appeal."

"Now would be a good time for introductions," I say. Both kids have Myriad brands on their wrists. Are they here to finish what the plane crash started?

"Or?" the girl asks with a tinkling laugh.

I think she's a Shell, but I need to touch her to be sure. "Or I prove the way to a person's heart is through their ribs."

She smirks at the boy. "Dibs! I get to use that threat the next time we're up against Ts."

"Ten." Killian steps into my line of sight, and my heart leaps. "You're here."

The girl has a similar reaction, I think. Her features soften, and the rise and fall of her chest quickens.

Acid-tipped daggers scrape at my insides. Are the two romantically involved?

Killian's gaze remains locked on me, intense and blazing. "Ten, I'd like you to meet Charles, my Flanker, and Elena."

Elena. "You are Sloan's Laborer."

"I'm also your worst—"

"Enough." Killian takes my hand, the scent of peat smoke and heather delighting my senses—I'm like an addict who just got a fix. He leads me into a palatial tent. "Dinnae be disturbin' us," he says over his shoulder.

The walls are made of jewel-toned scarves, and there are faux-fur blankets and plush pillows scattered around the floor. A small circle of fist-sized stones rests in the center, light glowing from each, illuminating the entire tent. A large wooden tub consumes the far left corner, steam rising from the water.

"Is this a Myriadian safe house?" I ask.

"Merely a temporary camp. Troikans can enter, if they so foolishly choose."

"The threat to Archer is noted," I say drily. Now, time to get to the main reason I'm here. I place my hands on my hips and glare at him. "Thank you for staying with me in the plane."

He gives a casual shrug. "I'm as brave as I am strong."

"But *no* thank you for staying in the plane," I add with bite. "And did you really just compliment yourself?"

"I did. Because you never do."

The accusation makes me blink. And laugh. I shouldn't laugh in the midst of such a grave discussion. "Did you get in trouble for staying with me?"

He turns away, blocking my read of his emotions. What he can't hide? The rigidity of his posture. "I don't want to talk about this."

"Too bad. Did you. Get in. Trouble?" He should know me well enough to know I never give up.

"Yes," he hisses. "Yes."

Guilt winds around my neck like a boa. "What was done to you?"

"That, I won't tell you."

I jump in front of him, but he darts out of range—only to return in a hurry.

"You have fresh bruises," he says, voice hardening. "Why do you have fresh bruises?"

He won't answer my questions, but expects me to answer his? Sorry, but that's not the way I play. "Why don't we discuss the crash…and your realm's involvement?"

His lips purse, letting me know he isn't happy with my sidestep. "If Myriad is responsible, no one has taken official credit. What makes you so sure Troika isn't at fault?"

I just…know. "How can one girl be the tipping factor in the war? How can one girl decide the winner?"

A tense pause. "How about we pretend there's only here and now?" He motions to a tray perched in front of a pillow. "I bought you a chocolate cake."

Cake? "Gimme!" Yeah, I'm *that* easy.

I rush over, only to skid to a stop when he adds, "Elena ate it while I was out. So you get fruit."

Bitch gonna get cut! "She's in a Shell. She doesn't need or even like human food."

"Shells can taste, just as they can feel."

Stupid Shells. I sit by the tray and dip a strawberry in the bowl of cream. As I chew, I'm pretty sure I have a mouthgasm. Archer has been feeding me well—steaks, shrimp, bacon—but he's neglected my sweet tooth.

Killian sits across from me, leans forward and gently wipes a bit of cream from the corner of my lip. A bit he licks away, making something low in my gut clench. My heart—the treacherous organ—drums out of control. My blood heats and the tingles only he can elicit return.

I'm trembling as I select another piece of fruit. Between one second and another, I tweak my plan: tell Killian here and now. "I came to thank you for saving me, yell at you for saving me…and to say goodbye."

Killian goes still.

"I'm asking for three hundred and forty-three days. Alone."

343 = 7 x 7 x 7

Seven days in a week. Seven dwarfs. Seven is often considered a holy number.

"I'll use the time to figure out my future," I say.

"No." He gives a clipped shake of his head. "Absolutely not. Even a day is too long. You need to make a decision, Ten, and you need to make it now. No more waiting. That's why I'm here before my spirit—"

Before his spirit…what? Had time to heal from a punishment?

"Killian," I say, the invisible boa squeezing again.

"Someone wants you dead. Letting you figure out your future when there's only a fifty-fifty chance you'll make the right choice is no longer on the agenda."

"That's a chance I'm willing to take."

"Well, I'm not." He shouts the words, his temper now fully engaged.

I blink in surprise. He's usually calm sophistication and wicked seduction.

He takes a deep breath, slowly releases it. "Let me give you another tour. Your gift to me for risking my life to save yours. You'll relax and enjoy and I'll *do something*."

This is a manipulation. One of his greatest abilities. But unlike before, when we first met, this isn't about signing me simply to win. He cares about me, a fact we both know.

"All right."

"Thank you." He's smiling as he stands, walks over and stretches out beside me. He urges me to my back.

My heart races as I rest my head on his shoulder. He drapes his arm around me, his fingers at the hem of my tank, and my breath snags in my throat. I've only ever lain like this with James, and the difference between the two boys astounds me. Body-wise, James was slim. Killian is all muscle. I feel surrounded…protected.

Light suddenly shoots from the device in his wrist and a picture forms on the roof of the tent. A skyscraper knifes toward a night-darkened sky. Stone, chrome and glass with multicolored lights glowing from each floor.

"This is where I live," he says. "The Tower of Many Labors. An Abrogate must train for every position, so for the time you train as a Laborer, you'll live here, too."

The video zooms toward a specific window, and I see a group of girls sitting around a table, eating golden wafers, animated as they talk. In another window, a father rubs his knuckles into the crown of a little girl's head. She snickers and bats him away.

A pang of homesickness surprises me. I used to have parents who teased me, and I miss them so badly.

"We work hard," Killian says. "We play harder. Everyone you see in the tower is off duty. They've either finished a case or they're on vacation." The video pans to the area outside the building, where candlelit lamps illuminate a gorgeous marble sidewalk. The outfits the people wear range from prim-and-proper to mega punk rock. Some of those people are walking while others are...floating?

No, they aren't floating but riding atop sleek, shiny hovercrafts. Nearby, someone is riding on the back of a lion that's as big as a horse.

"That's pretty cool," I say.

"Better than cool, and you know it."

Inside another building, a party rages. Music blares, and people bump and grind together. A Victorian maiden hangs from a cage. A Goth boy scales the chain dangling from the bottom, picks the lock on the door and slips inside. She rewards him with a kiss, as if he's just won a prize.

"We could have a lot of fun at a party like this," Killian says softly.

"We certainly could." The kind of party I dreamed of attending every time my parents demanded I stay home so I wouldn't endanger my life in the big, bad world. "If I'm being honest with you, though, nothing I've seen has changed my mind. I still want time."

"Don't give up on me. The tour isn't over yet."

The camera races down, down the street, finally swooping inside another tower. There are multiple columns, each made from a different jewel. Emerald. Ruby. Sapphire. Diamond. The waterfall—an inside waterfall, as if the tower presses up against a mountainside—has an ivory mermaid perched at the top, a shell tipped over and spilling...not water. Liquid gold? The walls are painted with different murals: cherubs on clouds, warriors in battle, a majestic dragon in flight. The couches have floral prints. Every chair frame is carved to resemble a different animal. The floor gleams like a sea of polished pearls.

The same pearls make up the edges of the hearth, which is the size of my old bedroom. Above it hangs a portrait of the most beautiful male I've ever seen. Golden curls surround flawless features that can't possibly be real. His eyes are vibrant blue and as clear as an ocean in the tropics. A crown rests upon his head.

There's a smaller portrait to the right of his. One of a woman with hair a darker shade of gold and eyes of burnished copper. She's smiling as if she knows a secret I do not, more mysterious than the one kept by the Mona Lisa.

On the left of the bigger portrait are one…five…ten… twenty portraits roughly four-by-four in size, so small I can't make out the faces from this distance.

"Our King and Queen," Killian says with unmistakable awe.

"The King…he kind of looks like…"

"Archer. Yes." Bitterness has displaced his awe. "Archer is one of his many sons. One of his biggest disappointments."

Wait. Stop. Go back. "Archer's dad is the King of *Myriad*?"

"A privilege Archer never appreciated."

Wow! Mind scramble!

I gasp as a small winged dragon lands on the King's shoulder. "The portrait—"

"Isn't a portrait but a type of hologram. Like the televisions humans watch."

Neat! The video zooms into the next room, a dining room as elaborate as the others. The King sits at the head of a long square table, dressed in what looks to be formal military garb. Form-fitting, with medals pinned along the wide expanse of his shoulders. At the sides of the table are nine kids; most look to be under sixteen. Two of the boys—twins—can't be older than thirteen.

"Meet our Generals. They weren't ready to ascend to their roles, but after their mentors were slaughtered, they had no choice."

Nine kids…and I'm to be the tenth. The complete cycle. The beginning of the countdown.

Coincidence? Fate?

"One day, you'll be seated at this very table."

I hear awe again… I hear envy. When—if—one day comes, will I hear resentment and bitterness?

The King stands and walks along the sides of the table, patting each kid on the shoulder. "You do your realm—your King—proud. Together there's nothing we cannot do. No height we cannot reach. No realm we cannot conquer."

The kids bang their silverware against the table in agreement. *Clank, clank.*

"He loves us," Killian says. "Only wants the best for us."

"And you love him." I'm certain of it.

He doesn't try to deny it. "Archer befriended me when we were very young, and he invited me to the royal palace on multiple occasions. Despite the King's busy schedule, he always made time for me while I was there."

A puzzle piece clicks into place. Archer rejected the man Killian clearly wishes was his own father.

What drove Archer to give up his parents and his realm? And Killian, his friend?

Just how devastated was Killian when Archer left?

"I'm surprised he, the son of the King, chose Troika

when he reached the Age of Accountability," I say before I start crying.

"Trust me. We all were."

The words sound as if they've been pushed through miles and miles of broken glass.

I take the conversation in a new direction. "Why do you have an accent but the King doesn't?"

"I spent a lot of time with the director of the Learning Center. What you would call an orphanage." His thumb brushes over my navel, making me shiver. "James grew up in the orphanage, too." His tone is hesitant, and I know he's doing his best to gauge my reaction.

I'm no longer hurt by memories of James, but… "Show him to me." This is an opportunity I can't pass up. An opportunity for closure.

"I knew I should have kept my mouth closed," Killian grumbles as the camera pans out. "Curiosity got the better of me."

We whisk down a darkened street, finally stopping at a pub…going through the door. Dark wood-paneled walls are illuminated by glow rocks that were made to resemble gas lamps. A glass floor offers a view of multiple bedrooms…beds…and the couples writhing on them. I'm about to look away—really—when I spot James. Handsome James, sitting at a table with two other guys. The three are throwing back cold ones and laughing uproariously.

"Her tits were…" One of the boys kisses pinched fingers, as if he's praising the taste of spaghetti.

The other two guys—James included—nod in agreement.

"I know she's signed," my ex-boyfriend says, "but I may arrange a meeting with her, anyway."

The third guy slaps his arm. "Leave some for the rest of us. I'm still pissed you stole my blonde."

"What can I say? She likes 'em big."

Okay. "I'm done," I snap, and the vision fades.

A thousand different emotions slam through me. The front-runners? Humiliation—such a stupid girl, falling for his act. Incredulity—so desperate for affection I refused to see the truth. Disappointment—people suck. Fury—I let a two-faced lying jerk hold me.

My taste in boys is seriously screwed up.

"I'm sorry." Killian's tone is raw with anger and regret. "I'll be killing him shortly."

"Don't bother. I'd rather *James* be the author of his own destruction." I roll to my side. "Archer told me about Dior."

He stiffens as he rolls to *his* side. Our gazes meet. We're so close. If he were human, I'd feel the warmth of his breath on my skin.

"Did you steal her to hurt Archer, win her soul, or because you had feelings for her?"

Resignation darkens his features. "I did it to hurt him *and* to win her soul. Strike at me, and I strike back twice as hard. But..." He reaches out, smooths a lock of hair from my cheek before lying down again. "I check on her occasionally. She used to laugh. She doesn't anymore."

Such a tangled web these boys have woven. "There has to be something you can do to help her. Not on Archer's behalf, but hers. She's part of your family."

He runs his tongue over his teeth. "You could make her freedom a condition of your contract."

Another manipulation. One so high-handed I'm actually shocked he tried it.

"All right. Cuddle time is over. I'm not changing my plan."

He grabs my wrist to stop me. "Ten—"

I use one of Archer's moves, swinging my free arm around, slamming my fist into Killian's jaw. When his head turns from the impact, I punch a second time, where the Shell is most vulnerable: the small control panel behind the ear, marked only by the tattoo of a square.

He goes still, and I know I have one minute, maybe two, before he's able to move again. "Disrupting the connection," Archer called it.

I stand, and Killian is only able to track me with his gaze. "This really is goodbye," I say, raising my chin.

"Afraid not, lass." His hand shoots out and latches on to my calf, yanking me off my feet. I tumble backward, landing on a mound of pillows. He's looming over me a second later. "Sign with Myriad."

"Go to Many Ends. And get off me!"

"Sign!"

"Screw you." I push him and climb to my feet under my own steam.

Before I'm halfway up, he hooks his foot behind my ankles and pushes me back down. "If you're not going to do the smart thing and sign, you need to learn to protect yourself."

"Archer taught me—"

"Don't care. He isn't the best. I am." Killian waves a hand over my prone form, all *here's your proof.* "Lesson one. Always strike your opponent while she—or he—is down."

I glare at him. "Archer said the exact opposite. I'm supposed to help my enemy up and possibly win a lifelong friend."

"That's the perfect thing to do. If you want to be stabbed in the back later."

Maybe. Maybe not. I thought the same thing while living at the asylum. But look at Sloan. At meeting one, we fought. We tried to kill each other. Now we protect each other.

Killian offers me a hand.

I hesitate. "I'll let you teach me a few tricks, but that's it. Afterward, I'm gone."

"Very well. I'll follow."

Stubborn, frustrating boy! I reach out as if to take the offered hand only to kick out my leg.

He falls and I somersault on top of him, my knees pinning his shoulders, but he's wily and more agile than I'm expecting. He swings his legs up and under my arms, pushing me to my back. When he crosses his ankles above my head, his calves pressing against my face, I'm effectively caged. He can smother me but opts to bend his knees at my sides and sit up.

The moment I have the smallest bit of freedom, I sit up, too. He's straddling my waist, which means he keeps the advantage.

Time to up my game. "Killian." I smile at him, running my hands slowly up his chest.

He closes his eyes for a moment. "This isn't going to end well for me, is it?" he says, his tone dry.

"No. It's not." I lock my hands at his nape and use all my weight to fall backward, bringing him with me, bucking my hips midway down to roll him, placing my body on top of his.

Fingers suddenly fist in my hair and yank me backward. As I fall, I catch a glimpse of black hair and furious features. By the time I land, Elena has a gun aimed at my chest.

With a roar, Killian launches at her, slamming into her and knocking her to the floor beside me. The gun goes off, but he has a firm hold of her wrist, ensuring the bullet tears through the roof of the tent rather than my flesh.

He rips the gun from her grip, stands. "You don't touch the girl. Ever."

"She was attacking you." Elena jumps to her feet. "She could have damaged your Shell."

"Which sounds like a me problem. She's mine. Mine to deal with. Not yours. Never yours."

She raises her chin. "She may be yours, but *you* are *mine*."

Killian stares at her for a long while before he laughs. A scary laugh. Then he goes quiet, and that's even scarier. "I'm not. And now I'll prove it."

He raises the gun and—

Boom!

chapter sixteen

"With us, all things are possible."
—Troika

Elena collapses, the bullet striking her between the eyes. No blood spews or leaks from the wound, and by the time she hits the floor, she's self-destructed, nothing but ash floating up, up through the new lunar panel in the tent.

"How could you…" I begin.

"She isn't dead. I simply decommissioned the Shell, hit it in a spot that doesn't damage the spirit inside. It's a safety measure for the times a Laborer doesn't have the strength to leave the Shell but must." With barely a pause, he cups my cheeks and adds, "Are you all right?"

"I'm fine." And I am. The cold-blooded murder of a Shell isn't really a big deal in the scheme of things. "I guess she got what she deserved for eating my cake, huh?"

"The cake. *That's* your main concern? I don't think I'll ever understand you." He empties the chamber of the gun, tosses the weapon aside and walks a circle around me. A slow prowl. He's a predator who's spotted his next meal.

"You could have died tonight. Elena could have pulled the trigger. At this rate, you *will* die, and soon. Death clearly stalks you. How many signs do you need? Choose Myriad, Ten. Now."

"What I need is time."

"You've had time. It's done you no good."

Dang him! "Have you ever regretted your decision to stay with Myriad?"

He stops in front of me, saying, "Only once. When I lost Archer." He pinches my chin and lifts, forcing my attention to remain on him. "What do you *want*, Ten? What can Myriad give you? A purpose? A place to call your own? Vengeance against your parents?"

"I can have each of those things in *this* life, on my own."

"So. You want what you can't find here." He releases me. "You want a guarantee."

Yes! "I want to not regret my decision forever." *Pressure...*

"No one can give you a guarantee."

"I know!" *Growing...* "Here, at least, I can tell myself that what happens is temporary. In the Everlife, I can't do that. It's permanent."

"Until Second-death."

"Well, I gather it's much, much harder to kill a spirit than a human."

"Maybe *I'll* be killed if I fail to sign you."

Pressure...exploding. Another manipulation. The last one I'll tolerate.

With a screech, I take a swing at him. He ducks and my arm glides through air. But I'm already drawing back my other arm, already swinging it. This time, I make contact. My knuckles drive into his cheekbone. Pain shoots up my arm and pools in my shoulder as he wipes the Lifeblood from the corner of his mouth.

"Look at you, giving in to your emotions the way Myriad suggests," he taunts. "Doesn't it feel good?"

"*Felt* good," I yell. "Now I'm stuck with a broken hand." And guilt! I always complained about Vans's hair-trigger temper, and today I acted just like him. Guilt is the worst, as much an enemy as fear!

Killian is gentle as he latches on to my wrist, studies my throbbing hand. "The bones aren't broken, just bruised."

I draw my arm to my side, my anger far from appeased. "Are you going to be killed if I choose Troika?"

He sighs. "No. But the fact that you belong in Myriad hasn't changed. It's meant to be."

Meant to be. Meant to be.

The words reverberate through my mind, and I go still. For years, my mother told me, *We make things happen.* Then one day she came home and announced, *I was wrong. If it's meant to happen, it will happen. If it's not, it won't.*

She changed her mind, because Myriad changed their stance. *Truth evolves*, they like to say.

Even my dad agreed. *We learn as we grow.*

While that's certainly true, shouldn't spiritual laws be rooted in a firm, uncompromising foundation?

Next, I remember what Archer once said to me. Believing in Myriad's idea of fate allows people to shift blame for every travesty, every disaster and every decision to an outside force. It means that, no matter what choice I make, what is meant to be will happen, which ultimately means my choices are inconsequential.

So...no, I don't believe in fate. No outside force is pulling my strings. I might have been born with a purpose, a divine destiny, but my decisions—even my indecisions—are mine. My actions—and lack of action—are mine. Because, at the end of the day, the consequences are mine alone to bear.

Deacon was right. I had the answer all along. I just didn't want to see it, because I didn't want to have to make the choice I was supposedly fighting to make.

But okay. All right. I'm learning, and I'm strengthening. I'm also changing. What should never change? The truth. Truth should remain the same, always and forever, a steady base at my feet; otherwise it was once a lie—once a lie, always a lie—and I have nothing concrete to stand on, only sinking sand or gossamer silk that tears at the first sign of pressure.

That's another point in Troika's favor. They never change what they believe. What's right for one is right for all.

And Myriad's tiered packages? The ones I once praised? One life should not be more valuable than another.

Surprise! I like Troika.

I reel. I reel *hard*. I've struggled to get to this point for so long, and now I'm here, and it's wonderful but...even in the midst of my revelation, I'm still not ready to pull the trigger and make covenant. Do I really want to war with the people of Myriad?

There's a *thump* outside the tent. What the—

Killian shoves me behind him, again blocking me from possible attack. The entrance swishes to the side and Archer and Deacon stride inside.

Well. Though I feel as if I've been beaten up inside, I

leap forward to stand between the longtime adversaries. "I'm fine, Archer. I don't need a rescue."

"That's not why I'm here."

Killian's hands tighten into fists. "You shouldn't be here at all."

Archer steps toward him, and Killian steps toward *him*. Deacon grabs hold of Archer, and I flatten my palm against Killian's chest to shove him back.

"Everyone…just…*stay calm*."

The anger drains from Archer as he focuses on me fully. "There's been a new development. Your mother… I'm sorry, love—"

"Love?" Killian demands.

"But she's sick," Archer finishes.

"Sick?" I press my hands against my stomach. "What's wrong with her?"

A moment passes before he admits, *"Baiser de la mort."*

No, no, no, no, no. "Someone *poisoned* her? Who? How?"

"I don't know."

My heart explodes inside my chest again and again, an endless bomb capable of unfathomable destruction. My mom is sick. She's…she's dying. I shouldn't care. The woman paid good money to lock me away, to have torture after torture heaped upon me. In a year, she visited me a total of three times, her work more important than her only child. Only toward the end did she seem to remember my existence.

And yet I still remember the woman who wiped away my tears anytime I skinned my knee as a child, the woman who braided my hair, hugged me close and told me she loved me more than the sun and stars.

I have to see her. Screw my quest for time and solitude.

My gaze locks on Archer. "I'm leaving within the hour. Don't try to stop me."

"Why would I want to stop you? I'm going with you."

"*I'm* going with you," Killian says, his voice nothing but metal shards and fire.

Someone is trying to kill me, and I'm smart enough to know I can use the protection while I'm so distracted. From both sides. "Here's the deal, the only one I'll offer. You both vow you won't hurt the other and you can both go with me."

"No," Archer says. Succulent, to the point.

"Hell, no," Killian says. Piss and vinegar.

"Otherwise, I go alone," I finish. Yes, I'm smart enough to know I can use the protection, but I'm also stubborn enough to go without it.

Archer purses his lips. Killian curses.

All business, I say, "How long will it take us to reach LA?"

"Until we know who wants you dead, we'll have to drive. No planes. No public transportation, period." Killian shudders. "We can make the forty-two-hour drive in roughly thirty-six. Maybe."

Definitely. "We'll take turns driving. And just to reiterate, you boys won't insult, attack or hurt each other during the trip. That's all I'm asking."

"Yes. That's *all*." Killian glares at me.

"You aren't asking." Archer crosses his arms over his chest. "You're commanding."

I stare him down. "I regret nothing. Now. I'm going to the cabin to gather my things and talk to Sloan. If you're both here when I return—alive and unharmed—we'll take off."

I head outside to find the sun rising, chasing the incoming storm away. I pause to catch my breath, for once unable to lose myself in the vivid shades of pink and gold painted over the sky.

A moan draws my attention to the ground. Charles is sprawled in a pile of leaves, twigs littering his hair. Archer must have hit him where it hurts. I leave him to his recovery and make my way to the house, happy there isn't another tornado brewing.

Sloan is waiting for me in the foyer, pacing. She's dressed in a black tank, black jeans and a pair of combat boots, her ponytail swishing from side to side.

"Hey," I say.

She closes the distance and pulls me close for a hug. "I heard Archer and Deacon talking. I'm sorry about your mom."

At first I'm not sure how to respond. Slowly I wind my arms around her and hug her back. Taking comfort, but hopefully giving it, too. "Yeah. It sucks."

"You're going to see her?"

I nod.

She sighs. "This is where we part ways, then."

I open my mouth to protest. *No! We stay together.* But resignation settles in and settles fast. This had to happen at some point. Her decisions are her own, and I won't try to make her do what she doesn't want to do just so I can keep my friend at my side.

"You heading home or staying here?" I ask.

"Heading home. I wanted to wait till after my birthday,

but I'm too impatient. Don't be surprised when news stations blast stories about the Aubuchon family home burning to the ground soon after the prodigal daughter returns. No estate, no reason to marry."

The pain in her voice is raw and ragged. "Change your mind about marrying the first unsuitable guy?"

"Yeah." She fluffs her hair. "No one deserves me."

That's my girl. "I'm sorry about your family," I say, and I am. Every child should feel invaluable. Loved without strings.

"I know you understand."

"Yeah. I was a ticket to money and fame, nothing more." I give her another hug. "Stay safe, or I'll be ticked. We still don't know who tried to kill us."

"No worries. I'll have a bodyguard. Deacon agreed to come with me."

"Good." I hate the thought of her out there alone.

An excited gleam sparkles in her eyes. "I think I'm gonna give him the honor of being my gentleman lover until we reach Savannah."

I choke on a laugh. "Gentleman lover? Really?"

"What? I didn't think it'd be polite to call him my show pony."

We smile at each other, snicker really, and I make my way up the stairs. In my bedroom, I brush my teeth and hair and stuff the clothes and toiletries Archer gave me into a bag. I grab the stash of protein bars I've been hiding *just in case*, then roll my scalpel and a few kitchen knives in the shirts to prevent clinking.

I head downstairs, determined. To my surprise—and

really, I'm surprised that I'm surprised—Archer is waiting for me in the living room.

He scowls. "It's safe to say you were the target of the plane crash. Someone wants you dead and plans to use your mom to draw you home."

Yeah. He's probably right. "That someone knows me well, because I can't not go see her."

"She's going to die. Going to her won't change—"

"She's not going to die!" Deep breath in…out. "You don't know the future. I survived *baiser de la mort*. She can, too."

"You survived a weakened version. She was given a full dose."

My chin trembles, and I shake my head. "You don't know that."

"I do. I've been in contact with her friend's TL, who's stuck around to monitor her progress."

Her friend's TL? My mom doesn't have a Troikan friend. Well, not to my knowledge. "Tell the TL to give her Lifeblood."

"She has. Many doses in fact. But Lifeblood isn't a cure-all, Ten. It's a spiritual strengthener. A power source. It can speed up the healing process, but it can't repair what's damaged *beyond* repair."

I hear his unspoken words—*She's beyond repair.*

I stalk past Archer, banging my shoulder against his. "Are we gonna chat all day or start driving?" I'm out the door before he can respond.

I march across the yard. Outside the Troikan perimeter, Killian is standing next to a black SUV. He's wearing sunglasses, hiding his eyes, the one real feature found on a Shell. His dark hair is tousled by wind.

I move around him to throw my bag in the backseat of the vehicle.

He comes up behind me. I feel him. Not the heat of his body, but him. All him. I turn, and he's *right there*. So close we're pressed together, two halves of a whole.

"Back off," I say through gritted teeth. "This isn't the time to attempt a manipulation."

His lips thin into a straight line. "I'm worried about you. I want to offer…comfort."

"No, you want to take advantage of a terrible situation. We both know *comfort* isn't in your wheelhouse."

He flicks his tongue over an incisor. "I think it is. For you."

I'm too raw to play nice. "I'm not special to you, Killian."

"You are."

"I'm not. You made that very clear today." I glare up at him. "You did everything in your power to bend me to your will. But I'm not part General, okay? I'm just me. Just Ten. I don't believe in fate, or Fusion, and I never will."

He's silent for a long while, tension vibrating from him. Finally he says, "You *are* special. When you look at me, I dinnae feel as if I'm alone. You make me think, and you make me better." His accent is thicker than ever before, a muscle ticking in his jaw.

I sigh, expelling my anger. "Killian—"

"Nae." He takes a step back, putting distance between us, hated distance, necessary distance. "I tried to manipulate you, yes, but only because I want the best for you. I want your future settled. Safe."

Zero! In my raw state, I lashed out and hurt him. I hurt him badly, and I'm so ticked with myself.

He climbs behind the wheel and slams the door, making me flinch.

Archer suddenly appears, stepping from the invisible wall. He doesn't glance in my direction but claims the front passenger seat.

With another sigh, I take the middle of the bench directly behind the warriors who are probably thinking of all the ways they can murder each other. One wrong word could set them off.

Grass and gravel spray from the tires as Killian speeds over roadless terrain. He seems to have no concept of safety as he snakes around corners and bounces over stumps and rocks, but the guys aren't trying to kill each other and no one's hurling curses at me, so I consider it a major win.

Soon the trees are replaced by buildings, each taller than the last. Eventually my eyelids grow heavy, and I yawn.

Gotta stay awake. "Are we going to sit in silence the entire drive?"

"Yes," they snap in unison. Then they growl at each other.

"Forget I asked." I spend the hours counting. Cars. Trees. Buildings. Clouds. When we stop to charge the car's battery—gas is no longer needed, thanks to the realms—I borrow money from Archer to pay for the power.

"Wait, and I'll go with," he says.

"Stay with the car and ensure nothing's tampered with. *I'll* go with her." Killian wraps an arm around my waist and pulls me forward.

Archer ignores him. "What do you want, Ten?"

"For you guys not to fight about this."

He looks as if he wants to protest, but nods to Killian.

I stalk away, and Killian rushes forward to open the door. "You my bodyguard?" I ask as he motions me inside.

"Yes. You're welcome."

There are eleven people inside. Four are girls, and they stare at him. He pretends not to notice.

"There are three Shells." He whispers the words straight into my ear, making me shiver. "I don't like this. Hurry."

"How can you tell who's what at a glance?"

"I'm *that* good."

Yeah, yeah.

I go straight to the candy bars and grab five of my favorite.

On my way to the register, I notice the digital newspapers flashing this week's headlines. For an extra five dollars I can upload the latest stories straight into my cell phone. Well, if my cell were activated.

Psychic Arrested. Never Saw It Coming!

Man Kidnaps Ex-girlfriend. Demands She Do His Ironing!

Dead Man Found in Cemetery. Town Distraught!

Pass on Marijuana? Issue Being Discussed by Joint Committee.

Then my dad's picture flashes over the screen of *Realm Politics Today*.

The senator's mistress is pregnant! No one is surprised, considering his wife, famed artist Grace Lockwood, left him, preferring to live in seclusion for over half a year. Hiding away with a lover, perhaps? Dr. Dewayne

Reynolds, who is also married to someone else, was spotted on the premises more than once. But there's a good chance Mrs. Lockwood and Dr. Reynolds have already split because Mrs. Lockwood is back with her husband. When asked about the senator's love child, she had no comment.

I'm—utterly—flabbergasted. Soooo much happened while I was gone. My dad wasn't lying when he said my mom was living in seclusion. He didn't wait for her to return, either. He had a fling, and the woman is now having his baby.

Soon I'll have the brother or sister I always wanted but never expected.

I smile. I curse. My dad found a loophole to population control since the law is geared toward women. Only they are limited to one child.

My dad might have even found a new bargaining chip for Myriad.

I taste blood and realize I'm biting my tongue. My sibling will *not* be used the way I was used. I'll die first.

"Did you know?" I ask Killian with more bite than I intended. "About the mistress's baby?"

"I knew only about the affair." His tone has as much bite as mine. "I requested reports on his activities, and they must have been redacted. Someone's keeping secrets."

His words spur a memory. My mother's flash-scribe.

I know I haven't come to see you in forever, but there's a very good reason. A beautiful secret. One that's taught me how to be a mother again.

While she was speaking, a baby was crying. "I wonder

if the mistress already had her baby." Was my mother allowed to claim responsibility for it?

Killian places his hand over the digital paper, his eyes closed. He's downloading the story?

"No," he finally says. "The mistress is only seven months along."

I open my mouth to say more, but the guy in front of me looks over his shoulder for a moment. Our eyes meet before he turns forward then back to look again, lingering this time. He starts to grin.

Killian moves in front of me. "You'll want ta keep your attention ahead," he tells the guy. "The sooner the better. For you."

The guy's cheeks redden, and he swings around.

I'm not sure if I just witnessed a display of jealousy or the equivalent of a dog peeing on my leg. But either way, I'm smiling when I shouldn't have anything to smile about.

My turn comes up, and I pay with Archer's wad of cash. The cashier stuffs everything in a bag, and Killian, my gentleman bodyguard, grabs the handles. I've just pivoted to head for the door when a weight slams into me from behind. There's a stinging pain in my back then a throbbing pain in my hip as I slam into the counter.

With a growl, Killian spins to push the culprit away from me. "Be careful."

"Sorry, sorry. I tripped." A teen who looks like he's suffering from a cold wipes his nose with a tissue, a ring too big for his hand glinting in the light…before sneezing all over Killian. The kid apologizes again, and he *does* look sorry. He also looks miserable. Poor guy.

Killian stares at his soiled shirt and grimaces.

I snort as I'm dragged to the exit. Then I remember my sibling.

"What's wrong?" Archer asks.

Rather than lie with the typical girl response—*Nothing, I'm fine*—I settle inside the car and angrily unwrap my first candy bar. If ever a girl needed sugar therapy...

I'm only halfway through when a horrible fog fills my head. A terrible ringing erupts in my ears. My heartbeat...warps, reduced to nothing but flutters, as if someone reached inside me and nailed the organ to my rib cage. Pain radiates from my left shoulder to the tips of my fingers.

Too young for a heart attack.

Muttering enters my awareness.

"—voice gives me a headache. Shut up." Killian.

"How about I cut off your ears instead?" Archer.

I'm not sure if Killian responds. The pain in my shoulder increases exponentially, and I gasp. Buckets of sweat pour from me and yet the blood in my veins freezes. I open my mouth to cry for help—*please!*—but all I can manage is another gasp. Then I *feeeel* my heart welcoming death, fluttering one moment, going still the next. My lungs seize up, and suddenly I can't breathe, *can't breathe, need to breathe.*

The fog in my head grows thicker until—

The fog vanishes in an instant. And so does the pain. Suddenly I'm weightless, and I'm falling...falling...*thud.*

TROIKA

From: A_P_5/23.43.2

To: L_N_3/19.1.1

Subject: Now What?

I'm with Ten, and we're headed to LA to see her dying mother. Killian is with us and the urge to attack now and apologize later is strong. Please advise.

TROIKA

From: L_N_3/19.1.1

To: A_P_5/23.43.2

Subject: My Best Advice

Don't do anything I wouldn't do.

General Levi Nanne

TROIKA

From: A_P_5/23.43.2
To: L_N_3/19.1.1
Subject: Wow! Thanks!

Are your pearls of wisdom actually plastic?

TROIKA

From: L_N_3/19.1.1

To: A_P_5/23.43.2

Subject: All Right, How About This?

Don't just protect the girl—get to know her better. I realize you like to maintain a bit of distance with your assignments because of what happened with Dior, but caring for someone doesn't weaken you, son, it makes you stronger. To love is to have a reason to fight for something better.

Also, Miss Lockwood's grandparents are Troikan Watchers and they've informed me there's talk in Myriad of another attempt on Miss Lockwood's life. Do not leave her side.

TROIKA

From: A_P_5/23.43.2

To: L_N_3/19.1.1

Subject: Seriously

Corroded plastic. But I won't leave her side by choice. You have my word.

TROIKA

From: Unknown

To: A_P_5/23.43.2

Subject: Hi

She died. You should have saved her. Why didn't you save her? She died at 10:17 on November 12 of this year. Details attached.

TROIKA

From: A_P_5/23.43.2

To: Unknown

Subject: Who Is This?

How did you access my rank and ID?

And how could she—whoever she is—have died on November 12 at 10:17 of this year? That date is a week away.

As for your attachment with "details"? It's a crudely drawn map to a crack house. Thanks, but no thanks.

chapter seventeen

"Truth evolves. What is true today may not be true tomorrow."
—Myriad

I roll over bumpy ground, air exploding from my lungs.

Gleeful laughter assaults my ears just before something hard slams into my stomach. A boot? Then a bird squawks, and the laughter stops. Footsteps. A man screams in pain. A second later, a lot of someones are screaming.

Get up! Get up! Danger!

I pry open my eyelids, expecting to see Killian and Archer with blades at each other's throats. At the very least, I should be inside the SUV, surrounded by paved roads, trees and buildings. Instead I see moonlight and ember-bugs, gnarled trees with toothy leaves that are snapping at me.

The Realm of Many Ends?

No, no, no. I'm not dead. Not again. I can't be.

But I am. Clearly.

My heart—finally working again—trips in panic. There are no monkey-skeletons in the sky, at least. Did they already capture prey? I draw in a deep breath, but the thick smoke and black clouds burn my throat, making me cough. A storm is brewing. In a place like this, I don't think I'll be treated to ordinary rain.

Weapon up. Now. The more the better.

Right. I search the ground, find a fallen twig. The moment I grab it, a sharp sting causes the muscles in my fingers to spasm. I drop the twig and watch as three beads of blood well in my palm.

Three...a triad. The noblest of all numbers. The only number equal to the sum of the numbers below it.

Troika.

The wells are...puncture wounds? Crouching down, I study the short, wrist-thick piece of wood, only then seeing the little brown bugs crawling all over it. And—

Oh. Wow, wow, wow. Dizziness nearly topples me. As I fight to remain standing, a crack of thunder booms so loudly my eardrums actually rupture. Grimacing, I stand. Again I teeter. With a single step forward, I almost faceplant. Ember-bugs were waiting nearby and now strike en masse, burning me.

I wave my arms. Another crack of thunder causes pain to explode through my skull. I cover my ears, but as the third crack sounds, I realize nothing can muffle the power of the boom. My scream joins the thousands of others still ringing out. Tears streak down my blistered cheeks.

Ten's tears fall, and I call.

The childhood song consumes my awareness, the perfect distraction. *Nine hundred trees, but only one is for me.*

Something hard slams into my back, knocking me down. The ember-bugs scatter, but it hardly matters. The bird-skeletons are back, and they've come to finish the job! I jab my elbow backward, hear a grunt.

"Hold her."

Through my pain and injuries, the voice is muffled, but I'm lucid enough to know birds squawk and humans speak. I've got a human on my back and another human—the speaker—somewhere nearby.

Two against one.

Two sets of hands latch on to my wrist in a tight clasp. A shackle. I buck up, dislodging whoever is straddling me.

The boy at my right says, "We're trying to help you, girl."

Maybe he's telling the truth, maybe he isn't. Remembering what Archer and Killian taught me, I turn my wrists to grab hold of the hands still holding me. I use both as leverage, yanking on the owners as I hoist myself up, at the same time kicking back, nailing the other person—*three* against one—in the chest.

I'm released as the two at my arms stumble for purchase, and I end up in a crouch. I swipe up the bug-covered branch, ignore the new stings and throw it at the person—a guy, roughly six feet tall, brown hair, unfamiliar and dirty but definitely human. He catches the branch, instinct I guess, and grunts as the insects bite him. With him, the playing field is now even, at least. We've both been bitten. Poisoned? The dizziness…

I straighten and turn, my hands balled into fists, my legs braced apart. I'm ready. One boy and one girl left. The boy has shoulder-length blond hair. At least, I think it's blond. It's matted with dirt and blood, dried leaves woven through the strands. He's on the short side for a guy, though he's taller than me, and he's thin, as if he hasn't had a decent meal in eons.

The girl is shorter and cleaner with braided blond hair and the face of an angel, despite the streaks of dirt she's sporting. When my gaze moves to her, she ducks her head. She's timid. Noted.

"Idiot!" The shorter boy scowls at me. "We're trying to save your stupid life."

Another boom of thunder nearly sends me to my knees, yet the three amigos merely grimace.

"When the rain falls, you don't want to be out here," he continues. "Your skin will melt off your bones."

"If you knew me," I reply through gritted teeth, "you'd know trust doesn't come easily. So. How do I know you're not as bad as the animals, leading me into a trap?"

The scent of something fetid wafts on the breeze, and I gag. This is death itself, and it's closing in.

"Stay here or follow us," he says. "The choice is yours."

Always. "Who are you?"

"Out here? I'm food." He turns and runs into the thick of the forest. The other two follow him, and I don't have to think for long. I sprint after him, too, mimicking the zigzag pattern as they dodge chomping limbs and shimmery patches of air. The scent of death begins to fade.

Nine hundred trees, but only one is for me.

The song starts up again, but I shake my head to clear the words. *Not now. Concentrate!*

Finally, the shortest boy says, "My name is Brett."

"Kayla," the girl says.

The taller boy is next. "I'm Reed."

"I'm Ten."

"How'd you die?" Reed asks.

I flinch. "I don't know. You?"

"Ever heard of HART?" Brett jumps over a rock. "We were at a meeting, planning a peace rally. There was an explosion, and we woke up here."

I rack my brain for news reports but come up empty. Must have happened while I was locked inside Prynne.

"Where were you based?"

"LA."

"My old stomping ground. And you truly believed you could make the realms stop fighting and start hugging?"

Kayla throws me a glare and misses the rock in front of her. She stumbles. Unlike me, she falls to her hands and knees. Brett and Reed immediately rush to her side to help her up. They are like a well-oiled machine. Clearly, they've had to do this before.

A squawk sounds—the bird-skeletons!—and I automatically reach for my scalpel. Zero! When will I learn?

Eight times eight times eight they fly, whatever you do, don't stay dry.

Wait. *They* fly. They. The birds?

The song can't refer to this place…can it? Lina couldn't have known I'd end up here. *Right?*

Always spoke in past tense. As if the future had already happened.

Always knew I'd escape Prynne.

One of the creatures lands just in front of me, and I skid to a stop. Wings made of bone and metal stretch on and on, knocking down trees. The boys draw weapons—crudely made wooden daggers. Good, that's good. Four of us against one of them. Excellent odds.

Kayla crawls to the base of a tree and curls into a ball, whimpering.

Okay. Three against one. Not bad odds. But even now, the skin-melting rain is closing in. Except…do we *want* to get wet? *Eight times eight times eight they fly, whatever you do, don't stay dry.*

Don't stay dry. But…if the rain melts us, it isn't water; it's some type of acid.

So the rain is out.

"Water," I say. "We need water." It's worth a shot.

"No." Brett jumps from one foot to the other, preparing to leap. "The lake is more dangerous than the creatures."

Clawed feet remain embedded in the ground as the creature lunges forward, its neck stretching…stretching…its beak snapping at Brett, who dives out of the way at the last second.

"No one ever returns from the lake," Reed adds.

But the song—

Is probably meaningless. *Get over it. Concentrate.*

I'm weaponless. I can't help the boys fight, but I *can* act as the bait.

"Hey," I shout. "Over here. Come get me."

The creature focuses on me. At least, I think it does. The head swings in my direction, but the eye sockets are clear.

The boys understand my intent and dive on the creature as it steps toward me. Another squawk is followed by another crash of thunder, this one louder than any of the others. Warm liquid gushes from my ears. I scream as I fall—

"Ten!"

My eyelids spring open. Killian looms over me, the sunglasses gone, the gold flecks in his eyes bright. I pat my ears as the throb fades. I don't… I can't…

"You're all right. I'm here, I'm here."

Yes, yes, he is. He's here, and I'm alive. Thank Firstking!

I scan the vehicle. We're stationary, pulled to the side of the road. "Where's Archer?"

"Don't worry. He'll return shortly…had to run an errand."

Even though my synapses aren't firing at full capacity yet, I detect doublespeak. "Did you destroy his Shell?"

His teeth flash in a smile that's part delight, part malevolence. "Define *destroyed.*"

So, yes.

"I didn't punch him," Killian adds, "I just showed him my fists really fast."

We'll have to address that, but not now. Now I have to go back. "The Realm of Many Ends," I say. "There are kids there. They need me." If they aren't already dead… dead…dead again. I can't go back without dying.

I don't want to die.

He cups my jaw and I can't look away from him. He's too relieved, too gut-wrenchingly gentle. He acts irredeemable so much of the time, but he has these great moments of compassion.

"You were in the Realm of Many Ends?" he asks gently.

"I was. But how did I die?" The fog in my mind…the pain in my chest. Oh…zero. Bowel check!

I don't want the last memory people have of me in this life to be soiled pants.

I manage a discreet glance down. All clear.

"How was I brought back?" I ask.

Killian releases me to rub his forehead. "You were poisoned. I looked you over, found an injection site." He slides his hand under my back, tapping a sensitive spot. "Your heart stopped, and I poured Lifeblood down your throat."

Poisoned while I was alive? Impossible. "When could I…? How?" No one knows where I am. "Who?" I sound like an idiot, but I don't care.

"My guess? The kid at the charge station. He bumped into you on purpose, must have had a needle hidden under the stone in the ring he was wearing."

I remember the sting in my back. But…but… "Why?"

"Whoever wants you dead could have had someone waiting at every charge station between New York and LA." Killian closes his eyes, draws in a deep breath. "The realms are definitely tired of waiting for you to make up your mind. They won't give you more time."

"That sounds like a me problem, Killian. You can ease off—"

"No! I won't ease off." He gives my shoulders a little shake. "This is an *us* problem."

We stare at each other, silent, and I wonder if my expression is as tortured as his.

I know the realms are capable of murder. Not just because of the plane crash and the poison, but also because of the kids from HART. Someone feared their end goal enough to bomb them.

I sit up, fighting the dizziness that followed me out of the realm. Cars whiz past our SUV. The sun is in the process of setting, which means I slept—and dirt-napped—another day away.

"I'm sending a message to Madame Bennett," he says,

typing into his arm. "Telling her you're very close to signing with us."

"But—"

"It should buy you a little time. *If* the ones who want you dead are from Myriad. If not, and word of this gets out, Troika will strike again and strike harder."

I disagree. A sneak attack isn't Troika's style.

Know them so well, do I?

No, but I know Archer and Deacon. I know their laws mean something to them. I know how precious life is to them. "I don't want you to lie for me, Killian."

He stops typing and lowers his head toward mine, the scent of peat smoke and heather thick between us, heady and intoxicating, making me shiver. "I'm not. I do think you'll sign with us. Why wouldn't you? You'll have a place of honor, you'll be adored by the citizens...and you'll be one of mine."

I gulp.

"If that doesn't convince you—I hope that convinces you—just remember the horrors awaiting you in Many Ends."

Like I'll ever forget. "I'm rolling the dice on this." At least for a little while longer. If I really am a tipping factor of the war, backing the right people—the ones I'll have to live with— is more important than ever.

"You make protecting you an almost impossible task, lass."

"Don't protect me, then. I can take care of myself. I've been doing it for a long time."

"You shouldn't have to." He cups my cheeks again, his

grip stronger, his thumbs caressing. "It's a sad way to live, and I don't want that for you."

I curl my fingers around his wrists, holding him in place. "How do you know it's sad? You have Elena and Charles."

"They report directly to Madame Bennett. I'm on my own and have been since Archer left."

I slide my hands up his arms and cup *his* cheeks. "We'll look out for each other, then."

As he holds my gaze, something shifts in our relationship. I don't know what. I've never experienced anything like this. But I feel the change deep, deep inside. I think he does, too, and it throws him.

He pulls back, severing contact. "Let's get back on the road. Time is our enemy."

In more ways than one. "Agreed." I'm not worried about Archer. I know he'll find me. He always does.

Killian exits the car, walks to my door and, his motions jerky, "helps" me out and leads me to the front passenger seat. I buckle in as he takes his place behind the wheel.

We sit in silence…silence that continues as we pass a group of picketers outside a virtual-reality tour facility owned by Myriad. Though there are at least fifty people, and each of them carries a sign, there are two slogans. One reads The Many Are Doomed! The other reads Your Might Isn't Right!

Their efforts are wasted. They aren't going to convince anyone they're a better choice this way. If I were part of Troika, I'd—

What? Try to change this, definitely. But how? I've never really been part of something bigger than myself. Never been on a team or put the good of many over the good of, well, me.

"Are you hungry?" Killian asks me, shattering the quiet.

"Starved, actually."

He exits the highway and turns into a burger joint and inches along the drive-through line. He orders a hamburger and fries, and the girl who collects his cash gasps.

"Killian." Her eyes go wide with a combination of shock, hope and anger. "I thought I'd never see you again."

He stiffens, stares straight ahead.

"How are you?" She looks to me for a moment then yanks her gaze back to Killian. "Who's the girl?"

Finally he deigns to glance in her direction. "Our food?"

Oh, wow. He's cold.

The color drains from her face. She trembles as she hands him a bag with grease stains on the bottom. He accepts and drives on.

"Your kindness brought a tear to my eye," I say drily. "Is that what's in store for me?"

"I was cruel to be kind." His fingers clench on the wheel. "And I don't know what's in store for you. I'm in never-before-explored terrain."

To hide my own trembling, I dig out the burger. "She was once your target, right?"

"You mean assignment. And yes, she was."

"Did she know you were a Laborer?"

"No."

"And yet you still managed to sign her."

"I'm *that* good."

His favorite reply. I pop a fry into my mouth, swallow.

"Did you use your tried and true method of hitting it and quitting it?"

"Yes," he says with only a slight hesitation. "I slept with her. But unlike your precious James, I didn't tell her I loved her. I've never promised forever."

Ouch. "But you make girls *hope* for forever, even though you know there's no chance you'll offer it."

"Just because I haven't offered it doesn't mean I won't sometime in the future. I'll give the right girl *everything*."

I fight a wave of intense longing. I would love to be the right girl. But only if he's the right boy for me.

Am I? Is he?

"Why did Myriad want Miss Cashier so badly that they sent you, a precious resource? Why did they leave her to a life of drudgery inside a fast-food restaurant after she signed?"

"I don't know."

"Surely you can guess. You've lived in the realm your entire life, were favored by the King. You know their ways even when they refuse to explain their reasons."

He works his jaw. "Troika sent a Leader to her, rather than a Laborer, telling us she was singular to them. She turned him down. I swooped in and ensured the realm couldn't have her. And she doesn't need an exceptional Firstlife to do what we need her to do in the Everlife."

This. This is the boy who first arrived at Prynne. I don't like him. "What do you need her to do?"

"Join our army. Fight for us. Help win the war. But more important, stop her from doing whatever it was Troika wanted her to do."

How cold. "She didn't strike me as a soldier."

"But she *is* a voice. One whisper into the ear of another can spark another whisper and another whisper, until the noise is deafening."

"A numbers game," I say, lamenting the irony yet again. "Why are people like my dad given so much?"

"Some people—most people—accept our first offer. But others, those who have something we covet, are given preferential treatment. Your father's contract came with very few benefits. It wasn't until you were born that he was offered a new, better deal."

"A deal that turned a child into a commodity." My bitterness is showing.

"That reminds me," he says. "Eighteen years ago, Madame had a daughter, Ashley. A girl who'd been Fused and reborn multiple times already. She was the youngest General at the time, and she'd always wanted a brother. I was irresistible, which is why I was chosen. But she died soon after, and I was returned to the Center."

My heart hurts for him. How much loss has this boy known?

"You're feeling sorry for me again, aren't you?" There's no upset in his tone, only intrigue.

"Well, you were just a little boy, and you were abandoned. I wish you'd had better."

He reaches over, takes my hand and lifts it to his mouth. As he kisses my knuckles, a tingling warmth mists over me. "Anyway," he says after he clears his throat. "I recently discovered Madame thinks *you* are bonded with Ashley."

Oh, wow. Madame Bennett's personal stake in me makes even more sense. "That's kind of creepy. I mean, how many times have you made a pass at me?"

"I said *she* believes you're bonded with Ashley. I don't. I'm certain you're bonded with one of the other slain Generals."

"So, how many Generals are there at a given time?"

"Ten."

"What?"

"Ten."

"What?" I repeat.

He rolls his eyes. "Ten Generals at a time."

Ah. I snort.

"Now eat," he says. "Keep your strength up."

"Sure thing…bro."

He glowers at me. "That's not funny."

"It kind of is."

He glowers at me again, but a moment later his eyes go wide. There's flash of light. As I turn, Killian shouts, "Brace—"

Boom!

I'm thrown toward him before I'm thrown in the other direction, only my belt keeping me in my seat. My skull slams against my window, breaking the glass. Pain explodes through my head as different bones shatter. My vision goes dark, my mind an ocean of panic, vibrations from impact causing ripples of misery as I'm tossed upside down again and again until finally landing that way, basically hanging from my belt.

Wake up, Ten. Now!

The words scream through my aching head, the English accent familiar. Archer's back? I blink open my eyes. My vision is no longer black but it's still hazed…until I use a shaky hand to wipe away the blood. No sign of Archer.

Grab the semiautomatic in the console. Turn the safety off, aim and squeeze the trigger.

Irish accent that time. "Killian?" I look, but he's not here, either. However, bits of ash are floating through the car.

Ten! The gun!

Killian's voice again, though his Shell is gone. What happened to the car? To him?

A wreck, I realize as I stare at my crumpled door. We were in a wreck, and he decommissioned his Shell in order to survive and help me.

Two men are up there and both are armed. Take the gun, lass. Leave the car. In it, you're the perfect target.

Danger. Right. I struggle with my belt, but finally manage to unlatch it. I topple and slam into the roof. My shaking intensifies as I pry open the console. A gun falls out, and I swipe it up, careful to keep the barrel aimed anywhere but at me. Cool air blows through the opening where the window used to be, and I crawl through.

Catching my breath seems impossible as I trip forward and catalog my new surroundings—the vehicle has been thrown off the road and into a ravine. In the distance, there's a hill populated with a thick spread of trees. Along the road, shadows are chased away by a car's headlights.

Go!

A command from Archer.

My legs weigh a thousand pounds as I pick up the pace. A car door slams shut, then another. Footsteps sound.

Faster! Killian demands.

I don't want to leave you, but I must, Archer says. *Only for a few minutes. I'm returning to Troika to get a Shell and backup. All you have to do is stay alive. Killian—*

I won't let her be harmed.

They both sound agonized.

Are the men chasing me Shells? Or human? Does it really matter? Whatever they are, they hope to kill me. And they just might. The odds aren't in my favor. I'm injured, leaving a blood trail, while they're uninjured. I don't know the terrain. They might.

Running won't do me any good. Might even speed up my death. I have to strike now, while I'm still on my feet.

I stop and turn. A wave of dizziness sweeps through me—*nothing new, focus*—as I drop to my stomach. Perfect timing. *Pop! Pop!* Shots fired, a silencer used. I zero in on the direction the men came from and see a shadow headed straight for me. I take aim.

A little to the left, lass. Killian. He's still with me.

I take comfort from the knowledge as I adjust my aim.

Now!

I squeeze the trigger.

The loud boom causes my ears to ring, and the gun's recoil causes my wrists and shoulders to vibrate. The shadow collapses.

Good girl.

One down. One to go. But where—

The cock of someone else's gun tells me one thing: I don't have time to fire off another shot of my own. Not knowing what else to do, I roll to the side as fast as I can. *Pop! Pop!* A sharp sting in my side makes me hiss. Inhaling deeply, I aim and squeeze the trigger of my gun. My assailant hisses this time, but he merely stumbles back without going down.

When he stills, he raises his gun. I open my mouth to

pick a realm at long last—either realm. This is it. The end for me. But two flashes of bright light appear in front of me, and when they fade, bodies are in their place, shielding me.

Pop! Pop! Pop!

One of those bodies jerks, as if hit, and I catch a glimpse of Deacon's rugged features.

Wait. He should be with Sloan.

"The girl is protected." Archer, the other body, punches the shooter in the arm, sending the gun flying. His next blow is to the man's nose. As a pained bellow cuts through the night, I lurch for the gun. The moment I've got it, I aim both weapons. Archer has the man—a human, judging by the blood trickling down his face—on the ground, a booted foot pressed into his neck.

Deacon wraps a hand around my wrist to force me to lower my arm. "No."

"That's not our way," Archer says. "Death isn't the answer. Where there's breath, there's hope."

"Agree to disagree." Killian steps from the shadows into a beam of light cast by the car's headlights. He must have returned to Myriad to get a new Shell while Archer and Deacon disarmed the shooters. "They hurt the girl, and I'm not okay with that. They die."

He lifts a gun of his own and fires.

chapter eighteen

"Without pressure, there would be no diamonds. Without tests and trials, you wouldn't know your own strength—or weaknesses."

—Troika

My adrenaline crashes in an instant, leaving me to deal with every new injury I've sustained. I drop the gun as my knees buckle, my weight suddenly too much to hold up. Unlike the boys in the Shells, I'm only human.

Before I hit the ground, Killian is there, wrapping his arms around me and cradling me against his chest.

"I've got you," he whispers.

I rest my head in the hollow between his neck and shoulder.

"We could have questioned the shooter," Archer snaps. "He could have told us who's targeting Ten."

"He could have lied," Killian snaps back.

Archer takes a step toward him, his body primed for action. "Or you were afraid of what he'd say."

"I'm not responsible for the attempts on Ten's life." Each word drips with menace. "I would never—"

"No, but your realm is. You don't want her to know, because you don't want her to align with Troika. Better to end up in Many Ends," Archer says with a sneer. "Isn't that right?"

"I don't want her in Many Ends. And how many times do I have to say Troika is just as likely to put a hit on—"

"No! You know better, but you'll never admit it, even to yourself. And this is your problem, Killian. This has always been your problem. You want so badly to win, you've become blind to the truth. And I get it. I do. My father told us victors are adored and failures are abhorred, and more than anything you wanted to be adored by someone, anyone." Archer is shouting so loudly, his voice is echoing from the trees. "Well, *I* adored you. *I* loved you. But you changed, and not for the better. You turned everything into a battle. And even back then, I understood. You'd never had a family, and you craved one, craved unconditional love. But now you have to decide what's more important—your pride, or Ten's life. Because in this instance, you can't have both!"

Never had a family…craved respect, love. The words echo in my mind as Killian grows so tense I'm almost afraid he'll shatter like glass.

"Enough," I murmur. "What's done is done and can't be undone." The dizziness returns with a vengeance, and I moan as my stomach threatens to rebel. "We can only move on from here."

Silence. Good, that's good.

"Deacon… Is Sloan…?" I say.

“She’s fine. She told me to leave her, that I wasn’t sufficient eye candy.” I hear the offense in his tone.

I know Sloan. I know she finds the boy intriguing. There has to be more to the story. “Has she reactivated her cell phone?”

“No. Like you, she doesn’t want to be traced.”

“I’ll have a message sent to her on your behalf.” Killian brushes my cheek with his own, some of the tension draining from him. “Stop worrying about her and start recovering.”

There’s command in his voice, but also concern. The concern warms me, because I know he doesn’t feel it for everyone. Or often. “Some General I’ll be, huh?”

“A General leads and learns. You’re golden.”

Archer scrubs a hand down his face. “We have a safe house an hour from—”

“No.” Killian gives a single but violent shake of his head. “I’m taking her with me. We’ll see you tomorrow—at her parents’ house.”

“No safe house,” I say. “No time.” If my mom dies before I reach her…

“I’ll get you there,” Killian vows. “Tomorrow.”

“I can rest in the car as we trav—”

He presses his lips against mine, silencing me, the sweet taste of honey and sugar teasing my tongue. I’m shocked—*want more, need more*—and I’m unable to stop myself from kissing him back, rolling my tongue against his. I forget we have an audience. I forget I’m in pain and bleeding. The world ceases to exist. My head swims…and swims, but it’s different from the dizziness, exponentially better.

Lethargy sneaks through my veins and invades my limbs. "Killian—"

He raises his head. "Sleep now." He sounds so far away.

"No," I mumble. I've slept enough. Too much. But I'm unable to fight the need as I'm tugged closer and closer to a sea of nothingness.

"You drugged her?" Archer gasps out.

He did? At the moment, anger is beyond me. I'm warm, deliciously warm, two strong bands wrapped around me as I drift…drift…

I'm not sure how much time passes before I hear a soft whisper in my ear.

"What am I going to do with you, Ten Lockwood?" Killian's voice.

I continue to drift without an anchor—

A sharp sting against my cheek. A bug bite? I want to brush my fingers over my face, but my arm refuses to cooperate. Another sting, this one sinking deeper, past skin. Tingles erupt in my shoulder as if the nerve endings are finally coming back to life.

"Wake up." A third sting.

This time, my arms works properly and I grab—a wrist. My eyelids pop open, and I come face-to-face with Elena. I don't think, I just act, balling my free hand and throwing a punch. Her nose breaks, and she grunts. There's no blood. Right. The Shell. No lasting damage for her.

As I release her and sit up, she readjusts her nose with a hiss. I take stock. I'm in another palatial tent, the scarves surrounding me a vibrant shade of purple. The pillows scattered about are cobalt. There's a tub, but it's empty. In the center, glowing stones are stacked next to a tray of half-eaten fruit and crumpled candy-bar wrappers. More chocolate meant for me…that this girl has obviously eaten.

I'll do as I told her during our first meeting and go through her ribs. I'll—

Do nothing. I wouldn't touch Killian's chocolate with a ten-foot pole. It's a bribe for my forgiveness, nothing more. But…then I see one of the wrappers isn't completely empty and make a dive for it. Okay, okay. While I wouldn't touch the chocolate with a ten-foot pole, I will touch it with my fingers.

I stuff the goodness into my mouth and savor.

Kissed me simply to drug me. Anger ignites. *Not forgiven, Killian Flynn. Not forgiven!*

"Where's Killian?" I ask.

"He was called away on Myriad business." She smirks at me. "Right now, *I'm* in charge of your care."

Killian's attempt to look out for me, as promised, even though he's not here, won't soften me. "I can take care of myself."

"Says everyone ever. But it's only pride talking, so I never listen. Pride is a nasty bitch."

"So is greed. And gluttony." I arch a brow at her.

"Actually, I threw the pieces outside."

Spite is a nasty bitch. "You don't like me," I say. "Noted. The feeling is mutual. You can go now."

"I take orders only from Killian, and even then it's iffy." She flips her hair over her shoulder. "He told me to watch over you, so I'll watch over you. I'm guessing you're a flight risk."

She isn't wrong.

I stand, grunting as sore muscles and bruised bones protest. I explore the tent, cataloging exits, searching for weapons, and find a small room sectioned off from the rest of the tent by red scarves. Inside is a temporary bathroom: portable toilet, rags, a mirror, a toothbrush and a hairbrush, a bowl of water and a calendar that leans against the mirror.

Curious, I reach for it. A blue light appears in the glass. Not just a light but words. A note from Killian.

Stick around, and I'll allow you to punish me. Leave, and I'll do the punishing. Yours, K.
PS: I wasn't sure what you loved so much about the calendar Vans took from you, but I wanted you to have a new one.

Nothing he does or says right now should please me, but I *am* softening. This boy…oh, this boy. He's a wealth of contradictions.

I hug the calendar to my chest then brush my teeth and hair and use the water to wash up.

"You done in there?" Elena calls. "Or are you constipated?"

Nice.

I hide the toothbrush in the waist of my shorts and leave the relative privacy of the bathroom to find her seated and sharpening a dagger with a stone. An attempt to intimidate me, I'm sure.

"About time." She doesn't glance in my direction, just keeps rubbing the stone over the blade. "You're filling Killian's head with foolish ideas and you need to stop."

"Foolish ideas?"

"Yeah. How about this doozy? *Firstlife matters.* Oh! The

ever-popular *work with your enemy, because he'll* never *stab you in the back.* And let's not forget my favorite. *Winning isn't everything.*" The rubbing stops for a moment, only to start up again—faster. "You're going to make a terrible General."

"Agreed. That's one of myriad reasons I haven't turned in my application for employment." I smirk at her. "Myriad. Get it?"

The gaze she levels on me is pure irritation.

Humor not appreciated. Noted. "Wow. Look at us." I sit across from her, keeping the glowing stones between us. A buffer. I smile sweetly. "We're bonding. Practically sisters."

Her motions grow choppy. "If Killian fails to sign you, he could be decommissioned. You get that, don't you?"

I go tense. "He told me he wouldn't be killed."

"He lied."

He wouldn't do that…would he? Unless this is *her* attempt to manipulate me?

"Though we have no idea who arranged your execution, Killian lobbied for you, convinced the Generals and even the King you were worth any risk. He just needed a little more time. But. Since he fought for your life, your fate will now decide his."

A brief moment of dizziness, the confession rocking me. "When? When was all this decided?"

"After the plane crash, just before the car wreck."

He bought me time—with his life. And yet someone is trying to kill me anyway.

I want to shake him. And kiss him, for real this time. But mostly I want to shake him. What am I supposed to do about my future now? I can't allow Killian to be harmed because of my decision.

"Maybe I'll kill you both," Elena says, as if she's speaking to herself. "He'll Fuse with another soul and start over, and you'll suffer countless agonies in Many Ends until you die and start over, as well."

Okay. She's gone too far, threatening Killian. I lean over the rocks—notice they don't burn—and slam the tip of the toothbrush behind her ear. While her Shell goes still, I claim her dagger and stride from the tent, only to grind to a halt.

The sun is once again in the process of setting, the sky ablaze with colors—and framing my parents' house, a three-story mansion that's sprawled over two acres of land. The house is box-shaped, taller in the center, shorter on the sides, with some walls made of glass, others of white stucco. Flowers of every color bloom along the edge, and orange and lemon trees offer sweet scents and shade. The grass at my feet is soft and green, as plush as carpet.

My stomach clenches. Home, but…not home. Everything is exactly as I remember it, my absence completely unnoticed. I don't belong here. Not anymore.

Killian must have driven through the night and then some to get here.

A bright beam of light explodes in front of me and when it fades, Killian is standing there. He's scowling, his dark hair unkempt. Dirt mars his clothing and there are tears in his shirt, revealing the ripple of muscle underneath. He's so beautiful it almost hurts to look at him.

"Snake." I throw a punch at his jaw, and it lands. On impact, his head whips to the side.

He masks his features as he faces me. "The end justified the means. You're home, as promised."

"Well, I hope you enjoy the end, because my trust in you is destroyed. You tricked me!"

"For your own good."

"And you tied your life to mine!"

His eyes narrow, his lashes fusing. "Elena has a big mouth."

"Yours should have been bigger. You lied to me."

He raises his chin. "I told you the truth at first, and it was clear you felt I was pressuring you further. I took the pressure off."

So. The boy who praised victory above everything else refused to use his ace against me. Argh! Now I'm even more torn.

"I don't want you killed," I say, stomping my foot.

"That makes two of us."

Archer and Deacon appear in beams of light to flank his sides. He swings around, two guns palmed, cocked and aimed. The Troikans merely smile in challenge, daring him to take a shot.

The muscles in his shoulders knot with tension, but in the end, he lowers the weapons.

Elena comes charging out of the tent. When she spots Archer and Deacon, she hisses.

Neither boy pays her the slightest bit of attention.

"I have news," Archer says to me, dread heavy in his tone.

Everything else is forgotten. "Did my mother—"

"No. She's still alive. For now." His eyes are grim. "But, Ten…while you were at the asylum…when she left your father and remained in seclusion, even refusing to come see you…she had a baby."

What? "No." I shake my head. "My dad's mistress is going to have a baby. Not my mother."

A secret…

Taught me how to be a mother again…

A baby crying…

"I didn't say she was *going to* have a baby." Archer pins me with a look. "She *had* a baby. She carried and gave birth to your brother in secret a little over a month ago. Had anyone known, she would have been forced to give the child to a childless family."

I reel, my mind trying to make sense of everything being thrown at me. *I have a brother…*

Women are usually sterilized a year after giving birth to their first—and only—child. Time to ensure the baby survives infancy. My mom could have healed. There are always rare cases…

I have a brother!

"Your father found out this morning," Archer continues. "He's requested a meeting with his ML."

"No way." I'll die before my brother is used. I head for the house.

Archer latches on to my wrist. "I'll go ahead of you. In spirit. I'll clear the way."

"You'd better hurry."

He nods and a second later, his Shell goes still.

I look to Deacon. "Don't let Killian inside the house."

"Lass—"

I turn and stare at him, willing him to understand. "I'm kicking Archer out as soon as I reach my mom. I have to do this on my own."

Silence.

When he gives a stiff nod of his own, I take off. I'm a bundle of raw, exposed nerves as I fly inside the house, up the stairs, past the walls decorated with my mother's artwork. Her paintings are famous all over the world. But these are paintings of…me? I slow. Yes, me. My face has replaced the abstracts. Me as an infant. Me as a preteen. Me as a teenager. Even pictures of me at the asylum.

Ten. Hurry.

Archer's voice fills my head. Right. He's invisible, and whatever he's doing to distract the maids is working. They turn away from me just before I pass, allowing me to reach my mother's bedroom without incident.

The door is locked, but that hardly matters for Archer.

Try it now, he says.

I do, the knob hot enough to blister. He must have used his light and melted the tumbler inside the lock.

I burst inside the room. There's a human-size lump on the bed, motionless, a crib in place of the nightstand and a woman—not my mother—in a rocking chair beside it. The woman gasps when she sees me, clutching the baby she's holding tight against her chest.

"You must be Ten," she says, sounding relieved. She stands. "I'm Maggie, and I'm very happy you're here." Her hair is fully gray, and her features are heavily lined, her jaw offset by jowls. But her eyes…they sparkle like freshly polished emeralds. "You're as pretty as your pictures."

I don't know her. I don't trust her.

I step forward, almost challenging.

"I'm an old friend of your grandmother's. Knew your mother when she was a little girl." She smiles a sad smile and pulls the blanket from the infant's face. He's sleeping, his eyes closed. "Would you like to meet your brother?"

My stomach clenches, and for a moment, I'm unable to catch my breath. "What's his name?" The words are whispered. I don't want to wake him.

"Jeremy Eleven Lockwood."

I almost smile. Eleven. In the periodic table, group eleven consists of the three coinage metals: silver, copper and gold. Eleven is the first double digit of the same number. Often thought to represent balance.

Jeremy Eleven is…not pretty. Patches of hair have fallen from his scalp. His cheeks are sunken in, his lips swollen and tinged with blue. My hand shakes as I reach out. I brush my fingertip over the softness of his knuckles, and he opens his fist to latch weakly on to my finger.

If love at first sight is possible, I'm already head over heels. "What's wrong with him?" I ask, still whispering.

Tears well in her eyes. "Your mother didn't know she'd been poisoned until after she'd fed him. She…"

She must be devastated, is probably eaten up with guilt. But she didn't do this. A monster did. Someone who places no value on Firstlife.

Bile burns my throat, and I struggle to retain my composure.

A moan rises from the bed. "Ten?" My name is nothing but a gasp, barely audible.

I meet my mother's gaze, and there's no stopping my gasp of horror. To me, it feels as though we sat across from each other in Vans's office only hours ago. She looked good then, if pale. She looked *normal.* Now her cheeks are hollow, and her eyes sunken. Her skin is sallow and paper-thin. Like Jeremy, her lips are cracked and tinged with blue.

As though in a trance, I glide to her side and sink to my knees. She moves at a snail's pace, but eventually manages to reach up and clasp my hand. Her grip is shockingly weak, even considering the way she looks.

"My baby girl," she says. "They couldn't break you. I'm so glad."

A cluster of thorns sprout in my throat. "I'm sorry, Momma. So sorry for—"

"You have nothing to apologize—" A cough racks her body, blood spraying from her mouth.

"Shh. The past is over and done. Save your strength." Seeing her like this…whatever anger I still harbored evaporates, leaving only the love I have for her. I suffered because of the choices she made, but so did she. Regret is etched into every line of her skin.

A tear trickles from the corner of her eye. "I never should have…pushed you…should have let you…choose." She taps the spot just over her heart. "Let Jeremy…choose. Let him. He's your dad's… Didn't know I could…pregnant again. Think he fed… Lifeblood. Healed me. Had mistress…just in case."

She jumps from one point to another, but I'm able to keep up. When Jeremy dies, his spirit will be up for grabs. I can't let my dad choose for him. "Archer," I croak.

I'll stay with him. I'll escort him into Troika, and when he reaches the Age of Accountability, I'll allow him to choose without interference. You have my word.

"Archer?" Momma asks.

"A friend," I tell her, and it's the absolute truth.

"Friend…good…such a good girl…love you…scribe."

I'm not sure she knows what she's saying anymore. I gently trace my fingers over her cheek. "Rest now, all right? We'll talk when you wake up." *Please, wake up.*

Her panicked gaze lands on Maggie. "Scribe."

"I'll give it to her, Grace," the old woman says. "Don't you worry."

The reassurance calms her, and she closes her eyes. I watch her chest for a telltale rise and fall of breath—holding my own until…yes. She hasn't slipped away.

Maggie places Jeremy in the crib and pulls a small black device from her pocket. Another flash-scribe. She hands it to me and I press my thumb on the center.

Her voice fills the room. "My dearest Ten. I can never express my regret for all the horrors you've endured. Because of my mistakes! Because I allowed bitterness to harden my heart when Troika failed to save my parents. Or so I thought. My mother visited me, you know. In a Shell. She was granted permission and she explained the truth. The fault was hers. I think I finally understand what you shouted at me so many times. Our choices direct our path."

I blink back tears.

"Seeing you at the asylum, sweet girl, knowing what they planned to do to you, how much they would hurt you, I'm overcome by sorrow. The only thing I should have done was love you. You're a beautiful girl, inside and out, and I want only the best for you. But I wasn't the best mother. I didn't give you the best life, despite the money and fame, but I *will* give you the best future."

The tears cascade down my cheeks now, rivers of remorse and sorrow, leaving hot streaks behind.

"I've arranged to get you out of Prynne and bring you home. Your future—your Everlife—is your own. I wish... well, it doesn't matter now. Take care of Jeremy. He's your brother, sweet Ten. He's going to need you. Your father sees him as a second chance. A chance to meet the conditions of his contract without you. Loophole. Because of population control, the contract doesn't mention you specifically, merely his child. I'm so sorry, sweet girl. I want Jeremy to live. I want *you* to live. My prayer is that you have a long, long Firstlife, happy and content, and in your Everlife you are free of regrets."

I hunch over to contain a sob. Does my mother know she and Jeremy are going to die together? And soon? Is she trying to tell me that my dad now wants me dead?

Is he the one who arranged the plane crash? The car wreck? He must be.

I am bleeding inside as I stuff the device in my pocket.

Archer opens the door; he's back in his Shell, his expression grim. "Your father is here. You were noticed on camera. He's being told of your presence right—"

"Ten!" My father's voice echoes off the walls.

chapter nineteen

"The future belongs to us."
—Myriad

"Ten!" my father shouts. "I know you're here."

My mother is sleeping so deeply, she doesn't stir.

Maggie rushes to the crib and gathers Jeremy close. "I'm sorry to abandon you, but I don't want the senator to notice the boy and take him away from me."

"I understand," I say even though everything inside me screams to keep the boy near me.

"Don't worry, dear. The nursery is your mother's walk-in closet."

"I won't let him hurt you," Archer says.

As a Troikan, he can't harm a human without punishment and that's what it will take to get me out of here unscathed.

Trust him, a part of me cries. *He'll find a way.*

No. Sorry. I won't trust him, not about this. "Stay in the nursery," I tell him. "Do as you promised for my brother.

You and Killian taught me how to fight for a reason. Now let me fight. I'll be okay." At least physically.

My father has a way of wounding my heart.

"Ten!"

Archer looks as if he wants to argue with me.

I shake my head. "Nursery. Now."

He scowls, but as my Laborer, he can't stay where he's not wanted and he does as I requested. Perfect timing. My father storms into the room—and stops.

He actually smiles at me. "You're here." He closes the distance and draws me in for a bear hug. "You finally did it. Ten, I'm so proud of you. Thank you. Thank you for signing with Myriad."

Frowning, I wrench away from him. "Why would you think I signed with Myriad?"

He blinks at me. "Because you've been released."

"No, I escaped."

His brow furrows with confusion, as if I'm speaking in a foreign language. "But you signed with Myriad first."

"No. I'm still Unsigned."

He pinches the bridge of his nose. "Are you trying to hurt me? Is that it?"

A bomb of rage detonates—I have thousands on tap, collected over the past year. "*Me* hurt *you*? Daddy, you paid people to *torture me*. And I think… I think you tried to kill me."

His cheeks redden. "Everything I did, I did for your own good." He grips me by the shoulders and shakes me. "I wanted you happy in the Everlife. I wanted to be a family."

"We could have been a family here, in this life!"

He continues as if I said nothing. "But you wouldn't

cooperate. You weren't just ruining your life, you were ruining ours."

It's as good as a confession. Every internal wound he's ever given me splits open once again, and I cry out. "Did you poison Mom?"

"No! I would never hurt her."

He truly sounds offended. "But you can hurt me, right?" Something my mom mentioned peeks through the dark mire of my thoughts. "Lifeblood." Black market, I bet. "You fed her Lifeblood, and it healed her reproductive organs. And just in case that didn't work, you got yourself a girlfriend and got her pregnant."

His eyes beseech me to understand. "You don't understand. Every day, Madame Bennett pressured me."

Boo-hoo. "I know a little something about pressure!"

"Not like this. Every day she threatened me and cajoled. She even gave me a tour of Many Ends, which is where I'll end up if my contract is voided."

How could she give him a tour of Many Ends when the Myriadians have no way inside it? "To save yourself, you were willing to send *me* to Many Ends." How has the man who carried me on his shoulders so I could reach the sky become *this*? "You're a coward!"

He shakes his head as he backs away from me. "You don't understand," he repeats. "Madame Bennett was right. Prynne stripped away your weakness and left you with strength. You're going to be an indomitable Abrogate, and I helped you. I played a part. I should be praised, not castigated." He's not listening, choosing instead to focus on anything but the crux of the matter.

"If happiness is dependent on outside variables, it can't

last. Variables always change. Real happiness has to come from within. Right here." I hit my heart with my fist. "Sometimes you have to dig for it, and you have to dig deep. I know because I managed to find glimpses of it even when I was locked inside a cell, spied on and beaten."

"Enough!" He stalks to the door, but pauses to glance over his shoulder. "You're making it difficult to love you, Ten."

As long as there's breath, there's hope.

I'm not sure that's true. "I'll kill you before I allow you to use my brother."

The muscles between his shoulders bunch. "I'm going to lose everything. You get that, don't you?"

I dismiss him and stalk to the bed to wake my mother. I'm getting her and Jeremy out of here. As I gently pat her cheek, the coldness of her skin makes my stomach twist. Her lips are bluer than before…lips that are now curved into a smile I haven't seen since I was a little girl.

Dead…*no. No, no, no.* "Mom. Momma." I give her shoulders a shake.

Her eyes remain closed, her body as limp as a noodle.

I look to my dad, but he's already gone.

"Maggie," I shout.

She bursts from the closet/nursery, Jeremy tucked in her arms. Her eyes are red-rimmed, as if she's been sobbing. Pink lines streak her cheeks. Like me, she's been crying.

Archer is stoic.

"She's not responding," I say. "You have to help me…" What? Perform CPR? *Baiser de la mort* decimates the heart, reducing it to tattered remains. There's nothing to resuscitate.

Fat tears fill my eyes. My chin trembles. Mom is gone. She's gone, and there's nothing I can do to bring her back.

At the asylum, I dreamed of hurting her, of dishing to her what she dished to me. But here, now, I only want her healthy and whole. I didn't get enough time with her. Would do anything for five more minutes. Just five. To hold her hand, to tell her I forgive her. To hug her and be hugged by her.

Now she's in Myriad. Hopefully happy. But I won't get to see her until *I* die.

Will we be on the same side—or enemies?

Maggie eases onto the edge of the bed. "She held on as long as she could, hoping to see you." She chews on her bottom lip as tension stretches between us. "Ten." Sadness is like a rainfall in her voice. "I'm afraid Jeremy doesn't have much time, either."

My hands shake as I reach out. I gather the featherlight bundle in my arms and cradle the sweet boy to my chest. His eyes are closed, his dark lashes so long, they cast shadows over his cheeks. His lips are bluer than before, and he's wheezing. I've heard that sound before. The death rattle.

No, he doesn't have much time.

I'm going to lose my mom and brother in the same day.

Killian stalks into the room. He spots me with the baby, and his angry countenance softens in a blink. The compassion he projects almost kills me.

My tears fall freely as I peer down at Jeremy. One drop splashes on his cheek, and his lids flutter open, his gaze meeting mine for two precious seconds. He has my eyes. One blue, one green. I bring his little hand to my mouth to kiss his knuckles.

"I love you, little man." Another of my tears lands on the corner of his mouth, and if this were a fairy tale, that tear—born of true love, offered freely—would save him. But this is real life and next he expels his last breath, his head lolling to the side.

I know time is of the essence. Once the physical body dies, the spirit *will* leave it.

Killian reaches for him, saying, "I'll make sure he ends up with his mother, lass."

Even with my mom, Jeremy will be strenuously *encouraged* to stay in the realm when he reaches the Age of Accountability. And in Troika, he'll still have family. The grandparents I was never allowed to meet.

And… I want Jeremy to walk in the sunlight, to feel the warmth stroking his skin.

I shake my head…and…and…*do it, just do it*…and hand my baby brother to Archer, who is no longer so stoic. There are tears in his eyes, as well.

The unreadable mask falls over Killian, and I know I've hurt him yet again. I have to do what's best for my brother.

"He will know love," Archer says.

This is *killing* me. "Thank you."

Archer and Jeremy vanish in a bolt of light, and all I can do is stand in place, trying to see past my pain. But there's too much of it, and it's too intense, every bomb of emotion I've ever stored in my heart suddenly exploding at once.

With a screech from the depths of my soul, I launch across the room. My hands are on my mother's dresser. I yank with all my strength, and the entire thing falls to the floor. Wood cracks, and the knickknacks that were sitting on top of it shatter.

"Why hurt two innocents?" I demand. "Why? Who would do this?"

I turn to the nightstand and kick it over. The legs extend into the air, and I kick them, too. I kick and I kick and I kick until one of those legs detaches. Panting, I swoop down to pick it up. I could beat my dad with it. I could dish to him the same pain he paid to have dished to me. Vengeance will be mine at last. He will deserve every blow.

I tell myself these urges are temporary. They will fade, just like my fury. I tell myself I'm a hypocrite. I chastised Archer and Killian for giving in to their hatred, and yet here I am, desperate to do the same.

I tell myself all that—but here, in this moment, it doesn't matter. My brother is dead. My mother is dead, and my father is free to start a new family with his mistress. When the baby is born, he'll no longer need me alive. He'll depend on the contract loophole to save his future while destroying mine. I'll be at risk once again.

"No, lass." Killian snatches the stake from my grip. "You'll never forgive yourself."

I turn to him and, with another screech, beat my fists against his chest. "Who would do this? Who would hurt a baby?"

He doesn't try to shield himself, and he doesn't try to stop me. I pound on him with all my strength, pouring my rage and hurt into every blow. This isn't fair. *Life* isn't fair.

"I wish I had the answers you seek," he says softly.

"This isn't meant to be. Do you hear me? This *isn't meant to be.*" A child isn't supposed to die without ever living. A mother and son aren't supposed to be separated in the

Everlife, and yet my mother is in Myriad and my brother is in Troika.

"I know," he says, surprising me. "This was done deliberately."

When the last of my strength abandons me, Killian wraps his arms around me and gathers me close. I bury my face in the hollow of his neck. I sob for everything I've lost—everything this little boy has lost.

"This isn't the end for either of them, lass. You'll see them again."

He still considers the fact a comfort. I release a near-hysterical laugh. "Yes, but which one will be my enemy? My Troikan brother or my Myriadian mother?" Maybe I *should* have given Jeremy to Killian.

"Why didn't you let me take the boy to Myriad?" he asks. "You divided mother and son."

I look up and notice Maggie is gone…think I remember Killian hustling her out the door during my outburst. "For once, I made a split-second decision based solely on instinct. Do this, not that. Light versus dark." Right versus wrong.

He considers my words, sighs and kisses my temple. "I ensured your father…fell asleep before I came to your room. Come on. Let's get out of here."

He punched my father into unconsciousness, didn't he? "My path started here, and I'd like it to end here." Determination gives me a surge of strength. "I'm going to make my decision. Today." I'm not running. Not anymore. I'm meeting my present—and my future—head-on.

He brushes his thumbs over my eyes, capturing the remaining tears. "A good General leads an army. A great

General leads every individual member. Today, you are a great General."

"Maybe, but it's not because someone else inhabits my body."

"How do you know?"

The very question I once asked him. "Some things you can't explain. You just know. Right here." I take his hand and place it over my racing heart. "The truth is so bright the shadows of doubt are chased away."

"What of actual proof?"

"I'm *living* proof."

He's thoughtful as he twines our fingers and leads me into the hall. "If you want to stay, we'll stay, but not in this room."

"Let's go to my bedroom." I point straight ahead, only to realize he probably has the blueprint of the house memorized. "Did you hurt Deacon to get to me?"

"Are you kidding? I wanted to fight him, but he told me to do whatever was necessary to protect you and then he opened the door for me."

Surprise, surprise. Troika and Myriad worked together.

We enter what had once been my sanctuary, and everything is just as I left it. The king-size bed has a large white canopy. When I was a little girl who dreamed of living in the moonlight of Myriad and marrying a handsome prince, my dad would use my sheets to make me a castle.

My mind shies away from the memory. Too painful right now.

I pull from Killian's side to walk around, bypassing the chrome-and-glass nightstand to stop in front of the vanity, where I used to sit every morning before school to fix my hair and makeup. Over the marble fireplace hangs a portrait of white roses. While some of the roses are skillfully done, some are clearly *not* so skillfully done. My mother and I painted the portrait together. Our first—really our only—dual project. My chin trembles. I was seven at the time.

I walk to the bed and recline in the center. Killian parts the window curtains and peers outside—searching for trouble? He checks the seam of the pane and places a small black device on the lock.

"A flash-scribe?" I ask.

"Similar. This one creates sounds waves imperceptible to humans. It will keep spirits from entering the house and spying on you, but not Shells." He closes the distance and stretches out beside me, dragging me against his body, holding me close, offering comfort.

It isn't long before Archer appears in a blaze of light. He spots us and, as if it's the most natural thing in the world, stretches out at my other side.

Killian stiffens, but doesn't protest. I'm glad. I'm surrounded by pure male aggression, and I like it. I take comfort in it, the most I've experienced in a long, long time. These boys are my friends. I owe them so much. I mean, even though I've distrusted them, hurt them, snapped at them and insulted them, they've stuck by my side, even putting their own agendas aside.

"Jeremy is with General Levi, a man I respect with every ounce of my being," Archer says. "He'll be protected and loved as if he is Levi's son. In fact, Levi is already teaching your brother a new language. Does either of you know what *goo-goo* and *ga-ga* mean?"

I want to laugh. I want to cry. "I think they mean happiness awaits." I reach over, squeeze his hand. "Thank you."

He squeezes back.

Killian growls low in his throat, but again, he doesn't protest. He takes my other hand.

The name Levi strikes a chord inside me. "My TL, before I was sent to Prynne, was named Levi."

"One and the same," Archer says.

Good. That's good. I'd had no idea Levi was a General; he'd never announced his title, but he was kind to me.

Are you living your parents' dream…or your own?

"Why did you choose to leave Myriad when you reached the Age of Accountability?" I ask Archer. For my benefit, but also Killian's. I know he's agonized over it. "Especially since your father is there…and the boy you once considered a brother."

Killian doesn't just stiffen; he goes rigid.

"I was training to be a Laborer, learning to occupy a Shell and travel to the Land of the Harvest. A group of us accompanied our trainer on a mission, not to sign a soul but to ambush a handful of Troikans. Men and women who were helping Firstlifers plant a garden."

"I remember," Killian says, his voice tight.

"We slaughtered them." Archer's voice cracks. "We slaughtered them, and as one of the women lay dying, hemorrhaging inside her Shell, unable to leave it because I'd pinned her inside with an arrow, she smiled at me. Smiled, with Lifeblood on her teeth. She managed to gasp out *I forgive you*. Can you imagine? She forgave me, when I suddenly couldn't forgive myself. I was the victor, soon to be rewarded for my deeds, when I should have been abhorred and punished. I knew I couldn't go on that way."

Footsteps sound outside my door. In unison, we sit up. My heart pounds against my ribs as the boys unsheathe weapons I didn't know they carried. Either my dad has woken up…or my potential killer is on the way.

Crack!

Hinges on the door bust, shards flying in every direction. Three big, beefy men I can only assume are Shells rush inside the room, guns drawn.

"On your knees," one of them shouts. "Now."

Both Killian and Archer leap to their feet, blocking me from the line of fire.

"You want to live, you leave." Killian squares his shoulders. "Now."

He doesn't wait for the men to obey, and neither does Archer. The two hammer away on the triggers of their guns. There's no blast or pop, only a soft whoosh as a dart embeds in each of the Shells.

Darts…darts…

This one, the Stag, shoots darts that, when embedded in a Shell, trap the spirit inside and shut down mobility.

In a blaze of light, three new Shells appear on one side of the room, and three more appear on the other. They are armed, as well, and we are completely surrounded. Killian and Archer continue shooting, but they can't dodge the darts fired at them without making me a target.

They both take a round to the chest and drop to their knees.

"Will kill you…for this." Killian's voice is barely audible, but I hear the menace in his tone.

"Stop! Enough!" Not wanting the boys further incapacitated, I put my hands in the air and move in front of them.

"You heard her. Enough." A woman in a formfitting red dress and killer heels strides into the room. Madame Pearl Bennett.

Her expression softens as she meets my gaze. "Hello, Ten. I've missed you."

chapter twenty

"Do your best, not just what's good enough."
—Troika

Pearl enfolds me in a hug I can't bring myself to return. She smells just like I remember: a mix of roses and lilac. When she pulls back, she's smiling at me with fondness. "Were you hurt while the boys were restrained?"

Once upon a time, I really liked this woman. I think I even loved her. But she convinced my father to send me to Prynne. She requested unimaginable tortures be visited on me. Now she wants to chat as if we're long-lost pals?

I remain mute.

She turns to the Shells. "Collar Killian before he's able to cause any more trouble."

"Don't you dare—" Killian goes quiet when the Shell closest to him wraps a glowing band around his neck. Horror and rage shine in his eyes.

"Stop!" I reach for him, desperate to help him, even though I have no idea what the collar is or does. But judging by his reaction, it's bad. Really bad.

"While a human can command a Laborer, you have no authority over a Leader." Pearl clasps my wrist, holding me in place with surprising strength. "I know you're fond of Killian. You were always fond of him, but he's been a very naughty boy and needs to be transported to the Kennel."

Kennel? And what does she mean, I've *always* been fond of him?

The answer slides into place. Ashley. She thinks I'm Fused with her daughter.

"Don't you dare!" The muscles in Killian's face and shoulders go taut as he struggles for freedom. "You have no right."

"Please, Pearl," I plead, my hands forming a steeple. "Don't hurt him." I never begged Vans for anything, but then, he'd never had anything worth begging for.

"I won't. If you sign with Myriad right here, right now."

My gaze darts to Killian. He already knows my answer. His head is already bowed in defeat.

"I… I…can't. I'm so sorry, Killian." There has to be a better way. Caving to evil manipulation now means caving later.

"I'm sorry, as well." She nods to one of the Shells.

He types into his wrist, a blue light glowing. Then he places a hand on Killian's shoulder. Killian's head lifts and our gazes lock for a split second. I see regret, sorrow and challenge. I *feel* them, too.

There's so much I want to tell him. *I consider you my family. I'm grateful for all you've done for me. We were learning from each other, weren't we? I'm coming for you.*

A blast of light slams into the two. Between one blink

and the next, they're gone, and I hiss with a combination of fury and concern.

"Now. Time to deal with you. The prodigal son," Pearl says to Archer. "The fact that I admire your father is the only reason you'll survive this day."

"Don't hurt him. Please." I'll beg for him, too. *My boys.*

She pats my cheek. "I hear he's due to attend an Exchange." She motions to one of the Shells. "Send him home so that he can at last receive it."

As a gun is pressed between Archer's eyes, he says, "I love you, Ten. You are the sister of my heart."

"Don't do this, Pearl. You said he'd live," I shout, but the trigger is squeezed. *Pop!* Archer's Shell bursts into ash.

"We freed his spirit from the Shell," Pearl assures me. "That's all."

The escape hatch. Right.

She takes my hand and leads me through the house. We pass my dad, who's standing beside the front door. He won't look at me and even though this man tried to kill me—twice—his complete disregard wounds me all over again.

A limo is parked in the driveway. A man in a suit is waiting for us. He opens the back door and helps me inside, and Pearl slides in behind me.

"We're going to a spa, just like we used to when you were a little girl. Remember?"

The spa. On the day my mother and brother died. The day she placed Killian in a hellish situation. The day she sent Archer to face judgment.

"I hate you," I snarl at her.

She flinches, as though wounded. "You will not talk to

me that way. Do you understand? I'm your superior. And Ten," she says, her voice softening, "I'm your mother."

"My mother is dead." The words leave me, and I go still. A terrible thought hits me, and I can't escape it. "Did you kill her? Did you kill my brother?"

Her gaze implores me to listen, to understand. "I *am* your mother. You're Fused with my Ashley. I know it. The timing was perfect—a sign. And you glowed so brightly, as only Generals do."

"I'm not just a General. I'm an Abrogate." Or rather, a Conduit. The car motors forward, twisting and turning along the roads. "Eight other Myriadian Generals died the same day as Ashley."

"Yes, but *all* the Generals are—" She stops herself, clears her throat.

"All the Generals are...what?"

"It doesn't matter."

Oh, it matters. Apprehension radiates from her, as if she's revealed a secret she should have died to protect.

"All you need to know is that you *are* my Ashley." She stares straight ahead. "And that...that *woman* planned to break you out of Prynne, to keep you from me forever." Disgust and anger drip from her tone. "Yes, I poisoned her. Something you will one day thank me for. Your brother was simply an unfortunate casualty."

I breathe through my rage. I know what happens when the emotion pulls my strings. Chaos. Destruction. Which is unnecessary. Like everything else, rage is temporary, changeable. And if I allow it to control me, I allow it to make my decisions for me. In that case, I might as well be taken over by Ashley or anyone else.

But I can't just sit here.

"You remind me of my father. You don't see the harm in what you've done. Allow me to remedy that." Without any more warning than that, I yank the wire from my bracelet and leap onto her lap. With a few swirls of my arm, I have the wire wrapped around her neck—*thank you, Killian.*

I yank my arm as hard as I can, cutting into her jugular. "This is all your so-called love will get you. Resistance."

I'm about to release her, my point made, when her eye sockets clear and the Shell goes still.

The car stops abruptly a few seconds later, and the door opens. A scowling Pearl leans in and shoots me with a dart. As electric pulses beat through my body, making my muscles spasm, she shoots the useless Shell, turning it to ash, then slides into the seat, removes both my bracelets and throws them out the window. She frisks me for other weapons, finds none and relaxes in her seat.

The pulses taper off the moment she removes the dart from my neck, and I go lax.

"I don't want to kill you," she says, "but I will if I must. You and Ashley will end up in Many Ends, but one day you'll return to the Land of the Harvest. I can find you again."

"How?" As far as I know, once a spirit is lost in Many Ends, it's lost for good.

"I'll watch for signs."

"And the so-called signs are never wrong?"

A slight tremor sweeps through her before she shrugs.

My head cants to the side. "Do you have any family in Troika?"

"I do."

"You war with them?"

"I do," she repeats. "Troikans want to destroy everything I hold dear. They look down their noses at me, only seeing a heathen they've deemed unworthy of their precious light. As if *I'm* inferior."

"There are some who despise the animosity between the realms." Archer and Deacon defend their home, but they also love their enemy. I've seen glimpses.

"You're championing them?" Her eyes narrow on me. "If you continue to refuse Myriad, I'll be forced to kill you myself. And then I'll kill Killian." She arches a brow, suddenly smug. "You care for him. Just the way he planned."

She's trying—again—to manipulate me. To turn me against the boy I've come to admire. "I won't let you harm him. In fact, you have three seconds to release him from the Kennel and the collar before I sign with Troika. One."

Her eyes narrow. "You can't—"

"Two."

She has a choice. Reach for a dagger and end me now, or comply. I didn't lie. I *will* sign with her enemy.

"He will be released," she rushes out.

"Now. Today."

Her nod is stilted.

We lapse into silence, and I should feel triumphant. I'm actually sad.

I peer out the window, trying to figure out where we're going. I know the area. Designated for stupid-rich Myriadians. My mom shops—shopped—in these stores.

The limo pulls in front of a spa, as promised. I say nothing as I'm ushered into the warmth of the day. The sidewalk gleams as if it's made of marble—painted cement—and palm trees sway in a gentle floral-scented breeze. With towering white columns and a gleaming staircase that leads to a wide set of arched doorways, the building could pass for a castle.

Pearl stays at my side as we enter. Several staff members step forward, smiling friendly smiles and offering the beverage of my choice, everything from champagne to aged whiskey. I decline. Must keep a clear head.

No other customers occupy the lobby. Guess Pearl rented out the entire place.

There's a tiered waterfall just like the one I saw in Myriad, with a mermaid perched on top. There are seating areas scattered throughout with leather couches and plush chairs. The concierge booth is framed by two ginormous sculptures, one of a woman with a dragon tail wrapped around her to conceal her breasts and the space between her legs, the other of a muscled man holding a globe of the world. The walls are painted a lovely shade of gold, and the air smells of lavender and lilac.

"Don't think," Pearl says. "Just enjoy."

Until I see Killian, I'll have to play along, so I nod. The girls who offered me a drink usher me to a private room in back, with two cushioned massage tables, two tubs filled with steaming water—Killian would be thrilled, if he were here. Soft music plays in the background.

Both Pearl and I are stripped. I hate that I'm weaponless and surrounded by strangers, but I keep my mouth shut. I hate that Pearl can change her mind about waiting and strike at me at any second. I remain on high alert as I'm bathed, waxed, oiled and massaged. And in a way, it's nice. After all the running I've done, as many accidents as I've endured, I'm sore.

Pearl watches me expectantly. I think she believes a rush of Ashley's memories will flood me, I'll open my arms and shout, "Momma!"

Sorry. Never going to happen.

My nails are painted girlie pink. My hair is trimmed and curled, the sides pulled back. Makeup is applied to my face. I'm given a beautiful sheath dress, Grecian in style, white with pleats that begin just under my breasts and fall to the floor. The spaghetti straps reveal my pale skin from neck to finger.

"Your favorite," Pearl says from behind me. "Look."

I actually twirl in front of the full-length mirror and gasp.

"You are breathtaking." She twines our fingers. "I've put together a party in your honor. The kind you used to love."

I'm in no mood to celebrate my *greatness*, but I offer no protest as we return to the limo. We travel the same roads, going back the way we came—are we going to my house? Where my mother and brother just died?

Oh, yes. We are.

Keep it together.

As the limo parks in the driveway, I stare at Pearl. "Now you're just being needlessly cruel." Before she can deny it, I demand, "Is my dad still here?"

"No. I've had him moved."

That's something in my favor, at least. "And Killian?"

"He's inside, waiting for you." She smiles at me. "Perhaps you'll see someone else you missed a little more…"

What's she planning now?

The answer presents itself as I emerge from the vehicle and climb the porch steps. The front door opens, and James steps onto the porch. Beautiful James, who must have been waiting for me. James, who protected me from Vans, bringing me extra food and making plans to escape with me.

James, who lied to me every day of our association.

He's tall, but not as tall as Killian, with dark blond hair and big brown eyes. His black-as-night suit hugs his muscled frame lovingly, the dark color making the blues and greens in his tie pop. Blue and green, like my eyes. A romantic gesture? Barf. He's romanterexic.

He grins at me, as if he's happy to see me.

"He grew far too attached to you," Pearl says, coming up beside me, "so I removed him from your case."

Liar! He didn't grow fond of me. He failed to do his job.

"My mistake," she adds.

"What makes you think I want him?" I lift the hem of my dress and scale the porch steps.

"Tenley." James holds out his hand, expecting me to accept, probably melt. "I missed you so much." His smile begins to fade as I continue to stare at him. "I hated to leave you, but I had no choice."

"Really? Tell me. How do my tits look in this dress?" As he gapes at me, I say, "Excuse me," and sail past him. I enter the foyer.

People are everywhere, but there's enough free space to maneuver into the living room. Laughter abounds, and perfumes clash. I wrinkle my nose as I scan the sea of faces, searching for Killian.

James comes up beside me, clasps my arm. "Ten, please. You have to listen to me."

She likes 'em big.

I yank from his hold. "I don't *have* to do anything."

"Yes, you were an assignment. At first. But I fell in love with you and—"

"You never loved me. If you had, you would have told me the truth."

Irritation flares in his eyes. Irritation he quickly masks with faux hurt. "If I told you the truth, I would have lost you."

"You lost me anyway." I did love this boy, but only a mirage of him.

Feminine twitters draw my attention to the stairs. Killian stands at the top. He—is—gorgeous. Our gaze meet, and oh, the blood in my veins heats, sizzles and melts me. *He's here. He's unharmed.*

Slowly he descends the staircase, every female he passes stopping whatever she's doing to watch him. Some even try to gain his attention. A few reach out to touch him, but he's focused only on me.

"Him?" James snarls at me. "You want *him*?"

I'd forgotten he was standing next to me. I yank from his clasp once again, my heart pound, pound, pounding. Like James, Killian is wearing a suit: black, pin-striped and perfectly tailored to his Shell. When he's right in front of me, his heated gaze sweeps over me, making me shiver.

"You look..." His gaze slowly works its way back up. "There are no words good enough."

"Thank you." I smooth my hand down the sides of my dress. I decide not to tell him about Pearl's threat. I'm not putting him in a position to fight on my behalf and perhaps be returned to the Kennel. "And you...wow. Only three words are good enough. Delicious man-meat."

The warmth of his chuckle strokes my skin. "That's my favorite compliment ever."

James puffs out his chest. "Killian."

His amusement fades as he meets the boy's gaze. "You'll want to move. Now."

James sputters. Killian cants his head—that's it—and James backs a few feet away.

A girl I've never met sidles up and wraps an arm around Killian's waist. He stiffens and flicks her off, but she doesn't seem to mind the negative reaction, returning to rest her head on the crook of his shoulder.

She looks me over. "Is she your flavor of the week? Well, I approve. Those mismatched eyes are striking, aren't they?"

He wraps an arm around *my* waist. "Excuse us." As she stares in astonishment, he leads me away.

"Another conquest of yours?" I ask.

"There's nowhere in the world you can go and not find one. I told you I was very good at my job, and I meant it. But..."

I'm teetering on the edge of anticipation as I await his words. "But?"

"You aren't just a job." He stops to cup my jaw, peer deep, deep into my eyes. "I didn't like being parted from you today."

My knees go dangerously weak. "I could admit I didn't like being parted from you."

He gives me the slow, wicked smile he first unveiled in the asylum. "Could you, or do you?"

"I do." I lean into him, breathe him in. I'll never get enough of his scent.

James approaches—again—and clears his throat. Was he always this annoying?

Without looking away from me, Killian grabs him by the tie and shakes him. "Go. Away."

James slaps at his hand like a bitch but it does no good. "I have a gift for you, Ten."

"Tenley," I snap. "And you can stuff your gift—"

A smiling Sloan peeks over his shoulder. "Actually, I think you'll want to keep this one."

chapter twenty-one

"There is no line we won't cross to get the job done."
—Myriad

I push James out of the way and throw my arms around Sloan, so happy to see her I could cry. Who am I kidding? I am crying.

"Thanks for ruining my makeup," I tell her.

"Anytime." With a laugh, she pulls back and twirls. "Tell me you've never seen a more glorious sight and mean it or I'll hate you forever."

"I've never seen a more laborious sight. There. Did I say it correctly?"

She flips me off, but she's still smiling. A scarlet dress adorns her body all the way to her knees, where the material flares and flits with her every movement. Her pale hair is swept to the side of her nape in an elegant knot of braids.

She waves a finger from the top of my head to the bottom of my heels. "Even with the mascara streaks, you're a hot tamale. If I were into girls, I'd give Killian a run for his money."

I snort. "You just won a little piece of my heart."

"Like I didn't already own one hundred percent."

"I'd love a chance to—" James begins.

Killian punches him in the throat, causing the Shell's voice box to collapse. Suddenly all James can do is flap his lips open and closed, no sound emerging.

I pat Killian's cheek. "My night just got better. Thank you."

Grinning now, he leans in to kiss my ear. He whispers, "I want you to choose Myriad, but I want you to want to choose the realm. I'm not going to pressure you, and I'll prove it." He traces his fingers along my arm, causing goose bumps to rise. "Take Sloan to your room."

What? "No. I don't want to leave you," I whisper back.

"I'm going to keep Pearl occupied. There's something you need to see." He kisses my cheek and lifts his head.

My heart thumps against my ribs. Do I need to see a good thing or a bad thing?

"Ugh. Enough lovey-dovey crap already," Sloan says.

I force a smile as I face her. "Why don't we go to my room and get away from all this noise? We can catch up."

"Nutter, that's the best offer I've had all day. Which is saying something!" She links her arm with mine, adding, "That guy over there wanted to—and I quote—teach me the meaning of *ecstasy*."

"So lucky," I say drily. I meet Killian's gaze, silently telling him, *Stay close.*

His gaze says, *Nothing will keep me away.*

All right. Time to concentrate and figure out what he wants me to see upstairs. I lead Sloan away, saying, "Have you signed with Myriad?" Why else would Pearl allow her to come?

"No, ma'am. When we parted, I hit the road with Deacon, thinking my first order of business would be destroying my family once and for all."

"Right."

She stiffens, adding, "They were so broke they couldn't afford my stay at Prynne, so...they made a deal with Vans. While he convinced me to marry the man they'd picked out for me, he could have me anytime he wanted, as long as he didn't get me pregnant. I kept thinking my prospective groom would grow tired of waiting for me and marry someone else, and I'd finally be freed, but he never did."

My hand flutters over my heart. "Oh, Sloan. I'm sorry." The words aren't good enough.

"Guess I'm worth waiting for," she says, every word sharp enough to cut.

"I had no idea what you were going through." And I'd only added to her problems.

When we reach the top of the stairs, she says, "No one did, which was the way I wanted it. I hated him, hated the times he...visited me, and I don't think I could have lived with the humiliation if everyone knew what was happening."

"I'm sorry," I say again. What a horrible existence.

She waves the words away, the motion clipped. "Anyway, I fired my ML Elena for her attitude problem."

"You mean you fired her because she wouldn't do everything you demanded the second you demanded it?"

"Exactly. I love that you know me so well." She beams at me. "Anyway. My case was given to James. He was invited here, and he asked me to join him. I decided destroying my family could wait another day or two so I could see my friend."

A friend. I have another friend, one I made all on my own. A human who understands my predicament.

There's a crowd of people milling about on the second level, so we have to push our way through. Someone waves at us. Others smile. We just keep trucking. When a couple drunkenly spills out of my mother's room, I have to swallow a curse...but I can't swallow the next one.

"No way. This isn't happening." I stomp to them—*calm, remain calm*—and barely manage to stop myself from chewing off their faces. "You don't go in that room ever. Ever! Do you understand?"

Sloan grabs my shoulders and pulls me back. "Fits of temper can wait."

"I mean it." I scan the rest of the faces around me. "*No one* goes in that room."

People rush downstairs. Good riddance!

A guard is posted at my bedroom door. A big, beefy guy with a mean scowl. But he opens the door as if he knows me. As if he's been waiting for me.

I grin and bear it. For now. "No one goes in the other rooms."

He nods. "Your command, my honor."

I like his readiness to please, but I kind of hate it, too. I'm not who he thinks I am.

Once inside the bedroom, I shut the door with a hard kick and Sloan flips on the light.

"Take a breather," she says, "and calm down."

My heels clink against the hardwood floor as I walk to

the bed. I plop on the edge and sigh. Last time I was in here, Archer and Killian snuggled me.

I want to be snuggled again.

"Don't take this the wrong way, but...this place is kinda sterile," Sloan says, her lips curled in distaste.

"A decorator selected everything, and I was expected to keep it clean." A room should be a sanctuary, but mine became a gilded cage over the years.

There's a bottle of champagne chilling in a bucket of ice. What Killian wanted me to see?

I pop the bottle's cork and pour the contents on the white rug at the end of the bed. Last time I had alcohol, I got stupid. Well, stupider.

Sloan laughs. "You dirty the carpets while I plan to torch an entire house. How do we even like each other?"

I smile at her. "Maybe we shouldn't dig too deep."

"That's true." She sighs, the amusement leaving her with the breath. "Okay, so. Let's get down to the nitty-gritty. I need your advice."

The reason Killian sent me away? "Shoot."

"Well, I kinda threw myself at Deacon, and he kinda turned me down."

"Kind of?"

"He told me he'll never date anyone outside his realm, and no one in his realm would ever do what I'm planning—the torching, in case you need a reminder—so I sent him away. Then James showed up and I thought, as crappy as he is, maybe he'll make Deacon jealous and you know, spur the guy into motion. And I know, I know. I'm immature. Whatever."

"I don't hear a question."

"Well, you know how eager I am to avoid Many Ends."

"I do. And having been there—twice—I can officially give the realm a one-star rating."

"What! You died? *Twice?* Why am I just now hearing about this?" She stomps over and slaps my arm. "What was it like?"

"Well, if your worst nightmare and the black plague had a baby, and that baby grew up to marry the boogeyman, and they had a baby, that baby would be Many Ends."

"Wow." She plops beside me. "You want to know what's sad? That's only *slightly* worse than I imagined."

"What are you waiting for?" I asked. "Why haven't you signed?"

She nibbles on her bottom lip. "Myriad and Troika refuse to give me what I really want."

"Which is?"

"Vans's spirit. I hate him more than I love anything else." In that moment, she reminds me of a live wire—ready to strike the first person dumb enough to touch her. "Troika doesn't play that way, and Myriad says they can't get to him, that he died as an Unsigned and ended up in Many Ends." I can *hear* the hate in her voice; it's so thick I figure it must be choking her. "My only real option is to go to Many Ends myself."

No. I don't want that for her. "Holding on to the past prevents you from grabbing on to a better future."

"I don't care. You don't know the things he did..."

I reach out and take her hand. Her tremors vibrate into me.

A tap sounds at the window. I share a frown with Sloan before walking over to investigate. Nothing seems out of the ordinary, and yet there's another tap. I open the pane and lean out.

A boy I've never met is dangling from the edge, white-knuckling the ledge.

"Who are you?" I demand.

He meets my gaze and smiles. "Why don't you take a guess?"

You've got to be kidding me. Deacon's eyes. "What are you doing out there? Come in, come in."

"Don't mind if I do." He kicks a leg over the ledge and hoists himself the rest of the way. He plucks the device Killian attached to the pane before shutting the window. "I tried coming in as a spirit first. As you can guess, it didn't work."

I glance outside. There are armed men patrolling the backyard and probably the entire property. To keep Troikans away from the party—or me inside it? I draw the white curtains with a flick of my wrists.

"Who the hell are—" Sloan sucks in a breath. "Deacon?"

"The one and only." He shows off his ripped biceps. "What do you think of the new Shell?"

"It's…weird." He's bald and now that I have a full view of him, I realize he's mostly naked, his skin nearly translucent, causing him to blend in with his surroundings. His junk is wrapped with a loincloth, making him look like… "This is awesome! You're a Ken doll." I laugh.

"I am not." He glares at me. "And stop staring at my package, perv."

"Are all Shells so anatomically incorrect?" Sloan asks, and she's staring harder at his package than I am. "Or is this the real you? Should we call you Microman?"

"Only camo Shells are like this, thank you very much." He gets real serious real fast. "Once a month there's a ceremony for those in Troika who are deserving of punishment. The ceremony is about to start, and I'd like you to watch it."

This. This is why Killian sent me up here. Archer is about to experience the Exchange. He wanted me to see it, to turn my back on Troika once and for all. But…that doesn't explain why *Deacon* wants me to see it.

"I don't understand you," I say. "What's your motive for showing me this?"

"You once expressed curiosity about the Exchange. Now you can see it for yourself." He stalks to the bed and stretches out in the center, and wow, it's difficult to track him; I manage it only because his iridescent flesh ripples like waves in an ocean. "Come," he says.

Sloan reaches out and squeezes my hand before taking the spot at Deacon's left. My knees shake as I close the distance and lie at his right. He types in the light projected from his hand and, just like the time Killian gave me a tour of Myriad, an image appears on the canopy above the bed. An image that begins to expand, until the entire bed is surrounded by the most breathtaking garden I've ever seen. There are hanging vines of wisteria, honeysuckle and ivy. The fruit trees are in full bloom, branches heavy with peaches, oranges and lemons.

"Usually we can use cameras to guide you, but cameras are forbidden in this part of the realm. I'm linked to a friend of mine," Deacon says. "You're seeing Troika through her eyes."

"Her?" Sloan waves a hand, as if she doesn't care. "Whatevs. You two get married and have a million babies."

The friend is clearly walking, taking us deeper and deeper into the garden. We pass an archway, a patch of wild strawberries and blackberries, and navigate a maze of wildflowers. Someone comes up beside us, a grim-faced girl with freckles on her nose and fire-engine-red curls.

"Don't want to be late," she says. "Better hurry."

We clear the garden and come to a sea of people. No one looks as if they're over the age of thirty-five. There's not a gray hair or wrinkle in sight.

"They're so beautiful," Sloan says.

"Yes. Only the human body decays," Deacon replies.

"Why is everyone wearing a robe?" In Myriad, the people wore clothing from what I assume was the era of their Firstlife. But here, almost everyone is draped in a violet robe with gold trim, elaborate and ornate, absolutely stunning. Those who aren't in violet are draped in red. I count one, two, three…six. Definitely the minority.

"Ceremonial robes," Deacon says.

Up ahead is a dais and behind the dais a palace, the walls glittering like diamonds, the trim…*ah-maz-ing.* Sapphires, rubies, emeralds. Topaz, beryl, onyx and jasper, each pure and flawless. Three people exit the palace to stand in the center of the dais. They, too, are dressed in robes, but unlike the others, they also wear crowns.

A tall, strong man consumes the middle. I can't make out his features. There's a light behind him—a rainbow, as if he carries it on his back, like a bow and arrow—and it glows so brightly he's partially obscured.

Power radiates from him. So much that I can feel it

through the connection Deacon has with the girl. It makes my blood fizz, and my skin feels as if lightning is zinging over the surface.

"Behold. The Firstking," Deacon says, his tone reverent. "Creator of the realms. Father to the Kings."

At his left is a woman with long braided hair the color of newly fallen snow. Her features are more apparent, but I almost wish they weren't. Her beauty is overwhelming, overpowering, and as I stare at her, I'm tempted to edge closer just to touch her.

Look away, look away. The third person—a male—is younger than the Firstking. His features are clearer than the others, but he lacks their beauty. In fact, he's almost plain. But his eyes...oh, his eyes. They are striking, as blue as the morning sky, and when he meets my gaze—

I gasp. He's looking straight at me, as if he knows I'm watching.

He smiles in welcome.

"The Troikan King is the Firstking's firstborn son, known here as the Secondking," Deacon says with the same reverent tone. "The woman is the Secondking's future bride."

The Firstking, the Secondking and the Secondking's fiancée. Troika, meaning three. Numbers always tell a story.

Despite the masses, not a single word is spoken. Not a whisper is heard until the Secondking steps forward. There are brands on his hands. Brands that are larger than any I've seen, going deeper.

"My people...my heart. For justice to serve one and all equally, always and forever, there can never be an exception to the law." His voice is thunder, and every word causes every cell in my body to burn. "If a crime is committed, a crime must be punished." The Secondking's voice booms, sweeping over the crowd, strong and sure. "For every word, every action, there is a choice. Right and wrong. Life and death. Blessing and cursing. I made my choice long ago—to keep the law intact. Who among you has transgressed?"

The crowd parts in rows of four. One by one, men and women move to the bottom of the dais. I scan…there! Archer has taken his place among those at the dais, and it's then I realize the ones being punished are the ones wearing red. Their heads are bowed, their hands clasped behind their backs.

I count the red robes—thirty-three in total—and my stomach gives another twist.

Thirty-three, the numerical equivalent of the word "amen." 1+13+5+14=33. A normal human spine has thirty-three vertebrae when the bones that form the coccyx are counted individually. The atomic number of arsenic.

A moment passes. Nothing happens, and no one speaks.

Then, one by one, the people in red robes begin to drop to their knees. A few cry out in pain. Others tremble. All keep their heads bowed.

"What's happening?" I ask in a whisper.

"They are experiencing the pain the one they harmed experienced."

The Exchange. I suddenly have the answer I'd so badly wanted. Archer is experiencing Clay's death. In his mind, he is hanging from a tree trunk, snow hitting him in the face. He is waiting for me…he is falling…he is bursting inside like a melon.

My chest begins to ache.

"Through this, we learn how our actions affect others," Deacon says.

I hate the thought of experiencing something like this, of knowing firsthand the pain I caused someone else. But…in a way, the experience is a gift. Knowledge is power. And here…here is where compassion is born.

When it's over, the ones in red robes stand. The royal family joins them and speaks softly to each one. Hands are clasped. Hugs are given.

The red robes return to the crowd, their heads still bowed. Archer, however, pushes his way to Deacon's friend and meets the girl's gaze—meets *my* gaze. His expression projects torment and sorrow.

This is the first time I've seen him without the Shell, and I notice little difference. The tone of his skin is more bronzed. The ends of his hair are like molten gold. His lashes are longer, his jaw a little more square. He really is quite beautiful.

The two clasp hands and suddenly the view changes. I'm looking at the friend rather than Archer. A girl identical to the redhead we met before.

"Thank you," Archer says.

She rises on her tiptoes to kiss his cheek. "If you need me, all you have to do is ask."

The two part ways. Archer takes us back through the garden, his gait fast. Pain must not linger after the Exchange. Not physical pain, anyway. When he clears the other side, a neighborhood comes into view, the houses a hodgepodge of designs; they look as if they belong in different parts of the world. A Southern plantation is next to a Spanish pueblo, which is next to an English cottage.

Waiting in front of the planation is—

"Clay!" I exclaim.

He smiles at Archer, and he looks good. His dark hair is a mess, his eyes sparkling. He's wearing a white T-shirt that conforms to his biceps, which actually look bigger. Someone's been working out like a fiend.

"You asked me to be here," Clay says. "Well, here I am."

Archer enfolds him in a hug. "I'm sorry. I'm so sorry I put a feud before your safety, that I wasn't there to save your life."

Tears fill my eyes.

Clay pats his shoulder as he draws back. "I told you, man. All's forgiven."

A pause, and I think Archer really wants to apologize again. "How's training coming?"

"I'm learning to inhabit a Shell, and next I'll learn how to use the weapons. I've only been drooling over those Oxies since my arrival."

Archer pats his shoulder. "Light Brings Sight, my friend."

Clay grins. "Light Brings Sight."

The two part ways, and a weight lifts from my shoulders.

Clay is happy. He's got a bright future ahead of him.

Archer makes a beeline for the plantation, passing towering pillars…a massive set of doors, already open. The interior is a dream come true. Wainscoting and detailed frieze molding. Vibrant rugs and crystal chandlers suspended from arched ceilings. I want to study everything in more detail, but Archer doesn't focus on anything but the man standing at the foot of a winding staircase.

I know him. Levi. My former TL. There's not a strand of dark hair out of place, and his lips are turned up in a welcoming smile. He's dressed in a perfectly tailored suit. He's dashing, the epitome of charm and sophistication.

He pats Archer on the shoulder. "Hello, Miss Lockwood. Miss Aubuchon."

We both jolt in surprise.

"Ten," he continues, walking to a pretty woman who is holding an infant. "I thought you'd enjoy a peek at our newest little charmer."

Jeremy? I'm trembling. "Yes. Please, yes."

He picks up the baby, oh…oh! Jeremy looks so healthy. His skin is pink and his cheeks rounded. He waves his arms and kicks his legs, and he's smiling! He isn't swaddled in a blanket—maybe he doesn't need to be while in spirit form—but he's wearing a onesie that reads Turn On the Light!

"He's thriving," Levi says. "And he is already loved. I've never had so many females visit my home."

I place my hand over my mouth to mute my cry. This. This is joy.

Light in the house flickers, and Levi frowns. He hands Jeremy back to the woman. "Guard him with your life." He strides into another room.

Archer follows him. "What's going on?"

"One of our Conduits is in danger. We must—"

The connection to Archer, to Troika, is severed, cutting off his words.

"No!" I gasp out. "How is a Conduit in danger?"

The entire house shakes, a crack appearing in the wall. Am *I* the one in danger?

When the shaking stops, Deacon pushes us off the bed. "Someone's coming."

As we hop to our feet, a thump sounds in the hallway. Then the door bursts open and Killian strides inside the room. There's a cut on his temple, the flesh leaking shimmering Lifeblood.

"We need to go," he says to me. "Now."

MYRIAD

From: P_B_4/65.1.18

To: K_F_5/23.53.6

Subject: Not Your Smartest Move

Where did you take the girl, Killian? Bring her back or this won't end well for you.

MPB

MYRYIAD

From: P_B_4/65.1.18

To: K_F_5/23.53.6

Subject: Answer Me!

We've captured one of Troika's Conduits. He made the mistake of leaving the realm.

Bring the girl to me, or I kill the Conduit—and your mother.

MYRIAD

From: P_B_4/65.1.18

To: K_F_5/23.53.6

Subject: Too Late

The Conduit is dead. Your mother is next.

MYRIAD

From: P_B_4/65.1.18

To: K_F_5/23.53.6

Subject: Last Chance

Troika is severely weakened. Now is the time to strike! You've always wanted a chance like this. Come back, and you'll get it. Or I can return to Myriad and track the girl, which I WILL do. Afterward, I'll assign you to the Kennels for a decade—if I don't kill you outright.

chapter twenty-two

"We see who you'll be."
—Troika

Killian takes my hand. He's trembling and mumbling about Pearl being a bitch. As he tugs me from the bedroom, I cast Sloan a look goodbye, but Deacon is already hustling her toward the window.

"Jump," Killian says. There's a dark edge to him. One I've never seen before.

I obey and end up on the other side of the fallen guard. Judging by the fist-size lump on his temple and the trickle of blood running down his cheek, he's human rather than Shell.

Word about my earlier outburst must have spread, because no other guests have come up here.

"What are you doing, Killian?"

"Making sure you survive the night."

We pass my mother's room. At the end of the hall, he stops to pick the lock on my father's door. We rush inside. Well. Not everyone heard I'm on a rampage. Three people in different stages of undress leap from the bed when Killian flips on the light. He palms a gun, aims and fires off three consecutive shots. There's no boom, no pop, only a soft whiz. Darts, I realize. All three people collapse.

He pushes me into the walk-in closet. He throws clothes from one of the racks, and I kick off my high heels. If we're going on the run, I kinda need to be able to *run*. "Your dad needed a way out of the house if protests ever got too violent. There should be a lock—here."

Click.

A doorway opens up, revealing a dark, dank staircase. We enter, the door closing behind us automatically. The scent of dust pervades, tickling my nose and throat, and I sneeze.

"I don't want you in trouble, Killian," I say.

"My choice, Ten."

Zero! He's using my own words against me. "Why are you choosing to do this?"

"I told you. You'll make your decision without pressure."

I can't stop my next actions and have no desire to try. As soon as we reach the bottom, I throw my arms around his waist, hugging him from behind. "You are a wonderful person, Killian. Better than you've ever given yourself credit for."

He turns and clings to me for a moment, only a moment. A stolen treasure of time. Then he disengages and, as if nothing happened between us, continues down the passage. When we reach the end, he punches a code into the pad by the door. The door's hinges creak as he peeks outside.

"How did you know the code?"

"Archer spoke to Maggie, then to me."

The two are working together now? *Without* my aid?

Killian leads me into the haze of the approaching night, the security lights that surround the house shining from different walls. Not that it matters. He's an expert at evading every pocket of illumination. And the guards on patrol. Without incident, he gets us to the road, where a silver Porsche awaits. I'm surprised when Elena climbs out and throws the keys at Killian.

He utters a hasty "Thank you" before taking her place behind the wheel.

"I hope you're worth it." She glares at me. "He'll never recover from this. Neither will I."

"I— Thank you." I don't know what else to say, and know she won't accept an impromptu hug. I climb into the passenger seat. Tires squeal as Killian speeds away. "Killian—"

"I'll be fine." He reaches over and takes my hand. He's still trembling. Our fingers link, and I don't mean to, but I cleave to him. "I always am."

"There's a first time for everything. What if—"

"No. We can't go there." Can't operate in a state of fear. "Do we have a destination tonight?"

"Yes. Your aunt's house."

Aunt Lina. Loony Lina. "I haven't seen her in years." I wonder which version of her I'll find today. "Won't that be the first place Pearl looks?"

"Yes," he repeats, "but she won't find you there."

"I don't understand."

"Don't worry. You will. Pearl mentioned tracking you, which means she had a tracker put inside you. I should have known."

A tracker? "How?" I ask, appalled. "Where?"

He squeezes my hand. "Do you know what I thought the first time I saw you?"

There's a sense of urgency in his tone now, as if he has a wealth of things to say but only a short time to do so. "Let me guess. *Great, she's crazier than I heard.*"

His chuckle is soft but ragged. "Yes, but soon after that?"

"After I punched you in the throat?"

"During our date."

"No." I lose my breath. "Tell me."

"I thought of something Archer told me right before he defected to Troika. Something I hadn't allowed myself to think about until that day. About a horse—"

"Hey!"

He smiles at me. "A warhorse. It's a compliment."

"Well, then, let's hear the rest of this supposed compliment."

"The day Archer chose Troika, I told him we were enemies and I would come for him. I told him that his father would forever hate him, and that he'd make it a personal mission to destroy him. His response confused me, until today. He said, *The warhorse paws fiercely, rejoicing in its strength, and charges into the fray. It laughs at fear, afraid of nothing; it does not shy away from the sword. The quiver rattles against its side, along with the flashing spear and lance. In frenzied excitement it eats up the ground; it cannot stand still when the trumpet sounds. At the blast of the trumpet it snorts, 'Aha!' It catches the scent of battle from afar, the shout of commanders and the battle cry.*" Killian squeezes my hand. "Then he added, *When you fight for what you know is right, my friend, you already have the victory. There's nothing to fear.*"

I place my free hand over my heart, moved in a way I would never have expected. A warhorse, unafraid of battle, actually craving it, daring his opponents to fight him, his enemy's efforts only making him laugh, because he knows he'll win. "You thought I was brave."

"And kind. And odd."

"Hey!"

"You shook me up. The things other assignments valued meant nothing to you. The things *I* valued meant nothing. Only when I spoke of a past I'd rather not remember did you soften toward me, as if you saw something in me no one else ever had."

He shook me up, too. He's *still* shaking me up. "Do you want to know what I thought about you when we met?"

"Please, Killian, kiss me."

Ha! "Close. I thought you were the most beautiful boy I'd ever seen…and that I'd better invest in a chastity belt."

He barks out a laugh, though his good humor doesn't last long. There's something going on inside his head.

"I wanted to know more about you, and I was secretly thrilled about our date. I was intrigued by everything about you, from your cocky attitude to your tattoos. There's a pattern to the designs."

"Yes," he says, but offers no more. "One day I'll tell you about them."

The device in his arm lights up, but he snags a razor from the console between us—one I didn't notice before—and runs the blade across his arm, tearing the flesh out of the Shell. He grunts. The light fades…dies as thick, sparkling Lifeblood gushes from the wound.

Fighting past my shock, I place my arm over the wound, applying pressure. He *is* risking everything for me.

"She threatened my mother," he says tightly.

"Oh, Killian. I'm sorry. Is there anything you can do to stop her? Wait. Let me rephrase. What can I help you do to stop her?"

He flicks me a glance loaded with surprise. "I need to get inside the Annals. A building heavily guarded. When I know my mother's new identity, I can protect her."

I don't think I believe in Fusion anymore, but I don't have the heart to tell him his mother is probably gone for good already.

When the hemorrhaging stops, I peer out the window. Palm trees whiz past. The sun is a magnificent ball of fire as it sets in the horizon. Warm, golden rays stroke over me and absorb through my skin.

For the second time, he lifts my hand to his lips, kisses the scars on my knuckles. He's kissed my knuckles once before, but this time…this time there's something special about the action and I feel branded deep in my soul.

"You wanted to know more about me," he says, returning to our conversation. "Here's the truth, flat out. I've pushed you so hard because I don't want you to end up like me. A failure."

I frown at him. "When did you fail?"

"Once I was thought to be Fused with a General, too. That's why I was allowed to train with Archer. That's why the King would visit with me."

Dread fills me, but I say, "What happened?"

"I couldn't complete the final stage of training. The King was disappointed, of course, and he gave me a task meant to redeem me. I was given the name of a human…someone I was supposed to kill."

The dread becomes tinged with horror. "Murdering an innocent isn't right, Killian. Your realm needs reform."

"Then join us and reform us, Ten. That kind of change can be made only from within."

Ugh. He makes a good point. But what of Troika? They need work, too.

And, wow. When did I become Miss Know It All, as if my way is the best way?

I sigh. "Go on."

"I was given the name Dior Nichols."

Oh…zero. "Does Archer know?"

"No. He'd already defected to Troika, and it was well-known she was one of his assignments. Which is why the King wanted me to kill her, I'm sure. I hated Archer, but I saw the way he looked at the girl, and I couldn't do it. I couldn't send her to Many Ends. I turned her against him and signed her to Myriad instead, and while I succeeded, I failed my King. I was banned from his presence and placed under Madame Pearl's leadership as a Laborer."

No wonder failure at his job is so abhorrent to him. No wonder he pushes and pushes to win every assignment given to him. He seeks to prove himself worthy of love and respect.

His motive doesn't excuse his method, but he's not the boy he used to be. "You've learned from past mistakes. You know what's right and what's wrong, and you're taking steps to make up for it through your dealings with me."

The gaze he throws me reveals shattered eyes. Something

inside him is breaking. "How can you say such things to me?" His voice is layered with different degrees of pain.

"Because there are no conditions for the things I feel for you."

He whips the car to the side of the road. Acting on instinct, I unbuckle and climb over the console to straddle him. He stares up at me with surprise and hope—a hope that breaks what little piece of my heart was still intact.

I brush my nose against his. "Is the night-night drug always in your mouth?"

"Only when I bust the capsule behind my tooth. A capsule I haven't yet replaced."

"Good." I frame his cheeks with my hands and press my lips against his.

He opens immediately and rolls his tongue against mine. I taste sugar and a hint of cinnamon, and I'm instantly addicted. I want more…want to devour. We thrust and parry, and I moan as delicious sensation after delicious sensation pours through me.

It's a kiss worth every moment of confusion and uncertainty. Worth every sleepless night and tormented day. A kiss capable of restarting a thousand dead hearts. A kiss with the power to soothe the rawest of wounds.

He wraps his arms around me, one hand sinking under my shirt to stroke up my spine, the other flattening on my rear to pull me nearer.

No matter how close I get, I can't get close enough.

I gasp his name. I comb my fingers through his hair. Soft and silky, the strands make my palms tingle. Those tingles ignite sparks and those sparks swim through my veins, heating everything they encounter, until I'm burning up from the inside out.

"I *feel* you," he gasps out. "The heat of you…it's so good."

Unable to sit still, I move against him, actually grinding on him. He leans forward, pressing his chest against mine, and my back arches until I accidentally hit the wheel. The horn gives a short but loud blast.

I chuckle. He chuckles. Then the ground beneath the car shakes, and he breaks from me. His hands tremble as he smooths the hair from my cheeks. His eyes are glassy, his pupils so enlarged his golden irises are almost completely eclipsed.

When he manages to catch his breath, he says, "We don't have time for this. Archer and friends are fighting Pearl, trying to stop her from tracking you. They've lost a Conduit, the light in their realm dangerously dim. They are now doubly determined to save and recruit you."

I'm struck anew by the knowledge that so much happens in the worlds and the realms, so much I can't see and don't realize.

"Besides," he adds, "I don't want our first time to be in a car."

We *are* cramped and anyone can approach the windows, attack us while we're distracted.

"Since our first time will be my first time ever," I say, my cheeks beginning to burn, "I agree the car isn't the best choice."

He presses his forehead against mine. "You're just making things harder for me. And I mean that in multiple ways."

I snort-laugh, killing the illusion I'm cool about the subject, and return to my seat. The pressure to make a decision has never been stronger. I'll save Killian, or I'll save a realm. But I'm beginning to suspect I finally know the right path for me.

chapter twenty-three

"Fight for us, and we'll fight for you. Fight against us and you'll lose."
—Myriad

Lina is waiting for me at the door of her house, a small but well-kept bungalow with white shutters and blue trim. Quaint and utterly perfect. As a little girl, I sometimes dreamed of living here. Uncle Tim, her husband, allowed Lina and me to put bows in his hair and paint his nails.

Of course, Uncle Tim eventually ran off with another woman, divorcing Lina and her crazy ways.

Porch light shines over her, illuminating dark hair and a pretty face aged by worry. This is Aunt Lina!

Killian puts the car in Park and latches on to my hand before I can jump out. "I got you a present." He reaches into the glove box, withdraws two leather wrist cuffs. "I know how much you loved your old pair."

"Killian! Thank you!" Grinning, I hug them before snapping them in place. "I did love them."

"That smile… I swear it's going to haunt me for eternity." He sighs. "I'm not going in with you. I have to destroy the car."

I don't like the thought of being without him, even for a second, but I nod. There's no time to waste.

"I'll miss you," he says, and there's something about his tone. An emotion I've never heard him use before. "Will you miss me?"

"Very much." I lean over and press a hard, demanding kiss onto his lips, tasting him one more time, letting him taste me. "Hurry back."

When I pull back, his hand snakes around the back of my neck to hold me captive. "The things I feel for you come without conditions, too."

I give him a dreamy smile before hustling outside. The cool of the night embraces me as I run toward the woman I've missed more than air. Tears burn the backs of my eyes when she meets me halfway, throwing her arms around me.

"Ten! I'm so glad you're okay. I knew something was wrong when your dad refused to give me the name and address of the boarding school you were supposedly attending, but I had no idea…not until the girl, Elena, came to see me."

Boarding school. That's what he told family and friends? "I was in prison, Aunt Lina, but I'm okay now. I'm actually kind of grateful for the experience." I'm stronger, and I have the answers I've always craved. The direction. Killian. Archer.

"Come on." She draws me into the house, one of her arms remaining locked around my shoulders. "Elena said you have a tracker inside you. I need to—"

"Yes. Killian told me. Though I don't know how it's possible."

"I'll explain when we're in the shed." Aunt Lina leads me past the cozy living room with the floral-print couch, lacy doilies and cat figurines, past the kitchen with yellow linoleum and chipping and peeling cabinets, then into the backyard, where a wooden shed consumes half the space.

Inside it, I grind to a halt. This is a serial killer's wet dream. Sharp, shiny tools hang from the walls. There's a gurney with straps awaiting a prisoner.

"Do you trust me?" she asks.

"Yes." *Of course. Maybe. Probably.* Zero! Way to test my limits.

"I've worked for Myriad for twenty-two years. I've heard things…seen things. I know what I'm doing, honey. Lie on the gurney. Please."

I hesitate. "Will you get into trouble for this?"

"Nah. Who can prove I did it? Anyway, some things are worth the risk and you, my dear, are one of them."

I hope you're worth it. How many times have I heard those words lately?

I think back. Three. Three times. Not as many as I would have guessed. Still. A lot of people have gone to a lot of trouble for me, and what have I done in return?

My stomach roils as I do as commanded.

"This is for your own good." She binds my wrists and ankles.

I don't protest. Considering everything Vans did to me, my silence is a huge deal.

She bustles here and there, gathering everything she needs before she comes up beside me. "Once the tracker has been removed, I'm going to take you to a safe house. Human, not Myriadian and not Troikan."

Leave? "Does Killian know the address?" Does he know where to go if he returns and I'm gone?

"I told him. Well, I told the girl, Elena."

Elena better not "forget" to tell him. Or betray me. Ugh. So much rides on a girl I don't like!

"All right. Moment of truth." With a flick of her wrist, Aunt Lina angles an oval-shaped glass over my forehead. "You might want to close your eyes for this."

"No, I'm good."

"Okay then." A bright light clicks on, and oh, wow, in an instant my corneas feel as if they've been doused in bleach.

I close my eyes. Heat strokes me as she runs it over every inch of me.

"Let's try this again." This time, she stops at my left hipbone, where I've been burning since Levi shared *his* light with me. "Aha. Found you!"

The tracker, I'm guessing, and I guess I don't really have to wonder who or why or how. Anytime I acted up—and a few times just for fun—Vans injected me with sedatives. Oh, and we can't forget the handful of times he beat me unconscious. Pearl must have paid him.

A sense of betrayal and violation overwhelms me.

I hear a gurgle and figure Aunt Lina is slathering her hands with liquid latex. Once it dries, she rucks my dress to my chin and lifts a syringe filled with neon blue liquid. "This will numb you so I can make the necessary incisions."

"If I'll be numbed, why am I bound?"

"These types of devices cause a certain…mental reaction." She rubs me with antiseptic. A sharp sting slowly fades as she injects me. "You can open your eyes now. The light is directed on the site, not your face."

I watch as she picks up a scalpel and cuts into my hip with a steady hand. I watch, untouched by pain, as blood pours out of me. I missed the insertion, so there's no way I'm missing the extraction.

She sprays something clear into the wound and the bleeding stops. With the glass in front of her—the light illuminating my hip—she picks up what looks to be a pair of tweezers and slips the tips inside my wound. Again, there's no pain, but I do feel pressure.

Though her wrist is steady, the tool moves. A slight motorized buzz that fills my ears.

"Get ready," she says. "I've almost got—"

Click.

The muscles in my abdomen clench, and I cramp, but it's nothing I can't handle.

The sound of the motor intensifies as Aunt Lina leans over to grab a pair of surgical scissors with her free hand. The moment she makes the first snip, a cool flood sweeps through me. An avalanche that gains speed and power as it moves, before finally stopping inside my mind.

Why is she removing the tracker? I don't want it removed. I want to keep it forever and ever and ever. "Aunt Lina. You have to stop."

"Can't do that, sweetheart." Another snip.

I pull at my bonds. When I fail to gain my freedom, I arch my back and twist to the side, willing to do anything to get those stupid scissors out of me. "You have to stop. Okay? All right? I need to be tracked. I want to be. It's *important*."

"I want you to be still."

I only struggle harder.

Expression resigned, she climbs on the table and straddles me, digging the scissors in deeper. Frantic, I buck my hips and wrench my arms. What will it take to make her understand? I'll die without the tracker. It's a part of me. It's the *best* part. "If you do this, I'll hate you forever. Please. Just stop. Please."

"No, you won't hate me. In just a few seconds, you'll love me." Sweat trickles from her temple as she pulls the light back into position under eyes and snips, snips. "Just one more to go…" Snip. "Got it!"

She lifts the scissors to reveal a capsule pulsing with neon red liquid, wires sticking out of its belly like spider legs.

"That's mine. Put it back where it belongs." My voice is a guttural snarl now.

I blink rapidly as the fog inside my mind thins. Wait. I begged to keep the tracker? "Are you freaking kidding me!"

"A drug," she explains. "We call it Special K."

"K?"

"K is for *keeps*." She giggles like a schoolgirl, and I have to cut back a groan.

How close is Loony Lina from taking over?

She climbs off me and drops the capsule into a jar of thick black goo. "All right. Time to go." As she unstraps me, my core temperature begins to rise, the rush of cold abandoning me.

After she glues my flesh together and places a bandage over the wound, she helps me stand. My dress falls back into place. She moves the gurney aside by cranking an old, rusty lever, revealing a concrete floor with a drain. Only, the drain is a dial she fits her fingers on, turning this way and that, causing one of the cement cracks to expand, creating an opening just large enough for me to wiggle through, my feet balanced on stairs.

A dog barks in the distance. The sound of breaking glass provides terrible background music.

"I'm going to take a wild guess. They're here," she says.

She throws a backpack at me, and I fall as I release the ladder to catch it. Landing hurts, air gushing from my lungs. She climbs down, stopping to reach up and do the dial thing again. The cement closes, darkness falling over us.

A rustle of clothing. A brush against my shoulder, and I know she's standing beside me.

"Come on." Her voice reverberates on walls I can't see.

I can't even see my hand in front of my face. *Drip, drip.* I anchor the backpack in place and extend my arms to feel my way to…wherever. Contact. Cold, hard stone. Under my fingertips, a soft glow comes to sudden life.

"Oh, yeah. Forgot about those," she says, moving in front of me. "Oh, and we have to be quiet. They can hear us."

"Then stop talking," I whisper.

"Right." She runs a finger over her lips, pretending to zip them shut.

I touch another spot on the wall and more light springs up. We're in a small four-by-four room, empty but for dust and stagnant pools of water. Wait! There's a crawl space in the right corner.

She zooms in on it, and I stay right on her heels, different sounds floating to me. Toppling furniture. Falling tools. Footsteps. My aunt's shed is being ransacked.

Pearl's orders, I'm sure.

As we come out the other side of the crawl space, I dig through the pack, searching for a weapon. I find a cell phone, bandages, a bottle of water, protein bars, a change of clothes, a pair of shoes in my size and a gun with a clip of ammo—yes! I sheath the gun at my waist and stuff the clip in my pocket. The effort pulls at my newest wound, a warm cascade of blood trickling down my leg.

We've entered another black hole. I press my palm against the wall, hoping—yes! A soft glow saves me from curling into a ball and sobbing. We're not in a room this time, but a narrow tunnel. I straighten to full height and race forward, still following after my aunt. The more ground we gain, the shorter the roof gets, and soon we're both hunched over.

She giggles again, and I groan. No Loony Lina. Please, please, no Loony Lina. Not now.

A quiet squeak is the only warning I have before three rats dart in our direction. While she waves at the things, I have to bite my fist to silence a scream as they pass me. Then I have to concentrate on bladder control as I wonder what they were running from.

Can't stop. Have to keep going.

The tunnel twists and turns for miles, surely. The water level rises to our ankles. And it reeks. Oh, zero, it freaking reeks. I gag when a dead frog floats past me. Are there now different strains of bacteria and other microscopic beings crawling all over my skin?

I kind of wish I'd stayed in that shed to fight to the death.

If I'm splashing around in used toilet water, I might kill *myself.*

Finally the water thins and the tunnel expands, allowing us to stretch to our full heights once again. When we reach a dead end, I laugh without humor. *Oh, irony, you nasty whore. You've struck again.*

Wait! There's another crawl space in the corner. Aunt Lina shimmies through and again I'm right on her tail. We enter another four-by-four room with stairs that lead to a drain in the ceiling…and another drain. She climbs up, up…and reaches for another drain/dial thing.

She turns her wrist to the right, the left, then the right again and the drain turns with her. Success! A new crawl through opens up.

"Why do you have this passage?" I whisper. "How?"

"Always knew we'd need it," she says. "Knew where to live, knew when and how to dig into tunnels that already existed. They go all over the city. Troikans built them centuries ago!"

So how does she, a Myriad loyalist, know about them?

She disappears over the top. I climb the ladder. My biceps strain and my calves burn as I hoist myself into a bathroom—with three people inside.

I reach for the gun even as I take stock. Two males, one female. One of the men is asleep on top of the woman, who is also asleep. Both are covered in dried vomit. The third occupant is slumped against the wall and watching me through slitted lids. He doesn't appear worried (or interested) by our sudden appearance or my gun. There are empty syringes all over the floor, and a tourniquet is still tied to the watcher's arm. Drool leaks from the corners of his mouth.

No question, this is a drug house. I sheath the gun as Aunt Lina turns the drain, ensuring the cement closes and no one can crawl through.

"Change," she says, and starts stripping. There's a pile of clothes already waiting for her.

Right. We'll draw far too much attention in our fecal-is-the-new-black outfits.

We toss our soiled garments in the trash and shimmy into the clean clothes, mine coming from the pack. I'm unconcerned by my audience, certain Drool Man won't remember us, anyway—if he even knows we're here. As we head for the door, I notice the numbers painted all over the walls, different math problems written over and over again, every single one equaling ten. This can't be a coincidence.

"Come on." Lina tugs me to the door. She turns the knob and we enter a hallway. The lights are switched off, the space dim, but I can see multiple people sitting or lying throughout. Smoke wafts through the air, tickling my nose. I hold my breath as long as I can, preferring to leave sober. No one attacks us, at least.

I quicken my step, uneasy, and find the living room, the way out. There are more people here, some lucid, most snoring. Aunt Lina doesn't head for the front door but picks up a paintbrush from the floor, throwing fuel on my unease. She moves to the wall to trace the tip of the brush along one of the math problems, which equals ten.

"Lina," I say softly.

"You died." Her voice is higher, making her sound as if she's around five years old. Dang it! Not now! "I was sad."

Determined, I walk over and clasp onto her wrist. "Lina," I say as gently as I'm able. "We need to leave."

"You died." She faces me, but her eyes stare at nothing. "I was sad."

"I'm alive. I'm here, and I want to leave this place with you."

"You died," she repeats, and I'm not sure she's talking to me or to herself. "I killed you. I'm sorry." Then she slams the tip of her paintbrush into my jugular.

chapter twenty-four

"Just because you can't see us,
doesn't mean we're not there."
—Troika

At first, I'm too shocked to react. And I think my adrenaline is too high, whatever drugs Aunt Lina used on me still numbing me. But the "this can't be happening, I don't feel a thing" sensation doesn't last long.

My neck is suddenly on fire.

Pain shoots through me, buckling my knees. Loony Lina maneuvers me to the ground while I gasp for breath I can't catch.

"You sang it. Don't you remember? You sang it, and you saved them."

My wild gaze circles the room. *Help me!*

She sings, "Ten's tears fall, and I call. Nine hundred trees, but only one is for me. Eight times eight times eight they fly, whatever you do, don't stay dry. Seven ladies dancing, ignore their sweet romancing. Six seconds to hide, up, up, and you'll survive. Five times four times three, and that is where he'll be. Two I'll save, I'll be brave, brave, brave. The one I adore, I'll come back for."

As she sings, she smooths the hair from my face, gentle, so gentle. Such a contrast to the horror she just visited upon me.

I don't... I can't... I can't speak. Can't breathe.

Still she sings. "Ten's tears fall, and I call. Nine hundred trees, but only one is for me."

Suddenly I'm falling...falling...landing with a thud on the forest floor. Air leaves my lungs in a white-hot burst, making me dizzy, but I scramble to my feet and, blinking rapidly, scan my newest surroundings.

Welcome back to the Realm of Many Ends.

The gnarled trees sigh happily. The toothy plants grin, as if eyeing me with mental forks and knives. The emberbugs sting me, and I yelp. Today the sky isn't quite so dark, but that isn't exactly a good thing. There are thick yellow clouds in the sky, undulating violently.

I'm stuck this time, aren't I? Twice before, my body has died, and my spirit has come to this realm, but both times, the boys were there to save me. Today, I'm on my own.

Now I'll be forever separated from my mother...forever separated from my brother...forever separated from Killian and Archer. Tears of frustration spill down my cheeks. My hand trembles as I wipe the drops away and—

Ten's tears fall, and I call.

The words hit me like lightning. The song Loony Lina sang as I died. Could it be... No, no, surely not...but maybe...a survival guide?

You sang it. Don't you remember? You sang it, and you saved them.

Them? The other kids?

Ten's tears fall, and I call.

"Hello?" I call. "Is anyone out there?"

Silence greets me. Maybe I'm wrong, but...

"Hello?" I repeat a little louder.

A few yards away, bushes slap together. I tense, wondering if I've just summoned the worst of the worst, until a girl shouts, "Where are you?"

"This way!" The song *is* a blueprint to our salvation. It must be. "Follow the sound of my voice."

I talk and talk and talk about nothing and finally she steps from the shadows. I recognize her pale braided bun—Kayla!—and race forward.

"Stop," she screams, and I immediately obey. "Move to the right."

I do, avoiding a shimmery pocket of air. A pocket that stands upright like a nearly imperceptible doorway. "Thank you."

The moment I reach her, the peace-seeking activist draws back her hand to slap me. The blow is weak, because *she* is weak, but it still manages to turn my head.

"I've been waiting for you, hoping you'd come back." She glares at me. "My brother was captured because of you."

Okay. Should have seen that coming. I rub the corner of my lip. "I'm sorry. I tried to distract the beast. Tried to help you guys."

"Well, you didn't." She withers, wrapping her arms around her middle. "How did you manage to escape? A flash of light radiated from you, and boom, you were gone."

"My body was resuscitated." Now. The chitchat will

have to wait. *Nine hundred trees, but only one is for me.* "I'm looking for a special tree. One that won't hurt us."

"How did you— Never mind. This way." She jogs off and I follow, sticking close to her heels, ducking when she ducks, jumping when she jumps. Limbs reach for us, plants bite at us, but none are able to catch us.

"How do you know where you're going?" I ask.

"The land is a maze filled with hundreds of invisible doorways that lead back to where you started—or into a trap. You either learn to navigate or you become bait for the animals. You don't want to be bait. Your screams will join all the others as your organs are eaten…regrown… and eaten again."

Many ends…

As we continue to run, I pick up the pattern in her actions. There's *always* a pattern, nothing by chance. Eight steps, duck. Nine steps, jump. Ten steps, turn. Eleven steps, turn. Twelve steps—

This is a count up, I realize. As if I'm gaining more time the farther I go. And if I were to turn and head in the opposite direction—twelve steps duck, eleven steps jump, ten steps turn, nine steps turn, eight steps duck—it would be a countdown. Time running out.

Symbolic?

Boom!

The ground shakes, but I'm used to it and manage to stay on my feet. The trees and foliage shrink away from us, and in the distance, the mushroom cloud rises.

"Hurry!" Kayla pants. "The birds always know when fresh meat has arrived."

The first tingles of dread arise. One step, five, eight and spin. A loud gaggle of squawks cuts through the smoky air.

"How much farther?" I'm wheezing now.

"Almost...there." She's wheezing worse.

Eight times eight times eight they fly, whatever you do, don't stay dry.

One of the birds swoops down, its claws open, ready to latch on to Kayla. As I dive on her, knocking her out of the way, the tips of those claws scrap my back and I cry out. When we land, we roll forward. Up ahead, there's an anthill and a swarm of ember-bugs. We're going to end up in one or the other, because this is freaking Many Ends, and there's no escaping an opportunity for pain.

An-n-nd the anthill wins.

The little beasties have upraised eyes, like alligators, yet they have the belly and stinger of a bumblebee and the legs of a cricket. And if the drool dripping from their fangs—because yes, we can add vampire to the mix—means anything, Ten is on the dinner menu.

They converge on me en masse, crawling all over me, biting me. Screaming, I bat at my face, my arms. Kayla's screams soon blend with mine. We're being eaten alive, and we can't go on like this. It's too much, but the sad thing is, it won't kill us.

An ember-bug joins the party, stinging me, blistering me, but also killing some of the ants. An idea hits me. It's horrible. It's going to get me hurt. But I'll recover. Maybe.

I throw myself into the swarm of ember-bugs. They sting me repeatedly, and I'm pretty sure my skin is melting off, but the ants are dying, too, so I consider it a win. Though my eyes are so swollen that I'm nearing total blindness, I'm able to find Kayla through her screams and throw myself at her. Our limbs tangle, the ember-bugs attacking her, as well.

When the last of the ants are killed, I tighten my grip on Kayla and roll over the grass, rocks cutting into exposed muscle but also smashing the ember-bugs. By the time we still, I'm leaking so much Lifeblood I'm not sure I'll have the strength to stand.

"Almost…there," Kayla gasps. Her eyes and lips are as swollen as mine, and there are puncture marks all over her face, neck and arms. She manages to climb to all fours. "This way."

Squawks sound from the sky. The birds must be circling us. We're easy pickings.

I grit my teeth and climb to all fours, as well. Dizziness nearly topples me as I make my way forward, staying behind her through touch alone, my fingers brushing her foot every time I extend my arm.

Finally, blessedly, she stops. "Eat," she says, placing something in my hand.

I don't take the time to study it—why even try? My eyes are still too swollen to see more than shadows. I just stuff the thing—a leaf?—into my mouth and chew with what little strength I have left. The moment I swallow, however, that "little" strength multiplies.

My swelling goes down, and skin begins to grow over my muscles.

I realize I'm under a Wisteria tree. The largest I've ever seen, with a trunk the size of a freaking house. The flowers are magnificent, some deep violet, some soft pink and some snow-white, all thick and lush, absolutely perfect, hanging from the branches like clusters of grapes.

I stand and pull Kayla to her feet. The sweet scent of sugarcane permeates everything here.

"Eat," she repeats, plucking a handful of petals and stuffing them in her mouth. Soon after she swallows, the rest of the punctures fade from her skin.

I eat a handful of petals myself, the taste as sweet as the smell, something I hadn't noticed while I was in so much pain. I swallow, and my skin begins to tingle, my blood to heat. This is how she and the others survived so long, no doubt about it. But…how is the tree here, in such a desolate place?

"The birds don't come near us when we're in this shade," she says. "I don't know why. I only know this is the center of the realm."

"How many other spirits are here?"

"Thousands. Millions. I'm not sure. The birds carry them to the mountains. If you want to know how many others are safe, like us, the answer fluctuates as newcomers arrive, but right now there are only two others. Reed and a man I've seen in the forest. He runs from us."

"Kayla?" Reed steps around a car-size branch. When his gaze finds me, it narrows. "You came back."

"Unfortunately." And now I'd like to find a way out.

You saved them.

How?

Eight times eight times eight they fly, whatever you do, don't stay dry.

"Last time I was here, you told me there's a lake," I say.

Reed's smile is cold as he waves his hand in the direction he just came from. "It's just outside the shade, but the moment you reach the shore, the birds will descend."

"Even if I jump in?" *Don't stay dry...*

His laugh has a very sharp edge. "No. The birds won't get you if you jump in, but something else will. Everyone who's ever touched a drop of that water has been sucked into its depths—and come out in pieces."

chapter twenty-five

"If at first you don't succeed, kill your opponent."
—Myriad

I stand at the edge of the shade, my pockets full of leaves from the tree, Kayla and Reed beside me. The birds know what I'm planning. They must. They circle overhead, waiting to dive—to attack—the second I move.

Kayla gives herself a hug. "Are you sure you want to do this?"

Seven ladies dancing, ignore their sweet romancing. "There's a difference between wanting to do something and knowing I need to do it."

"Okay. Why do you *need* to do this?" Reed demands.

"I think it's the way out." I opt for honesty rather than evasion. As much as I don't want to get their hopes up, I do want to get their hopes up. Hope empowers. It's the reason we wake and the reason we rise. The reason we keep moving forward. "If you could leave, and choose one of the realms—"

"Yes," they say in unison.

"No longer interested in peace?" I ask.

"Peace will always be my first priority, but I know I can't achieve it here," Kayla says.

I don't have the heart to tell her she'll never achieve it. Troika and Myriad will never call a truce, and their battles will always spill into the Land of the Harvest.

Reed frowns at me. "Tell me you have a plan to survive whatever's in the water."

"I do. I'm going to figure it out when I get there."

He rubs the back of his neck.

"What do I have to lose? My life? Been there, done that." But what happens next? I don't believe in Fusion, not anymore. Not for anyone. But I'm in Many Ends. I don't think I'll get to enter into the Rest.

"I can't believe I'm saying this," Reed grumbles, "but I'm coming with you."

Kayla moans. "I knew you'd insist."

"You don't have to—" he begins.

"There's no way I'm staying if you're going," she interjects. "Don't even suggest it."

A little bubble of hope expands in my chest. There's more to the girl than I realized.

Reed nods. "Just...be prepared for the worst."

I hate the thought of risking their lives—and I use the term *lives* loosely—but if I'm right, and the song is the road map to freedom, this is our best option.

"I'm prepared," Kayla says. "Every day, I'm prepared."

"Your faith in me is humbling, guys." I run the wire of a wrist cuff through two belt loops in Reed's mud-stained jeans. Kayla doesn't have belt loops, so I press her finger through the small metal hook. "Whatever happens, you keep a tight grip."

Her nod is reluctant, but hey, a nod is a nod.

"Oh, a word of warning. There may or may not be seven women in the water, and if they try to romance you, you have to ignore them." I grab their hands while they sputter in confusion. "Okay, then. On your mark, get set, go!"

We bound forward, running as fast as we can manage. The birds swoop down, dive-bombing through the sky. And that's not even the worst. The gorilla-spiders spring from the shadows of the forest, using their powerful arms to gallop and increase their speed. I should have known they were out there!

Fight the panic. Stay focused. Any moment now they'll reach us...almost there... I leap to the side, dragging Kayla with me to avoid another doorway. Then I sprint for the shore, forcing Reed and Kayla to keep pace. We end up belly flopping, the top halves of our bodies in the water, our legs on the ground.

A gorilla grabs Reed's ankle. A bird sinks sharp claws into my back while another bites Kayla's calf, drawing Lifeblood. I kick my attacker and twist to throw water at the animals. The droplets splash over them, and like the Wicked Witch of the West, their flesh sizzles. We're released, allowing us to scramble deeper into the water, but there's no time to rejoice. No reason to bask in a sense of relief. In seconds, we're sucked into a whirling vortex, traveling down, down, deeper and deeper into the water.

As I attempt to kick my way to the surface, I swallow too much water and choke. We continue to spin, round and round, the wire wrapping around Reed's waist. Zero! My plan to keep us together might just sever him in half.

Finally, the spinning stops. I'm dizzy, but at least I can breathe again, the water sucked away from us—even from my lungs. We're trapped in the eye of a great and terrible storm, suspended inside a beam of jellyair, I think. Fish... *things*...swim around us; they have the face and torso of a human female. The shape, anyway. Rather than skin, they are covered in scales. Long strands of pink hair drift around shark-like bodies.

"Come with me," one says. As she speaks, two layers of dagger-sharp teeth are revealed, a piece of flesh trapped between the two in front.

"No, no, come with me," another says.

They giggle like little girls and continue inviting us over.

A third speaks up. "Let's be friends. Everyone could use a new friend."

Yes, yes, I'd love to go with them, would love to make a new friend. Sounds like the best ideas *ever.* Reed and Kayla must agree with me, because they're already paddling forward, reaching for the seven ladies dancing.

Seven ladies dancing, ignore their sweet romancing.

Loony Lina's voice fills my head, drowning out the giggles and the chatter. I shake my head to clear my thoughts and concentrate fully on the task at hand, only then realizing the "ladies" are licking their teeth, preparing to chomp into the first person to come within reach.

Zero! I yank on the wires, pulling the kids to my side. They fight me, actually kicking at me, desperate to join their new "friends."

In an effort to drown out the *sweet romancing,* I sing the

song out loud. The kids fight me less and less, the fish-girls growing more and more agitated, screaming and cursing, the long strands of their hair actually standing on end and crackling with bolts of lightning, as if they've stuck their hands in a socket.

When Reed and Kayla at last still, the bottom of the jellyair vanishes, and we're dropped.

Down, down we fall through a tunnel of darkness, finally hitting something sharp. We roll over dirt and rocks, the wires now wrapped around all of us, cutting both my arms to the bone. I hemorrhage, strength draining out of me at a rapid rate. I tremble, my limbs weakening as I untangle myself.

In my pocket, only one leaf remains; the others must have been sucked out with the water. Reed and Kayla, who also packed their pockets, come up empty. I tear the leaf in three and we each eat a section.

Warmth…my skin patching itself…a return of strength, but not a full recharge.

I work my way to my feet, and Reed and Kayla struggle to stand alongside me.

"Where are we?" she whispers. There's a tinge of horror in her voice—a tinge I feel myself.

"I don't know."

The room is lit by bone torches—flames crackling at the end of human remains. The ground isn't rock and dirt as I assumed but pulled teeth and…cat litter? The scent of baking soda does not prevail against unwashed bodies.

Walls tower all around us, but they aren't made of stone, wood or drywall. No, these walls are made of cages. Too many to count, one stacked upon the other. Inside each cage is a single spirit. The Unsigned? Those captured in the Realm of Many Ends? The occupants are contorted in different positions of pain, moaning with various degrees of torment.

Laughter suddenly rings out, and it doesn't come from the cages. Someone's coming!

"Six seconds to hide, up, up, and you'll survive," I command softly. "Climb. Now."

We scale the cages as if the ground is on fire, able to use the upper bars as handrails and use the lower bars as footstools. The caged people watch us, but they're too pained to comment. This is going to haunt me for the rest of my—death.

When three men turn the corner, we go still. I shake, beads of sweat trickling down my temple. The men don't bother to look anywhere but the bottom row of prisoners. Prisoners who are shrinking back, making the men laugh.

They stop at the cage on the far right, unlock the door and reach inside, dragging out a sobbing teenage boy.

"Please, no," the boy pleads. "Please."

"You know better." One of the men holds the kid's mouth open. "You don't speak to your betters."

Another man palms a dagger, reaches out and slices off the kid's tongue.

The sheer brutality of the act makes me suck in a breath. As the men drag the boy away, he fights as best he can, but it does him no good. He's too weak, and they are too strong.

I'm too weak to help. Three against one. Or three against three if Reed and Kayla help, but who knows if they will. I tell myself I'll be captured. We'll all be captured. We'll be locked away, and we won't be any good to anyone. It's a choice. A smart choice. I can come back for him. For everyone. I'll know the way to a safe place, and I can return armed to the max. Maybe. Hopefully.

But I remember the time Bow—Archer—fought the guards inside Prynne. I did nothing and guilt ate at me.

I might regret this, but—

I drop, my stomach floating into my throat. I pull the wire in my bracelet—*Thank you, Killian*—the second I land on one of the guard's shoulders. He grunts. As we fall, I wrap the wire around his neck but as soon as we reach the ground, I roll off him, the wire remaining in place, choking him. My arms are extended overhead, and I use them to pull myself around and kick him in the face. A face that's bright red, almost blue.

His eyes bulge as he struggles to free himself, making little gurgling sounds.

Another guard boots me in the stomach. Stars explode behind my eyes and pain shoots through me. He doesn't help his friend—if they're even friends—because the jerking motion of my body only tightens the wire.

Mr. Boot draws back his leg, preparing to deliver another strike. I prepare to take it like a girl. Better than a man. Reed lands on him, and the two topple in a tangle of punching fists.

The third guard releases the tongueless boy and runs. If he gets away, we're toast. He'll come back with others.

Sometimes you can offer someone a second chance. Sometimes you shouldn't.

I yank my arms with all my strength. The wire cuts

through the guard's throat—completely. Suddenly I'm free of my burden and running after the last man.

Kayla beats me to him. She knocks him down, whimpering and clinging to his back, even upon impact. He reaches back to grab her by the hair, but I latch on to his wrist before he's able to make contact with her.

Anger burns me while desperation cools me off. I'm one hundred percent conflicted about my next actions. Even still, I yank, pull the man out from under her and stomp on his head until he's as limp as spaghetti noodles.

I'm panting as I approach Kayla. "You all right?"

"Yeah," she says, but she doesn't meet my eyes. "I think so."

I maintain my calm facade as I look back at Reed. His opponent is motionless, as well. He's crouched beside the tongueless boy, who is just as motionless. Hemorrhaged already?

All for nothing! my mind screams.

I lift a mental chin. Salvaging my conscience—worth it. Worth all this.

The prisoners in the cages are buoyed and cheer for us, even when we *shhhh* them.

"If another guard comes, I won't have a chance to free you," I say, and finally they go quiet.

I work on a lock for one minute, two, the seconds agony, but there's no keyhole and I can't find another way.

"I'm sorry," I say. I have to get Reed and Kayla to safety. "I'll come back."

Next move?

Five times four times three, and that is where he'll be.

I do the math. Five times four is twenty and twenty times three is sixty. Sixty and that's where he'll be. He who?

Since Lina created the song especially for me, she would have known which wall I'd end up climbing when the guards arrived. She would have known my instincts. And my instincts are screaming to climb up sixty flights of cages.

I hate my instincts. "Climb," I say, returning to the spot I abandoned.

Kayla moans, shakes her head. "I don't think I can."

"Don't think, do." A motivational speaker I'm not. "It's the only way."

"You *can* do it," Reed tells her, giving her a boost. "You will."

We begin to climb…and climb…and Reed and I have to pull Kayla up several flights. A few times, one of the prisoners gathers the strength to grab hold of one of us and beg for help. Once again, I'm struck by the need to do what I can. I want to do something so badly I'm crying by the time we reach the thirtieth level. Only halfway. These people, they are emaciated, and they are filthy. They are injured and without hope. Every so often I stop to try to unlatch a few of the locks, but each time I fail, and it zaps even more of my strength.

Two I'll save, I'll be brave, brave, brave.

Right. Stick to the plan. *Get Reed and Kayla to safety, come back for the others.*

By the fortieth flight, I'm shaking uncontrollably. By the fiftieth, I'm ready to give up. I give myself a pep talk. *Been through worse, but came out stronger on the other side. So close to the end of the song—to victory.*

At the sixtieth level—I did it, I really did it!—my happiness is short-lived. I find myself staring into Killian's eyes.

Horror fills me, but so does elation, and I gasp his name. "What are you doing here?"

He grabs hold of the bars, his dirty fingers ghosting through mine. He's still in his Shell, a shiny golden collar wrapped around his neck, but I'm a spirit. "You died. How did you die? Damn it, Ten. I wanted you to live."

"Not my fault. My aunt kind of murdered me." Enough about me! "How are you here? You—"

"When did you sign with Myriad?" he demands.

"I didn't. You—"

"You must have. You're in the outermost part of the realm. The Kennel."

"No. And stop interrupting me!" Desperation gives my tone a sharper edge. "I'm in the Realm of Many Ends, same as you, and I want to know how you got here."

"This is Myriad, lass."

The two are connected through the lake?

"How do I get you out of here, Killian? Help me help you. Please."

A feminine hand shoots out the cage next to his, and Elena says, "You're the one I blame for this."

Zero! I can't leave without her, either.

"She isn't to blame." More agitated by the second, Killian says, "You need to leave, Ten. Keep climbing. There are only twenty levels to go, and you'll reach the top."

Only twenty? I whimper. "I'm not leaving without you. Reed! Kayla! Help me free him."

As we work (unsuccessfully) at the lock, Killian scrubs a hand down his face. "The Realm of Many Ends is connected to Myriad. I'd heard rumors, but I never believed them. How could I be so blind? But it makes sense, doesn't it? Why else would Myriad say it's better to remain Unsigned than to sign with Troika?"

"Let's worry about that later. For now, shut up and help me."

He reaches through the bars. "No. You need to leave—"

"Ten four." Reed starts climbing again. "I don't need to be told more than twice."

Killian's golden eyes beseech me. "At the top go left, left, right, left, right and kill anyone who gets in your way. Don't hesitate. You follow those directions and you'll reach a shimmery doorway. When we pass through it, we're taken to the Land of the Harvest. Because your spirits are unbound, I'm not sure where you'll end up."

Any place is better than this one, but I vehemently shake my head. "I told you I'm not leaving without you, and I meant it. You either, Elena." Hurried, a bit clumsy now, I wind the wire from my bracelet around the metal lock and begin sawing. Sparks fly.

"We'll be let out soon enough." He traces a fingertip over my knuckles. "We always are. You need to go."

"I'm making progress at last."

"Not fast enough."

He's tearing me up inside. "Killian, I can't—"

"You can. You will."

"Unless you're captured today, so you don't have time for this," Elena interjects. "Just do what he says."

Even as I shudder, the last of the song plays through my head. *Two I must save, I'll be brave, brave, brave. The one I adore, I'll come back for.*

Lina foresaw even this. She knew the difficult situation I would face.

There isn't another way, is there? "Okay. All right," I say, the words yanked out of me. "I'll go. I hate this, but I'll go." I unwind the wire as tears stream down my cheeks. "I don't believe in fate, but I think I believe in destiny." The path set before me, if only I make the right decisions. "I'm coming back for you."

He looks at me as if he wants to grip the back of my neck and kiss me. "The Generals now agree with Pearl. You're better off dead than signed with Troika. But if you sign with Myriad, Ten, you'll be one of us. You'll be protected. And you and I…we can be together."

I want that. I want to be with him. He isn't a boy, he's a warrior. He isn't someone I can push around, and I'm glad for that. When he looks at me, he sees who I am and he isn't scared. Because we're a match. We burn together—and he only wants me to burn hotter.

He'll walk through hell for me. I have no doubts about that. And I'll walk through hell for him. But I'm not signing with Myriad. This? These cages? They seal the deal.

I have to find another way to be with him.

"I'm coming back for you," I repeat. As I climb away from him, I'm sobbing, but I do what needs doing. I keep going, my determination giving me enough strength to heft Kayla up whenever she slips.

Finally we reach the top, and Reed, who is waiting for us, hauls us onto a stone walkway. Stone above, beside and below us. Every stone carved into the shape of a human skull. Empty eye sockets seem to follow me as I stumble forward, taking the lead. Left, left. Right. My knees shake. In this hallway, skeletons hang from the ceiling, each draped in a violet robe.

Troikan robes?

When we take the next left, strange symbols glowing on the walls, an alarm screeches to life.

Zero! We've been found out.

It isn't long before a stampede of footsteps sounds behind us. I glance over my shoulder as guards hustle around the corner. Six of them.

"Go, go," I tell my charges. "I'll divert our tail."

Kayla reaches for me. "No! We do this together."

"Reed," I say, and he understands.

He jerks her to his side, forcing her to keep pace with him. They make the next right, disappearing from my view.

I stop and spin, facing the guards as they barrel toward me. I'll fight to Second-death if necessary, but these men aren't getting past me.

A second later, the guards reach me and—

chapter twenty-six

"Today you live, tomorrow you die. Make what you do in the meantime matter."
—Troika

I jerk upright, my eyelids flipping open. Archer is standing beside me, holding my hand.

Relief bathes his features as he clutches my hand to his chest. "You're alive. You're going to be okay."

"Where am I?" My voice is a foggy rasp. I'm panting, my skin clammy. I'm also dizzy and weak. "Where's Kayla? Reed?"

He forces me to recline on a mound of pillows. "Let's start with you. You're in a Troikan safe house."

Another safe house…in a bedroom that's been turned into a makeshift trauma ward. Different machines circle us, some of them beeping in tune to my heart. Monitors are anchored to the walls, flashing numbers and symbols I've never seen.

"Kayla and Reed are in Troika, thanks to you," Archer says with a bright smile. "You saved them."

"No." I shake my head. "Killian. Killian saved them. But…how did you find them?"

"They passed through a veil in Myriad and their spirits ended up in the Land of the Harvest. They were screaming for help, and a TL happened to be nearby. The two pledged allegiance to Troika, a bond formed and the TL was able to escort them into the realm."

There's hope, then. There's hope for the Unsigned, even after they die. They can be saved! They just have to find their way out of Many Ends…out of Myriad.

I shudder. "Killian needs our help. He's trapped."

"You're in no condition—"

"I don't care. I have to go back for him. They put him in the Kennel, Archer. A dog cage." I bite back a sob. "I have to go back."

"You won't do anyone any good until you've regained your strength." He releases my hand only long enough to pull a chair to the side of the bed. "Your aunt *killed* you."

"Yeah. I remember." And wow. My throat hurts. I reach up, my hand trembling, and pat my neck. There's a thick bandage covering the hole the pointy end of the paintbrush left behind. When my shoulder gives out, my arm falls uselessly to the mattress.

Zero! Archer's right. I'm no good to Killian in this condition. To navigate the Realm of Many Ends, to climb those cages and race through Myriad, I have to be at my best. They'll be prepared next time, waiting and watching for me.

Even still, my sense of urgency doesn't fade.

"Besides," he says, "you owe me big-time. I saved your

life. And guess what I want in return? For you to stay in bed until you are *fully* recovered."

Rat. He asks too much of me. "How did you find me?"

"I received a message from someone who knew my rank and ID. This someone mentioned 10:17 on November 12 and a girl who dies at the crack house. I decided to check things out and found your body in a pool of blood."

"Lina sent you a message?"

"That's my guess."

"But how did she get your rank and ID? How did she get the equipment she needed?"

"Those are excellent questions she refuses to answer."

Well...maybe I already know the answers. Loony Lina isn't so loony, after all. She isn't polyfused but gifted. She saw into the future. She knew how to navigate two realms. "Where is she now?"

"Here. Locked up in the bedroom next door. She won't hurt you again."

She hurt me, yes, but she also contacted Archer so that he could save me. Right now, I don't know what to think about her. "How long have I been out?"

"Only two days."

Only? That's forty-eight hours Killian and Elena have spent inside their cages. If they haven't been freed. They seemed to think they'd be released sooner rather than later.

"Have you heard from Killian?" I ask.

"No."

So he *hasn't* been freed. My stomach sinks.

"Levi came here," Archer says, "shared his Lifeblood with you—it's stronger than mine and it kept your body alive while your spirit was in Many Ends."

"And Myriad. Archer, Many Ends is *connected* to Myriad."

He worries two fingers over the golden shadow beard on his jaw. "I know. Reed told me. All Troika is shocked, and all Myriad is denying the boy's claim. The realm doesn't want us to know they have access to the spirits of the Unsigned. Probably because they don't want us to know what they *do* to the spirits of the Unsigned."

Well, Killian knows the truth now. He'll set the record straight. Once he's free. I have to free him. "There are so many spirits locked in cages…not to mention the spirits being used as living bird food." And worse!

"I know that, too. The kids told us everything they'd been through."

"I have to help them. All of them." But now that I'm away from the Kennels and my adrenaline's on simmer, the task suddenly strikes me as impossible. Since I won't sign with Myriad, I'll have to remain Unsigned to enter Many Ends again. And next time, I'll have more people to find and free, monster birds and nightmare gorillas to fight. They won't give up their stashes of human-candy easily.

So the question is: Do I go ahead and sign with Troika?

I want to, it's how I was leaning before this, but if I go that route, I may not be able to find another way inside Many Ends. And I haven't yet gotten a very necessary promise from Archer. A promise he may not give me.

I want him to save Killian from Myriad's wrath.

"Sign with Troika, Ten." Archer must be reading my thoughts on my face. His stare turns mean. "We'll find a way to save the spirits in Many Ends. Together."

"Can we? The only way I know to do that is to experience Firstdeath again and have you bring me back." The risk! One day, my body won't recover.

"We'll find *another* way."

I want to trust him. I do. I didn't trust him in Prynne, and I didn't trust him when my father came storming into my room, and yet he came through for me anyway.

"Will you save Killian from Myriad's wrath? Because they've tied his life to my decision. If I sign with Troika, he dies."

Archer closes his eyes. "I can't. I can't get inside Myriad, and that's where they'll keep him."

"Then I'm going to remain Unsigned a little longer."

Now he glares at me. "Just because we can't see the solution doesn't mean there's no solution at all."

"You make a good point, but I'm weak, and this isn't the time to make a life-altering decision."

"There's no *better* time." But he sighs and mercifully changes the subject. "How about a celebratory poem?"

"You'd like it to rhyme, I'm guessing."

"Only because I deserve the best."

Ha! "If there's one thing I know, it's this. When I was dead, I was missed. You, Archer Prince, think I'm great, so much better than the numbers six, seven, eight. Even nine! Because it's time, it's time, it's time you faced facts—life without me seriously lacks. And before you get huffy and try to deny it, there's something I should probably admit. I *guess* I love you, even though you're a pain. But I'm pretty sure that means...I'm completely insane."

In an effort to rebuild my stamina, I walk the treadmill for ten minutes...twenty... All the while, I peer out the window. At the trees swaying in a strong breeze, at the sun shining over rolling hills. I want to be standing in a warm, golden ray—crave it. Actually, I want to be kissing Killian in a warm, golden ray.

I have to leave this safe house, and soon.

Two days have passed since I first woke in bed, and still there's been no sign of Killian or Elena. My frustration level is nearing detonation.

"Zero!" I punch the console, causing the machine to speed up.

Oops. Detonation achieved.

"Temper much?" Deacon strides into the gym, a built-on room at the back of the house, spacious but crammed with equipment. He's wearing a skintight shirt, his jeans ripped and his combat boots caked in mud. He crosses his arms over the monitor on the treadmill.

"Yes." I slow the speed so I won't be quite so winded during our conversation. "How are Kayla and Reed?"

"They're good. They've entered training to become Laborers."

They're both cautionary tales for the hazards of remaining Unsigned, so they should excel at their new jobs. Then again, there are morons like me…

I can't let go of my desire to return to Many Ends and save the spirits still trapped. I can't let go of Killian.

"You want to know who isn't doing so well?" he continues. "Sloan. She's missing. Has been since we split after the party."

Ookay. Way to stop me in my tracks. I punch the proper button and the tread slows even more…stops…and the incline lowers. I grab my towel and dab at my sweaty brow. "How does Archer always find me? Do that. Find her." I don't like that she's missing.

"You called for him. She hasn't called for me."

Right. "I think she planned to go home to finally torch her family's estate. Have you looked there?"

His nod is clipped. "First place I checked."

Zero!

Bang! Bang! Bang!

In unison, we turn toward the north wall. The wall blocking us from Lina—Aunt Lina or Loony Lina?

Bang! Bang! Bang!

I've seen her only once since leaving my sickbed, but she didn't even realize I was in the room, stared past me when I gripped her shoulders and shouted, "Why? How could you do that to me?" I left unsatisfied and angry.

"Want me to check on her?" he asks.

"No. I'll do it. Then we'll search for Sloan. And Killian," I add quietly. "Together."

He grunts. Not an agreement but not a rejection, either.

Bang! Bang! Bang!

Resigned, I stalk down the hall. At the end is Lina's room, the wall in front of me no longer made of plaster but of bulletproof glass. Amazing what kind of repairs and changes these Laborers can make in a short amount of time. Lina is pacing, her hands wringing together. She's been bathed—a female Laborer showed up yesterday not just to feed her one of those glorious mouth strips but to brush and braid her hair and change her clothes. She's now wearing a pretty pink dress with ruffles.

I place my hand on the ID panel. A laser shines between my fingers, warm to my skin. The lock on the door opens, followed by the door itself. I step inside, and Lina instantly calms.

"You shouldn't have trusted her," she says.

Loony Lina. Here we go again. While I know she somehow sees into the future, making sense of her statements is nearly impossible until after the fact. "Who shouldn't I have trusted?"

"Her. I'm sorry she died."

My stomach clenches. "Who died, Lina?"

"You died. I cried. He died. You cried. She died. So many died." A tear slides down her cheek. "Why didn't *I* die?"

As angry as I am with her, I don't like seeing her upset. And in a way, I'm glad the events played out the way they did. Had she not killed me, I wouldn't have freed Kayla and Reed. I wouldn't have learned Myriad and Many Ends are connected. I wouldn't have any clue what happened to Killian.

Warm breath brushes my face, and I blink, only then realizing Lina is in front of me. Zero! Concentrate!

"Lina," I say. "Help me understand. Please." If she's suicidal, she must understand her own condition. And it must be horrible, living with all that death in her head, knowing what will happen, but being unable to prevent the disasters from coming to pass. "Please," I repeat.

She opens her mouth, snaps it closed. "So many names. So many disasters. So many deaths."

"Who dies—died—next?"

Her eyes stare at nothing…or a future I still can't see. "The public execution."

Finally! We're getting somewhere. Though I want to shake her, I remain still. No matter how frantic I feel, I can't risk sending her back into the abyss of memories that haven't yet happened.

"The boy…the Laborer. The human girl," she says.

My blood grows cold. A public execution. A Laborer and a human girl. There is only one missing male Laborer, and only one missing human girl. "Killian? Sloan? What happens—happened—to them?" If I know, I can save them. I have to save them!

"The public execution," she repeats. "Madame…she killed him. Him, the Laborer. You cried. I'm sorry."

No, no, no. "Where is—was—the execution?" I can barely get the words out.

"The road…the steps…you looked so pretty in your white dress."

The white dress? From the spa? Is she confusing two different days in the same location?

Her hand darts out and clutches mine, surprising me. "The war…it's coming here. Trickling, trickling, then comes the flood."

Present tense. This is the first time I've ever heard her use it while in this state. Why now? "What war? The one between Troika and Myriad?"

"You can't stop it. No one can. The dragon strikes. The lion roars." Her grip tightens on me. "What happens tomorrow changes everything."

Tomorrow is the execution? Urgency drives me as I kiss her cheek and mutter, "Thank you." I rush to the door.

"You died, I cried," she says.

Back to past tense. Because we're no longer touching?

I turn and find her pacing again, wringing her hands, her eyes once again staring into the distance. I will help her. Somehow. First, though, I have to help Killian and Sloan.

"Deacon," I call as I lock the door. "Archer!"

I run toward the living room, heading for the gym, where I last spoke with Deacon, but he meets me in the kitchen. "I think I know where Sloan is, or where she's going to be, and I'm positive she's in danger."

In a flash of light, Archer appears beside his friend. He's pale, his lips drawn tight.

"Pearl is planning a public execution," I say.

Archer nods. "Word has been sent to all Troika. Killian and Sloan are scheduled to die bright and early in the morning."

"Myriad, as terrible as they are, will never allow Pearl to kill an Unsigned human in public," Deacon says. "It's bad for business."

"Sloan," Archer replies, his voice sad, "signed with Myriad a few hours ago. Her spirit now belongs to them."

Deacon closes his eyes, his shoulders slumping.

My friend signed with my enemy. And they *are* my enemy. They are hurting those I love, planning to do worse.

I pinch the bridge of my nose, feeling as though I'm partly to blame for Sloan's decision. I should have spent more time with her at the party, should have discussed our futures in more detail.

But really, what good would I have done her? She saw the Exchange, same as I did. She knew the great value Troika places on all life.

Still. I love her, and I'm not going to watch her die. "Gather your troops," I say. "We're going after them."

They don't hop to, but pause to share a look.

"What?" I demand.

"You know Killian and Sloan belong to Myriad." There's remorse in Archer's voice, and that's a step in the right direction, but he still sucks right now.

"They are people, regardless of their realm. If you won't help them—won't help me—fine. I'll save them on my own."

"And you'll be walking into a trap," Archer says. "Word of the execution was sent to us simply to draw you out of hiding. That's Pearl's MO, as she's proved. Here, at least, you're safe. She can't get to you."

"I don't care."

I stalk to my room to bag up the weapons I've collected. A few daggers, an Oxi, a Stag, two kitchen knives. That done, I strap on my leather bracelets.

When I turn, Deacon is leaning against my door frame. "All right, you've talked me into it. I'm going with you. For Sloan, not for Killian."

I'll take what help I can get, however I can get it. "What about Archer?"

"Let me tell you something, little girl. Troika has legions of armies, but every single one is otherwise engaged, especially now that we're down to only one Conduit. These armies are stationed throughout your world and our own.

They fight to protect a race of people who do not see them or even think to thank them. They have very little time off—if any at all. They work tirelessly. They're injured often. They don't need more to do."

"I commend them," I say, even though I don't know why he's telling me all this. "What about Archer?" I repeat.

"He went to ask the King for an army."

chapter twenty-seven

**"You have a Secondlife, but not a second chance.
Choose wisely."
—Myriad**

That night, Deacon and I head for the spa to set up shop. We're about a mile away when we come to a roadblock, Myriad Shells on patrol. We backtrack with every intention of reaching the designated area from the other direction, only to find another roadblock. An attempt to sneak past it will either prove really stupid or really smart.

Thing is, once we're out for the count, we're out. The end.

Eventually, we decide to back off. Pearl planned for everything, placing her people everywhere. On top of buildings. At every entrance and exit of every road and building within a one-mile radius. She's serious about my capture. Or rather, my murder. By killing me and sending me to Many Ends, she's certain Ashley will one day get another chance to enter Myriad. She's desperate, and that desperation is going to be her downfall. I can't sink to the same level.

I have to stay calm. Stay ready.

We return to the safe house to wait out the night, pacing, pacing…until finally morning dawns, the execution scheduled to begin in less than an hour. As soon as we see Killian and Sloan, Deacon is going to do the beam-me-up-Scotty thing, transporting me straight to the scene of the crime. He tries to talk me out of going that route, but I'm determined. Even when he tells me the human body always has a poor reaction to traveling from one point to the other in only a blink. Whatever. I'm willing to risk a little motion sickness.

Reporters from all over the world are on the scene. Video feed dominates every wall in the living room, the projections offering us a panoramic view of the festivities, and we watch as the street fills with a sea of humans wanting to witness the horrific event. It's as if this is nothing but a game.

Public executions aren't held often, but they are held and they are legal. Realms are allowed to punish signees who violate contracts as they see fit. Because Secondlife is a sure thing, the deaths aren't considered terribly serious.

I've seen three in my lifetime, and I remember my parents throwing popcorn at the screen.

Come on, come on. We're already armed for the most brutal of combat—I'm wearing half the weapons that were in my bag. All I could hold. There's a time for peace, and there's a time for war.

Threaten my loved ones, and it's war. No question.

Deacon's mouth curls in distaste. "Everyone looks so excited."

He's right. No matter which direction the camera pans,

smiles abound. Someone even brought a beach ball to toss around the crowd.

Where is Archer? Why hasn't he returned?

Cheers suddenly erupt along with whistles and catcalls. Tensing, I scan the walls, circling the room until I find the source of the merriment. At last, Killian and Sloan are dragged to the "stage," the plateau at the top of the marble steps in front of the spa.

I'm expecting them, but the sight still horrifies me. I take a moment to study the scene.

The gold collar is still wrapped around Killian's neck, trapping his spirit inside the Shell. A Shell that is now utterly flayed, flaps of skin hanging by threads. He is a beautiful but morbid sight, covered in so much Lifeblood he looks as if he's bathed in glitter. His tongue...his tongue has been cut out—I know because it's pinned to his shirt. His wrists are shackled to fetters even now being anchored to the columns beside him, his ankles bound to fetters on the ground.

His body forms an X. The Roman numeral for ten.

X marks the spot.

One of Sloan's eyes is swollen shut. There's blood matted in her hair and caked around her nose and mouth. She cried so much and so hard, her face is swollen, tear tracks having left welts on her cheeks. She, too, is shackled with fetters to form an X.

A third person is dragged onto the plateau, and I gasp. My father's head is down and though he's uninjured, his arms are fettered behind his back. His dark hair is rumpled, and tears stain his cheeks.

He's placed a few feet away from Pearl, who looks like

an angel. She's wearing a ceremonial robe like the Troikans', though hers is as white as snow, her pale hair falling to her waist in perfect waves.

Just then I'm struck by a truth so real it might as well be a bolt of lightning: there is no greater evil than the one that cloaks itself in virtue.

Pearl doesn't waste any time. She lifts a gun, aims and squeezes the trigger. The loud boom causes the crowd to go quiet. My dad's body jerks, and he collapses. "This man attempted to cheat his contract, and such behavior will never be tolerated."

Another gasp escapes me, and my hands fly up to cover my mouth. My dad lands on the ground and stays down, his eyes open but unfocused, a quarter-size hole leaking blood between his eyes. Nausea churns in my belly, and my knees begin to knock. *He's dead.* My father is dead. Just. Like. That.

Tears begin to pour down my cheeks. I might not have liked the man, and he might have tried to kill me—this might be what he deserves—but the little girl I used to be still loved him. That little girl will always love him.

"I'm so sorry, Ten." Deacon gives my shoulder an awkward pat, as if he doesn't know how to offer comfort. "I had no idea she had your father."

My hands fall to my sides and fist. Meanwhile, the crowd cheers as if she's said something amazing.

Pearl peers into the camera and smiles. "If you sign with Troika, they die."

She's speaking directly to me. She knew I'd be watching, because she'd taken great pains to spread the word this morning.

The cheers from the crowd grow louder. I think I hear a few shouts of protest.

Oh, yes. I do. Multiple people are holding HART signs that read What If You're Next? Stop the Madness!

Pearl holds up her hand in a bid for silence and finally addresses the masses. "I come to you with a heavy heart." Her voice—now soothing—drifts through the living room. "Myriad's love for you is boundless and as always we want only the best for you. Yet here I stand, admitting we failed you. The two traitors beside me were welcomed into our fold only to betray us—betray *you*—to Troika, the enemy intent on our destruction."

A chorus of "boo" erupts.

She places her hand over her heart. "These two tried to hurt you, my people, my family, and that will never be tolerated. I will always fight for you—fight for what's right for you, what's best. Today, the traitors will face my wrath. Their attempts to harm those under my protection will end."

Cheers again.

Fools! How can they not see the villain she is?

Who am I kidding? I missed it for years.

She looks straight into the camera, as if she's peering straight into my soul. "We will proceed…unless anyone wishes to raise an objection?"

"We go now," I tell Deacon. "We can't wait for Archer any longer."

He doesn't protest, and I'm grateful. "All you have to do is survive, Ten. She won't hurt them as long as you're breathing."

By that reasoning, I should stay here. But we both know that isn't an option. If I do, Pearl *will* hurt Killian and Sloan.

"I'll survive," I vow. Whatever it takes.

He wraps his arms around me—but nothing happens.

I frown. "Are you sure this will work?"

"Of course. Shells were patterned after human bodies. I'm waiting for you to close your eyes."

Please. I'm not missing a moment of this. I've been to Many Ends; I can handle anything. "Go!"

Bright, blinding light basically incinerates my corneas. The foundation is ripped out from under me, and I'm thrown like a baseball across a field, the world around me nothing but a blur. I'm—

"Here," Deacon says.

I hear gasps of surprise, but it takes me a moment to focus. My stomach churns, erupts. I hunch over and spew out my guts. More gasps, only these are laced with disgust. There's a patter of footsteps as people rush to get away from me and my gross.

As I straighten, wiping my mouth with the back of my hand, the world comes into view. Deacon landed us right in front of the plateau, just a step below Pearl. His Oxi is already aimed. He fires.

Three Myriad Shells rush from the sidelines to form a wall in front of Pearl, the blast nailing the guy in the middle, the air around him suddenly smoky. He tries to wave away the fumes as his comrades jump away from him, leaving him to decay. Clumps of his hair fall from his head, and his skin begins to age rapidly, wrinkles appearing, spreading, digging deeper.

The guy on his right shoots him between the eyes and the Shell explodes into ash.

Click. Click. Click.

I don't have to look to know that every Shell in the audience is now aiming a weapon at me. Are bullets in the chambers, or darts? Does she want to kill me right from the start, or try one more time to convince me Myriad is better than Troika?

I keep my attention on Killian. He's shaking his head no, his golden eyes—those beautiful eyes—beseeching me. *Leave. Don't do this.*

A part of me dies at seeing such a strong boy so helpless.

"I'm here to bargain," I call and his head falls forward in defeat.

Four seconds pass before Pearl steps forward, her chin high. Four types of blood. Four horsemen of the apocalypse. Four stages in a human Firstlife: conception, birth, life and finally death.

I'm going to deliver her Second-death.

"The time for bargains has passed." She nods at her men. "Hobble her."

Hobble, not kill. She is confident she has the edge.

As a thousand explosions ring out, Deacon whisks me away on a beam of light. I'm blinded for a moment, and my stomach rebels the second we land—directly behind Pearl.

I retch all over Deacon's boots, not that anyone notices. Or hears. Shells and humans are too busy toppling from the blasts. Without us there to take the blows, they end up shooting each other.

Deacon raises the Oxi, the barrel aimed at the back of

Pearl's head, but she didn't earn the title of Leader by sitting behind a desk.

She senses him and ducks, spins, a Stag palmed from a pocket in her robe. As she fires off a shot of her own, Deacon shoves me out of the way and vanishes, and the dart embeds in the building behind me. I waste no time, unsheathing a dagger and tossing it. The tip slices through her wrist, her version of muscle clenching and unclenching, forcing her to drop the weapon.

A *pop, pop* sounds at my left. Sharp pain erupts in my neck, electric pulses shooting through me, making me jerk, rendering me useless. Pearl smiles as she pulls the blade from her wrist, then nods in thanks to the Shell who pegged me full of darts.

Can't have failed so easily. So quickly.

She walks toward me, saunters really, pep in every step. She's proud of herself, even a little giddy. My gaze scans… Deacon is fighting a crowd of Myriad soldiers. A split second after he disappears, they disappear. A split second after he reappears, they reappear, the battle never pausing. Someone is always punching, throwing elbows or knees.

"Help," I manage to gasp.

"Yes, help her," Pearl calls. How smug she sounds. "Anyone?"

Deacon glances my way and appears behind Pearl a second later, but that's what she wanted him to do—draw out and conquer. She dives low when he swings at her and as she rolls, she nails him with a dart.

He drops, his body twitching. *No, no, no.*

My fault!

No. *Her* fault. She stands, giving me another of those

smug smiles, my dagger still in her hand. "You were right, you know. You can't be Fused with my Ashley. Which means we were wrong about the other Generals. We have to be wrong."

Other Generals? Plural? "Wrong about what?"

She ignores me, saying, "I'm supposed to bring you in if at all possible. I don't think it's possible."

The darts send electric pulses through every muscle in my body. It's agony. Worse than anything Vans ever put me through. Before Many Ends, it would have overwhelmed me, and I might have tapped out.

My trials were my darkest hours, but now I'll use them as the foundation of my triumph.

As Pearl raises the dagger, I push through the pain. My determination is unparalleled, the sun stroking over me, seeping into me…strengthening me? I manage to kick out my leg, knocking her feet out from under her. She falls, crash landing on a step. The pain grows worse, but my determination grows with it, the sun continuing to stroke me, warming me from the inside out. I'm able to reach up and yank the dart out of my neck.

She and I stand in unison, facing off. Another dart—two, three, four—sink into my flesh, and I drop to my knees. But only for a second. Only long enough to pull out each one and stand again.

Surprise and fear darken in her eyes. "You shouldn't… No one should… How…"

The sun continues to stroke me as I bend down and pluck out the darts in Deacon. I keep my eyes on Pearl. "Your pride dragged you here while my determination carried me. I'm a force to be reckoned with, and today is the day of your reckoning."

Backing away from me, she shouts, "Kill them! Kill Killian and Sloan."

A moment of surprise. She's flipped the script and changed her game play. I was the ultimate target, but because she's at a disadvantage—despite the army surrounding her—she's determined to strike at me any way possible.

I cast a panicked look at Deacon, who is still recovering. He's gone a second later, reappearing in front of Sloan while I dive for Killian. Shots ring out as blinding white lights appear all over the plateau, all through the street, even in front of Killian and Sloan. Shells! An army from Troika!

Archer stops the shots from hitting Killian. Or rather, his sword does. In one hand, he holds a sword of mesmerizing blue-white fire. The one I've asked him about, the handle actually growing from his palm. In his other hand, he holds a shield, and with a crisscross motion of his arms, he either burns the darts and bullets—*everything* fired his way—or blocks them. Nothing gets past him. He remains unharmed, Killian saved from Second-death.

My relief knows no bounds. Nor does my irritation. "You're late," I say to Archer.

A slight smile teases the corners of his lips. "Actually, I'm right on time."

Pearl is busy typing into the light in her wrist. Messaging for help?

I lumber to my feet, brush the dirt and pebbles from my palms. "You ready to hear my bargain now?" I don't give her a chance to respond. "Let Killian and Sloan go, and you'll live. Fight us, and you'll die."

"How about my bargain instead?" Behind her, other lights slam into the ground, new Myriad Shells appearing, each holding a crude-looking spear or bow and arrow. Guess the Generals don't want us taking out one of their Leaders, even though she's acting against orders. Or is she? They could want me dead, too, stories of Pearl going rogue nothing but lies for the people. "We fight, *you* die."

An instant later, Shells dive on Shells. Weapons slash. Limbs fall.

I'm allowed only a glimpse of the carnage, a ring of Troikan warriors appearing around me. Each clutches a blue-white sword of flames, slashing at any projectiles that are fired in our direction as a swarm of Myriad Shells surround us. I'm Unsigned, and yet they're protecting me as if I'm one of their own.

One of the Troikan soldiers falls, his Shell littered with arrows. Another warrior crouches down, gathers his friend close and vanishes in a beam of light. The others tighten the circle, and I wonder why the fallen Shell wasn't ashed, the spirit inside freed. The arrows must make it impossible, like the collar Killian wears. Yes! That's it. Killian once told me a story about a Troikan woman he killed. He trapped her spirit inside a Shell. She hemorrhaged to death, unable to escape.

How many are going to die today?

Is Killian being guarded as fiercely as me? Probably not. He's on the other team. Then again, this Troikan army isn't just here for me, but for two who should be their enemies.

Still. I can't just sit here, doing nothing. Seeing no other recourse, I crawl out from between the legs of my protectors. *Sorry, folks.* Chaos reigns all around me, swords of fire swinging, body after body falling, ash floating on the breeze. Spears and arrows whiz past. More bodies fall and ash. Grunts, groans and screams create a macabre soundtrack. And that's only what I can see and hear! No telling what's happening with the spirits around us, invisible to humans.

I scramble as fast as I can, my prize in sight. A single warrior is guarding Killian and in this case, one is enough. Archer dazzles me with his skill. I've never seen him like this, a lethal savage, a weapon in his own right and a terrible beauty to behold. He doesn't meet my gaze, but I know he knows I'm there, his every motion well-placed to prevent me from being grazed by the sword as I close the rest of the distance. Finally I'm in front of Killian and—I'm already crying. I'm crying so hard. He's a mess, more so than I realized.

I cup his face and he uses up massive amounts of strength to lift his eyes. His irises…the beautiful gold is lighter than before and fading even now. I don't have to be told what's happening. He's dying inside the Shell.

"I told you I'd come for you. I'm getting you out of here." I tug at his collar to no avail. I press against every inch, searching for an open sesame. There isn't one. "You're going to heal. I'm going to doctor you up so gently you'll swear I've been to medical school."

I think he says, "Go," but it's hard to tell.

As I work at the fetters on his ankles, the heat singeing me, I say, "I'm staying put. Ten Lockwood isn't leaving another man behind. Especially her man."

By the time the cuffs snap open, my hands are covered in blisters. I meet his gaze, which is a little brighter now and full of determination—good, that's good—before I turn my attention to his hands.

"Hurry." Archer swings the sword this way and that, burning darts before they can soar past him. "The Myriad Shells are herding the humans into the line of fire, using them as shields."

I know him. He can't—won't—harm a human.

I work as fast as I can, frantic, and finally Killian's wrist cuffs open. With another moan, he sags against me. I ease him to the ground, place a soft kiss on his Lifeblood-stained lips and whisper, "This next part might hurt. I'm sorry."

Not knowing what else to do, I thread the open fetter through the collar, letting the outer heat soften the metal. I then thread through the wire in my wrist cuff and begin to saw with all my might. The wire was the only thing that made any headway with the Myriad locks, so why not the collar, too? Sparks fly, metal shavings raining down. Killian grimaces. It's burning him, but it can't be helped. I keep going, and finally the collar falls to the ground in pieces, freeing him from bondage.

"Now! Ash his Shell," I tell Archer. *Set his spirit free!*

He swings around to face me, the sword raised and ready—but he never renders the blow. His body jerks and his eyes go wide as three arrows cut through his back and peek out his chest.

chapter twenty-eight

"If you don't stand for what's right, who will?"

—Troika

A scream of denial splits my lips. Archer is still jerking, as if his spirit is struggling to escape the Shell but can't.

I glance up at the person who did this to him. Not a person, a monster. Pearl grins at me as she lowers her bow.

She did this. And she will pay.

"N-no," Archer says.

One word, but I realize I'm allowing hatred for Pearl to pull my strings—allowing *her* to pull my strings. That's Myriad's way. Not my way. A road leading to an end I don't want.

Forget her. I squeeze Archer's hand. He's more important. I'll guard him from another attack, even at the cost of my own life.

Pearl reaches back and slides an arrow from the pouch now hanging over her shoulder, but she doesn't have time to aim. A sword of fire cleaves her head from her body, killing her.

I feel nothing. Not even relief. As her head soars down the steps, her body topples, revealing a panting Deacon behind her.

"Archer needs Lifeblood," I tell him. "Now!"

He takes a step forward, but Myriad soldiers are so enraged by the death of their Leader, they release their human shields to race up the steps and attack Deacon en masse. He herds them to the bottom of the steps, away from Archer.

How am I supposed to save him?

Sloan is free on the other side of the plateau, at least, leaning against a column and crying. She can't help me, either.

I focus on Archer and the arrows, accidentally jarring him, and the hum of a motor erupts. He arches his back, bellowing in agony.

"Can't move arrows...blades in shaft...drip poison... every time you pull." Killian's voice! He rolls to his side, facing us. He'd been drinking Lifeblood from one of the fallen soldiers, his mouth glittering. His tongue is already growing back, his skin weaving back together. "He needs Lifeblood."

"I know! But no one has any to spare and—" Wait! I do. *I* have Lifeblood. I'm not just a body. I'm a spirit. "Killian, how do I get my spirit out of my body without dying and going to Many Ends?"

"You don't." His voice is stronger now. "You can't."

"I must! If I don't share my Lifeblood with Archer, he'll die."

Killian inhales sharply, his features tortured. "I'll give you ten seconds, no more. The moment your spirit leaves your body, your body will die. It won't revive until your spirit returns, and the longer you're separated, the less chance there is it has the strength to accept your spirit when you attempt to return unless you're flooded with Lifeblood, but as you can see, it's in short supply right now."

I don't understand how he thinks he can give me ten seconds. Then his Shell goes still, the eyes clearing. He's gone? But—

An invisible hand clutches my heart in a vise grip. I'm yanked forward—no, not my body, I realize a second later, but my spirit. Suddenly I'm crouched before Killian. The *real* Killian.

Only a split second passes as I look at him, though it seems like an eternity. *So beautiful*... Muted sunlight shines over him, chasing away the dark shadows trying desperately to cling to him, and my breath catches. His hair is jet-black silk, the locks long enough to hang over his brow, the perfect frame for features that have been chiseled by a master. His eyebrows are just as black and the perfect thickness. His eyes, those golden eyes with the crystalline flecks, are pure male aggression, intense...perfect. His perfect blade of a nose leads to the perfect shadow of stubble. His top lip is the same plumpness as his bottom lip, the two a perfect pair. His skin is a perfect bronze, as if it's been painted on by perfect brushstrokes.

Perfect. Yes. That's what he is. Perfection made flesh. Or spirit.

Scars wrap around his neck like a boa, but there are tattoos strategically placed to mask them. More lines and stars. They are raised, seemingly alive. I reach for him, and see that parts of me are glowing. The beams are muted, but there, as if I'm shedding the same shadows clinging to Killian.

"One," he says. He has hold of my shoulder, but slides his grip to my wrist. He's the one keeping me from returning to Many Ends, isn't he? "Two."

Zero! The countdown.

I turn to Archer—who is aglow, even through the Shell, so bright my eyes tear. One by one, I rip out the arrows. He flops around like a gutted fish, too weak to bellow again. I look around for a weapon, realize I couldn't touch one anyway. Like to like. I'm spirit right now, not tangible to the Land of the Harvest.

I bite into my wrist, actually tearing into my flesh like a dog with a bone.

"Six," Killian says, his grip on me tightening.

"Just a little longer!" I place my wrist over Archer's mouth. My Lifeblood pours into him, slides down his throat as strength drains from me. I glance up, at the battle, and what I see takes my breath away.

I see Shells, and I see spirits. It's the battle between the spirits that is the most brutal. Spirits aren't just on the ground; they're in the air, hovering as they fight. Swords of blue fire against swords of red fire. I don't have to wonder who is Troikan and who is Myriadian. The Troikans seem to absorb sunlight while a dark film covers the Myriadians.

These men and women…they aren't just sun against moon but truly light versus dark. I tried to have the best of both worlds, while doing to others what I hated others for doing to me. Pushing my own agenda. I wanted peace. They didn't. My choice versus theirs, when I only had half the story. Even now I realize there's so much about the realms I don't know.

"Nine."

"Wait!" I say. "Please. Just a little longer. He needs more—"

"Ten." Killian is merciless, yanking me backward and basically stuffing my spirit back into my body, and I'm too weak to stop him.

I gasp as spirit and body connect, my first thought of Archer. I scan his Shell. Despite my Lifeblood, his flesh isn't yet repairing itself.

"Archer," I say, my chin trembling.

"Okay. It's okay."

No! There has to be something else I can do. There just has to be. "Deacon!" I shout.

Archer gasps in a breath, blinks open his eyes. He blindly reaches for my hand, and his fingers curl weakly around mine.

Our gazes meet, and tears refill my eyes, only to splash upon his cheek.

"The Rest," he says and gives me a smile I will never forget. Satisfied. Content. He's lived a good life. "Finally."

"No," I say with a hard shake of my head. "You stay here, and you stay with me. I need you. You have more to do."

"You will be…fine without me. Take care… Deacon, Killian…and yourself…don't forget yourself. The law."

"Stop talking like we're saying goodbye." My tears fall faster. "Deacon," I shout again, scanning the battlefield, seeing no faces I recognize. "Someone! Help Archer! He needs more Lifeblood."

The battle continues to rage. I can no longer see the one raging between the spirits, and I wonder who is winning.

Archer's smile slips a little, now both sad and eager. "Not much time…tell me poem. Happy. Rhyme."

As my insides are ripped to shreds, I close my eyes. He isn't going to make it, is he? My Lifeblood just isn't strong enough. Maybe because I'm Unsigned. Maybe because I'm still recovering from my own injuries. Maybe because of a thousand other reasons. I might never know the truth, but one thing is suddenly clear: his death is because of choice. Pearl's choice to fight me. My choice to save Killian and Sloan.

And now, Archer will pay the price. My decisions—my indecisions—have never affected me alone, as I so confidently told myself what seems a lifetime ago. They affect everyone I love, everyone in my life. Even those I will someday meet. Even those I will never meet.

I mocked Pearl's pride, but look where my own brought me. Look where my own brought my friends.

The knowledge washes through me, horrifying me, utterly destroying me, but I fight past the overwhelming influx of regret and sorrow. For now. I have to. Archer needs me. This wonderful guy needs me to be strong for him, to ease him into the Rest. After everything he's done for me, I can do this for him. I *will* do this for him.

I will mourn tomorrow.

"A poem. One just for you." I smooth a shaky hand over his brow, like a mother soothing her child before bed. "Year after year I hated my life. No matter where I looked, I only saw strife. Oh, poor me, I had no one to live for… until you arrived and taught me to soar."

His lashes flutter shut, the sadness vanishing from his smile, leaving only happiness. So much happiness, despite the battle raging around us. Thankfully, Troikans have taken up posts around the dais, preventing Myriadian soldiers from closing in. "More. Please."

I continue. "You saved me from the worst kind of death, as if you breathed into me my very first breath. You, Archer Prince, oh, how you shine. Now and forever, you'll always be mine. I'll miss you, dear Bow, for the short time we're apart." My chin trembles as I say, "Take care of this gift…for I give you my heart. You are loved, I love you. Because of you, I've been made new."

"Yesss," he says again, the drawn out *s* tapering off as he expels his last breath.

His head lolls to the side, and his grip on me goes lax. I imagine his bright, bright glow fading completely.

He's gone. He's really gone.

I collapse onto his chest, sobs racking me. He deserved so much better than this.

"Ten," Killian shouts, horror in his voice.

I straighten and turn to him. He's sitting up, diving in front of me.

"No," he cries, but it's too late.

Something sharp cuts through his back, comes out his chest, enters mine and rips through my back, pinning us together. The pain is incredible, and it spreads through every cell in my body in seconds until I'm wholly consumed.

She stabs you in the back, Lina said.

I expected the attack to come from Pearl, but she's dead. I gaze up in horror—and discover Sloan.

Tears glisten in her lashes. "I'm sorry," she cries. "I'm so sorry, but they offered me something I couldn't refuse."

The only thing she'd wanted was revenge against Vans, despite his death. Either Pearl lied to her or she has—

had—a way to get to Vans, something Killian and Archer were unable to do.

"I hate him more than I love you. I'm sorry," she repeats with a sob of her own.

A sense of betrayal nearly chokes me.

"Ten." As Killian tries to pull himself from the spear, the motor hums, cutting at him, cutting at me, leaking poison. "Sorry, I'm sorry."

With a roar, he yanks backward, freeing himself from the spear. When he rights himself, he repeats, "I'm sorry," then grabs on to the shaft and jerks with all his might.

I scream as blades cut, cut, cut at me. Finally, though, the spear leaves me.

As blood rushes up my throat and chokes me, I manage to turn my head and watch as Killian swings the spear. Blood-soaked metal glints from the shaft—as it slices through Sloan's stomach. Her eyes go wide, and her knees collapse.

She's not going to survive the day, either.

I want to hate her, but as one second ticks into another, I realize I'm just sad for her. Her decisions, like my own, brought her here.

Killian crawls to me. I'm panting and wheezing. The death rattle. This is it, isn't it? The end. I'm going to die. I'm going to die *today.* Only minutes…seconds?…remain.

I once told my life story in a nutshell, but some of my numbers have changed.

Seventeen—the number of years I've lived. *Existed* is no longer a strong-enough word.

Two—the number of boys I've grown to adore since my escape from Prynne. Archer, the family I've craved for so long, and Killian, who took a shattered heart and put the pieces back together.

Three—the number of friends I've lost in my quest for the truth.

One—the number of lives I have left.

Three—the number of choices remaining for my eternal future.

"Ten, you won't survive this." There's a tremor in Killian's voice. "The poison…it's in my system, too. My Lifeblood won't help you."

Baiser de la mort, the kiss of death, even now rushing through me.

He frames my face with his hands. He's trembling.

"Go," I manage. "Get…help…for…you." *Don't die with me!* I have a Secondlife. He doesn't have a third.

"I was wrong about so many things." He gives my lips a soft kiss. "The victor isn't always adored and the failure isn't always abhorred. I failed to sign you… I lost…and I'm glad for it. Sign with Troika, Ten. It's where you belong."

Another flood of tears streams down my cheeks. This boy hates losing, and yet he's letting me go.

"We'll be…enemies," I whisper, my body going numb. "You'll be…killed."

"Better you're my enemy and happy than my friend and miserable. And don't worry about me, lass. They can try to kill me. They have before. I always come out okay."

I won't be happy while he's trapped in Myriad, perhaps placed in the Kennel for good. But I won't be happy in Myriad, even with this boy at my side.

Only one other option. I remain Unsigned and return to Many Ends…where I may or may not be able to save the spirits trapped inside. Without Archer, I never would have revived after the last visit.

Archer once asked me to trust him. He said we'd figure out a way into Many Ends, a way to save the spirits. And if I can get inside Many Ends, I can get inside Myriad. I can save Killian. Maybe he can go to court.

New plan, new goal.

He presses my hand against his chest, where the wound from the spear still gaps open, his beautiful Lifeblood making his skin glitter. If he doesn't leave the Shell soon, he could very well die inside it. But I know him, and I know he won't leave it—or me—until I've made my final decision.

I squeeze his hand with as much strength I can muster. "I'm coming...for you, Killian. Again."

"Ten—"

I smile at him. "I pledge my life to..." I suck in a breath, knowing deep down it's my last, and as I release it, I whisper, "Troika."

★ ★ ★ ★ ★

There are worse things than death,
as the next part of Ten's journey will prove.
Don't miss
LIFEBLOOD,
book 2 of the EVERLIFE *series.*
Only from Gena Showalter and Harlequin TEEN.

A CHAT WITH GENA SHOWALTER Q & A

Q: Starting a new series sounds daunting and exhilarating. What was your inspiration for *Firstlife* and how do you feel about this brand-new series?

A: I love scripture, and there are numerous scriptures about a kingdom not of this earth, kingdom vs. kingdom—a war between spiritual forces—and the power of choice. Life and death. Blessing and cursing. Light and dark. Those themes combined, and the idea to write a book where life as we know it is just a dress rehearsal and real life actually began after death—where two realms are in power—was born. The idea was a fire inside of me. It burned, and it consumed. I *had* to tell the story of Firstlife.

Q: How hard was it to create two such different realms and make the choice between them difficult for Ten? How did you handle that?

A: As my editor can tell you, this wasn't just hard for me—this was Horrible Agonizing Rough Demanding. (HARD) I wrote many drafts of this book, adding layers to each realm, doing my best to build two vastly different societies with equal appeal.

Q: You write stories for both teens and adults. What is different about the way you approach writing for each age group, and what is the same?

A: This might come as a surprise, but I approach every book in the same manner. I don't consider my audience while writing a first draft, because I know I'll never be able to please everyone. I write for an audience of one. It is the characters that set the tone for the book. Teenagers and adults have different mind-sets, different experiences and pasts, different expectations, and they stop me from pushing when it isn't time to push.

Q: Who is your favorite character in *Firstlife* and why?

A: My romance reader/writer roots are about to show. I favored the guys. Archer and Killian. Why? Because I'm a cougar! Meow! (I mean, Roar!) I adore those sexy bad boys and their golden hearts. And muscled bodies. But most of all, I adored watching Killian realize he couldn't win Ten with his seductive charm. He actually had to expose his true self to interest her—and by doing so, he gained her appreciation and ultimately her love at no tangible cost. It changed him.

Q: Truth now. Which realm would you sign with and why?

A: I'm a Troika girl, through and through. I like me some light. I like the value they place on human life. I like that they will fight for someone's right to choose, even if that someone chooses their enemy. But mostly, I like the unwavering justice. There are no favorites. There are no exceptions. Truth never changes.

Q: Where did you get the idea for Ten's obsession with numbers? How much fun was it to incorporate all the number facts into the book? Will numbers remain important to the Everlife novels?

A: Ten's obsession with numbers wasn't something I planned—despite her name!—but as I wrote that first draft, the obsession grew organically from her character. I had so much fun hunting down numerical facts as well as numerical possibilities. And yes, the numbers will remain important throughout the Everlife novels...will be even *more* important!

Q: Without giving away spoilers, can you give us a hint as to what's next for Ten and crew?

A: Ten's welcoming to Troika, Killian's punishment for his actions, dealing with the loss of Archer, Ten being trained for every job in the realm—a Conduit without knowledge has no light to share—and the war between the realms heats up with worldwide repercussions. And that's just to kick things off!

Thank you, Gena!

QUESTIONS FOR DISCUSSION

1. If humanity discovered beyond doubt that there was life after death, how do you think people would react? How would or wouldn't the value of human life change?

2. Ten believes Firstlife matters and Killian at first does not. Who is right, and why does Killian's perspective change? Discuss elements in the book that support your answers.

3. Killian and Archer were friends before they became deadly enemies. What turns the tide in their relationship and motivates them to form a new relationship? Point to specific scenes in the book to inform your answer.

4. Killian has relied on his charm and attractiveness to convince his targets to sign with Myriad. When that doesn't work with Ten, what changes does he make in his approach and why? How well does that work with Ten?

5. Symbolism plays a huge part in the book—or does it? What symbolism, if any, did the author use to represent another idea via association or resemblance? What themes did the author explore?

6. What passages in the book struck you as the most insightful? The most profound?

7. Ten comes to learn a single decision boils down to only right and wrong—for her and those she loves—and the consequences of making a mistake can have eternal repercussions, and yet indecision can come at an even greater cost. Do you agree with her? Why or why not?

8. What do you consider Myriad's strengths? Weaknesses? What do you consider Troika's strengths? Weaknesses? Use examples from the book to support your answers.